WHAT

YOU

DON'T

KNOW

WHAT
YOU
DON'T
KNOW

JOANN
CHANEY

FLATIRON
BOOKS
NEW YORK

WHAT YOU DON'T KNOW. Copyright © 2017 by JoAnn Chaney. All rights reserved. Printed in the United States of America. For information, address Flatiron Books, 175 Fifth Avenue, New York, N.Y. 10010.

www.flatironbooks.com

The Library of Congress Cataloging-in-Publication Data is available upon request.

ISBN 978-1-250-07553-6 (hardcover)
ISBN 978-1-250-07554-3 (e-book)

Our books may be purchased in bulk for promotional, educational, or business use. Please contact your local bookseller or the Macmillan Corporate and Premium Sales Department at 1-800-221-7945, extension 5442, or by e-mail at MacmillanSpecialMarkets@macmillan.com.

First Edition: February 2017

10 9 8 7 6 5 4 3 2 1

For Mom and Dad,

who always said

I should write

THE

CRAWL

SPACE

HOSKINS

December 19, 2008

If this were a movie, it would start with this shot: two men climbing out of an older-model brown car, dressed in cheap suits and cheaper shoes. One of them is wearing a hat, a black panama, and it makes him look a little like a time traveler from the 1920s. But this isn't Prohibition and this isn't Miami; this is Denver in the year 2008, and it's cold outside, so the man in the panama looks foolish, although you wouldn't tell him that, not if you want to keep your asshole firmly intact, because this man might look foolish but he's also one mean motherfucker, you can tell that if you manage to get a good look at his eyes. You might think it was a woman who gave him the hat, who teased him into wearing it, telling him he'd look so handsome in it, so debonair, but you'd be wrong. This man's name is Ralph Loren, a name that sounds like a bad joke but isn't, because nobody teases Detective Loren, *nobody*, even if they're pretty and young with tits out to *there*. Loren doesn't have a sense of humor—it's not that he has a weird one, or a mean one; he just doesn't have one at all. He was born missing that part of his insides, and life is a hard row to hoe without a few laughs along the way, but you don't miss what you never had. At least that's how the saying goes.

But it's the second man you should watch, the one climbing out the passenger side, the tall man with the big shoulders and the beginning shadows of a beard. This man comes around the front of the car, not bothering to avoid the dirty snow piled up at the curb but plowing right through it. He'll regret this later, when he's back at his desk, his socks wet and cold and frozen between his toes. Paul Hoskins is that kind of man who doesn't think too hard about what he does and regrets these decisions later. He's always been that kind of man and he always will be, until the end of time, amen.

"We're finally doing it, huh?" Hoskins says, looking up at the house they've come to visit. It's large and brick, a house taller than it is wide, with a big bay window over the front yard. It's traditional, not the kind of house you'd normally find in Denver, but this housing addition was built back in the '80s, thrown up quickly for the crowds rushing in from all over—California, mostly, if you listen to the locals, all those jerks and their terrible driving skills—and it doesn't look cheap, not like some of the other houses on the street. There are trees and shrubs planted in tasteful clusters around the property, although the foliage is faded and brown now, with nets of colored Christmas lights wound through the branches. There's a man-made pond out back too, with a slat-wood dock and a rowboat made for two. There are fish in that pond, and frogs, but the water's covered over with a thin sheet of ice now, and Hoskins wonders if all that has to be replaced every spring, if a delivery truck swings by with foam coolers full of wildlife. "Time to get the bad guy?"

Loren sighs, pushes back the flap of his jacket, and flips away the strap keeping the gun secured at his waist so he can get to it fast if he needs. These two are cops, detectives and partners; they've been together a long time and they'll be stuck that way awhile longer, although neither one is overly fond of the other. But they're kept together because they work well, they *click*, and that doesn't happen as often as anyone would like. A good partnership is a lot like a good marriage, and as anyone can confirm, a good marriage is hard to find.

But even in the best marriage, things can go very wrong.

"It's about damn time," Loren says. "If I never see this dipshit again, I'll die a happy man."

They walk up the long driveway, which has been neatly cleared of snow by the kid next door for ten bucks, and up to the front door. It's big and solid, oak, and the opaque sidelight is dark. It's early, not quite seven in the morning, and everything is quiet. Inside the house looks dark, lifeless, but Hoskins catches a faint whiff of brewing coffee and his stomach growls.

"Ready?" Loren asks.

"Yeah."

"Yeah?" Loren says, mocking. "When's your ball sac gonna drop? That high-pitched voice you got makes me want to punch you in the face."

Hoskins doesn't respond to this. He's been taking this kind of shit from Loren for the last ten years, and he's learned that it's best not to respond. Safer. Loren can shovel it out to anyone who'll listen, but he certainly can't take it. The last time they had it out was three years before, when Hoskins made a smartass remark about Loren's mother—that's what you do, if you want to piss a guy off, you go right for his mom, even if you don't know her, even if she's dead—and Loren broke his nose. There'd been an investigation, and a reprimand. A few visits to the department psychologist. But they'd still been forced to work together. If Hoskins had learned one thing about his partner, it was this: Keeping quiet is better. It wasn't that he was afraid of Loren, and he'd be able to hold his own in a fight, but if it came down to it, if you really got down to the brass knuckles (which is how Hoskins had thought the saying went since he was nine years old), he thought it was better not to speak if there wasn't anything to say. His father used to tell him to keep his pie hole shut more often, and the old man was right: Silence often made things easier, kept it simple.

Loren rings the doorbell, pressing his thumb down on the glowing button so hard his finger goes white above the first knuckle, and then immediately starts knocking. Loren is not a patient man. He's a pot of water ready to boil over on the stovetop, a balloon pumped too full of air. His fists make a heavy, dull sound on the door that makes Hoskins's head hurt, but he doesn't say anything.

It takes a bit—thirty seconds, maybe a few minutes, Hoskins doesn't know—before the door is pulled open. Hoskins had thought Jacky Seever might be in a bathrobe at this time of day, or a pair of tightywhities, stained yellow at the crotch, but instead he's in a suit, same as always. Seever's the kind of guy who'd mow his lawn in a suit; he probably sleeps in the damn things. Three-piece suits, all the same unvarying shades of slate gray or dark blue, slacks and a coat, a vest with a silver watch peeking from a pocket. The suits are all well tailored and pricey; they make Seever look like a man-about-town, and those suits may be the reason why Hoskins hates Seever so much, because he'd never be able to afford anything like that, not on a cop's salary, but it's not the only reason. It's Seever's suits, and it's his fingernails, which he keeps neatly trimmed and buffed, and it's his hair, parted on the right and sprayed until it's as hard as concrete. And the glasses—Jesus Christ, it's those glasses, wire-rimmed transition lenses that get darker in brighter light, that's what Hoskins first hated about Seever—those fucking glasses. Anyone who wore those glasses of their own free will was an asshole. Hoskins grew up poor; he's got a natural distaste for guys who strut around, flashing their bankrolls and Seever's one of those guys, but he's also worse, because he's got money, but he's also a snake in the grass. *A phony-baloney*, like his old man always says. *Or in Latin, phonus-balonus.*

"Officers?" Seever says. He asks everyone to call him Jacky, but Hoskins has never been able to do it. For him, this lousy fuck will never be anything other than Seever. "Early, isn't it? Is there something I can do for you?"

"Oh, you fat bastard," Loren says mildly, taking a step forward so Seever is forced back, has to make room to let them in. Seever's a small man; he wouldn't be able to keep them out if he tried. So he doesn't. "You know why we're here."

There's powdered sugar dusted across the front of Seever's vest, strawberry jelly smeared between his knuckles. Sloppy. He's been eating more these days, and with greater frequency. They've watched Seever duck into restaurants and gas stations, come out with plastic carry-outs of steaming food, cases of Diet Coke. Seever eats when he's under stress, and when he realized the police were constantly watching him, trying to nail his ass to the wall, he amped it up. Even in the last week he's gained. His belly is softly ballooning over the waistband of his slacks, straining the buttons on his tweed vest. The whole getup would fit someone in better shape, it might've fit him before but it doesn't now, and now the shirt doesn't quite conceal the underside of his gut, which is covered in wiry black hair and purple stretch marks. Reverse cleavage.

Hoskins follows his partner into the house, pausing long enough to shove a slip of paper into Seever's hands. A search warrant. It says they're looking for marijuana, but they don't give a shit about drugs. It wouldn't matter to them if the kitchen wall were built with bricks of Mary Jane. But they needed a way to get into Seever's house, they'd been spinning their wheels for weeks, trying to catch Seever at more than cramming food in his face and scratching his ass, and it's the best Judge Vasquez could give them. The best any judge *would* give them, because none of them liked Loren, not that Loren gave a flying fuck, but it sometimes made things difficult, so it was Hoskins who'd petitioned for the warrant, who'd had to put on his smiley face and explain the situation, Hoskins who'd had to beg for help. But that's how it was with Loren, how it'd always been. Loren wanted what he wanted, and someone else had to get it for him.

"Weed?" Seever says, the warrant pinched between his pointer finger and thumb. By the looks of it, he might've been holding a square of used toilet paper. He reads it, laughing, a sound that's like glass breaking. "You're not going to find any of that here."

"That's all right," Loren says. He's smiling, or at least pulling his lips back from his teeth, although it makes him look more like a rabid dog than a man. "I have a feeling we'll find what we're looking for."

Seever closes the front door, shutting out the cold morning light, and Hoskins is blind for a moment. This isn't good. The blinds are all drawn, the interior of the house is dark. His eyes haven't had time to adjust. He wonders if Seever knows this, if he'll take this particular moment to lose his shit, to try to kill the two cops who've come to put him away for the rest of his life. But Seever doesn't move, only stands inside the door, his hands hanging down at his sides, because really, no matter how he acts or what he says, Seever is a coward.

"Where do you want to start?" Seever asks. He's pleasant, unconcerned. "Upstairs? Gloria's at her mother's place for the weekend, so you can—"

"The crawl space," Loren says. "I want to see that."

But the crawl space is flooded, filled with rank water and unidentifiable bits, floating clouds of grease. Standing over the cutout in the laundry-room floor, Hoskins watches their three reflections in the black water, waves his hand so his twin down below does the same.

"Sump pump's broken," Seever says. He's smiling. Slyly, Hoskins thinks. Like he's managed to fool everyone. "I've been meaning to get a plumber out here, but I haven't found the time."

Loren coughs wetly into his fist. He has a cold that won't let go, not this time of year, and not after all the time he's been spending outside, sitting in his car, watching Seever and waiting for this moment. Hoskins and Seever stand patiently as he coughs and wipes his mouth with the old tissue he's pulled from his pocket.

"Think you're pretty smart, don't you?" Loren says. "You think you got everybody fooled, but I got your number."

"What's that?" Seever says, but there's something in his eyes, creeping in around the corners. He's starting to look like a cornered dog, wide-eyed and scared, and this is just the beginning.

"That plug needs to be replaced," Loren says. He takes off his hat, hands it to Hoskins. Then his coat, and hooks his fingers under the noose of his tie, yanks it loose. "Bully for you, I know how to do it. My old man was a plumber, used to take me out on calls with him."

"I'll get someone—"

"Nah, I can drain this puppy right now," Loren says, because he knows what's down there, under those floorboards and the standing water. They all do. "It'll save you some cash, not having to call someone out. Besides, I'm not in a hurry. How 'bout you, Paulie? You got somewhere to be?"

"Nope."

"And you, Seever?" There's a black speck on Loren's teeth, right at the front. A single grain of coffee, or a fleck of pepper. "You got a hot date?"

Seever shakes his head. That sly smile is long gone.

"Great," Loren says. He bends at the waist, unties his shoes and pulls them off. There's a hole in his left sock, and his big toe peeks through. He tosses the shoes away, and one bangs against the side of the washing machine. Then he sits, dangles his legs over the square hole in the floor, and slowly lowers himself into the standing water. "I'll have this fixed up in no time, then we can wait for it to drain. Maybe you could get me some of that coffee, Seever. That'd be nice."

The house gives Hoskins the willies, although at first he can't decide exactly why. It might be the strange, dank smell that occasionally finds its way to his nose, lurking under the smell of the pine from the Christmas tree or the vanilla-scented candles, or it might be the mountain of glass flower vases in the garage, stacked nearly to the ceiling in one corner, dusty and smeared. In the end, Hoskins thinks it's probably the photos that bother him the most. There are photos everywhere, framed and nicely matted, mostly of Seever. His wife isn't in many of them—she's the one behind the camera, squinting into the black box and clicking, capturing her husband's image a thousand times. If they'd had children, or even dogs, it might've been different. Instead, here's Seever in sunglasses, holding a glistening trout in two hands. Seever at Disney World, standing awkwardly in the shadow of the huge silver golf ball. Seever at the Grand Canyon, at the Golden Gate Bridge. Always standing close to something important, monuments right over his shoulder. It makes Hoskins nervous, seeing Seever's face plastered all over the house, his piggy eyes watching everyone who passes.

It's in the bathroom, when Hoskins is drying his fingers on the stupid little tea towel, trying to avoid the rough patches of embroidered roses, that he notices the photo propped up on the toilet tank. Why anyone would want a photo staring at them while they're relieving themselves is beyond him, but what does he know? Nothing.

It's Seever in the toilet photo, of course. Posed in front of his own house this time, the brick walls and big bay window behind him, the house numbers nailed up beside the door clearly visible. He's smiling, his arms thrown wide, a bouquet of red carnations clutched in one white-gloved hand.

He's dressed up, like a clown.

"I love visiting those kids in the hospital," Seever had told them, weeks ago, before he got nervous, when he still thought the two cops following him everywhere was nothing more than a good joke. He'd seen them parked, watching him, and he'd saunter up for a chat, shoot the shit about the weather or how the Broncos might do in the next season. This time, they'd followed him to one of the restaurants he owned and he'd invited them in, sprung for lunch. They sat in a booth, Hoskins and Loren on one side, Seever on the other, and had meatloaf and buttered peas, apple pie and coffee. "Making those kids smile— that makes me feel good."

They knew all about his volunteer work; they'd watched him at the hospital, going into the rooms where kids lived, either waiting to get better or waiting for their terribly short lives to spin out. There were kids that weighed hardly anything at all and had no hair, kids who'd been burned and beaten, kids who'd been goofing off outside and had broken a leg. At first, they'd been sure Seever was a pervert, a *kiddie-diddler* on top of everything else, but he wasn't. The kids liked him, he did a good job. Seever was a weirdo, a fuck-up in most every way, but he was good with kids, he seemed almost normal when he was in costume, bouncing around and squeezing his nose and twisting balloon animals.

"Why a clown, Seever?" Loren had asked, dumping a spoonful of sugar into his coffee. He seemed genuinely puzzled by this. "Most kids are scared shitless by those things."

"That's not true," Seever said. The top button on his shirt was undone, and Hoskins could see the gold crucifix nestled in the hollow of his throat. "Kids love clowns."

"I wouldn't be so sure about that."

"Oh, everyone loves a clown," Seever said, winking. "They're every-one's friend. You know, I think a clown could get away with murder."

It takes four hours for the water to drain, and the moment the soft dirt floor is visible they send a technician down. He's wearing a plastic suit with a mask, yellow gloves. He has a small shovel in his hand, the kind you might use to plant flowers in a garden.

But he's not planting flowers. And he's not looking for marijuana either.

He's down there less than ten minutes when he calls up, frantically, and it's Hoskins who drops down the hole this time. He pulls up the legs of his trousers and duck-waddles to the tech, who's squatting in the farthest corner.

"It stinks over here," the tech says. "Don't toss your cookies. Not down here."

And it does stink, bad. It makes Hoskins think of the time his ex-wife threw raw pork in the garbage, saying the meat had turned and they couldn't eat it, and the bin had sat out in the summer sun for days, the meat slowly rotting in the heat, filling the neighborhood with a smell that turned stomachs and made dogs go apeshit.

"What is it?" Hoskins asks.

The tech points to the ground at his feet, a shallow divot where he's pulled back the dirt. There's a piece of fabric there. Flannel, blue and white. A T-shirt, probably. Most of it still tucked in the ground, out of sight. And beside the fabric, and partially wrapped inside it, is an arm. It's rotted enough that Hoskins can see all the way down to the bone in places, but there's still flesh there, the torn skin blackened and curled around the edges, like paper that's been singed by fire.

"It's here," Hoskins shouts, moving back, away. The smell is so strong, too strong. He's going to be sick. "We found it."

He hears a scuffle above his head, feet thumping on the floorboards. There's a shriek of pain, and then Loren is speaking. Hoskins can't hear the words, but he recognizes the tone, the familiar sounds of his part-ner. And then, louder, bleeding over the sound of Loren's voice, is Seever. He is crying.

SAMMIE

December 29, 2008

If there is one thing Sammie Peterson has learned over the years, it is this: Everyone thinks the pretty girl is a moron.

That's what they think of her, she knows, she can feel those thoughts coming off the men as they work, as if there are cartoon bubbles floating over their heads, right there for her to read. They've invited her to stay in the crawl space while they dig, to get a better sense of the crime scene, to watch what's going on so she can report it all more accurately in her articles, but she doesn't like it down there. It's too small, too *close*, even though they've ripped up most of the floorboards and moved out the washer and dryer, so the crawl space isn't actually under the house anymore but a part of it, a place where the men can stand upright as they look at what Seever has left behind, their hands perched on their hips or folded across their chests. And they watch her when she *does* venture into the crawl space, she can feel their gazes on her ass and her breasts and her mouth, but hardly ever on her eyes. She's heard them talking, even though they've been quiet about it, whispering to one another while they're smoking outside or walking to their cars. They don't like her, not only because she's from the *Post*, and all cops hate a reporter snooping around, but also because of Hoskins. They've been careful in front of other people, acting like they hardly know each other, never touching, never talking, even when they could get away with it, but somehow everyone still knows.

"Have you told anyone?" she'd asked, not that long before. They were in his bed, the TV on but muted. She likes having the TV on while they have sex, likes to have the room filled with flickering light. "About us, I mean?"

"Why would I do that, princess?" he asked. "It's none of anybody's business."

"It—it feels like people know."

"Like who?"

"Like everyone."

"It's probably Loren," Hoskins had said, and he'd been smiling, but there was nothing kind about that smile, nothing familiar. Hoskins was a good guy, and that smile didn't belong to him. But then she blinked and it was gone. "That guy knows everything and can't keep his mouth shut."

"Might be."

"It's fine," he said, reaching for the glass of water on his nightstand. She wished she could see his face. "You're worrying over nothing."

But she's not all that worried, except when she thinks about her husband finding out about Hoskins. Not that she's afraid of Dean, or that he'd do something bad, but she doesn't want to hurt him, doesn't want to see the look on his face if he finds out. It's *everyone else* knowing that bothers her, because she knows what they're all saying, she's heard them say it.

Slut.

Whore.

The men think she's fucking Hoskins so she can get into Seever's house, so she can watch the investigation firsthand and write her articles for the *Post* and make them all look like fools, because that's what the scum media does. The men all like Hoskins, they think he's a hell of a good guy, but they're not fools. They see exactly what's going on. They've all seen the kind of tail Hoskins can typically pull, and Sammie's pretty far out of his league. She's a *dime*, a solid ten, and she could do much better. She's only fucking him so she can get in here, they tell each other. She's only sucking his dick for a story.

And it's true. Some of it, at least.

But Sammie wouldn't admit this, not even if someone put a gun to her head and demanded the truth. It's not exactly something that she's proud of, that she lets Hoskins touch her, that she puts on a show for him and then goes home and tells her husband lies so she can one-up every other reporter out there, panting to tell a good story. Besides, no one understands the position she was in at the paper, how it was to be there, day after day. Writing boring book reviews and fluff pieces on the local dog show, when all she wanted was to write a good piece, one that *mattered*. One that could make a difference. She'd hear her editor handing out assignments, but he'd pass right over her every time, and she'd go back to typing up her piece about the knitting club in Highlands Ranch that was donating their blankets to the homeless, or the dog with the prosthetic leg. She'd spent her whole life wanting to be a reporter, she'd thought she'd be big-time, that she'd be a glittering success, and when she'd been hired at the *Post*, she was sure she'd made it. The rest would be simple. But nothing in life is simple, and so she'd been patient, and she'd waited, and when she saw an opportunity she took it.

But it *does* embarrass her that all the men talk about her, that they call her names and treat her coldly when all she's doing is her job, in the best way she can. So what if it involves sex? If she were a man, no one would care. They'd probably congratulate her, give her an award. Her connection to Hoskins allows her to duck under the police barricade every morning while the rest of the journalists are stuck in the cold, standing on the street far back from Seever's house, with their notepads and recorders and cameras, and some of them have set up trailers and folding tables with steaming urns of coffee and cold doughnuts. There are journalists out there, important people with household names, flown in from New York or L.A., they have tents built in some of the yards and they spend all day out there, in the hopes that something might happen. She's heard that some of the neighbors are charging the media a day rate for squatting in their yards, a flat fee for every time one of them needs a toilet. But she gets to walk right past them, all of them, gets to see everything that's happening inside, is already writing her next article in her head as another body is zipped up in a black bag and carried out of the house.

This is something else Sammie has learned: If you're going to fuck someone, at least make sure they're important.

So the men keep whispering to one another as they dig up more bodies, and Sammie keeps writing, and she keeps fucking Hoskins. Keep on keeping on, as they say.

It's strange to be in Seever's house, surrounded by all the photographs of him, to see the dish towels his wife had hung from the hook beside the kitchen sink before she was forced to leave, and the ceramic Christmas tree still in the center of the dining-room table, one of the plastic lights sitting askew. But maybe it's only strange for her because she used to work for Seever, years before, practically a lifetime ago, before college and jobs and marriage, she'd been a waitress at Don's Café, one of the restaurants Seever owned. She'd already been working there a month when she saw Seever for the first time, when he stopped by to look over it all, make sure everything was running fine. He was wearing a nice tweed suit, expensive-looking, and his fingernails were polished and clean. He was handsome in those days, with his heavy brow and deep-set eyes and generous mouth, but even back then she'd noticed the weakness around his chin, the softness of his body, and she'd known he'd surely run to fat at some point; he was that type. Seever hadn't said anything to her that first time—he'd come in during the lunch rush and it'd been too busy for introductions, with everyone running back and forth between tables and the kitchen with trays of chicken-fried steak and creamed corn, potatoes, and okra.

She actually met Seever the second time he came in, shook his hand and told him her name. He was in a clown costume that time, dressed up to entertain kids in the restaurant with his clumsy dancing and clumsier balloon animals. He looked silly; most men would hate to be all done up like that, but he seemed to enjoy it. That was the thing. He liked to make the kids laugh and clap, even if the joke was on him, and there was one little girl who abandoned her plate of pancakes to dance with Seever, and he spun her round and round like a ballerina, until her skirt stood straight out from her body and she was out of breath from laughing so hard. Sammie had watched the whole dance with the rest of the customers, a pot of coffee in one hand and a big smile on her face, the same as everyone else, but Seever had still singled her out when it was over, because he'd seen her looking—of course he had, he was always watching, even if it was only from the corner of his eye.

"You like kids?" he'd asked, coming up as she was clearing off a booth. He bent down, grabbed an empty straw wrapper from the bench and handed it to her.

"I don't like them so much when they're screaming," she'd said, smiling. "But your dance with that girl was pretty cute."

"Samantha, isn't it?"

"Everyone calls me Sammie."

"I like that."

Later he twisted her a dog out of pink balloons, although it didn't look like much of anything except two pink balloons. She didn't tell him that though. And that afternoon, before he'd left for the day, he gave her the yellow daisy he had tucked into his lapel.

Seever was already killing at that time, Hoskins told her, although he was working carefully, picking his victims at random, people no one would miss, no one who could be connected to him in any way. It wasn't like years later, when Seever had gotten lazy and sloppy, when he thought he was invincible and he'd let Carrie Simms escape, and things had started to unravel. Sammie sometimes wonders what Seever had been thinking when he gave her that daisy, if he'd been thinking about taking her to his house and tying her up, doing bad things before he killed her, the way he'd done with so many others. But when she thinks about Seever now—the Seever she thought she'd known, the guy in the expensive suit with the gilt-edged smile—she can't imagine him killing anyone, even though she's a writer, and aren't all writers supposed to have big imaginations? And of course she knows, like everyone else, she's been trained by a lifetime of television and movies and books that the bad guy is usually the one you'd least expect, the one who seems the most innocent, the guy who laughs a lot and opens doors for ladies and is never, ever rude.

Seven bodies have been taken out of the crawl space so far—five women and two men—and they'd all hoped that lucky number seven was where it would end, that they'd find nothing else down there but dirt and worms. Victim seven had been removed the day before last, patches of red hair still clinging to his weathered skull, a punk-rock shirt hanging around his wasted chest. Later, they'd learn that the kid's name was Kenny Fitz, that he'd run away from home, like he had a million times before, but this time he'd never come back. Later, Kenny Fitz's mother would give Sammie a photograph of him to run in the *Post* alongside her article, and Sammie would hate to look at it. The photo was a glimpse into the past, at the grinning kid who'd one day accept a ride from a guy wearing a tweed suit. She wished she could go back in time, warn the kid, tell him to go home, hug his mom and get his shit together. But she couldn't, and she hoped that Kenny Fitz hadn't known what was going on at the end, that he hadn't been aware of anything when Seever had wrapped that extension cord around his throat and tightened down for the last time. She hoped that Kenny had spent his last few moments thinking good thoughts. About his mother. Or the dog he'd left behind, who still slept on Kenny's empty bed, his snout twitching and his paws paddling uselessly through empty air.

"Someone cared about this kid. Loved him. You know how I know?" Hoskins said this after the boy's body had been slipped into a plastic bag and wheeled away, before they knew who he was. Hoskins hadn't been eating much, or getting much sleep, and she could see it in his face, in the gray skin under his eyes. "It's his teeth. That kid's got good ones. Lots of fillings. He had braces at one point. Good teeth aren't free. Someone paid for all that work. Someone who loved him."

They find the eighth body the next day, while Sammie is in the kitchen, pouring herself a cup of coffee and listening to one of the technicians bitch about his job.

"When I blow my nose these days, nothing but black shit comes out. It's filthy down there. I don't know how much longer I can take this."

"Sorry," she says. She wonders how many times a day she says that single word. "It sounds terrible."

"*That's* what you should write about. How fucking bad it is down there. I feel like I'm stuck in a nightmare and I can't wake up."

She'd discovered, not long after starting her daily visits to Seever's house, that it was best to let the guys complain. At first she'd tried to reason with them, to point out they were doing their jobs, that they were getting paid to hunker down in that crawl space and dig corpses out of the ground. It wasn't like anyone was expecting them to work for free. But the men would get angry when she said things like that, so she started keeping her mouth shut, acted sympathetic and apologized when the complaints started. That went over better.

"It'll be over soon," she says.

"I certainly fucking hope so."

Someone shouts from the crawl space, words that she can't understand, and she jumps, startled, and slams her hip into the counter, hard enough to bruise. She ignores the pain and sticks her head into the laundry room, where the crowd of men are, excited and high-fiving, pumping their fists in the air.

"They found another one," the tech says, peering over her shoulder. His breath smells like wet cardboard. "Fuck, yeah. There're more."

She turns slowly, goes back to the kitchen. Her coffee is knocked over, although she doesn't remember doing it, and the mug is on its side, lazily rollicking back and forth on the counter, as if it's being pushed by a ghost. She grabs the roll of paper towels and drops to the tile floor, trying to ignore the excited chatter from the next room as she reaches for the steaming puddle.

HOSKINS

January 5, 2009

They've got a crew at Seever's house, digging up the crawl space and cataloguing everything that comes out of the ground. It's slow work, thankless. So far they've found eleven bodies, and that's only one corner of the room, in a section a few feet square. Quadrant one, they call it. Nine of the victims are women, and one matches the description of a girl who'd gone missing in Fort Collins in 1988. Twenty years, Hoskins thinks. How many people could Seever have killed in twenty years?

"I didn't kill anyone," Seever says. The three of them are together. Hoskins, Loren, and Seever. We are family, Hoskins thinks. I've got all my brothers with me. They're in an interview room, one that's so tight it's claustrophobic, and the air vents blow out either hot or cold, but never a temperature that's anywhere near comfortable. "This is all a big mistake."

"So those eleven people we've pulled outta your place are a figment of my imagination?" Loren asks. He's sitting opposite Seever at the small metal table, a cup of coffee in front of him. He hasn't offered Seever anything. Hoskins is by the door, his arms folded over his chest. He can't stop thinking about the last victim they pulled out. She had twine wrapped around her wrists and a scarf around her neck, one end of it crammed in her mouth. She'd choked on it, the coroner said, sucked it in and it'd snaked most of the way down her throat. She'd drowned in watered silk, the fabric printed with blooming red poppies.

"Is that all you've found?" Seever asks. He's agreed to talk to them without a lawyer, isn't all that concerned with his defense. He's not stupid, just crazy.

"So there're more?"

"Oh, I'm sure."

"How many are we gonna find down there?"

"Zero."

"How many did you murder?"

"All of them."

Hoskins rubs his fingers across his lips. They're dry, cracked. His hands smell like the soap in the station's bathroom—cheap and generic, but familiar. This isn't the first interview they've done with Seever, and it won't be the last. Not by a long shot. He's a sanctimonious son of a bitch, and he likes to play games, to toy with them. He talks in circles, sometimes telling the truth, but most are lies, bullshit made up for his own amusement. Jacky Seever's under arrest, he's guilty, no one in their right mind could think otherwise—but he's still all loosey-goosey, his hair slicked back from his forehead like he's goddamn greased lightning, an easy smile on his face like he's got nothing to worry about. Like he expects to be heading home soon, pulling up a kitchen chair and tucking into his dinner.

"What'd you do with their fingers?" Loren asks, and it's a good question, a valid one, because every victim that's been carried out of the crawl space has been missing at least one. Left hand, right hand, it varied. Seever didn't seem picky. It was a detail they hadn't released, Hoskins had even kept it from Sammie because she'd run it in an article if she had the chance. He thinks he might love Sammie, but love doesn't mean he's stupid. Sammie believes people should be told everything, that nothing should be held back, but not for the common good—just her own. She would want to feed the detail of the missing fingers to the public, serve it up like a waiter carrying a silver platter and lifting away the lid with a flourish.

"Fingers?"

"Yeah, dummy. You got some weird kink with fingers? Seems to me like you prefer the middle ones—you stick them up your ass to get off?"

Seever smiles. He likes to talk, there are some times he won't shut up, but Hoskins has a feeling they'll never hear the truth on this, and maybe it doesn't matter.

"I have a question," Hoskins says. It's the first time he's said anything, because Loren does most of the talking in these interviews; he's better at it, he knows what to ask. Hoskins is more like window dressing, backup if it's needed, a witness in case something bad goes down. Someone to keep an eye on Loren, make sure he behaves.

"What's that?" Seever asks. His eyes are greenish-brown, and there's a bright spot of gold in his left one, under the pupil.

"Why'd you bury them all in your crawl space?" Hoskins asks. If this interview doesn't end soon, if he doesn't get out of this room, he'll be sick. He felt the same way in the morgue, looking at the victims so far, their bodies laid out on the metal tables with the raised edges, so if the bodies leaked or bled there wouldn't be a mess to clean. "Why keep them with you?"

Seever blinks.

This is the million-dollar question. Sammie asked Hoskins this the night before, when they were in his bed. She had a bowl of trail mix balanced in the crux of her thighs, and even though he hates eating in bed, hated finding the sunflower seeds and nuts in his sheets after she was gone, he lets her do it.

"If Seever hadn't kept the—the dead people—"

"The victims," he'd corrected her. "Or the departed. That's what you should call them."

"Why'd he bury them all under his house? It's not like he has a good explanation for how all those bodies got down there. No one will ever think he's innocent."

"He's not trying to convince anyone he's innocent," Hoskins said. "He doesn't deny anything."

Sammie was wearing one of his shirts, and the collar hung loosely off one shoulder. He ran his fingers along her chest, down into the dip above the delicate bone. She closed her eyes, tilted her head back so the fine line of her neck was exposed. He often wondered what Sammie was thinking.

"Did you go down to your crawl space sometimes, pay them all a little visit?" Hoskins asks now, mildly. There's a rushing sound in his ears, and it seems like he's looking at Seever through binoculars, but through the wrong end. Seever looks so far away and tiny, although he's on the other side of the table, only three feet away, but he thinks that if he were to reach out and grab at Seever, his fist would swipe uselessly through empty air. "You'd go down there and gloat and laugh and jerk off?"

Seever swallows, his throat making a sharp clicking noise. Then he looks away.

"How'd you do it?" Loren asks, and Hoskins can hear the impatience in his voice, the waspy hum of anger below the surface. Maybe Seever can't hear it, but he hasn't worked with Loren for the last ten years, hasn't learned to gauge Loren's temper like you would the temperature of bathwater before climbing in. "Where'd you pick them up?"

Seever leans forward, his elbows on the table. He's wearing one of the orange jumpsuits all the prisoners wear, and the front of it is filthy, smeared with dried food and dirt. Seever was always so particular about his clothing, and now that's gone to shit. Incarceration isn't nice for pretty boys. Seever props his elbows up on the table. He looks eager to talk, and Hoskins expects that they'll get more lies out of him, more games and bragging, but instead, they get the truth.

"I got them from all over, wherever I could," Seever says. "I never attacked anyone. They all came home with me because they *wanted* to."

"I guess you expect me to believe that they *wanted* you to tie them up and kill them, too?" Loren asks.

Seever doesn't answer this, just laughs, that high-pitched titter that digs right into your brain and doesn't let go, and that's what sets Loren off. That's what they tell the boss man later, that Seever had laughed, he was always laughing like a maniac and Loren couldn't stand it anymore. But it's more than the laugh, Hoskins knows. It's the last seven weeks they've spent following Seever around, watching and waiting for him to slip up so they could finally arrest him.

They were first led to him by an anonymous call; a woman gave them Seever's name and address, said he was up to something, that she'd seen people going into the house and never coming back out. So they'd started watching him go to work and go to the bar and go home, peering at him through binoculars while he sat on the lip of his bathtub and clipped his fingernails into the toilet bowl. They started watching Seever because they had no one else to watch, no other leads, and they had to do *something*; the city was screaming for an explanation. Twenty-three disappearances reported in the last seven years in the Denver-metro alone. People disappeared all the time, but not like this, without witnesses or bodies, and there were stories about cults and Satan-worshipping floating around, of white slavery. Hoskins had heard the stories himself, and he'd laughed, because it was all so stupid. There had to be an explanation for all the missing people, he can remember thinking. Something sane and reasonable.

So they started following Seever, because of that one call, and they could've stopped at any time, but there was something that kept them after him. Because Seever was weird, there was something off about him, something *wrong*. It was Loren who said this, who said Seever was hiding something, that he was up to no good, he wasn't sure Seever was behind all the missing people, but the dude was bad news. And Loren was to be trusted, he had a nose for the work, he knew how to read people. Loren didn't like Seever, didn't like the way he'd shake hands and hold the sweaty grip for a moment too long, didn't like the way he'd gel his hair so the rows left behind by the comb's teeth were still plainly visible. Loren wanted to bust Seever for something, *anything*, even if it wasn't anything big, because he wanted to see the guy squirm, wanted to laugh in his face when they shoved him into a cell in his fancy suit and left him there to sleep on a cot and shit in a toilet with no seat. Oh, they could've busted him anytime for drinking—Seever liked to toss back a few at the bars most nights before heading home, they could've pulled him over a dozen different times—but Hoskins made Loren wait.

"I don't know," Hoskins had said. He was usually the one who plowed forward without a second thought—*prepare for ramming speed, look away if you're squeamish*—but this was different, there was some niggling doubt, a pricking in his thumbs that told him to slow down, to wait. To watch. If Seever was guilty of something big—and as they spent more time watching him, Hoskins was sure this was the case—and they jumped on him too soon, he'd be lost. Seever had money, he had friends; people liked him. They could slap him with a DUI, but then they'd have to back off, because otherwise he could claim they were harassing him, that the police department was out for blood on an innocent citizen, and they'd never be able to get him for anything else. "It would probably be better to wait."

"Bullshit," Loren had said, smacking his palm hard against the steering wheel. They were in his car, parked outside one of Seever's restaurants, watching the shadowed figures moving behind the glass, eating and laughing and sometimes doing nothing at all. "We could have him behind bars tonight."

"That won't get us into his house," Hoskins said, drumming his fingers on the dashboard and staring out at the white stripes painted on the asphalt, as if he were bored. "Let's say he is the one behind all these missing people. We'll never know if we never step foot in his place. Then we'll be the assholes who let this dipshit slip through our fingers."

Loren wouldn't take orders, he didn't like to be told what to do, Hoskins had learned that not long after they became partners. Loren would only go along with something if he thought it was his own idea, so Hoskins played the game; he was the one yanking the puppet strings, although it had to be done softly, with care. None of Loren's other partners had figured this out; Loren had stomped all over them and none of them had lasted, not until Hoskins. Because a partnership can't work with two snarling pit bulls—one of them has to play the part of the leash.

So Loren considered, spent a day mulling the whole thing over, then went to Chief Black, said he'd thought about it, and he'd decided the best thing to do would be to wait, to keep watching Seever and look for a good time to sweep in and nab him, and the boss man agreed to give them more time. Later, people would congratulate Loren on having that kind of foresight, on knowing when it was best to pull back, on having such good *instincts*, and Loren never once tried to correct anyone. Hoskins wasn't mad—that was life with Loren, what he'd come to expect. You had to give a lot to Loren to get a little, and the glory wasn't as important to Hoskins as it was to do his job the right way. The ends justify the means, or, like his father used to say, it doesn't matter what you put in your mouth, it's all shit in the end.

Be vewy, vewy quiet, Loren would whisper when they were parked across from Seever's house at night, struggling not to fall asleep. *We're hunting wabbits.*

It was funny at first, and then later, not so much.

Seven weeks of Elmer Fudd, seven weeks of watching Seever shovel food down his mouth-hole and stroll out to the curb to check his mail and chat with the neighbors, who all seemed to like Seever, who thought he was a pretty damn good guy. It was all going nowhere. Loren was persuasive but he wouldn't be able to convince Chief Black to let them watch this one guy forever. They needed a break. And they got one: a nineteen-year-old girl named Carrie Simms, the only person who'd ever managed to escape the crawl space.

But those seven weeks of Seever before Simms strolled into the station, fifty hours a week of him, sometimes more, there were nights Hoskins would dream about Seever slipping into bed with him, his hand hot and inviting when it snaked over his hip, reaching for his dick, and it didn't matter how hard Hoskins fought, he couldn't get free of him. They'd only been watching Seever, but he'd still managed to worm his way into their heads like a parasite, and Hoskins knew *that* was the real reason Loren jumped out of his chair and punched Seever right in the face, making his nose crunch flat and blood spray everywhere. Loren didn't do it because Seever was a killer—they'd arrested plenty of those before, men who'd done terrible things to their wives and children and complete strangers—but because Seever was like the chorus of a terrible song, set on infinite replay. He was the awful taste caught in the back of your mouth, the one that can't be rinsed away. The bloodstain in the carpet that won't ever come out.

Hoskins grabs the back of Loren's shirt and hauls him back, the two of them stumbling clumsily together, and Seever's shrieking, one hand clamped over his gushing nose, and he's looking right at Hoskins, because Loren's out of it, his eyes are closed and his lips are moving, counting slowly back from ten like the department psych told him to do when he felt ready to lose his shit.

"This isn't over," Seever screams. His voice is thick and syrupy from the blood pouring down his throat and over his lips to the collar of his jumpsuit, but Hoskins can understand him perfectly. "It'll never be over."

February 21, 2009

Thirty-one. That's how many bodies they have when the crawl space is all dug through and the backyard is plowed up and the concrete floor in the garage has been smashed to pieces and trucked away.

"I hate that bastard," Hoskins says. He's tired, big bags hanging under his eyes. He's been spending lots of time with Seever, hours and hours of interviews and questions, just the two of them, because Seever won't talk in front of Loren anymore. Hoskins doesn't tell her much, but she knows that Seever told him where to dig under his garage, and they'd found a skeleton there, that he'd been brought out to his house to show them the area in his yard where he'd buried another. "If I have to spend one more minute with that bastard, I'm going to lose my shit."

She doesn't say anything to that, because she always liked Seever, she still can't believe he's a killer. But you can never know what one person is capable of, she thinks. Like her husband. Dean isn't stupid; he knows something's going on, he's been watching her. He doesn't trust her anymore, and that bothers her, although it probably shouldn't, because why should he? Look what she's doing—to him, to their marriage. And to Hoskins. She can't forget Hoskins, who is tired and cranky most days, is not as often in the mood for sex but still clings to her. He's the kind of man who needs a woman in his life. If they'd met years before, she might've ended up with Hoskins instead of Dean, but thinking that makes her feel idiotic, because why should she always think about her life in terms of men? But she's never been without one, not since her first kiss in the seventh grade, and maybe she's like Hoskins—she can't live without a man in her life. But she doesn't have one man, she has two, and something's bound to give sooner or later, it's only a matter of time. Dean's asking questions and Hoskins is pressuring her to file for divorce, to move in with him, and she can't commit either way, because someone'll end up hurt, and is it so bad this way? It's the first time in her life that she doesn't want more, she'd be happy if things would stay the same, but then Hoskins makes the choice for her, says he's met someone else, that it's serious.

"What's her name?" Sammie asks. She hadn't thought it would be this way. She should be the one breaking up with him, that's how she'd always imagined it happening. Not this, over dinner, with another couple at the next table, eating silently, and she knows they're listening, and there won't be any tears or screams from her; Hoskins picked the perfect spot to do this, to escape unscathed. Without a scene.

"That's not important."

"It is to me." But why should it be? she thinks. Isn't this what she was looking for, this chance to step cleanly out of this relationship and back into her marriage? There's no reason to hang on. There's no reason to go to Seever's house anymore; there are other stories to write, it's time to let go.

"You don't like me seeing other women?" Hoskins says, smiling. "You go home to your husband but it's not okay if I have a girlfriend?"

"I never said that. I just want to know her name."

"If you don't want me seeing anyone else, move in with me. Leave him."

"I can't do that. You know I can't do that."

"Yes, you can. Pack yourself a bag of clothes and leave. I can buy you whatever else you need." This is Hoskins in a nutshell, she thinks. He wants to be the hero. If he lived in the Old West, he'd be wearing a white ten-gallon hat and she'd be hog-tied on the train track, screaming her fucking head off. "I'll take care of you."

She doesn't think there's another woman. There can't be. Hoskins has spent every moment of the last few months wrapped up in Seever, and in her. He hasn't had time to meet anyone else. He's making this up, she thinks. So she'll get jealous and leave Dean. Hoskins wants to settle down, he's told her that before. And she wonders why she always meets men like this, her whole life it's been this way—men who want more than she has to give. Where are all the men who want nothing but sex, to have some fun and move on?

"I need to go," she says, yanking her napkin off her lap and cramming it right down on her salad, *smush*, so she hears the lettuce leaves crack under the pressure.

"Were you listening to anything I said?" Hoskins asks.

"Yeah."

"And?"

"I don't know."

"You don't know what?"

"I don't know."

"So that's it?" he says. "You're all done with me?"

"No."

"Then leave him. Come home with me."

"I can't."

"I don't understand." And he wouldn't, she thinks. He doesn't know what it's like to be married to a nice man, a *good man* who makes her happy most days, and then have Hoskins, who she might love, but she can't leave Dean, because that choice would be irreversible, and what if it turned out to be the wrong one? It's not as if she could take it back. She's right in the middle, and it's safe there. She has her cake and she eats it too, like her mother would say if she knew all this was going on, but her mother would die if she did find out. Die of shame. She'd never be able to show her face in church again, that's what she'd say. *I have a whore daughter and I'm never getting into heaven.* "You got what you wanted, I guess? You got the story, you're getting the good assignments, and now you're done?"

"No." She shakes her head and bites on the pad of her thumb, but the truth is that she *is* getting the good assignments, that now Dan Corbin considers her a *serious* journalist. She gets calls from other reporters at other papers, hoping to squeeze information out of her, asking for her contacts, her sources, when it wasn't all that long ago that she was the one making the calls. She owes it all to Hoskins, but there's something inside her that hardens when she thinks about that. She's a miser, loath to give up anything to pay her debt. Especially when she knows exactly what Hoskins wants—he wants her. "That's not how it is."

"You'd lie to get anything you want," Hoskins says, and he stands up fast enough that his drink knocks over, spilling water all over everything, and a waiter rushes forward, wanting to help, to save the meal, but that seems as if it's happening far away, completely separate from this moment. "God, you're an ugly bitch."

Later, at home, Sammie will cry over what Hoskins has said. It isn't the part about being a liar that hurts, because she *is* a liar, she already knows that. But who isn't? Mostly it's the ugly thing that'll bother her. Because she's *not* ugly. Everyone, her entire life, has told her how pretty she is, how beautiful. It's a part of who she is; it's as much of her identity as her fingerprints or the freckle on her right hip. Her beauty has been the one thing she can count on, her fallback when everything else is going wrong. She has never had anyone call her *ugly*, and it hurts, although a part of her thinks that Hoskins is right, that she *is* ugly, that everyone sees it and tells her the opposite, she doesn't know any better.

"This isn't over," Hoskins says, vaguely, not really looking at her but over her shoulder, and it scares her—if they weren't in public, if the couple beside them wasn't openly staring now, not even pretending to mind their own business, if the waiter wasn't hovering over the table, patting down the wet spots he can reach, she might've screamed. Because those aren't Hoskins's words. They're Seever's, that's what Hoskins had told her, that Seever had said that, it was his catchphrase, he repeated it every time they spoke. "This'll never be over."

Then he leaves, turns and walks off, out of the restaurant and into the warmth of the afternoon. The couple hurriedly go back to their meal and the waiter starts clearing the table, everyone is busy not looking at her, *Move along folks, nothing to see here*, and she feels like she's been slapped, stunned, and she wishes someone would look at her, even if it is with pity, but no one does. It's like she's not even there at all.

March 17, 2009

On Tuesdays she goes to the grocery store, stocks up her fridge with plastic totes of salad greens and skim milk and ground coffee. She still hasn't gotten used to shopping for one—it's strange, not to buy all the things Jacky used to eat, the potatoes and cheeses and gallons of rocky-road ice cream. And all the red meat. She hardly ever eats meat now. There are even times she forgets to eat altogether, when she'll come into the kitchen in the morning for a cup of hot tea and find it completely untouched, and she'll realize that she didn't eat at all the day before. This never fails to surprise her, because it doesn't seem like eating is something a person could forget. She doesn't buy much at the grocery for that reason, and even so it sometimes goes to waste, the lettuce leaves melting into black goo at the bottom of the produce drawer, the quarts of milk separated and sour.

It's Tuesday, but she's not going to buy food. Instead she's going home, to the big house on the northeast corner of Sycamore Street, the brick place on a quarter-acre lot with the thirty-foot evergreen planted right outside the front door. That tree cost a small fortune to plant, and the roots would break into the foundation and the sewage lines at some point, but she'd once told Jacky that she wanted to live in a house with a big tree right outside the front door, and he'd stored that information away, kept it for later. Jacky always had a good memory for those kinds of things, and he loved surprises, and she was surprised when he bought the house, even more surprised when she woke up to the sound of men planting the tree in the yard a week after they moved in. Jacky liked to make her happy, he said that was a husband's main job. To make his wife smile.

"I'm sorry for all the times I've made you cry," he had said, a week before he was arrested. She was packing, carefully laying out outfits and rolling up socks to tuck into the shoes already in her open suitcase. They'd done a lot of traveling over the years of their marriage, and she'd become an expert at packing. Toiletries in gallon freezer bags, in case they exploded, which they were so apt to do when flying into Denver. A pillbox to keep her jewelry in, the compartments keeping the necklaces from getting tangled. Socks tucked into shoes to save space.

"What was that?" She'd been busy with her packing, trying to keep all the last-minute details straight. She was going on a trip with her mother, to see the arch in St. Louis, or farther on, to Chicago. The trip had been Jacky's idea, and later, she realized that he'd been so adamant about her going because he knew what was going to happen and he didn't want her around to see him arrested. "I'm sorry, I wasn't listening."

"I'm sorry for the times I made you cry," Jacky had repeated, slowly. He was sitting in the armchair by the window, looking out on their quiet street. There was a car parked at the corner, the same place it'd been every day for the last few weeks, and she could see the shoulder of the man sitting behind the wheel, his fingers drumming on the dash. She hadn't said anything to Jacky about the car and the men who were always around, but she knew he already knew, and that they were cops. She knew that by the clothes they wore, the way they wouldn't meet her eyes when she drove by. They'd been married for almost thirty years but Jacky still thought she was oblivious, that she didn't notice the little things. It was the running joke between them, and she'd always gone along with it, but she'd noticed the cops, their shifty eyes and their suit jackets that were cut too loose around the waists to hide their weapons, and she'd known something was going on.

"What're you talking about?" she'd asked, but he hadn't answered her, that's the way Jacky was sometimes, he'd move from one thing to another before she had time to catch up. He'd ignored her question and helped her pack, and she didn't remember that he'd said it until he called her from jail. She *had* spent a lot of time crying in the early years of their marriage, but after Jacky was arrested, she didn't cry at all.

But the house. Her house. Jacky had bought it because the restaurants were doing well. He said it was an investment in the future, that living in a rental was like flushing money down the toilet. It wasn't a nice house to begin with—the carpets were filthy, the walls were covered in tacky wallpaper, and there were spiders living in the highest corners—but Jacky said that was her job, to spruce up the house, to call in the contractors and the cleaners, to shop for furniture and curtains and knickknacks. Fluffing their nest, that's what Jacky called it. She'd thought they'd spend the rest of their lives in that house, they'd finally have kids and grow old and complain about having a second floor because of their stiff knees and they'd talk about selling, that's all it would be—*talk*. But none of it happened. There was never a baby, no matter how hard they tried or how many doctors they visited, and here she is now, forty-nine years old, living in a dumpy furnished apartment while her husband sits in prison and her beautiful house is empty. It wasn't the life she'd imagined for herself, but it's what she has, and nothing is going to change it.

She'll never live in her house again, the police say. She'd spent so many years planning, so much time bringing home paint samples and walking slowly through furniture showrooms. It hurts her to think that she'll never have a home that works so well at Christmas, when the dining room would be crammed with friends and family, the fifteen-foot tree glittering in the front window. Or those times during the summer, when they'd barbecue out back and neighborhood kids would be tearing around the yard, catching frogs in the pond and jumping off the dock Jacky had built, their tongues stained red from Popsicles. Her pastor always said that a person should let good memories of better times help them get through the bad, but that was before Jacky was arrested, before Pastor Ed had taken her aside and quietly suggested that it might be best for her to worship at home, that *He* would always listen to her, no matter where she was. Turn the other cheek, that's what she'd always been taught, so she didn't go back to church again; she stayed at home and watched televised sermons on Sunday mornings and prayed quietly before every meal and bed, but she would've liked nothing better than to see them all dead, to see Him smite them all for turning their backs during her time of need. But she waited, bided her time, because He repays. Sooner or later, everyone gets what they deserve.

"When will I be able to move back in?" she'd asked a few weeks ago. She was tired of the apartment. Corporate housing they call it, but it was as bad as staying at a motel. Worse. It kept her up at night, wondering how many people had slept in the bed, had used the chipped dishes in the cupboard and sat on the stiff sofa.

"What do you mean?" the cop had asked. There were two of them, and they always traveled in pairs, like a matched set. They were the ones who'd sat in front of her house, and one was younger and handsome, but the other was mean. She could never remember either of their names, didn't even try. She didn't like them. "You can't move back in there."

"What're you talking about? That's my house. I own it."

The two men looked at each other, seeming amused. She hated them for that. Like she was a child demanding a toy she couldn't have, because she didn't know any better.

"The house is going to be torn down, Mrs. Seever," the young one said. At least he was polite, not like the other one, who was always watching her, a weird smile on his face. "Completely demolished."

"No, it's not."

"Yeah, I'm afraid it is."

"Jacky said I could live there, even if he was in prison."

"Jacky doesn't get a say in things these days," the old one said. Loren, she remembered. Detective Loren. He was grimacing, his lips pulled back far enough that she could see every tooth in his head, and most of his gums. "You lose your vote when you murder a bunch of people."

"I don't understand."

"The house has been sold."

"But I live there."

"I guess your sweetie-pie husband never told you that you're dead broke," Loren said. "He had his lawyer sell everything to pay for his defense. The house. His car. All your assets. You didn't think that fancy lawyer-man was defending Jacky out of the goodness of his heart, did you?"

She tightened her hands on her purse, her nails sinking into the leather.

"But those all belonged to *me* too," she said. "He couldn't have sold it all without me knowing."

"Technically, nothing belongs to you," Loren said. "Your name wasn't on anything, so Jacky was able to do whatever the hell he wanted. And he did. Without ever letting you know."

He was right, she realized. Jacky had always taken care of every-thing, all the finances, all the paperwork, and she'd never been involved. Not once. She'd never known how much money they had, how things were going, but it had always been easy to believe that everything was fine, because it always seemed to be, and she'd never questioned anything as long as her credit cards still worked and her checks still cleared without issues. He'd bought the house without her, as a surprise, and he'd always gone to the car dealership alone. The only paper she'd ever signed with Jacky was her marriage license, and that's all he'd needed to bring her up in the world, then tear her down so low.

"But the diners—" she started, but then paused. She hadn't set foot in any of them since Jacky's arrest, had never even called to check on them. There'd been so many other things to deal with, and Jacky had assured her that he had the managers running things, that she didn't have a single thing to worry about. *I'll be out of here before you know it,* he'd told her during one of their visits at the county jail. *You don't have to lift one finger. Don't worry.* "Are they gone too?"

"Yes," said the young cop, shooting her a pitying look. She could've killed him for it.

"Who bought the house? And the diners?" she asked. "I'll buy them all back. They're mine."

She regretted saying the words as soon as they left her mouth, because she thought—no, she *knew,* she couldn't afford to be naïve, not anymore—she had nothing left. If Jacky had sold the house and the restaurants, all behind her back, of course he would've cleaned out their bank accounts too. If she was lucky he might've left her enough to live on for a while, but who was she kidding? Jacky was the one in prison, but she might as well have been too, and she'd built it herself, slid every brick into place with her own two hands. A prison built out of complete and utter stupidity.

Sucker, that's what her father would've called her. He would've smacked his lips together pleasurably when he said it. A goddamn sucker.

"The diners sold to new owners, and the house was bought by some foundation here in town. They work to improve the quality of life in Denver, and the plan is to destroy the house," the young cop said. He seemed embarrassed. "Have it leveled completely. I've heard talks about a playground being built there. Maybe a community garden."

"Why would they do that?" she cried.

"Because their check cleared, and they can," Loren said. "And because people need to forget what happened there."

"Forget what?" she said. She'd been scrubbing at her mouth with a tissue, meaning to wipe away the lipstick she'd forgotten to apply, and her lower lip had cracked open and begun to bleed.

"They need to forget your husband's a fucking psychopath."

"Jacky never hurt anyone in his life."

"Is that what you think?" Detective Loren said. She glanced at the young cop, wishing that he would speak more, he was so much nicer, but he was standing by the door, his arms crossed over his chest, watching his partner. "Do you know what your sweet, harmless hubby told us a few weeks ago?"

"No."

"One of the girls he killed—Beth Howard, I think. Is that right, Paulie?"

The young one shrugged.

"Anyway, this girl, she's walking home with a bag of groceries. And your husband, kind man that he is, offers her a ride. And she takes it. Maybe it was hot outside and she had a long way to go, or he propositioned her, or she was just a lazy idiot. But we'll never know."

"I don't understand why you're telling me this," Gloria said, pulling her purse closer to her body, taking some comfort in its weight.

"So *Jacky* brings Beth Howard home, where he does what he does. I won't go into detail—I'm sure you've seen the news. You know what he was doing."

"I didn't know." She stopped, cleared her throat. Something is stuck there, hot and heavy, but she'd rather choke to death before asking these men for a drink. "I didn't know anything."

"Paulie, you mind getting Mrs. Seever something to wet her whistle?"

The young one ducked out, came right back with a can of Coke. Gloria took it, cupped her hands around the aluminum, but didn't drink. The can was warm.

"Anyway. Where was I? Oh, yeah. Ms. Howard's dead, and I'm pretty sure everyone agrees that your husband had something to do with it." She hadn't thought it possible, but Detective Loren grinned, his lips stretching so far it looked like the top half of his head was ready to topple right off. "Ms. Howard was a kindergarten teacher, by the way. When she went missing, every kid in her class wrote us a letter, because they loved her so much. It was real touching, wasn't it, Paulie?"

"This doesn't have anything to do with me," she said stiffly.

"Wait, I have a point. So after Jacky was done with Ms. Howard, do you know what he did?"

"I need to go now."

But that bastard cop, with his mean eyes, he wasn't going to let her go until she heard everything he had to say.

"Jacky slid that girl under your bed. You spent eight hours sleeping six inches above a young woman your husband had killed." A bead of sweat ran down Loren's forehead, into his eye, and he swiped it away absently. She realized he was enjoying this, watching her squirm. He'd be able to tell all his buddies about it later over beers, she could practically hear them laughing at her expense. "Jacky liked keeping his victims close, even when he was done with them. Damn. Maybe if you'd given it up a little more—if you would've occasionally bent over and took one for the team, he wouldn't be where he is now."

She didn't say anything. She could feel a migraine coming on, a screaming-bad one, she'd spend the next ten hours in bed with a damp washcloth draped over her eyes. She considered taking the Coke and throwing it right in Loren's face, bounce it off his forehead. She wanted to hurt him for blaming all this on her, make him bleed.

"You can certainly go into the house and collect your things," Detective Loren said. "But there's no fucking way you can live there anymore."

So here she is, on a Tuesday, usually her grocery day, pulling into the driveway as if this is still her home, the keys jangling loosely in her palm and she walks to the front door. There's a car parked at the curb, the engine idling so the air conditioner keeps chugging away—it's warm for March—keeping the two men inside out of the heat. The one in the passenger seat raises his hand, and she nods in return, although she'd much rather flip him the bird. They're cops. There are always cops here now, keeping watch over the house until it's torn down, which is a waste, she thinks, because *why not* let the bums and delinquents have a turn before it's all razed to the ground? She's heard that people have tried to break in, because they want to write ugly things on the walls in spray paint and kick holes in the doors, or they want to steal something, a morbid piece of Jacky Seever to show off to their friends.

She unlocks the front door, goes inside. She was last here the week before, with two young men and a moving truck, and they'd carried out everything she'd pointed at, loaded it up to take away, even though they were nervous, they'd heard all the stories about the house, and the crawl space was still exposed although the cops had nailed a tarp over the open hole and roped it off. She had them box up her photographs, and the set of Christmas china with the scalloped edges and the sprig of holly imprinted in the centers. All the furniture in the guest bedroom, the nice wicker set with the lace coverlet. She'd slept in that bed sometimes, when Jacky's snoring got too loud, or when her insomnia was particularly bad and she didn't want to keep Jacky up, and it was nicer than the stuff in the master bedroom, more comfortable.

"The police confirmed that a few of your neighbors complained of a bad smell coming from your house on several occasions. Is that true?" That was one of the questions from that newspaper reporter, she couldn't remember her name, who had showed up two months before. Gloria had tried to close her door on the girl when she'd said she was from the *Post*, but then the girl had said she thought Jacky was innocent, that he was being raked over the coals for no good reason. That was why Gloria had let her into the apartment, had set her down in the tiny living room and served her coffee and cookies, the crispy butter kind in the blue tin.

"I remember that happening once or twice. On hot days."

"Okay."

"We always had a rodent problem," Gloria said. "Jacky would set out poison, and the mice would crawl up in the walls and die."

The young woman frowned, tucked a strand of hair behind her ear. She was young, very pretty. By the look of her flat stomach she didn't have any children; she might not have been married. Gloria didn't ask—it would've been rude.

"Mice?"

"Yes. Having that pond out back attracted all kinds of pests."

"Did your husband tell you that? About the mice, I mean?"

Gloria sat back in her chair, a hideous shiny black leather thing with silver buttons punched up the arms, a monster that was supposed to be southwestern-style but was only ugly. It struck her that this girl, who was drinking her coffee and taking polite bites of her cookies, didn't believe that Jacky was innocent at all, and probably thought she was a liar too.

"Yes. That's what Jacky told me."

"And you believed him?"

Gloria bit down on the inside of her cheek, hard enough that it would be tender and swollen all the next day, and sores would form on the broken skin, causing her misery for a week.

"Why wouldn't I believe him?"

"Your husband confessed to murdering thirty-one people, Mrs. Seever, right in your own home," the reporter said. "I find it difficult to believe you had no idea what was going on."

"The police cleared me as a suspect, if that's what you're getting at."

"Not at all."

Gloria stared at her.

"You look familiar," she said. "Have we met before?"

"I don't think so."

"Jacky would've thought you were pretty," Gloria said. "He would've been interested in getting to know you better."

The reporter left in a hurry after *that*.

Inside is cool and quiet, with the musty smell that always happens when a house is shut up for too long. She's already taken everything she wants out of the house, but she still wanted to come back, to say goodbye. She was happy in this house.

Gloria goes upstairs, slowly, because her knees have begun to ache some in the last few months, and turns into the master bedroom, second door on the left. Here is their big bed with the cherrywood headboard, and the filigree metal lamps she picked up from an antique dealer. She'd read that men naturally sleep on the side of the bed closer to the door, so they'd be able to protect their spouse, but she'd always slept in that spot. She wonders what that says about their marriage.

She gets down on her knees and flips back the edge of the duvet so she can see under the bed. It's not a comfortable position. The shag is rough on her cheek, and from this close she sees little black smudges caught in the carpet fibers. Dirt, or makeup. Jacky used to always complain when she'd sharpen her eyeliners, and the shavings would end up on the carpet, because they'd never come out, not even after a good scrubbing.

There's nothing under the bed except a few dust bunnies, a scattering of bobby pins, and a book. The book has been pushed way back, and she has to strain to reach it, her fingers scraping fruitlessly against the spine before she finally manages to hook it. It's a book for pregnant women, with advice on morning sickness and colic, breastfeeding and choosing the right brand of diapers. She can't remember buying it, although she must've, because no one else knew that they'd spent most of their marriage trying for a baby. Most everyone assumed that they were one of those couples who'd decided to pass on kids, that they'd forever play the doting aunt and uncle to everyone else's children and spend all their free time and money on travel and good wine. But everyone was wrong; Gloria had wanted children for so long and then it was too late, her insides had dried up and shriveled from disuse, and nothing could be done. Although now, she thinks, she's glad there was never a baby.

She flips through the book, looks at the pages full of words and sketches of a vulva, which looks more like a strawberry cut in half than anything that might be hiding between a woman's legs. It's warm in the house, stuffy, and she lies down, rests her head on the soft length of her upper arm. The floor is hard, but she still starts to doze, because it's so warm and she's tired and this is her home, this will always be her home. She was nearly asleep when something under the bed moved, and when her eyes flew open there's a young woman staring at her, only inches away. A woman with a heart-shaped face and mousy-brown hair, wearing a blue dress printed with sprigs of white flowers. It's Beth Howard, Gloria knows it. Beth Howard, the girl Jacky kept under the bed, and she'd be pretty except she's dead; her face has a shrunken look about it, like a softening, wrinkled apple left for too long in a dark cabinet. But her eyes are alive, mad and glittering, two tarnished marbles pushed deep into her white face.

"He took everything from me," the girl hisses, and Gloria sits up with a jerk, the muscle in her right shoulder wrenching in pain. She scoots away from the bed, her hands scrabbling for purchase against the carpet, until she backs into the armchair she always kept in the corner. From the chair she can see that there's nothing under the bed, nothing at all but certainly not a dead girl. It was a trick of her imagination.

Gloria leans against the armchair wearily, pulls her legs up to her chest and settles her forehead against her knees. She looks like a girl when she sits like this, young and vulnerable, the girl she used to be. The girl hiding behind the couch while her father held a gun in her mother's face.

She has her eyes closed and is breathing deeply, trying to get herself under control. In through the nose, out through the mouth, like the gym teacher used to tell them back in high school. And then, she smells it. What others had sometimes complained about but she never noticed. The smell of rot, the cloying, wet scent of flesh boiling with maggots.

It's my imagination, she thinks. It's all in my head. I don't smell anything.

She waits for it to pass, bundling her hands into fists and pressing them against her eyes. It makes her think of a trip to the zoo when she was much younger, standing inside the moist heat of the monkey house and feeling the bile rising in her throat before that horrible smell finally faded into the background, still there but tolerable, and she thinks this will be the same, but it only seems to get stronger; it might be because of the heat, the big brick house would always get so hot during the summer unless the AC was pumping away, but it's a moot point, because she can't take it any longer. She stumbles out of her bedroom and down the stairs, reaching desperately for the front door, barely able to keep from vomiting, or from screaming.

May 18, 2009

Carrie Simms, the girl who escaped Seever, doesn't want to testify at the trial. She's painfully thin and small, with a face like a mouse. She's normally easy, agreeable to most anything, but not on this.

"I can't be in the same room with that guy," she says. Her hair has grown out in the last few months, and she wears it hanging in her face, strands of it poking into her mouth so she seems to be gnawing on it, making her seem younger than she is, and shy. "Every time I see that bastard on TV I feel like passing out."

Simms had wandered into the station the third week of December, when the holiday decorations had already been up for long enough that Hoskins was sick of looking at them. He'd spent Thanksgiving watching Seever's friends and family through the big front window, passing baskets of dinner rolls and slices of turkey breast around the dining-room table. They were having a good time in there, warm and laughing, and it was those situations that made Hoskins hate his job, because he should've been doing the same thing, he should have a wife and kids but instead he had nothing, his ex-wife had left because he was always so wrapped up in his work, he was never around. When he finally called it a day he stopped by his father's house, but the old man was asleep in front of the television, kicked back in his La-Z-Boy with a can of beer nestled between the armrest and his thigh. And when Joe woke up, he didn't seem to recognize Hoskins at first; he was nervous and a little scared, and that depressed Hoskins even more, because that was his life, sitting in front of a suspect's house alone and then being forgotten by his own father. Even Loren had someplace to go for the holiday, although he wouldn't tell Hoskins where.

He expected it to be the same for Christmas. More watching Seever, alone, while everyone else was opening presents or drinking nog, and he was thinking about this as he looked at a sprig of mistletoe someone had stapled to the ceiling near his desk. He was just about to get up on his chair and rip it down when Simms came in, wanting to tell someone her story. He didn't believe her. Not at first. Simms was a high-school dropout who'd fallen into drugs, mostly meth, and she'd been arrested for prostitution a few times, once for assault. She'd called po-lice eight times in 2005, saying she'd been robbed, trying to file claims for TVs and stereos and expensive things she'd never owned. She was nineteen but looked forty-five, she was a junkie who needed a fix, and she said she'd ended up with Seever because she was more than will-ing to suck dick for cash, and that's what she'd offered him. She'd climbed willingly enough into Seever's BMW, he'd given her shots of tequila, a hit of coke, and a handful of pills, and then she'd blacked out. When she woke up she was naked and hog-tied, and the guy who'd been so friendly at the bar was suddenly a different person, and he had a big bag of all kinds of things, things you can't buy in a store but only through catalogs that arrive in the mail wrapped in heavy black plastic so the mailman can't see what kind of kinky shit you're into. Seever had big plans, he was practically bouncing on his tippy-toes with excitement, like a kid at Christmas. It had gone on for days before Simms was able to escape, when the twine around her wrists was loose—partly because Seever was lazy and hadn't double-checked his knots, but mostly because Simms was so damn skinny. She'd man-aged to wiggle free from the ropes and she'd run, not paying attention to where she was going or where she'd been, or even to the fact that she was only wearing panties and a ripped undershirt.

"Why didn't you come to us with this right away?" Hoskins had asked. "You said it happened—four months ago? Beginning of August? Why'd you wait so long?"

"I don't know," Simms said. A few minutes into their conversation she'd asked for blank paper and a highlighter, and she'd sat there, still talking, running the marker over the white sheet until it was com-pletely yellow, and then she'd started on the next one. The pinkie fin-ger on her right hand was gone, only a badly healed stump was left; she said Seever had cut it off, although she couldn't remember him doing it, she'd been unconscious when it happened, woke up and it was gone. They didn't believe this, not at first; it seemed like another lie, another fantasy. Simms was missing teeth and had the scabby skin of a meth-head, she had track marks all up and down her arms—on anyone else, a missing finger would've been startling, but on Simms it was barely worth noticing. Hoskins didn't believe her story about Seever cutting off her finger until he saw the other victims being hauled out from under the house, their hands mutilated, the stumps sometimes still weeping with pus and blood and rot. "It's not like I want to advertise that some dude spent two days jamming a dildo up my ass and talking about the hole he's digging in the crawl space for me."

He didn't believe Simms at first, mostly because she was the girl-who-cried-wolf and had called the cops so many times before. Simms was more comfortable with lies than she was with the truth; a lot of people were that way these days. They wanted to be involved but not *too* much, they didn't want to rock the boat, but still wanted justice. That was why the police station got so many anonymous tips. Everyone wanted a piece of the pie, but no one wanted to put their name on it. But Hoskins wasn't sure, so he called Loren into the office to hear her story, even though he'd taken a long weekend for the holiday.

"You called us after it happened, didn't you?" Loren asked Simms. He was tipped back in his chair, his eyes halfway closed so he seemed half asleep. Hoskins had seen Loren raging and angry in the interview room, and he'd seen him cool and professional, but he'd never seen him like this. Bored, almost. "Did you make that anonymous call so we'd look at Seever?"

For the first time, Simms laid down the marker. She wrapped the fingers of her right hand around her left wrist, so they looked cuffed together.

"No."

"It had to be you who called."

"It wasn't. I never called."

"What made you decide to come in now?" It was the same question Hoskins had asked, and it'd made her angry, sarcastic, but she reacted differently with Loren. It was strange to see, because most people were either scared of him or repulsed, but Simms was more at ease with him in the room.

"I keep thinking about biting," she said. Her head was ducked, her chin practically against her chest, so they could barely hear her words. "I want to bite down on soft things and make someone scream."

They loaded Simms into Loren's car and drove her to Seever's house, parked down the street. Seever was outside, walking down his driveway to grab the *Post*, and Simms's breath caught in her throat when she saw him. Hoskins didn't believe her story until he saw her eyes bugging out of her skull and her fists crammed against her mouth, he thought she might be having a seizure but she was just terrified, trying not to scream.

They still didn't have enough to arrest Seever, but it was more than they'd had before. Years before, Jacky Seever had been detained for marijuana possession, and that's what Hoskins told the judge they were looking for. Judge Vasquez knew the truth, Hoskins could see it written plainly on the man's face, but they still got their warrant—not to look for murder victims, but to search the premises for marijuana.

It was all they needed.

It's over, the boss man says. Chief Jonathan Black, the biggest pain-in-the-ass boss Hoskins has ever had, doesn't want to hear it. The Seever case is closed.

It's a PR thing, Hoskins knows. A budget thing. They'd been searching for Seever for so long, it's time to move on. There are other murders, other crimes. They can't keep this up.

It's time to hand it over to the people, Black tells them, and it's true—Seever's not theirs anymore. He belongs to everyone. Outside the jailhouse where Seever's awaiting trial there's a huge crowd, carrying homemade placards and bringing out their folding chairs and cases of bottled water, and it almost seems like a party, except the celebration is more like an orgy of hate, the people smile rabidly, flecks of spittle at the corners of their mouths. Denver has been waiting for the moment when the monster gets pulled out from under the bed and into the light, and that is now; they don't want to wait for more, they want to see this one brought to justice.

Hoskins leaves through the jail's side door, pausing to watch the swelling crowd gathering out front. There's a girl there, wearing a jacket printed with pink bunnies. She can't be more than five. She's holding a sheet of poster board, awkwardly, because it's too big for her small arms, but she doesn't put it down, doesn't want to miss out on the fun. There's a poem written on the board in straggling black letters, and Hoskins hopes she doesn't know what it says, hopes that she can't read yet:

Roses are red
Violets are blue
Good morning Jacky
We're gonna
Kill you!

Jacky Seever was brought to trial on June 1, 2009, charged with thirty-one counts of first-degree murder. Seever wore a brown tweed suit on that first day, as he was wont to do, and a blue silk tie. No photographers were allowed in the courtroom, but an artist in the audience sketched plenty of images that appeared in the *Post* alongside Samantha Peterson's articles. In some of the sketches, Seever is stone-faced, with a sheen of sweat on his brow. In others, Seever looks weary, even remorseful—although it is up for debate whether that's how he actually felt.

The trial itself lasted less than six weeks, and it was the focus of an entire nation. It had been a long while since the American public had been riveted by one person, and they were hungry for blood and gore, and a good story. They got it. A respected member of the community. Thirty-one victims. Nineteen of those had been identified, and the weeping families would tell anyone who'd listen about their murdered loved ones. Cable news stations had a constant feed on the trial, and every newspaper in the country had sent a journalist to cover the story. Local hotels had no available rooms, and anyone who had nowhere to stay found themselves camping out beside the homeless in Civic Center Park, only to be rooted out by the cops in the middle of the night.

The prosecution asked for the death penalty.

It took only three hours for the jury to make their decision. Fast enough that they were done in time to grab an early prime-rib dinner and shrimp cocktails at the Broker. The American public was relieved—a monster had been condemned, and they could finally get back to their regularly scheduled programming.

Jacky Seever was sentenced to death by lethal injection.

But a crime like this isn't only about the killer. There are others to consider. The victims. Their families. Detectives Ralph Loren and Paul Hoskins, who were both given a commendation and a goodish raise for Seever's arrest. Sammie Peterson, who became something of a local celebrity because of her articles covering the case. Gloria Seever, who had to learn how to live in a world without her husband. Those are just a few, because a crime like this has a wide reach, and you can never know how many are actually affected. That's how things like this are—a drop in still water that starts a ripple, and it spreads in every direction, going on and on, probably into infinity, never flatlining but starting other ripples that head in completely new directions. Sooner or later, the original ripple will slow, it will lose much of its urgency, but it's still there.

It'll never be over.

THIS
ISN'T
OVER

November 27, 2015

After seven years, nearly everyone has forgotten about Jacky Seever. Except Carrie Simms. She's spent every day of the last seven years thinking of Seever, of what he did over the days he'd kept her tied and gagged in his garage. Those kinds of things aren't easy to forget, and sometimes she wakes up in the middle of the night, her head aching because she's had her jaw clenched tight, trying to keep from screaming. A dentist gave her a hunk of plastic to stick in her mouth when she sleeps, like something hockey players wear to keep their teeth from shattering, but she doesn't need a guard for her teeth, she needs one for her brain, to keep it quiet, to keep from dreaming about Seever. A dream-guard, that's what she needs. Or a lobotomy. Carrie used to be the kind of girl who talked a lot, laughed loudly, but over the last seven years she's become mostly silent, a woman who doesn't want to be noticed. She's only twenty-six, but her roots are mostly gray already, there are deep lines radiating from the corners of her eyes, and her hand sometimes aches, as if longing for the lost finger.

But she's alive.

She sometimes thinks back to her life before Seever, or **Before Seever, BS**, as she likes to think of it, in big capital letters and bolded. She doesn't remember much of that life, only that she was sometimes hungry and cold, and almost always stoned out of her gourd, and the people surrounding her were a constantly rotating cast of nobodies, people she'd see once and then never again. That was all **Before Seever**, and she thinks that if she'd never met Seever in that bar, if she hadn't gone home with him that night, she'd already be dead, from drugs or something, and it would've been her own fault, no different from suicide. Seever had meant to kill her, but in those few days she'd spent in his garage, her wrists and ankles tied together, an old rag stuffed into her mouth and sometimes one looped over her eyes, she'd learned an important lesson: She wanted to live. It sounds stupid, it sounds cliché, but those terrible hours spent with Seever made her life that much more precious, and when she finally got out of that garage and ran, her bare feet slapping against the concrete, when she was terrified that she'd look over her shoulder and he'd be there, ready to take a handful of her hair and drag her back into the darkness, those were the most beautiful moments she'd ever experienced. She's not thankful for Seever and what he did, not really, but maybe she is, just a little.

She's cleaned up now, no more drugs, no booze. She doesn't work—her grandfather died the winter before, so she lives off what he left her and student loans, so she goes to school, training to be a vet tech, because she's always liked animals, they don't laugh and snicker and stare at the hand that has a stump instead of a pinkie finger, as if it's the most horrifying thing they've ever seen. Animals have never tried to hurt her, not the way Seever did, or the way her uncle used to when she was young. If an animal attacks you, they have a reason, they didn't do it because they thought it was fun, they didn't want to see you hurt for no reason at all. Animals don't laugh when you scream, and they don't stroke your hair afterward and promise that it'll all be over soon although it's a lie. She lives alone, renting a guest cottage behind a bigger house, it's probably meant to be a garage or a shed but was renovated, the washer and dryer sit in a closet and she can barely get the doors open to throw her clothes in and there's only a stand-up shower stall in the bathroom, no room for a tub, but she doesn't care. One day, she thinks, she'll graduate and get a job, live somewhere better. Maybe she'll even find some nice guy and go out on dates—or she'll get a pet. A dog—a dog would bark if someone tried to break in, a dog would be good protection. Or she could get a cat. Probably a cat. She'd wanted to get a cat after she'd moved in, and she asked the owner, an old Korean guy who traveled a lot and liked to play golf, but he'd said no, that he didn't want a cat pissing on the carpets, her security deposit wouldn't go *that* far.

"So you think Seever's wife knew you were there?" Detective Hoskins had asked, and she'd wanted to have an answer for him, but she wasn't certain.

"I don't know," she'd said, and she'd felt Hoskins looking at her closely, trying to figure out if she was lying or not, but she wasn't, because that was the truth, she didn't know. She sometimes wondered if she was really alive, or if she was taking part in some virtual reality and her real body was curled up in the fetal position somewhere, floating in a sac of fluid and hooked up to a giant computer, like in that movie, the one she can never remember the title of. Because that's what her life had been like—one long, never-ending bad movie. She could only hope that she'd wake up at some point and find out that none of it had happened.

She doesn't have a TV, can't afford one, so she usually reads a book before bed. A library book, because she can't afford to buy them, not now. She sometimes falls asleep with the book still open and her bedroom light on, a habit Mr. Cho has been lecturing her about, because he doesn't like to see her waste electricity, even though she pays her own bill. So she tries to turn off the light before she goes to bed, although she's not a big fan of the dark, never has been. When she was small the kids were always playing that game Bloody Mary, and once, at a slumber party, the other girls had shoved her into a dark bathroom and there were a few terrifying moments when she couldn't find the light switch, when she was sure that the big mirror above the sink would light up witchy red and a woman would appear, holding a big knife, her cracked lips spread in a silent scream. It was always dark when her uncle snuck into her room, and Seever had liked to keep a blindfold on her, so she'd never be sure where he'd touch her next, and he'd chuckle when she jumped or shied away. But Mr. Cho doesn't know all that about her uncle or Seever, and she isn't going to fill him in; he's concerned about the electric bill, so she tries to sleep in the dark, because that's what adults do, she needs to get over it. Her uncle is dead and Seever is locked up in prison and she's fine, she's *fine*, she's safe and she's alone and no one can hurt her.

Falling asleep isn't her issue. It's *staying* asleep. There are the nightmares, lots of them, usually about Seever, and sometimes the dreams are replays of her actual memories, but she can't tell the difference between what's happened and what she's imagining, not anymore. Like the memory she has of being blindfolded, of lying on a piece of carpet, although she could plainly feel the cold concrete beneath, and hearing a door whistle open, and she thought it was Seever, that he'd already come back for more even though he'd just left, but maybe it wasn't him at all, because Seever loved to talk, to hear his own voice, and whoever was there with her that day never said a word. But there was a *scent*, the faintest whiff of perfume, it made her think of the purple flowers that had grown in bunches beside her mother's front door, and when she started groaning for help, trying to form words around the cloth taped into her mouth, there was a puff of warm air and the creak of the door again, and the scent was gone, like it had never been there at all.

"You should think about talking to a professional about all of this," Hoskins had told her after Seever was locked up and sentenced and everyone had dusted off their hands and was finished with the whole thing, and she was supposed to go back to normal like nothing had ever happened. "It might help."

"I could tell you the same thing," Carrie said, and Hoskins had actually looked *surprised* at that, as if he hadn't realized how bad he looked, how much weight he'd lost.

"A doctor could prescribe you something to help you sleep," Hoskins had said, and how she'd laughed at that, because she'd been clean for almost a year by that time, no drugs, no booze, no problem, and people never seemed to realize how easy it was to slip back into that shit, that one sleeping pill could lead to a beer before bed, just to relax, and then it would be three beers and a half-dozen pills, and it would be a quick slide from there; she'd been down that path before, but now she was clean and she wanted to stay that way. So she puts up with the insomnia, *deals* with it, and now here she is, three in the morning, shivering under her blankets and wide-awake, the stump where her finger had once been throbbing, staring out into the dark bedroom. She was dreaming about Seever again, she thinks, the way he smelled, that cheap cologne he wore, and the rasp of his stubble against her bare shoulder as he'd lain behind her, his arms crossed over her middle, holding her close. He'd take her blindfold off then, so she could see his arm hooked around her stomach, look around and see the big red toolbox standing against one wall, and a big stack of empty vases in another. She'd never been violent, even when she had some drug or another raging through her system, but she thought that if she could get to that toolbox or that pile of glass, she'd have a weapon, she'd cut Seever's throat without a moment of hesitation, then she'd slice off his lousy dick and cram it in his mouth, give him some payback for everything he'd done, not that that would be enough, not by a long shot. But she never got a chance to even try, not until she escaped, and the only thing she could think about then was getting the hell out of there, not revenge.

She can't stop shaking. The dream was so real that she can still smell Seever, along with something else, and she realizes it's the smell of her own sweat. It's hard to believe that she'd sweat so much when her room is so cold, and she starts to sit up, thinking the furnace must be broken, that she'll have to bother Mr. Cho while he's out on his golfing trip in Phoenix, and an arm slips around her neck, pulling her back down into the pillow so fast she doesn't have a chance to scream.

"Don't worry, I'll make this last," a voice says, stubble brushing against her earlobe, his cologne so strong that she's practically choking on it. It's Seever, she thinks, and she tries to fight him but he's got the upper hand; she was surprised and not ready, but really, hasn't she been expecting this all along? Seever's not in prison at all, he's here with her, in her bed, he's going to finish what he started, and this is not a dream.

MOVE

ON

If this were a movie, you'd know time has passed because the words would be printed right there on the bottom of the screen for you to read: *ix years later.* And this scene would open up over the city of Denver—the camera would sweep over downtown, taking in the strangely curved glass walls of the Wells Fargo building and the golden dome of the Capitol, and the snakelike curve of I-25 as it unfolds north and south. And the mountains, always the mountains, huge hills of purple and blue on the western horizon, their caps dusted with snow. We would see all this and dive down with dizzying speed, toward Colfax Avenue, where most of the city's porno shops and the massage parlors are located, where there's always graffiti and loud music, and if you know enough, if you're desperate enough, you may know where to park your car and honk so the hookers'll come out and show their faces, among other things. On Colfax, not far from the rush of the interstate, is a coffee shop, plunked right down in the corner of a Walmart parking lot like an accident, way out where the donation bins and the RVs sit, where the piles of papers are stacked for recycling, and on windy days it's a hot-ass mess, a hurricane of smeary newsprint and words. The coffee shop looks like a refrigerator box thrown on its side, like a playhouse for a kid, but it's a real, legitimate business where a customer can pull their car right up along the side and watch through a window as their coffee is being made. The coffee is overpriced and tastes like shit, and there aren't many choices. No pastries or granola or protein packs. Nothing like that. Just coffee.

But what the place lacks in options, it makes up for in other ways. The employees, mainly. They're all women—girls, really—and they work their shifts in bikinis. Sometimes lingerie. It's part of the concept, to satisfy the customer. Get some coffee, get an eyeful. Like a Happy Meal for adult men.

Det. Paul Hoskins is a regular customer.

"Same as usual, honey?" Trixie says, leaning out the window. She speaks with a Southern accent, but Hoskins knows it's a put-on, nonsense she's picked up from TV, because she occasionally slips right back into the flat, toneless drawl most people seem to have these days. She's wearing a hot-pink bra and a black thong. Her tits look ready to tumble right out into the open, and he can see the beginning of a pimple in her cleavage, red and irritated.

"Yeah." The girls all know he's a cop; they say it makes them feel safe to have him come through every morning. His coffee is always on the house.

Trixie hands Hoskins a steaming foam cup—she must've seen him coming, got his drink ready. Large coffee, straight black. Loren always used to give him shit for drinking it like that, called him a *real man* and asked him how much hair he had on his chest and then dumped three packets of sugar and a dollop of cream into his.

"Thanks," he says. "Slow morning?"

"It'll pick up," Trixie says.

"You got any big plans for the weekend?"

"Not really." There's a sketch on the side of the foam cup, a cartoon mug with long, sexy legs sprouting from the bottom and big, juicy lips around the midsection. That's their logo—a cup of coffee that looks ready and more than willing to give a blowjob. Hoskins sometimes wondered if any horny teenage boys jacked off to that logo. "Hey, I brought in some doughnuts this morning. You want one?"

He doesn't think Trixie's her real name—what kind of parent would do that to their kid?—but he's never asked. It gives the girls a sense of security to give out a fake name, although it's a false sense, especially in this day and age, when anyone can find out anything. But he understands. Telling a little lie to make life easier.

"What do you got?"

"Couple powdered sugar. One—oh, two glazed. Something with filling. Looks like raspberry."

He'd found out about this place from a woman he'd dated, Vicki, or something like that, he can't even remember her name, who'd read about it online and then went into one of her rants—she said that's what the world was coming to, people would get their rocks off anyplace they could, even if it was their morning coffee. But Vicki was also the kind of woman who wished she could live back in the 1950s and wear an apron, and thought most men were perverts, any woman with a good body and a low-cut shirt was a whore. She had opinions, she had a big mouth, but she was mostly insecure. Insecure and needy, and he'd put up with it, not for any good reason but mostly because she kept coming back. He couldn't even remember how they'd started dating, or where he'd first met her. She'd finally broken up with him, went through his bathroom cabinets and dresser drawers and packed up everything she'd left behind over the six months of their relationship, shouting that she was through with his *shit*, that he was a bastard who'd never be able to hang on to a woman, that he'd never find anyone better than her. He'd heard it all before. She dumped him because he was *damaged*, because being with him was like dating a robot, but he figured it was really because of the coffee cup he'd forgotten to throw away, Vicki had seen it and known he'd been going to *that place*, and if there was one thing she wouldn't put up with, it was a boyfriend who liked to stare at half-naked women while they poured his coffee. So Vicki had left, but she still sometimes texted him, wanting to *check in*, she'd say, and he knew he could get her back, if he wanted.

He didn't.

"Are you offering me a doughnut because I'm a cop?" he asks.

"Oh, I didn't mean it like that," Trixie says, the smile dropping right off her face. There're two scratches on her shoulder, deep ones. Could be from a cat, although they don't look it. "I thought you might like one."

He reaches through the window and touches her arm. It's cold outside, and Trixie's arms are studded with goose bumps. She looks unsure for a moment, and right below the uncertainty hovers another emotion: fear. He's seen it plenty of times over the years, usually on women who get treated like punching bags by the men in their lives.

"I was kidding," he says. "Sorry, bad joke. I'll take the raspberry one, if you don't mind."

She smiles again, but it's weak. He'd like to ask her out, to take her to dinner and maybe go to bed with her, to trace a finger down the length of her naked spine. But it's not a good time to ask, it seems like it's never the right time, but especially not when she looks like this, like he punched her in the belly, quickly, the ol' one-two, knocked all the air from her lungs and left her green.

"Have a good day," she says, handing him the doughnut wrapped in a napkin. When she leans over, he sees the tattoo on her hip, above the lacy waistband of her panties. Five-by-five, he thinks it says, that old way of saying that everything was all good, but he's not positive, it's blurred and sloppy, the ink gone purplish and soft.

"Thanks. See you in the morning?"

"Nah, I've got the day off."

"Okay."

He pulls into traffic, turns right, toward downtown. It's still early, the sun's barely out, but his cell phone is already ringing. He grabs it out of the cup holder where he leaves it, glances at the screen. It's Loren. He doesn't answer. They're not partners anymore, it's been nearly two years since their split, but Loren still calls him plenty. To shoot the shit, Loren says, but that's a joke, because when did Loren *ever* just want to chat? Never, that's the answer. No, Loren calls because he likes to remind Hoskins of what he used to have, what is now out of his reach. Or maybe he phones because he doesn't have a partner anymore, there's no one he can talk to these days. Loren's been burning through partners left and right since Hoskins left, no one has ever been able to stand working with Loren and that hasn't changed, something that Hoskins finds strangely comforting.

So Loren rings every few days to tell Hoskins about his caseload, what's going on. Most recently, his calls have been about the two women who were pulled out of the reservoir two weeks before. Neither of them had been weighed down, the killer either hadn't thought of it or hadn't cared, but they'd been tied together with twine, looped around each of their necks, keeping them tethered, so they'd be found at the same time.

"Those gals used to hang out around Seever's place before we arrested him," Loren had said. "You remember those two? Said he'd hired them to weed the garden, to sweep his driveway?"

"No." But of course Hoskins does, they'd interviewed those girls after Seever's arrest, along with anyone else who'd been associated with Jacky Seever, and those two, barely out of high school, were walking dynamite. After the interview was over, when Hoskins stood to show them out, the two of them had come right up to him, one on each side, making a Paul Hoskins sandwich, and offered to meet him after work, to let him have them both in bed at the same time. Either one of them—or both—could've ended up buried in Seever's crawl space, but neither seemed overly concerned about it, and he'd thanked them for coming in and showed them out, but he'd been sweating as he did it, trying not to look at their ripe bodies and their puckered mouths. Did he remember them? God.

"I don't know who you're talking about."

"Yeah, you do. These two were snatched off the street, they were kept alive for three days before they were dumped, Paulie. Tortured and raped. The bastard cut off their fingers, just like Seever used to do."

"Coincidence," Hoskins said. But he was sweating, shaking a little. That's how news about Seever made him feel—like a nervous kid. "They were in the wrong place at the wrong time. It happens."

"That suggestion makes you an asshole."

"I don't care. I don't want to hear about Seever, or any of this."

"You miss it. I know you do."

"No, I don't," he'd said, but was that true? Yes. Sometimes. "Leave me the hell alone."

It takes ten minutes for him to get to work, to the same building he's been working in for the last twenty-two years. After Seever's arrest, he got his own private office that looked out over downtown, one with big windows and a door with a lock. He was in that office for almost five years before he was told to pack it up and pound sand; he was punted off the eighth floor and down to the basement, to an office that's dry and clean and decent, he's lucky to still have a job, to still have a paycheck coming in, but it's still the basement, down where you hide the things you no longer want to see but still want to keep around.

Everyone thought it would be Ralph Loren who eventually lost his shit, who'd end up being kicked out of the department for doing something stupid, because that was Loren's jam, that was always what he did. There were rumors that before Loren had joined the Denver PD, when he'd been working undercover out in Miami—or was it Atlanta?—that some big-time drug dealer had pissed him off and Loren had shoved a bong so far up the guy's ass that it'd ruptured something inside, and that's how he'd ended up in Colorado, transferred halfway across the country for his own safety.

But it was Hoskins who was put on an unpaid suspension, because he'd hit a woman. No, not *just* hit her—he'd punched that bitch right in the mouth and wrenched her arm up behind her back until she squealed like a pig, and she'd ended up with a cracked tooth and some bruised ribs and a bald patch where he'd snatched the hair right off her scalp. Hoskins wasn't the type of guy to hurt a woman—he'd never done it before, and he had no plans to do it again—but he hadn't been able to *not* do it, because that woman had killed her daughter; she'd starved the six-year-old and then beat her until her skull was broken open like an uncooked egg. Oh, it was bad, but it was somehow worse because that woman wasn't a crackhead, she wasn't a desperate hooker with a drug problem or insane—she was just mean, liked to see her kid in pain. That woman had a nice house with a minivan parked in the driveway and wore fucking *cardigans*, and they'd found the little girl stuffed in her own bedroom closet, knees drawn up to her forehead and her sunken eyes closed like she was sleeping, and the woman stood there and said she was depressed, that her husband had been stationed overseas by the military and she felt out of control, that she hadn't known *what* she was doing, that someone should've checked on her, that the girl's *school* should've noticed something was wrong, that this whole tragedy could've been prevented. And Hoskins had lost it, *big-time*, because he was tired of the excuses, he was worn out from his job, from seeing terrible things and dealing with terrible people, but it was Seever he was thinking about when he hit that woman. It'd been years since Seever, but he still dreamt about him, still caught himself reliving all the conversations they'd had, mostly one-on-one, because Seever had refused to speak with Loren after he'd punched him, wouldn't breathe a word if Loren was anywhere around. Hoskins was the only one he'd have, and once Seever got going, once he opened his mouth and let it rip, it was almost impossible to shut him up. Seever told Hoskins almost everything he'd done, everything, and Hoskins wishes he could forget it all, wipe his memory clean, because knowing things another person is capable of, well, those things stay with you, they *change* you.

I liked to hear them scream, Seever had said.

He'd been a different man before Seever. A better man. But Seever had managed to rip that part of him out, with his teeth. Chewed him up and spat him out.

"Why'd you let me do it?" Hoskins asked Loren, later, after the woman had hired a lawyer because he'd used *excessive force* and demanded Hoskins's head and he'd been quietly moved out of Homicide and into the basement office, where he was away from prying eyes. He was a department liability; they couldn't fire him but they couldn't *not* fire him, so this was the next best thing. "You didn't even try to stop me."

Loren had shrugged. Hoskins had heard that it was Loren who'd pushed for Hoskins's transfer instead of a termination, and it'd gone through because Loren had influence, he had the higher-ups firmly by the balls, and when he wanted something he usually got it.

"Sometimes the shit gets to be too much," Loren said, and that's all he'd ever say about it, but Hoskins thought it was as close as Loren would ever come to telling him that he understood.

Her phone rings on a Tuesday, although she misses the call, has to let it go to voicemail. Her cell is tucked into her bra, the screen pressed against the side-swell of her breast, and she feels it vibrate when the call comes through. She doesn't get a chance to look at her phone for the next hour, because it's not allowed when she's on the clock, when she's supposed to be working. Girls have been let go for less than that, and she needs this job.

This is what happens when newspapers become obsolete, when your editor says there's an *economic fluctuation* and they can't afford you anymore but you still have bills to pay—a mortgage and a car payment, groceries, you're a grown-up, those things come along with the territory—and it doesn't matter that you have a degree, a damn *master's degree*, because you aren't the master of anything, especially not your own fate, and you can't find any work writing, not if you'd like to make actual money.

So you take what you can get.

It's been almost eight months since Dan Corbin laid her off, and she was unemployed for three months, ninety days of not knowing what to do with herself except sit in front of the computer twelve hours at a time and email her résumé to a thousand places and fill out a million applications, and then she ended up here, in a shop in a big fancy mall in south Denver, not because of her education or her background but because of how she looks—at least, that's what she thinks, because she doesn't have any experience selling cosmetics, and none in retail. *You'll catch on quick,* the manager said when she was hired. *Be confident. Customers trust confidence.*

It was true, she caught on, she learned, and what she didn't know she pretended to know, and customers seemed to like her, although it would've been easier if she was a gay man or a foreign woman, because that seemed to be the law of beautyland: The gay men and eastern European women know all. But it was all right. It wasn't writing, and it wasn't exciting, and there were times she'd be applying eyeliner to a client or swatching every possible shade of red lipstick to the back of her hand if the customer would just buy something, please God *anything*, and she'd think: This is my life. This is all there'll ever be, forever and ever. I'm going to get old and wrinkled and ugly, and I'll still be showing women how to contour their cheekbones and fill in their eyebrows.

Sammie is taking antidepressants.

She sits in the food court during her lunch break, at a table near the center of the action, where she has a good view of everything. It's noon, there are twenty-four days until Christmas, and the holiday crowds are hungry. If you want to judge a person, she thinks, watch how they shop. That will tell you everything you need to know.

"Nothing to eat today?"

She's scrabbling down the front of her shirt, digging for her phone, but then stops, smiles at the young man standing nearby. His name is Ethan; she doesn't know his last name, doesn't know much about him except that he works at one of the restaurants in the food court, a deli that serves sandwiches and coffee, fresh cookies. He's dating one of the girls she works with—Kelly, who has big hips and a bigger mouth, the kind of girl who thinks the world owes her a favor, the kind of girl who constantly sticks her foot in her mouth and doesn't realize it but just keeps on yapping—and he comes into the store a lot to visit his girlfriend, brings her drinks and snacks. A nice kid. A few years out of high school, trying to figure out what he wants to do. He'd recognized her from her photo they'd printed in the *Post* beside her articles, and it was flattering when he was so excited to meet her, he told her he always wanted to write, he has plans to go back to college and get a degree in journalism. He's always asking her questions, about the newsroom, the crime desk, all the pieces she'd written. He's like a kid, always wanting to know more. And she's told him a lot, shared more than she probably should've, because no one else ever wanted to hear her talk about her time at the *Post*, they wanted her to live in the present and look toward the future. *Move on.* But Ethan, he ate it up and begged for more.

"Not today."

"I can grab you a sandwich, if you'd like. It's no problem."

"No, that's okay."

He'd asked Sammie out a few weeks before, and then reneged the offer before she had the chance to say a word. He hadn't meant for it to sound like a *date*, he said, because that wasn't it. He had Kelly. He just wanted to pick Sammie's brain about writing, about making it a career. He might end up taking a few classes at the community college. He'd never managed to succeed at anything, he'd said, except making one hell of a pastrami sandwich, and that wasn't going to fill his mother with pride.

"I'm a loser," he'd told her once. "I can't do anything right."

"That's not true."

"It is. Sometimes I think you're my only friend."

"You have Kelly."

"And you have your husband." Ethan laughed. He didn't laugh often, and she liked the way he looked when he did. If she'd been ten years younger and single, she would've taken him to bed, Kelly or no Kelly. Maybe in spite of Kelly. "And here we are."

Her cell phone is vibrating again.

"Sorry, I need to see who it is," she says, digging down her shirt again. Ethan takes a few steps away, and stops. Waits, like he wants to talk more when she's done. It's probably Dean, calling to check on her, see how her day is going, and it's a 303 area code, but it's not her husband. It's the Denver *Post*. It's Dan Corbin, her old editor.

"Sammie, thank God you answered."

"What?" she says. She'd never thought she'd hear from Corbin again, even though she'd sent him several emails letting him know she'd be interested in coming back to the paper if the budget got better, but he'd never responded. There's something especially cold about being ignored by email.

"It's Corbin," he says slowly, and she realizes he misunderstood, he thought she couldn't hear him. "From the *Post*."

"Yeah, I know."

"Okay." He pauses. Any normal person would ask how she'd been, if she'd enjoyed her Thanksgiving. But that wasn't how Corbin operated. He's one of the smartest people she'd ever met, but his social skills have always been shit. "Listen, the seven-year anniversary of Seever's arrest is coming up."

He pauses for dramatic effect. Corbin always did like some flair, but this time it's deserved. This is the phone call she's been waiting for, she's spent more than half a year wondering when Corbin was going to pick up the damn phone and dial, and now here it is.

"Okay."

"And his execution date is coming up. What is it—a year from now?"

"Thirteen months, I think." It's not a guess. She knows the exact date Seever is scheduled to die—January 13, 2017. Friday the thirteenth.

"Well, with these things coming up, there's been a renewed interest in Seever."

"Okay." She nods, smiles, because that's what she'd learned years before, that people could hear a smile in your voice, once she'd had a boss who stuck a mirror to the side of her computer so she could watch herself when she was on the phone. She's still smiling, but she wishes Corbin would cut the shit and ask her to come back. To resurrect her career with what started it—Jacky Seever.

"Our subscriptions were higher than they'd ever been when you were writing about Seever, and I think rehashing his crimes in some new pieces could be a good thing. Help generate business, get us back to where we used to be."

It's all too good to be true.

"It sounds amazing," she says. "And I still have all my old files, all the photos. I'd be happy to come back."

There's a moment of silence, and Sammie thinks that they might've been disconnected, until Corbin gives a kind of laugh, rough and hoarse, like the bark of a dog.

"I think you're misunderstanding me, Sam. I'm not asking you to come write for the *Post* again. I was under the impression you'd given up writing. Sam, you there?"

"Yeah, I'm here," she says, and it's incredible how normal her voice sounds, like there's nothing wrong at all, but Ethan is looking at her, concerned. I must look upset, she thinks vaguely. Like I got bad news. Like I'm being told someone set my house on fire and murdered my dog. Jesus. She swivels on the plastic seat, turns away so she's watching the guys at the pizza counter twirl their dough and slice up the pies. "Then why'd you call me?"

"I wanted to see if you'd help Weber out," Corbin says. "Get him up to speed on Seever, share your sources—or point him in the right direction."

"Weber?" she says. "You gave this assignment to Chris Weber?"

"Yeah. You remember him?"

"Of course I do," she says, shaking her head. Chris Weber was a complete jackass. A moron who'd been raised to think his shit didn't stink. He was a big ol' boy, tall and broad but not fat, liked to wear sweatshirts with the sleeves pushed up past the elbows. He was the type of guy people expected to see working the crime desk, and Sammie had hated him from the moment they'd met. "He's a fucking tool."

"Sam, he's been doing solid work."

"I haven't seen any of it."

"You still read the *Post*?"

"Occasionally." Oh, the lies. She still has the paper delivered, she reads it every morning as soon as she pulls herself out of bed and brews a pot of coffee, from the front page all the way to the back, every single word. Dean didn't like it, called her a baby with a pacifier, and maybe that was true, but she told him to go fuck himself and did it anyway. Sometimes she'd read the paper and then get on her computer and pull up the online versions of her old articles, although they were getting harder to find, buried in the backlog of Internet garbage, and she'd read them, slowly, so it became that she'd memorized nearly every word she'd ever typed. Her photo, the expensive one she'd had done by a professional that helped readers remember her face is gone, but her name was still there, and it always would be; at least they couldn't take that away from her.

"His first big piece comes out tomorrow, front-page stuff. Take a look when you get a chance. It's good. He's a hell of a reporter, all I'm asking is that you help him out. Throw me a fucking bone, Sam."

"What's it about?"

"You know I can't say."

"Quit being an asshole, Corbin. You're already running the damn story, it won't be a secret for long."

"Did you hear about those two women pulled out of Chatfield Reservoir a few weeks ago?"

"Yeah," she says. The story had caused a big flurry—two women murdered, possibly raped, then dumped in the water. A couple on an afternoon walk had spotted them and called the cops. "I didn't think any details had been released on them yet. Even their names."

"Weber tracked down some cops out drinking, bought them some beers, pumped them for information. Got the whole story."

"And what is the story?"

"The two gals the cops pulled out are Tanya Brody and Selene Abeyta."

It takes her a minute to recognize the names, less than a minute, but then she remembers. She'd interviewed both the women after Seever's arrest, although back then they'd been girls in their senior year of high school, and they'd spent quite a bit of time doing chores out at Seever's place for cash. They'd both agreed to talk to her about Seever, and they'd come to the interview together, because they were best friends forever, they didn't do anything separately.

Thank goodness we did, Tanya had said. *If he'd caught one of us alone, we'd probably be dead right now.*

He always gave me the creeps, Selene had said, and the two girls had laughed at that, snidely, although Sammie hadn't included that in her article.

And now, seven years later, they were dead. They'd died as they'd lived—together. Sammie could remember the two of them, laughing and squealing as she interviewed them, excited about their fifteen minutes of fame, taking the chewed gum in their mouths and trading it with each other. Back then, she'd found the pair irritating, she'd been glad when they'd left, even though they made for a good story.

"Are you serious?" she asks.

"Serious as a heart attack," Corbin says. "Missing for several days before they were found. The cops didn't give specifics, but they said those two were murdered the same way Seever would've done it."

"They think Seever's involved somehow?"

"Maybe. Seems fishy, two women who he might've been grooming as victims showing up dead. You used to think Seever might've had a partner. You might be right, and the guy's finally decided to finish what they started."

"Maybe."

She pushes her tongue into the corner of her mouth. There's a toddler a few tables over, making one hell of a mess with fries and ketchup while his mother is busy texting and flipping through emails. She stands up, walks toward the big stone fireplace in the middle of the food court. It's warmer there, and less crowded.

"Sam? You still there? Damn phone, we must've—"

"I'm here," she says shortly. "I'm still here."

"So you'll help Weber? He could use it on these pieces he'll be writing, and the book—"

"Book?"

"Oh, yeah." Corbin sounds embarrassed, like this is a secret he'd been meaning to keep and let slip. "This guy I knew back in college is a literary agent, he was in town this weekend and I was telling him about Seever, and these two women. He was definitely interested, thought he could sell a book about it without a problem."

"But there's already been a book about Seever," she says. That book should've been *her* book, but the two men who'd written it had been faster, they'd been able to jump on the opportunity and wring the life from it. That's how it was with writing, Sammie had discovered. You had to be quick on the draw or you'd be left in the dust, and no one gave a damn.

"You and I both know that book was shit," Corbin says. "And Seever's crimes—especially if he's connected to these new murders—I think it's a big enough story to carry another book. A good one. And my friend agrees."

This isn't how this was supposed to happen. This is not how Sammie imagined all this going down, all those times she'd been standing in the shower, waiting for the conditioner to soak into her hair, acting a scene out to herself like Corbin was right there with her, begging her to come back to the *Post*. No, this is not how she'd thought all this would play out, but Sammie's quick, already thinking one step ahead— she's one hell of a chess player, and that's all life is, isn't it? One big game.

"What if I did some poking around myself?" she asks, speaking slowly at first. "What if I wrote up a piece on Seever, or something about these new murders? Something better than Weber could put out. Would you run it?"

"I don't know," Corbin says, but she can already hear the excitement in his voice, and she has to wonder if this is what he was planning all along. Because Weber doesn't need her help, he'd been in the business long enough to know his head from his ass, he would've figured it all out no problem. No, this sort of thing is right up Corbin's alley—pitting two reporters against each other. He wants to watch the struggle, col- lect the big reward at the end. If Corbin could turn his life into reality television, he'd plot and scheme and get everyone voted off the island. "I already promised this to Weber. It wouldn't be fair."

"I don't think a good story has to be fair," Sammie says, and she knows this'll seal the deal, because Corbin's not fair, he's all about the business, and if she can bring him something good, something that makes people drag out their wallets and pay, she's in. "I think it has to be good, and it doesn't matter much who writes it."

"I always admired that about you," Corbin says. "You'll do anything to get your way."

You'd lie about anything to get what you want, Hoskins had said, and it makes her wince to think of it. Almost the same. Close enough.

"I'll be in touch with some ideas," Sammie says, and hangs up, because it's always better to be the one ending the conversation, no awkward goodbyes needed. And she's already thinking ahead, trying to figure out her next step, and imagining Weber's face when he realizes that she's snatched his job right out from under him. Petty, she knows, but it'll be good. Not good. Fucking *spectacular.*

"You're going to be writing for the paper again?" Ethan asks from behind her, and she jumps, startled, and then throws her arms around his neck. She's excited, so she ignores the way his arms slip around her waist, how close he's holding her. That's all background noise, because she has a chance, and all anyone needs is one. Mice can squeeze through holes less than half their size, they can wriggle into places you'd never expect, and she'd done the same thing before; it'd been a fight to cover Seever the first time, she'd had to do things she didn't like, but she could do it again. It's right there, in front of her. The hole she has to squeeze through. She just has to make herself fit.

December 2, 2015

His basement office is small and dark, and the fluorescent lightbulbs in the ceiling fixture are the kind that mimic daylight, but they seem too bright, overly fake. They hurt his eyes and give him headaches, they're like something you'd put in a mental institution, or in a spook house, but he doesn't complain. Even if he did say something, if he sent an email or a handwritten note up the ladder to administration, he'd be ignored. Once upon a time he was the golden boy, a rising star in Homicide who'd managed to bring down a serial killer. And then, in the blink of an eye, he was lower than dog shit, he was dismissed from his position and sent to work on cold cases, going through the old files that still needed to be put in the computer system, one by one, until his brain felt ready to explode.

"Those cold cases are still open investigations," Chief Black had said. He was trying to make the move sound appealing, but couldn't manage to sound entirely convinced himself. "You're still technically a homicide detective. You're an extension of the department."

So here he is, two years after his fall from grace, plugging away on the cold cases, opening up the old brown folders with the creaky spines and the corners that had long ago splintered from age. Squinting at old photographs and deciphering the handwriting of detectives who'd retired before he'd even joined the force.

February 26, 1970: A pretty cheerleader never made it home from a high school basketball game and was found raped and murdered six miles from her home the next day.

June 23, 1979: A nineteen-year-old was shot in the head in Washington Park as he slept under a pine tree.

October 28, 1996: A skeleton was found on the side of the road in north Denver, still bound with rope across the midsection and legs. The coroner guessed it had been there for over a year before being found. The body was never identified.

If Hoskins were still up in Homicide, he'd be investigating those two girls pulled out of the reservoir. He can imagine what the two of them looked like, swollen with water, their tongues black and fat. Their eyes gone, because fish get hungry. He'd skimmed the article about them that morning, not that he could miss it, not right on the front page of the *Post*, about the connection the two victims had to Jacky Seever, the possibility of Seever having a partner, someone who was still free, raping and killing. The whole thing was ridiculous—or maybe it wasn't. Sometimes truth is stranger than fiction, Hoskins knows that for a fact, but he also knows this: Seever never worked with anyone. Not a lone wolf, Hoskins would never call him *that*, but more like a weasel, a creature that seems harmless but will rip off your face if given the chance.

At least, he thinks, the article wasn't written by Sammie. There have been times over the years that he'd yank the newspaper out of its blue plastic sleeve and unfold it to find her face staring up at him, a tiny, blurry photo printed beside her byline that was still clear enough for him to make out the hard line of her jaw, the sarcastic twist of her lips. Enough to make something inside him give a lurch and then settle down to silence once more. He hasn't seen Sammie's face in the paper for a while now, but he's still surprised that she wasn't the one to cover these two new murders, that she wasn't the one to connect their deaths to Seever. He wonders at it, but not too much. He's finally reached a point when he doesn't think about her all that often, and he'd prefer it to stay that way.

"I'm gonna grab some lunch," Ted Johnson says, sticking his head into the office and startling Hoskins out of his daze. Ted works in the next office over, and Hoskins isn't sure what he does—something to do with the department's computers, with the software. Tech stuff, the shit no one else seems to understand. He can usually smell the cheap cologne Ted always wears before he actually sees him, because the kid must bathe in the stuff. "Want me to grab you something?"

"I'm good," Hoskins says. "Thanks for asking."

"You doing okay?"

"I'm fine."

"You've been quiet, that's all." Ted takes a step into the office, and stops. He's holding his wallet in his hands like it's a purse, and Hoskins knows exactly what sorts of comments Loren would've made about *that*. Hoskins guesses Ted's in his early twenties, sports those tight jeans and the low-top sneakers all the kids seem to wear these days, and not even ironically. If the kid lived in San Francisco or Seattle, he'd be working at some tech company, changing the face of the Internet. But in Denver, Colorado, Ted's another unseen cog in the wheel of the police force, hidden away underground. "You want to talk?"

Hoskins is stunned for a moment, and then laughs, actually *guffaws*, because when was the last time he had anyone besides the department psychologist ask if he *wants to talk*? He was partners with Loren for almost fourteen years, and he was never the kind of guy to *talk*; if you started *sharing* with Ralph Loren, he would've told you to stick your feelings right up your poop-chute.

"What's so funny?" Ted asks, frowning, and it makes Hoskins think of when he'd first been moved down to the basement and Ted had introduced himself. He'd asked Hoskins to call him Dinky, because that's what his big brothers had always called him, and all his friends, and that had made Hoskins laugh, hard.

"Why Dinky?" Hoskins had asked. "Out of every nickname in the damn world, why that one?"

"You ever seen those vacation movies? You remember the dog that got tied to the bumper and dragged?"

"Yeah."

"One time this kid hog-tied me to his bike," Ted had said. "He dragged me down the street, and I lost most of the skin on my arms, had gravel ground into my face. The doctors had to pick it out with tweezers."

"Nothing's funny," Hoskins says now, wiping at his eyes. "You surprised me. Same shit, different day. You know."

Ted nods, still frowning, but Hoskins knows that Ted *doesn't* know, because he's a kid; he's still wet behind the ears and he doesn't know shit about much of anything. Ted still lives at home with his parents, still drives the car they bought him for his sixteenth birthday, spends most of his free time with his eyes glued to the screen of his cell phone. He's a nice enough kid, smart and hardworking and eager to please, but he's also naïve. Probably still a virgin.

"Hey, I guess I do need one thing," Hoskins says. "Do you have access to old autopsy reports? I need stuff for the Grimly case, back in '92, and I can't figure out this damn computer."

"I can get into *anything* in our database," Ted says. He's excited, now they're on familiar ground. "You need some hard copies of it, or would an email be okay?"

"If you'll get it to me on a floppy disk, that'd be great."

Ted frowns.

"I'm pretty sure your computer doesn't even have a port for a floppy—"

"I was kidding."

"Oh."

"An email would work," Hoskins says. "I can print it out myself if I need it. And it's not any hurry. Take your time."

"Okay. Oh, hey, I just remembered—I was looking through the files on Seever, and he did some messed-up stuff," Ted says, casually, although by his tone, it sounds like he's been waiting to bring this up. That's how people are, once they realize that Hoskins was one of the cops who arrested Seever, they think he'd like nothing better than to tell them all about it. If given half the chance, people would squeeze him for every bloody detail. "It's really interesting, that he—"

"Who gave you permission to read through those?" he says angrily. "Those are classified files."

I don't think about Seever anymore, he'd told the department's headshrinker a few weeks before. *Not unless someone brings him up. But everyone always wants to talk about him. Like nothing else has happened in the world in the last seven fucking years.*

A lot of detectives find themselves affected by a particular case, she'd said, toying with the bracelets on her wrists. They made a metallic chiming sound that put his teeth on edge. *Especially with a larger-than-life figure like Jacky Seever, it's normal to—*

Didn't you hear me? I don't want to talk about him.

"Nobody gave me permission. But I know you worked that case, and—"

"Keep your fucking nose out of those files," Hoskins says. "And just because I was on that case, doesn't mean I want to rehash it with your ass."

Ted blinks, and for a moment Hoskins is sure he's going to cry, he's still young enough for tears. He considers apologizing for a moment, then doesn't. Better to let the kid figure out things on his own.

"All right," Ted says. "Well, I'll be back."

"Okay."

Ted looks at him one more time, sullenly, and disappears. A minute later, Hoskins hears the elevator doors slide open and closed, and then he's alone.

"How's he doing?" Hoskins asks. "Is he having a good day?"

He's on the phone, calling home to check on his father. Good ol' Joe Hoskins, who'd spent forty years as a floor supervisor down at the Brewery in Golden, who used to play poker every Tuesday with his work buddies and knew how to blow rings with his cigarette smoke, moved in with his only son in the early spring, when they decided he was no longer fit to live alone.

"He's pretty clear today," the woman says. Hoskins can't remember her name. She's the latest in the many women he's hired to care for Joe, mostly retired nurses, someone to hang around during the day and keep the old man out of trouble. "He had eggs for breakfast. A cup of coffee."

"Decaf?" he asks. If Joe has any caffeine, shit gets hairy, but they have to hide it from him. Replace his regular coffee with decaf without him seeing, dump most of the beer out of the bottles in the fridge and water it down with apple juice. It seems stupid, and it's a lot of work and sometimes feels pointless, but those little tricks make it easier to live with Joe. That's what his life has become these days—careful deception.

"Yeah," the woman says, slowly, so Joe must be sitting right there, listening. He's a different man these days, not the same father Hoskins had always known. Joe's like a kid sometimes, childish and demanding, other times he is silent and angry. He's not often sly, but when he is that worries Hoskins the most, when he looks in Joe's eyes and can see the wheels turning, see some plan coming together. When his father looks like that it reminds him of Seever, before the arrest, when he thought he was invincible, that no one could ever touch him.

You hear about that gal who disappeared down in the Springs last year? Seever had said once, when he'd sauntered up to where Hoskins and Loren were parked, a cigarette stuck delicately between his pointer and middle fingers, the way a woman would smoke. *Anyone ever find her?*

They *did* find that girl, later, down in Seever's crawl space, but it'd all been a good joke for Seever then, a real chuckle factory, as he liked to say. And Seever was sly, sly as a fox, as a goddamn weasel, and there were times when Joe would look that same way, like he had some tasty secret he was hiding, and Hoskins would feel a cold trickle of fear on the back of his neck, and he'd feel bad; it's his *dad*, after all, but there's something about that look that makes him afraid. And what else was he supposed to do? His father's crazy, Joe's losing his fucking mind and it isn't his fault, it's the shitty luck his DNA had dealt him, but he's still his father.

Still, Hoskins sleeps with his bedroom door locked.

"Did he take his pills?" he asks. Same questions, same phone call, every day. He'll call again, in a few hours, to make sure Joe has eaten lunch, that he's taken a nap in front of the TV. "Did you give him the paper? He needs to do the crossword."

"I know," the woman says flatly, and he can hear the impatience in her voice. She'll quit soon, he thinks, and it won't be long before he'll be searching for someone else. Another name he won't be able to remember. "He's doing it now."

"Does he have his slippers on? It's cold in the house."

"Yeah."

"And he keeps scratching that spot on his arm. Could you put some cream on it?"

"I already did."

"Okay."

This must be like having a kid, he thinks. Calling the babysitter to make sure everything's going all right, no one's playing with matches or shit in their pants, worrying over everything. It's been this way since his father fell off the ladder while pruning a tree in his backyard, and there hadn't been any broken bones or damage, not even a scratch, but there'd still been a brain scan, just in case, and the doctor had thrown around lots of big words and charts and had shown them the X-rays on his laptop, and Hoskins and Joe had nodded and pretended to understand, although they had no clue what the fuck was going on. And afterward, when his father was at the front desk scheduling another appointment, Hoskins asked the doctor to explain it all again, in a way he could understand.

"There's calcium depositing around your father's brain," the doctor said. He wasn't looking at Hoskins, but down at his phone, scrolling through his endless text messages. He was already done with the conversation, moved on to other things, and Hoskins considered snatching the phone from his hand and throwing it through the window. "If we hadn't done the CAT scan, we might not have found out until it was far too late."

"Found out what?"

The doctor looked up from his phone, smacked his lips together wetly. God, Hoskins hated doctors, hated everything about them. The expense of them, and the time they took, but mostly he hated the way they made you feel like such an idiot, like you were too stupid to even be worth their attention.

"The calcium is affecting your father's brain," he said. Slowly, as if Hoskins might be the one with the dysfunctional upstairs. "He's going to start forgetting things, even more than he already is. Suffering from dementia. His brain impulses will slow down, so he won't be able to get around as well. It could happen a little bit at a time, over many years so you might not notice, but your father's got a pretty advanced case. The calcium's been building up for a long time."

"Jesus. What are we supposed to do?"

The doctor shrugged.

"There's no known treatment for his condition," he said. "There's nothing you can do."

"So we're waiting for him to die?" Hoskins asked, and the doctor had to have heard the anger in his voice, the fear, or maybe he didn't notice it at all. Maybe the doctor had heard so much of it over the years that he'd become deaf to it.

"I suppose we are," he said. "But you could say the same thing about everyone. We're all waiting to die, aren't we?"

His father was going to lose his mind, had possibly been losing his mind over his entire life, slowly, one piece at a time, and this was a curious thing, that a disease had hidden in the structure of his DNA and decided to finally make itself known; it'd been there all along and no one had ever noticed it, because everyone loses their keys and forgets to turn off the oven, maybe Joe did it more often than most people, but how was *that* supposed to be a reliable sign of what was coming? But Hoskins, he was losing his mind because he was a cop and he'd seen terrible things and it happened a lot, cops went apeshit all the time, but that felt like a half-assed excuse, because it was his *job*, wasn't it? He'd signed up for the whole damn thing and he'd known exactly what he was walking into; he'd been trying to get into Homicide since the day he'd been sworn in and it'd driven him to the brink and still he missed it, he sometimes wanted back in so bad he could taste it.

Or, Hoskins thought, he was losing his mind for no reason at all.

He finds ways to keep it together. Just one way, really, although there might be more ways, methods he hasn't yet discovered. Not drink, he'd tried that, most cops have found their way to the bottom of a bottle at one point or another, but it didn't work for him. He was a lousy drunk. He didn't smoke and he didn't sleep with whores and he didn't shoot up and he didn't gamble. He didn't take the prescription the department psychologist had prescribed for him either; they made his tongue fuzzy and his hands tingle in a way he didn't like, and he didn't care much to talk about his feelings, but he still went to the head doctor once a month, partly for show, because people thought you were trying to get better when you went to the doctor, although that wasn't entirely true in his case.

"Avoidance behavior," this woman had immediately said, not ten minutes after they'd first met. She'd been asking all sorts of questions, one after another, and marking his answers on her notepad, although she held it so he couldn't see what she'd been scribbling. "You don't care for conflict, so you avoid it."

"That's what you think?"

"I think it's interesting that you'd choose to go into law enforcement, when confrontations clearly make you anxious."

"Can I ask you something?" he'd asked, and she'd smiled, but sourly, so he knew that she had to let him speak but she wasn't happy about it.

"Of course."

"Isn't there some sex thing called the pearl necklace?" he'd asked, and she'd flushed in embarrassment, because she was wearing a blouse that had been left mostly unbuttoned and a thick rope of pearls that hung low, so your eyes were drawn down, way down into the cleft of her cleavage. Her name was Angelica Jackson, but Hoskins couldn't stop calling her *Ms. Jackson*, like the old song. Ms. Jackson if you're nasty.

None of that shit made anything better for him, and he might've gone bananas if he hadn't started walking when he felt himself losing it. It sounded like the most fucking *stupid* thing on the planet, he was like one of those old guys who show up at the mall before business hours in a sweatband and tennis shoes to cruise the perimeter, but it worked; it was the only thing that did. He couldn't run—well, he *could* run, and sometimes he did run at the gym, hopped on the treadmill and cranked it until his eyeballs felt ready to burst like pimples and ooze down his face—but running only made it worse, his brain would start working overtime, like it was trying to keep up with his legs, and when his head got working like that he'd think about going out onto the street and grabbing someone, *anyone*, and shooting them right in the face—not between the eyes but right in the face, so there'd be nothing left and then he'd do the goddamn mashed potato in the mess it left behind. But when he walks he doesn't have thoughts like that, everything becomes soft and distant and vague, like he's looking at the world through gauze.

"Why are you so afraid of losing your mind?" Ms. Jackson had asked him. "What do you think will happen?"

But that wasn't the right question, because he knew what would happen if he lost his mind, it'd already happened. He'd grabbed that daughter-killing woman, not because he'd felt some moral obligation to teach her a lesson or because the little girl's murder bothered him in a way he hadn't felt before. No, he'd beat the shit out of that woman because he'd wanted to; he'd wanted to hear her scream and beg for him to stop, he wanted to see her bleed. There was something pleasurable in it, feeling the soft push of her flesh under his fists and the snap of her bones; he thinks he could've kept doing it until she was dead, and that thought horrifies him, but there's another part of him that smiles and rubs its hands together gleefully, and that part of him was left there by Jacky Seever, was pushed deep into his soul like a seed and left to germinate, to grow into something poisonous and deadly, a white-bellied mushroom that only grows in the dark.

His office phone rings when he's pulling on his coat, and he stares at it for a long moment, because how long has it been since someone called *him*? Up in Homicide the phone would be ringing constantly, all day and all night, but his cases are long cold, and anyone who ever cared about them has long since stopped calling. He considers ignoring it and heading home, but then finds that he can't. If he doesn't answer it, he'll spend the rest of the night wondering who it could've been. So he picks up.

"Hoskins?"

"Yeah?"

He doesn't recognize the voice, not at first, takes him a moment, but only because it's been so long since he's heard it. Chief Jonathan Black is still technically his boss, but he doesn't have constant contact with the man anymore, not like he used to. At first it was a relief, not having to give a daily report on his investigations and fill Black in on his progress, but then he realized that he never had to tell anyone what he was doing because no one cared. And somehow being ignored was almost as bad as having the boss man breathing down his neck.

"It's Black."

"Yeah, got it."

"How've you been doing down there?"

Hoskins doesn't know how to answer this. The easiest answer is that he's *fine*, everything's fucking *grand*, as long as the direct deposit keeps dumping into his checking account every other Friday and his health insurance is still valid and the balance in his retirement keeps ticking upward, he can't complain. But then again, maybe he's not fine. He's stuck in the basement forty hours a week, in an office with no window, and no hope, flipping through murder cases that are sometimes older than he is. He's started taking the photos out of the files and taping them to his office walls; some of them are pictures of victims before they were killed, smiling at prom or at a family barbecue, but mostly it's the crime scene pics he puts up. Photographs of a woman on a bare mattress—the only way anyone seems to be killed on a bed, with the sheets and blankets missing—her bottom half naked, legs splayed and eyes closed; old black-and-whites of a field, overgrown with grass and weeds, with the body of a small child facedown in the packed dirt; a man lying over a sewage drain, his eyes open and glittering, seemingly alive except for the strange way the soft flesh of his neck was peeled back, the knife's cut so deep that it'd almost separated his head from his shoulders. These photos might be a sign that he's not okay, this macabre gallery staring down at him five days a week; maybe it's not okay to be constantly looking in the face of death.

"I'm fine," Hoskins says. "I was about to head home, Chief. Is there something I can do for you?"

"I guess you heard about the two floaters out at Chatfield?"

"Yeah." He tosses his coat over the back of his chair and sits. Kicks back his feet. "I read about them this morning, in the paper."

"And Loren told you, didn't he? He keeps you filled in?"

Hoskins presses his lips together, doesn't say a word. He might be a cop, but he's not a goddamn snitch.

"You don't have to answer that," Black says. "Loren's never been able to keep his mouth shut. But in this case, I don't give a damn."

A part of Hoskins is glad to hear that Black won't put a stop to Loren's calls, there's a part of him that likes those calls from Loren, looks forward to them. Wants to hear the latest goings-on. It keeps him in the loop, but that loop is the problem. The reason why he can't move on.

"Listen, I'm calling because another victim's been found, looks like she's connected to the first two."

"Okay." Hoskins knows exactly where Black's going with this, and he has the sudden urge to hang up the phone, to throw on his coat and *run* out the door, *don't let it hit your ass on the way out,* and pretend like he never got this call.

"It looks like Seever's work."

"Seever's in prison."

"I *know* where he is, Hoskins. But now we have three women who're all connected to Seever in some way—and they're all dead."

"So why're you calling me?"

"I want you working this case with Loren."

"No."

"You seem to think that was a request," Black says. "Believe me, it's not."

"My answer's still no." Hoskins stuck his thumb in his mouth, chewed on the skin around the nail bed. It was a habit that used to piss his father off, and Joe would smack him upside the head when he caught him at it, complain about how nasty it was.

You afraid the nail-biting's gonna keep me from landing a husband, or something? Hoskins had asked once, and Joe had laughed, more out of surprise than anything else, and he'd laid off on the nagging. For a while.

"The scene's down in Lakewood, on the east side of 470," Black says, as if Hoskins hadn't refused. "I need you out there in the next half-hour."

"You've got lots of detectives upstairs," Hoskins says. "Give it to one of them." He's trying to worm his way out, but he already knows he's going. Not just because Black is giving him an order but because he *wants* to go, no matter what he says.

"Do you know that Loren hasn't been able to keep a partner since you went down there?" Black asks. Angrily, but also amused, but Hoskins guesses that to be the chief of police you can't have the stick crammed up your ass all the time. "He can't seem to figure out how to play nice with anyone else."

"So let him work alone. He's a good detective. He took down Seever, he'll figure this one out."

Black laughs. "Why do you do that, kid?" he asks.

"Do what?"

"Why do you play down the work you did? Why do you let Loren take all the credit?"

"I don't know what you're talking about."

"Yeah, you do," Black says, softly. "You might think you've got everyone fooled, but you're wrong."

"Loren's a good detective."

"Yeah, I heard you the first time," Black says. "But so are you. But you'd be better off upstairs, we both know that. With Loren."

"Tell me more," Hoskins says, only half-joking. "Flattery will get you absolutely everywhere."

"You're really going to make me do this?" Black asks. "Maybe you'd like a handjob while I'm at it?"

"I've seen all the calluses you've got on your palms. I don't want your hands anywhere near my dick, thanks. It'd be like sharpening a pencil."

"Look, I'm sorry I put you down in the basement, but it's the only way I could keep you on the payroll after that stunt you pulled," Black says. "Is that what you want? An apology?"

"I don't want anything."

"You're the best fucking detective I've ever had on my team," Black says quietly and quickly, like he doesn't want to take the chance that someone else might hear what he's saying. "I need you on this case with Loren. He's got a few suspects in mind already, and I need an arrest made, all these loose ends tied up as soon as possible. No one else can handle this the way you can."

"This is—"

"Listen, that article those assholes at the *Post* published this morning is scaring plenty of people. I asked them to chill out, give us some lead time on this before they start up, but you know how those reporters operate, and they'll throw this city into a panic. If the people around here start thinking this is *Seever Junior*, that's going to cause a lot of issues. You remember what it was like before."

Hoskins closes his eyes. He does remember those weeks before they arrested Seever, when the city had gone batshit. Everyone had been scared, people were turning on one another. Gun sales skyrocketed. People were being killed in their own homes, because they'd gone to the toilet in the middle of the night without turning the lights on and spooked a family member. People were acting like Jack the Ripper had come to Denver; everyone was waiting to hear about the next disappearance, expecting to turn a corner and see a monster coming down on them with a knife and a grin, no one ever expected it to be Seever the Clown, sitting pretty behind the wheel of his German import in his fancy suit.

"And this latest victim, it's Carrie Simms," Black says, quickly. Like he wants to get the words out fast, get the bad taste out of his mouth.

"Carrie Simms." Hoskins's heart, it takes a turn in his chest again, quick and slippery, then stills.

"Simms, Hoskins. The girl that got away from Seever."

"I know who she is. Are you sure it's not suicide?" Hoskins asks. It's all he can think, women like Simms sometimes didn't recover well from trauma, and she was already fucked up, even before Seever got a hold of her. Seven years was a long time to wait to kill yourself, but you could never know what people would do, or how long they would wait to do it. Sometimes a human was nothing more than a ticking time bomb, and sometimes it took time to detonate.

"It's not suicide."

"Fuck."

"That's what I said," Black says. "I'll text you the address. Loren's already out there."

"Okay."

"You didn't think I'd let you molder down there for the next twenty years, did you?" Black says. "You didn't think you'd be done with this forever?"

There's a peach tree in her backyard, stunted and small. It never bears any fruit, because the climate in Denver isn't right for it—the summers are too short and never get hot enough, the winters are far too cold. The soil is too sandy and rocky. She sometimes wonders who planted the tree to begin with, what hopeful person flipped through a Burpee catalog and ran their finger along the slick pages and stopped on a peach tree, already imagining the taste of the fruit, the way the juice would explode from the flesh at the first bite and run down their arm, dripping all the way to their elbow. And then that tree came in a brown box, the roots wrapped up in a burlap sack, and it was planted in the backyard, in the sunniest corner, but it only grew a little every year, twisting and bending like an old man, and nothing ever bloomed on those scrawny twigs. And there it still is, right outside the dining-room window, bare branches shaking in the wind. She's thought about having it cut down, clearing that spot and having a concrete pad poured, where she could put out some nice lawn furniture in the summer, but she never seems to get around to it. It's not as if her schedule is crammed full, but she forgets the tree, doesn't think about it again until a time like this, when the cold is creeping in through the cracks around the windows and the peaks of the mountains are covered in snow.

She's been in this house for the last seven years, creeping around like a mouse, hoping that no one in the neighborhood would recognize her, make the connection, and so far she's been lucky. It would be easier to pick up and move to another town where Jacky wasn't much more than a story on the evening news, a city where people didn't accuse her of being some kind of dragon lady, and she'd tried to move, rented a house in California after Jacky was sentenced, drove out caravan-style behind the moving truck, through the mountains and desert and into a part of California that was so green it made her eyes hurt. The house she'd rented had a pool shaped like a kidney bean in the back, and the privacy fence was covered in a creeping bush that blossomed in great clouds of pink. It was all so quaint and normal, and no one recognized her; she never once heard someone mention Jacky's name—Jacky's case was national news, she still sometimes saw it mentioned, even so many miles away, but it wasn't as bad, and California had plenty of its own problems.

There was an elementary school down the street from her house in California, and in the afternoons Gloria would slowly walk past the chain-link fence and watch the kids playing, shouting and jumping, fighting. Their screams would give her a headache but she walked by anyway because it reminded her of Jacky, who'd always liked kids so much, especially the little ones in diapers, while she'd never had a knack for it. She still remembers the year Jacky dressed up as Santa Claus and went around to all their diners, carrying bags full of candy and toys for the kids, and how they'd shrieked when they saw him, sometimes in terror, but even then they'd refused to leave. And she'd come along, dressed as Mrs. Claus, but only because Jacky had insisted, and when he got an idea in his head there wasn't any use arguing with him about it, he would never give in. And later at home, while Jacky was in the shower, singing Christmas carols in his off-key tenor, she'd looked through the handful of Polaroids deemed rejects because all the parents had passed on them, and saw that while Jacky was grinning like a kid in every one of them, her own mouth was screwed up so tight she might've been sucking air through a tiny straw. That was the difference between her and Jacky, though. He was always trying to be Mr. Good Times, always wanted to make everyone happy. Not that she didn't want people to be happy, but she didn't have the enthusiasm her husband did.

She was in California five weeks when she decided to leave, to move back to Denver. California was too much. Of everything. The stores were always too crowded, the lines at the gas pumps were always too long. The sun was too bright. It was too warm, and what a waste that was, since half her wardrobe was for winter. And there were so many different people everywhere she looked, men booming in Spanish and tiny women with black hair and slanted eyes, and plenty of blacks, more blacks than she'd ever seen in her life, playing basketball on the streets and braiding one another's hair and laughing, big whooping laughs that bounced off the walls and came back to her ears again. A gay couple lived in the house across the street, two black men who were very kind, but she couldn't even speak to them about the weather without imagining what they did in bed, how they enjoyed each other, so she tried to be extra careful about when she went out, not wanting to get caught in an extended conversation at the mailbox.

And besides, Denver was her home. She'd been born there, lived her whole life there. She hadn't realized that a place could be a part of someone until she was in California, where everything seemed a smidge off, the brick in the wall that wouldn't quite line up with the rest, and it was enough to make her miserable.

And she still wanted to be close to Jacky.

So she moved back. Bought a house in the Whittier neighborhood, where she was able to stretch the inheritance her mother had left her further. It was an area where the neighbors were less likely to care who you were as long as you didn't cause trouble, where people still knew how to mind their own business. It wasn't all that far from one of their diners, the original one her father had opened, although it wasn't theirs anymore, or even hers, but had been sold off long before to pay for lawyers and fees and whatever else the courts had cooked up. She doesn't leave the house all that often, and she tries not to drive past any of the diners if she can help it. She doesn't want to see something that used to be hers and never will be again. So she stays home and watches the peach tree fighting for life in the cold.

She visits Jacky once a week. Visiting is allowed for only a brief window on Wednesday mornings, so she wakes up early to make it to Sterling on time. It's a long drive. For a while she tried listening to audiobooks as she drove, but she'd found her mind wandering, and she'd realize that half the book was gone and she had no idea what'd happened. She started listening to music, any kind, and then to nothing at all, it never mattered, only the howling of the wind as her car sliced along the interstate ever reached her.

"How can you still care about him?" a girlfriend asked, not long after Jacky was arrested. She'd lived with her mother for a while after the house was torn down in the tiny apartment her mother had rented since her father had died. "You don't have to deal with him anymore. File for divorce."

"I don't want to talk about this," Gloria had said. She was tired of these phone calls, sick of being told what to do by women who barely knew her. She'd gone to church with them, had gone shopping and traded recipes and gossiped, but they didn't know her, and they certainly didn't understand her marriage.

"He's a monster, Gloria. He could've murdered you in your sleep. Have you ever thought of that?"

She carefully replaced the phone in the cradle. When it rang again, she ignored it. She'd turned the voicemail off, so there was never an answer, and sooner or later whoever was calling would get tired of the endless rings and hang up.

"I'd like some tea," her mother had said, from the armchair she hardly ever left. Almost a year later Gloria would find her in that chair, her head canted strangely to one side and her mouth twisted into a cruel maw, dead from a stroke during the night. Her mother had never said a word about Jacky since his arrest, never asked questions or tried to talk about it, and Gloria thought that it might've been because her mother understood. Her parents had been married for fifty-two years when her father passed, and she thought her mother had a good idea of what she was going through because her father was difficult; he could be terribly mean, but when you were married you made things work, that was your job, you dealt with what was handed out, you made the best of what you got. It was like that old country song. *Stand by your man*, that's how it went, and it wasn't that way anymore, people bailed and filed for divorce at the first sign of trouble, but she hadn't been raised that way, she'd made a promise and she was going to keep it.

"There's a good sale on squash right now," Gloria says. "I have to go back tomorrow, pick up some more before it goes off."

"What kind of squash?"

"Spaghetti. And acorn." She pauses. "Some college students moved in across the street last week. They've been throwing parties every night, and it keeps me up."

"Why don't you call the cops?"

She makes a face, picks at a loose thread hanging off the bottom of her skirt.

"It's not that bad," she says. Of course, Jacky doesn't know that someone broke into her home a few months ago, stole everything of value. Her TV, her phone, even her clock radio. And the paintings Jacky made in prison, the ones she brought home every week and piled up in the garage—most of those were gone too. She'd filed a police report, and two cops had come out, they'd laughed when they realized who she was, then left without taking any notes, without taking her seriously, and she knew she'd never see any of her stolen belongings again. "I'm sure the police are busy with much more important things than my silly complaints."

This is how it is every Wednesday with Jacky—an hour of boring conversation about nothing at all. About the grocery shopping she did the day before, the TV shows they both watch. He tells her about the menu in the cafeteria for the week, and about the guy two cells down who'd had a heart attack the week before and still isn't back from the hospital wing. It's exactly how they'd be talking to each other if Jacky wasn't in prison, the mundane conversation of marriage, one week's worth of talk compacted into sixty minutes over two old rotary phones as they look at each other through a pane of bulletproof glass. It's the only way Jacky can get visitors, because he's considered dangerous; the guards think Jacky might hurt her if he got the chance, they treat him with special care.

She still wears her wedding band. Jacky can't.

"Have you gone into any of the restaurants?" he asks. He asks this same thing every week, but she can understand. They were a big part of Jacky's life for so long—owning and operating half a dozen successful restaurants was no small feat—so she usually tries to be gentle. She decides to ignore the question this time, acts like she hadn't heard it at all. "Are they clean inside? Have the menus been changed?"

"Have you been painting?" she asks. Jacky blinks. He was always the talkative one in their relationship, the one who'd lead the conversation. Years before, they'd be out for dinner and they'd meet another couple, or some acquaintance, and Jacky would introduce his wife, and then Gloria would fade quietly into the background. But things have changed, and she's the one steering the ship, jumping from one subject to another, asking questions, pushing Jacky to talk. He's severely depressed, the prison doctor says. He has heart problems, weight problems. He's on a cocktail of medications, they keep changing it up, and he's sometimes blurry, faded. Confused. She has to take control during most visits, or he'd sit there like a lump, or end up repeating the same story. "Do they have a package for me at the front?"

"Yeah," he says.

"How many did you do this week?"

"Four, I think." Jacky pauses. "I need paint."

"What colors?"

"Red, mostly."

The artwork started as a kind of therapy, because Jacky needed something to do behind bars, and he wasn't a reader, he'd never been much for exercise. So she'd brought charcoals and paper and paint and sponges—Jacky wasn't allowed access to paintbrushes, they were too sharp and could be used as a weapon—and she'd thought it might be a complete failure but it was worth a shot, because Jacky wasn't doing all that well, in fact, he wasn't doing well at all. During his first six months at Sterling, Gloria had been in a terror that she'd get a call from the prison, telling her that Jacky had hanged himself, or that he'd managed to drown himself in the toilet. And maybe things would've been better that way, God knows there were plenty of people who would've danced in the streets and set off fireworks if Jacky Seever were dead, but he was her husband, and she loved him. She still worried about him, she still found herself in the men's section at the department store, shopping for undershirts and socks, even though Jacky didn't need them anymore, the prison supplied them. It was old habit, but that's what every marriage is. Habit.

"Red? Black too?"

"I don't know. Probably."

"Okay."

The whole art thing was an idea, nothing more, but it'd worked, and Jacky turned out to be *good*, he had an eye for it. And there was a market for paintings made by men like Jacky, especially the nasty ones, and Gloria had found an art dealer up north who specialized in those sorts of things, although she'd sell him only one at a time, when she needed the money, because selling the paintings had been like admitting Jacky's guilt, like flaunting to the world that it was all true, he'd killed and he'd loved it, he was reliving it through his art and she didn't care. The paintings were awful but they were also a godsend, because she suddenly had money again, and there were no more long days of wondering how she'd be able to provide for herself once her inheritance ran out.

She kept selling to the art dealer until the rest of the paintings were stolen from her house, and he still occasionally calls and asks if she has anything new, but those calls are few and far between. People have lost interest in Jacky; they've moved on over the last seven years.

What we need is someone connected to your husband to get mur-

dered, the art dealer had told her once, and she'd actually laughed at that, although the memory of that laugh kept her up for most of the next few nights. *That would move his work, put some cash in our pockets.*

It was terrible, but it was also true, like most terrible things are. People died every day, and if that person happened to be connected to Jacky, well . . . It was an awful thought. But it *would* sell paintings, even the ones of flowers and mountains and bowls of fruit and blocks of smeared color that were all Jacky seemed to make these days. So she still stops at the front desk every week when she leaves the prison, where the guard with the mouthful of big plastic teeth is always waiting with Jacky's newest canvases, all bundled up, ready to load into her trunk, and she's considered telling him to throw them away, that she doesn't need more junk in her house, but she doesn't. She takes them, every time. Another old habit that won't die.

She goes straight home after visiting Jacky—she skips the squash at the grocery store, doesn't feel up to it, her eyes hurt and her legs are tired—and opens the package of paintings. There are five canvas squares. More landscapes. Flat gray land and swirling skies, full of color. Oranges and reds, mostly, swirled together, so they look like madness. She thinks the paintings are probably the view out Jacky's cell window, the thin slice of the real world he can still see.

The paintings end up stacked in her garage, where they stay, collecting dust.

"You're that Seever woman." It is the next morning, and Gloria is at the supermarket, although it's not her regular grocery day, because what else does she have to do? She's tapping the squash, picking it up and smelling it. She doesn't know how to look for a ripe one, isn't sure that it matters, and the woman who walks right up to her catches her by surprise. She is young and plain-looking—not at all pretty, not with the dark circles under her eyes and the spit-up stains on her shoulders. "Gloria, isn't it?"

"Yes," Gloria says before she can think to deny. Jacky's lawyer had suggested she change her name, but she'd never gone through with it, and after a while it had seemed silly.

"How could you do it?" the woman asks, and Gloria knows exactly what she means, right away, it was a question she'd heard before. So many times over the years.

"I never did anything," she says quickly. It's the same old response, the one she gives everyone. "I never knew what was going on."

"You're as guilty as he is," the woman says, and her baby starts whimpering from its seat in the cart, glassy-eyed and flailing. "You should be right next to him when he gets the needle. That's what you deserve."

The baby cries out suddenly, and throws its bottle so it hits the floor and goes rolling away. Gloria goes after it, her face hot. This isn't new, she'd been approached like this before, heard it all. But it isn't something a person gets used to. Not in a million years.

"Here. Your baby dropped it," she says, holding out the bottle, but the young woman shrinks away, her face horrified, as if Gloria had taken a shit in her hand and was offering it up like a gift.

The woman won't take it but hurries away, and Gloria is left with the bottle in her hand, the milk in it still warm.

She grills a steak for dinner that night, even though she doesn't like red meat all that much and she'll spend the whole night suffering with heartburn. She drinks a beer with the steak, although she would've preferred wine, and has a bowl of ice cream for dessert. Because it's what Jacky would've eaten. She still sleeps on the left side of the bed. She keeps three extra rolls of toilet paper beneath the sink in the bathroom, stacked in a small pyramid, because that's how Jacky liked it. There is no part of her world that doesn't revolve around him still. There must've been a period in her life when she was her own person, when her entire identity wasn't wrapped up in being the wife of Jacky Seever, but she can't remember that time. Not anymore. She doesn't exist as her own person anymore. After Jacky's arrest, people were always asking if she knew, how she couldn't know what he was doing, and they treated her like she was guilty of a crime too, even if it was a crime of ignorance. Because that's what marriage does. It locks two people together, forever and ever, until they're dead, and even after.

Lies Sammie regularly tells:

That she wants to have kids.

That she's glad she doesn't work at the paper anymore, that the stress was too much for her.

That she's considering going back to school.

That she never eats dessert.

That she always takes her vitamins.

"Are you feeling okay?" one of the girls asks her. She should've had a coffee during her lunch break, something choked with caffeine, because this is an important question at this job. If you're sick, you cover it up, make yourself radiant. You can't sell makeup to anyone if you look like shit.

"I'm fine." Lie.

"You sure?"

"I'm just tired."

This is the truth, although she knows everyone will assume she has the beginnings of the flu, because it's winter and it's retail and no one uses enough hand sanitizer or sneezes into their elbows like they should. She's tired, although she went to bed early and slept like the dead, and the truth doesn't seem like a good enough excuse, but it's all she's got.

"You didn't get enough sleep?"

"I don't know." Sammie looks at her hands. The nail on her thumb is cracked all the way down to the bed, sore and swollen, but she can't stop fiddling with it. She wishes the girl would shut up because her thoughts are all a jumble, she can't get them straight. She wishes she were at home, looking through her files on Seever, figuring out what to write about.

"Everything okay at home?"

"Yeah, everything's good." That's the thing about working with all these women, she's come to realize. They never shut up. They never stop asking questions. They want to know how you're doing, if you're angry, if they've done something wrong. And if there's a juicy bit of gossip there, something they can use against you, they'll do it. It's like snake handling. You never know if the damn thing is going to turn on you, sink its fangs right into your hand, and watch you die.

"You're not sick? I have vitamin C in my purse. The chewy kind."

"No, I'm fine."

She folds a stick of gum into her mouth and turns away, heads back onto the floor. It's been busy in the store, even before opening there was a line outside, customers waiting to be let in. There's nothing worse, she thinks, than eager retail shoppers, pounding on the glass and foaming at the mouth to get at the merchandise. There's something so embarrassing about it, so tacky, and she can't stand to look when they first come streaming in, giddy with excitement. There's a bigger crowd than usual today, because there's a new line of products being released—eye shadows and lipsticks and blushes, all limited edition, which will work the crowd into a frenzy, because everyone wants what they might not be able to have.

"I'd like to try that one," one customer says, sitting down on Sammie's stool. She's wearing Crocs and pushing a stroller, and the baby inside is red and ugly and squalling. The woman's pointing at a bright-blue eye shadow, one that she'll probably buy and never wear again. "It'd be good for the office, don't you think?"

Some women are defined by their husband, some by their children, but Sammie had always thought she was defined by her work, by the words she'd put out into the world. And the Seever case—that'd put her at the top of her game, she'd had reporters from all over the country calling, wanting to horn in on her success. She could've gone anywhere after those days, should've taken one of the offers at the bigger papers in Philadelphia or New York, even L.A., but she'd stayed because she felt a loyalty to the *Post*. Denver had become her hometown even when it wasn't, because it was where she wanted to be. But instead of moving up she'd gone to this, one woman after another in her chair, every one of their faces running into the next, so there were times when she'd look around the shop and be unsure who she'd already spoken with.

"What are you wearing?" the next customer asks. "You're so pretty. What's that lipstick you have on?"

"It's this one right here, one of my favorites," Sammie says, picking up a tube. "Let's put some on you. It's called Liar."

Seever had made her career, and he could do it again. Remake her. She still thought about him often, still flipped through the scrapbook she'd made of all her articles on him, her name in bold print under her blurry photo. Thirty-one victims were found on his property. Twenty-six of them were female. Seever preferred women, but he'd happily taken whatever had come his way.

"You don't have something with fuller coverage? I can still see that scar."

"I don't see anything."

"It's there. Right *there*. You're not looking close enough."

Not all the victims had been identified, even after seven years. Eight of them had been buried without a name, without anyone to mourn for them. The cops guessed it was because his victims were from all over, not just Denver, and a lot of missing people were never reported. They were homeless, or prostitutes, or people no one gave a shit about. When they were gone, they stayed gone. And Seever had been on the road a lot, traveling for business, and his routes were nearly impossible to trace. He'd been at it a long time, before cell phones and credit cards, before surveillance cameras had appeared on nearly every building. He'd been a ghost.

"I'd never wear that color lipstick. It's fine for *you*, but I'm a mother. You understand, right?"

She'd interviewed most of the families, walked through their homes, sat at their tables and drank their coffee. They showed her photo albums and old stuffed animals. They'd cried, and she'd patted their backs, handed them tissues. They'd wanted to share their pain, and she gladly took it, turned it into words. She'd visited the families, looked at the photographs of the dead, inhaled the dirt that'd covered their bodies down in that crawl space. Those experiences were like thread, and she'd taken them, braided those threads together and pulled them tight, laid one perfectly against the next, and that weave became her stories.

"I've had a terrible morning," a woman says. She has hard eyes, a mean mouth. "I don't want anyone to know there's anything wrong. I want you to make me look good."

This is nothing, Sammie thinks. These women and their petty

problems, their flaws they want covered, their little insecurities. They don't know what real suffering is. They've forgotten their coupons or they don't know what to make for dinner or they don't like how their hair looks. They tell her all these things because they want someone to care, but she doesn't, not after what she's seen.

"My ex-husband won't leave me alone," another one says. "He wants to fuck me again. One more time, he tells me. That's all he wants."

She needs to talk to Hoskins. That's where this all started, how she got going on this path to begin with. They haven't spoken in almost seven years. She doesn't want to see him, but she does want to see him. She feels both ways, neither. But if Weber's information is right and the two women pulled out of the reservoir are somehow connected to Seever, Hoskins will know for sure, he'll know exactly what's going on.

"How much does that cost? For one lipstick? Are you kidding me?"

"Excuse me," Sammie says. "I'll be right back."

She goes to the bathroom, stands in front of the sink, and washes her hands. The light is dim and soothing, not at all like the glittering bulbs out on the floor. She wets a paper towel, presses it carefully to her eyelids so she doesn't smear her eye shadow, the careful line of kohl. When she'd first been hired, she'd come in with nothing on her face at all, and she'd seen the shocked looks the other girls had given her, the disgust.

We sell makeup, her boss had said. *I don't think it's too much to ask that you come in with some on your face.*

The bathroom door opens, and one of her coworkers comes in. It's Kelly, Ethan's girlfriend.

"What's wrong with you?" Kelly asks, letting the door shut and crossing her arms over her chest. She's so young, and so stupid—the type who'll always think that if she bullies and complains enough, if she screams the loudest, she'll always get her way. And sadly, it usually works.

"What do you mean?"

"We have customers out there."

"I know."

"So what're you doing?"

Sammie looks at Kelly in the mirror. She hates this. Being questioned by a girl with shorn punk-rock hair who's almost half her age.

"Do you really need me to answer that?"

"What I need you to do is get back to work."

There's a cough from one of the closed stalls.

"Right away, boss," Sammie says, sketching a salute, wanting to end with flipping the girl the bird but resisting it.

"Oh, you think you're real funny, don't you?"

"Yeah, I'm a real comedian."

"I hate it when bitches like you get hired," Kelly says. "You think you're so much better than the rest of us. You think you can do whatever you want and everyone will fall down at your feet and worship you."

"What're you talking about?" Sammie asks coolly. But she knows, she's seen the way Kelly's eyes narrow when she sees them talking, the way she'll immediately make her way over and butt into the conversation.

"You're not better than me."

"I never said I was."

Kelly considers this, leans back on the sink, and crosses her arms over her chest.

"A guy came in the other day, asking for you," she says. "He said you used to write for the paper, about all those murders that happened a few years back. He told me he wanted to talk to you about the case."

"Who was it?"

"He never said."

Sammie sighs.

"What did he look like?"

"A real creep." She smirks. "The kind of guy who'd sneak up on you in a dark alley and tell you what a pretty mouth you have."

"What did he want?" Sammie asks, puzzled. She doesn't have a clue who'd show up here looking for her. Or who even knows she's here.

"I guess there's so many men hunting you down you can't keep track of them," Kelly says. "And I bet all these guys have wives or girlfriends."

"What are you talking about?"

"You're so full of it. You should get down off your high horse before you fall and hurt yourself."

Sammie pushes past the girl to get out, gritting her teeth and resisting the urge to clap her hands over her ears because the girl is still talking. She isn't crying, she's not the crying type, but she's angry, and it's a few minutes before her hands stop shaking.

When she leaves work she heads downtown, weaves through the afternoon traffic, and slips into a parking lot, where she has to buy a ticket from a machine and stick it on her dashboard so she won't get towed. She walks quickly up a side alley to Sixteenth Street, where the lampposts are wrapped in twinkling white lights and the pedestrian shuttles are running nonstop. It is crowded on the street, people swarming past, going home from work or to work from home, doing some holiday shopping, grabbing an early dinner. The country is supposed to be in a recession, but you'd never know it here.

It's cold, but it's not far to where she wants to go. She ducks inside, and the gold bell above the door jangles merrily. The bookstore is warm and well lit, and she stands just inside it for a moment, rubbing her hands together. She hasn't been in this building for a long time, not since Seever's trial, when she was invited to read some of her work, excerpts from the book she'd been writing on Seever, bits that hadn't made it into the paper but she'd squirreled away instead. Back then everyone had assumed she'd be announcing a book any moment, and the back room of the Tattered Cover had been completely packed with folding chairs, standing room only, the people were crowded in at the corners, their heads tilted as they strained to hear her read. She'd been flushed, nervous, and she'd forgotten to pee before starting, so all she could think about was her hot, heavy bladder throbbing against the bottom of her belly, but it'd gone well; there'd been plenty of applause and later a few people had asked for her autograph on copies of the *Post*, above her byline. But then, before Sammie's head had been able to stop spinning from it all, that other book about Seever was published, written by two guys who'd never even been to Colorado, who'd done some searching online and wrote a few hundred pages. And they'd referenced *her* articles, for God's sake, they'd ripped off her material and got away with it, and then it was over; no one wanted another book about Seever then, especially not with all those kids going missing out east, and a string of murders in Florida. Jacky Seever was big news then, but he wasn't the *only* news, and the public was hungry for some new piece of gore to snack on. The book about Seever, she thinks, the one not written by *her*, was the beginning of the end, but at least it didn't sell well. It wasn't made into a movie, *thank God*. So it isn't *all* bad.

She walks through the bookstore, the old wooden floorboards creaking under her shoes. The thin green carpet is bunched up in some places, so she has to be careful not to trip. But it's the books she's looking at, the endless shelves of them, going from the floor all the way up to the ceiling in some places. It makes her dizzy, all these words together in one place, it always has, even when she was a kid and would visit the public library during the summer, and their air conditioning would be cranked and the water fountain icy cold, but she'd still be sweating and almost ill, because it was all so overwhelming. But in this store she knows exactly where she's going, she does this every time she comes in, but now it feels like it means something more, now that she might have a chance. She goes to the corner where the nonfiction is kept, and she runs her fingers along the spines until she finds the exact spot where her book about Seever would be sitting. *Should* be sitting. Will be. She worms her pointer finger in between two books she's never read and holds it there, feels the spot where she's supposed to be, where she's going to be.

She's parked outside Hoskins's home, idling across the street in the gray shadows between the streetlamps. It's a little shoebox house near downtown; it looks tiny on the outside but is huge inside, like it's been enchanted with some weird magic. It's different from the last time she saw it. Better. He's been putting some effort into the property. Trimming back the branches on the evergreens and hanging drapes in the windows. Sweeping the snow off the walkway out front. She can remember when she'd first met him, right after Seever was arrested, when Hoskins was running on nothing but nervous energy and caffeine, when he didn't have time for anything but his work. Things have changed a lot over seven years, and she'd heard about his suspension, it'd been covered in the paper although she wasn't the one to write it, she'd turned down that assignment because it seemed too weird, too close to home. She knows he lost his position in Homicide, but she's not sure if he still works for the PD. Or if he still lives here.

Almost six in the evening. There's a car parked in front of the house, another in the driveway, but she's not certain if either belongs to Hoskins. He might've changed cars in the last seven years. The lights are on in the back of the house, where she knows the kitchen is. He might be making coffee, or dinner, pushing ground beef around a frying pan, although the thought of him cooking a meal strikes her as funny. She never saw Hoskins use his kitchen; she once opened his fridge to find nothing inside, not even an old box of baking soda. Nothing but the frosty blue light. The fridge could've been brand-new, recently unboxed and plugged in, except for the outside, which was peeling back at the corners from wear and tear, and the white-powder coat was flaking away to the metal beneath. The empty fridge had made her laugh at first, and then it upset her, made her sad, although she didn't know why. When she'd first started dating Dean, his fridge had been filled with food, and she'd found it comforting. Slices of cheese and wrapped butter in the door, plastic containers of leftovers stacked neatly on the shelves under the cold light. She used to open Dean's fridge just to look, to run her eyes over all that food like a greedy kid in a candy store.

She's made her decision—she'll get out, go to the front door. Wing it from there. She has no idea what she'll say, but she's always been good on her toes. She'll make it work.

What she actually does: nothing. Before she can turn off her car the front door opens and Hoskins comes out. He looks the same. A little older, but the same. Or maybe he's changed a lot, and she doesn't know the difference. She remembers the big freckle he had on the inside of his thigh and the streak of grays in his pubic hair, but she can't seem to remember what color his eyes are. The other things she remembers about Hoskins: The smell of cologne on his bare chest. The big vein on the underside of his cock. The way his eyebrows would jump up his forehead when he laughed, as if he was surprised into amusement. The grunt he made when he came.

She isn't excited to see him, like she thought she might be, or even nervous. Instead, she doesn't feel much of anything. He walks across his front yard, pushing through the snow so he can get to his car that much faster, and a woman comes out behind him, waving her hands and saying something. She looks like she's wearing scrubs—a nurse? The woman might be his girlfriend, or his wife. For the first time, there's a twinge in her chest. It could be jealousy, but that doesn't make sense, because it's been seven years—isn't that long enough for her not to feel a thing? It's like one of her girlfriends used to say back in college: Once you fuck a man, he's yours forever. Even if you wish he was dead.

She watches the woman go inside the house, Hoskins get into his car. He's moving in the quick, jerky way she recognizes. It's the way he moves when there's something big going on, when the adrenaline is pumping furiously through his veins. She could come back again later, when he's home again, but instead she decides to follow him, to see exactly what's going on, where he's headed in such a hurry. Get the scoop, like they supposedly say, although she's never heard anyone actually use that phrase, not once in her whole life.

He'd been in Homicide for all of a day when he pulled Loren as a part-ner. Luck of the draw, he was told, although later he'd find out that it was because no one else could stand to work with him, even though he was a good detective, he had more arrests under his belt than anyone else.

"You like being a cop?" Hoskins had asked him once, not long after they'd started working together. They were sitting in Loren's car, parked behind a dry cleaner, eating tacos. Loren turned to look at him, bewildered, and Hoskins turned red. It was a stupid thing to ask, like something a second-grader would ask the cop coming to talk about Chester the Molester and stranger danger, but he had to know. "I mean, you seem pretty good at it."

"I fucking hate it," Loren said immediately.

"Then why do you do it?"

"Because I'm good at it," Loren said, the ghost of a smile hanging around his hard mouth. Hoskins didn't care much for that smile.

"So? I'm sure you're good at other things."

"Nope. This is it." And Hoskins knew that a person could be good at something and also hate it, but after a while he realized that Loren loved police work, really got off on it, no matter what he said. It wasn't serving the public and helping his fellow man that did it for him, and it wasn't that he got to put one over on the dipshits of the world and parade around like a hero. And it certainly wasn't the money, because cops make shit; teachers and cops, cleaning up everyone's messes, got the shaft in the payroll department. No, for a guy like Loren, it's not about the money or anything else.

It's about the hunt.

Like one of their early cases together, looking for a man who'd raped and killed three women in their own homes in the middle of the day. There were no signs of break-in, no leads to go on, nothing. It took Loren some time to get going, three women were dead before he got geared up, but then it was on, *on like Donkey Kong*, and the hunt started. Hoskins had never seen anyone operate the way Loren did, had never even heard of it; it wasn't so much *investigating* as it was *transforming*, the way an actor, a good one, will become the character they're playing. Loren didn't do it very often, but when he did, when he hunted, he was all in, all or nothing. He changed his clothes, his voice, his habits, everything, so he became the person they were looking for. Loren called it *getting in his head*, but to Hoskins it seemed like more of a metamorphosis. A butterfly struggling free of a cocoon and spreading its wings for anyone to see.

Sometimes it was guesswork, sometimes they had nothing to go on, like that early case with the women killed in their homes. But Loren was watching, he was taking in everything, waiting until it felt right. And then he bought a suit at a department store and borrowed a Lexus from a local dealership, and he made Hoskins wait in the car when he went up to a nice house in a fancy neighborhood, not unlike the ones where each of the dead women had been found. A woman answered his knock, a housewife who was home alone, her kids were at school and her husband at work, and Loren had smiled and asked to use her phone because his cell had gone dead and he was late for an appointment. And even though Loren had the face of a rabid bulldog the housewife had taken one look at his nice suit and the Lexus parked at the curb and she'd let him in, had even closed the door behind him. Because money talks, even when its mouth is shut tight. And Loren could've done anything behind that closed door, he could've raped and killed the woman, or sat down for tea, but instead he called Hoskins, who pulled his vibrating cell from his pocket and stared at it for a moment, with the same expression he would've had if he'd pulled out a poisonous snake.

"This is how he's doing it, Paulie," Loren said, his voice pleasantly low through the phone's speaker. Hoskins tried to imagine what was going on inside, if the woman was standing by, waiting for him to finish his call, but Hoskins thought she'd probably turned her back, gone into the other room, wanting to be polite, even if it was her own home. "He doesn't have to break in. They let him in. *Invite* him in."

And Loren was right, he always was, they went knocking on doors again and a neighbor of one of the dead women came forward and said they *did* remember seeing a white car in the neighborhood around the time of the crime, a late-model Audi, something like that, and the man behind the wheel was handsome, with good hair. *I didn't think about him before,* the woman said, spreading her hands and shrugging. *I guess he didn't look like a criminal.*

· So they brought out a sketch artist, and the neighbor did the best she could, although Hoskins thought "handsome with good hair" wouldn't get them anywhere, it was about as useful as being told the guy was wearing fucking *pants,* but the drawing and description of the car caught someone's attention, and they arrested a guy a week later, a polite young man with a good job who drove an expensive car and liked to hurt women; his DNA matched that left at the scenes, the timelines matched, and it was case closed, everything was neatly sewn up. All because of Loren and his spooky ability, and his love of the hunt.

Hoskins never thought he'd be working in Homicide, never thought he'd be side by side with Loren again, and he'd thought he didn't care so much, that being in the basement, eight hours a day, five days a week thumbing through dusty old files and plugging them into the computer wasn't bad, but now, cranking the key in his car and listening to the engine labor in the cold, he thinks there's a good chance that he misses the hunt too.

When Hoskins pulls up in front of the house where Carrie Simms's body has been found, where Loren is running his investigation, he wonders if he might still be in bed, if this might be the most realistic dream he's ever had. It's the silent, flashing blue-and-red lights of the patrol units, and the steady, fast thump of the blood through his head. He hasn't been at a crime scene in a long time; he thought it might never happen again. That's what happens when they kick you out of Homicide—you can kiss that job good-bye. There's no coming back from the grave until you're resurrected for being a good detective, for doing your job right. Rewarded for his merits, although Hoskins wonders if this might be a punishment in disguise.

But it's not only being here. It's also the woman coming his way, who'd pulled in behind him and immediately climbed out of her car without bothering to turn her headlights off. At first, he thinks it must be one of the neighbors, home from work and wanting to know what's going on, but there's something familiar about the way she swings her arms as she walks, the tilt of her face up toward the sky. And then the woman pushes through the shadows and stops in front of him, her face lit by her car's headlights so she looks like a ghoul.

"Holy shit," he says, not bothering to keep his voice down. What's the point? She's got to know how surprised he is. "What the fuck are you doing here?"

Sammie Peterson. It's been seven years since he last saw her, when he'd tried to force her into making a decision, and that was a mistake, because she'd chosen her husband over him. It'd pissed him off, being passed over like that, so he'd gone to her house and knocked on the door; he'd known she was inside but she still wouldn't answer, so he'd sat in his car, the engine off while he broiled in the afternoon sun, waiting. Hoskins likes to think he's a good guy, *rational*, but every man has a point when the wires get crossed and things go bad, very bad, and that was his point, because he loved Sammie—hell, he didn't *love* her, he was *in love* with her. So he'd waited until her husband came home, and Hoskins had told him everything, standing out on the sidewalk while the sprinklers ran and some neighborhood kids pedaled by on their bikes. Told Dean how he'd been fucking Sammie, how she'd basically worshipped his cock, how she'd taken it up the ass and in the mouth and in any position he wanted, how she'd loved it, how she'd *begged* for it. And Dean hadn't said anything at all to any of it, just shifted from one foot to the other until Hoskins was done and then went inside and shut the door firmly behind him. He'd been expecting Dean to argue, to fight him, something, and he'd gone home disappointed. But after that he'd started letting go, stopped driving past her house and thinking about her, except sometimes, when he'd wake up with a thudding headache and no memory of his dreams, but he'd know, somehow, that they'd been about Sammie again.

"What're *you* doing here?" she asks, and that catches him off guard, because he should be the one in charge, he's the police and this is a *crime scene*, but he wasn't expecting her, especially not like this, casually sauntering up as if they don't have seven years separating them, as if time has stopped and rucked up so they're back there now, before it was ever over.

"I'm a cop," he says rudely, that's always been his safety net when he's uncomfortable—bad manners. "And this is a crime scene."

"I *know* that," she says. Pauses, and smiles. "Sorry. It was a stupid question."

The house they're in front of is big, older. A Realtor would describe it as *rambling*, he thought. The mailbox at the bottom of the driveway was built to look like a cat, and then painted orange with black stripes. It's meant to be cute, whimsical, but Hoskins guesses it probably irritates the neighbors.

"What do you want?" he asks, still looking around, trying to get a feel for the place. This is how he's always tried to do this—he keeps his eyes open, even before he gets inside, because he never knows what he might see. It's not the space immediately surrounding a victim that's the crime scene, some cops forget that. "You need to get the hell out of here."

"Don't be like that," Sammie says, touching his hand. She doesn't wear a wedding ring, even after all these years. "I wanted to tell you I'm sorry. For what I did to you."

"What?"

"I'm sorry." She looks embarrassed. "I never got a chance to apologize for how I treated you back then. I'd take it back if I could."

He looks at her. She's wearing all black, even her coat's black, and she's got makeup on. He's never seen her done up before.

"You came out here to apologize?" he asks.

"Yeah."

"It's been seven years. Seven years, and I haven't heard a word from you."

She bites her lip, looks abashed.

"Yeah, sorry it took so long," she says.

"Did you follow me here?" he asks.

She looks up at him, then away. Toward the house, where a cop is walking around the edge of the property, stringing up yellow tape. This is a crime scene, that tape says. Something bad happened here. Already there are people wandering toward the house, people who live in the neighborhood and others who happen to be driving by and were attracted by the flashing lights, they have their cell phones in their hands, ready to take pictures and videos to repost on the Internet, they're hoping for some gore, that's what the world is coming to, Hoskins thinks, one big voyeuristic funbag.

"Yeah, I did," she says.

"Don't do that. Ever. Don't ever do that again."

"But I need to talk to you."

"So, talk."

"Right now?"

"Why not?" he asks. "You came rushing out of your car like a bitch out of hell to catch me. You must have something important to say."

"I need to sit and talk with you, I have questions—"

"Listen, I'm not interested in dealing with the *Post* anymore. If you want a quote or something for an article, you'll need to get in touch with PR. They're handling that shit now."

"It's not about an article." She's starting to look flustered, angry, and he likes that. He always liked getting Sammie worked up, get the blood rushing into her face and her tail feathers ruffled.

"Yeah, sure." He doesn't believe her, because that's what it was always about for Sammie—about her work. About getting ahead.

"It's not."

"All right, princess. I believe you. Calm down."

"I'm telling the truth."

"Okay. Then what do you want from me? You got a six-year-old kid stashed in your backseat who looks like me? I don't make enough to pay you child support."

She snorts.

"I'd forgotten about you calling me that."

"What? A bitch out of hell? To be completely honest, I still call you that all the time."

Sammie laughs, a little too loudly, and covers her mouth with her hand. He'd forgotten how beautiful she is, seven years will do that. He catches himself staring, looks away. Her face, that's what he'd first been drawn to, those eyes that have the slight uptilt at the corners, and he'd started sleeping with her, congratulated himself on his good luck, all the while assuming that she was dumb as a bag of rocks. But that beauty is all for show, because Sammie's funny, she's charming, and she's also smart. And over the years he's learned that smart can be dangerous.

"Well, isn't this a surprise. A nice reunion, seven years in the making."

Hoskins sees the shock on Sammie's face before he turns around, she's looking at something behind him, at *someone*, and she looks ready to scream, to turn on her heel and run. She's staring at the man standing behind him, a man in a three-piece suit and wire-rimmed glasses, a man with buffed nails and his hair parted sharply to the right. It's Jacky Seever, but it can't possibly be, because Seever's locked up in the prison out in Sterling, the next time he'll walk outta there'll be his last, when they take him down to Cañon City for his execution. Some cops out in Cleveland had tried to "borrow" Seever a few years back, hoping to pick his brain, figure out what makes a killer tick, but they couldn't get clearance for it, because Seever's home is where his ass is, and his ass isn't going anywhere, no judge in Colorado is going to let that happen.

But here he is.

"You look good, Paulie," Seever says, but it's not Seever after all, it's Ralph Loren, that's what Hoskins tries to tell himself, it's *Loren*, back to his old tricks, he's seen him pull this one before, many times, *get-a-grip*, it's Loren, Ralph Loren. Then, the headlights on Sammie's car turn off, they time out, and they're all plunged into darkness.

And Loren, because he knows that he's scared them, Loren can read people like a book and he's a sick fuck who gets off on making people squirm—he laughs. Loud and hard, like a crazy person.

"You still sucking dick to make your deadlines?" Loren says. He's chewing gum, smacking it in his jaws, enjoying it. "I can't believe how fast you media assholes get the word out. It's like bleeding in the ocean—you just have to wait, the sharks'll show up sooner than you'd think."

"What the hell is all this?" she asks, pointing at the suit, the hair. She doesn't like Loren, never has, but this puts him in a whole new light. She's always thought there was something off about Loren, and Hoskins had told her about his tricks, that he liked to dress up like his suspects, that his investigation style was *strange*, but it's one thing to hear about it, and another to see it. She can't get her heart to stop racing in her chest, or her hands to stop sweating, even though she knows this isn't Seever standing in front of her, her brain knows it, only the rest of her body won't listen. "What kind of sick fuck are you?"

"Oh, I love to hear a pretty lady talk dirty," Loren says. "Make me bend over and grab my ankles, and I'll bark like a dog for you."

"God, you're disgusting."

Hoskins hasn't said anything yet, he still looks pale and shaken, like he's seen a ghost. Maybe he has.

"Want to see what a disgusting dog I can be?" Loren drags the word out, rolling it over his tongue, so it's more like *daaawg*. A disgusting *daaawg*.

"I don't want to lose my breakfast, thank you," Sammie says. "Your costume is quite enough."

"There won't be a problem with you losing anything, if you take it up the—"

"Jesus Christ, *enough*," Hoskins says. There are two spots of color high in his cheeks, bright red. He's angry, she can tell by the color and the glitter in his eyes, and she also knows that Loren bugs the shit out of Hoskins, that they have the kind of explosive relationship that only the PD would get behind, because they're both good cops, so wouldn't pushing the two of them together make a dream team? "It's too early to have to listen to this bullshit. Can you both shut up?"

"Same old Paulie," Loren says, dropping a hand onto Hoskins's shoulder. "I missed you, *padnah*."

"Isn't this sweet?" Sammie asks, looking back and forth between the two. "I hate to break up the reunion, but I do have some questions—"

"Oh, I thought you knew," Loren says, giving Hoskins's shoulder another squeeze. "When you dump a guy, you stop getting whatever information you want for your shitty articles. So buzz off, lady."

"Get off me," says Hoskins, shrugging out from under Loren's hand. "Don't touch me."

Loren frowns, pushes his glasses up the bridge of his nose in a gesture so much like Seever that she stares at him for a long moment, fascinated. He's good; he must've spent time practicing it, standing in front of the mirror and analyzing himself, wanting to be perfect. But it makes her wonder what kind of man mimics the appearance and gestures and voice and *everything* of a man who was best known for being a monster.

"You didn't have any trouble finding the house, did you? You been out here before, Paulie?"

"What?"

"Where were you yesterday? Around this same time?"

"Are you fucking kidding me?"

"Just wanting to clear you as a suspect. A man can never be too careful."

"Chief Black called *me*," Hoskins says. His face is beet red. "He asked me to come out here. To help *you* out."

"The *fuck* he did," Loren says. "I don't need anyone's help."

"Call Black, then. Tell him that. I'd be happy to head home, right now," Hoskins says, crossing his arms over his chest. But he's staring at the house, hard, and Sammie thinks he's dying to get in there, to see what's going on. To put on his Sherlock hat and poke around. "I've got plenty of other things I could be doing."

"Did someone else get murdered?" Sammie asks, and the two men look at her, as if surprised that she's still there. "Is that what's going on? Is it someone else connected to Seever?"

She doesn't have anything to take notes on, and that's a damn shame, she thinks, because there's something going on here, and she doesn't see any news crews around, not yet. She's first on the scene, but she's unprepared. It won't happen again.

"Paulie, tell your girlfriend to go home," Loren says. Hoskins's face is pointed at the house, but he keeps glancing at Loren, like he's afraid to look away for too long.

"She's not my girlfriend."

"Is Seever somehow orchestrating these murders from prison?" she asks.

"Jesus," Hoskins mutters, scuffing his shoe against a dirty pile of snow. "That's what we need in the paper. A conspiracy theory about Seever playing puppet master from death row."

"Hey, that reminds me." Loren snaps his fingers and turns to Sammie. "I go visit your old buddy Seever sometimes—he loves to run his mouth, and there's not very many people who go see him these days. He's got this list of visitors, you know, Seever had to okay it, the judge had to approve. They can't just let anyone in to visit that jerk-off. I'm on it. Hoskins is too. His wife, his lawyer. And you're on it. Samantha Peterson. Now, why would you be on the list, even after all these years?"

"I don't know," Sammie says. But she *does* have a good idea—it was Dan Corbin who called Seever's lawyer and got her put on the visitor list years before, thinking that she'd go out and visit, get a few quotes directly from Seever. It'd been a hassle to do, Dan had made sure to tell her. Lots of red tape, documents to sign. But she could never bring herself to visit, didn't think she could stomach it. She hadn't realized she was still on the list, but it's something she can use to her advantage. Pay Seever a visit, get a direct quote from him. Access to Seever could open up all kinds of doors.

"From the way Seever was talking about you, I think he was hoping you'd come by for a conjugal visit."

"Shut up," she says, meaning to sound vicious, but instead her voice is too high pitched, they can probably hear the lie in her voice. She looks down, fiddles with her car key.

"Sounds like you and Seever had some good times," Loren says. He isn't going to let this pass, he's going to keep picking at it like a scab. God, she hates him, standing there in his Seever getup, grinning like a fool. "He's got some good memories of you saved up in his spank bank."

"I didn't think Seever would give you the time of day anymore,"

Hoskins says to Loren. "And now you're visiting him out at the prison?"

A slow smile blooms on Loren's face.

"We're good friends," he says. "We have ourselves some nice, long chats. He'll talk to anyone who'll listen these days. About what he did, what he'd like to do. About *her*."

"Stop," Sammie says.

"Does it turn you on to see me looking like this?" Loren says, brushing off his shoulder. "Is that why you're blushing? Getting all hot and bothered at the sight of your old fuck buddy?"

Sammie looks at him, horrified, and he drops a wink, slow and somehow indecent.

"What the hell is going on?" Hoskins asks, looking back and forth between the two of them. "What are you talking about?"

"Oh, you didn't know?" Loren asks. "I can't believe she never told you. Of course, you might've thought twice about banging her if you'd known."

"Known what?"

"Well, Jacky Seever knows Sammie pretty well. Biblically, you might say."

"What?" Hoskins says, but she can already see the realization dawning on his face, slowly creeping in. He looks the way people do when they get bad news, when they're told someone they love has died. The knowledge comes slowly, and then all at once, like an avalanche pouring down the side of a mountain.

"Seever and Sammie used to come together to perform acts of sexual congress. They were boinking. Shagging. Fucking. Whatever you want to call it."

"Is that true?" Hoskins asks, looking at her, and it doesn't matter what she says, he already believes it. And the worst of it isn't the truth—it's the look on Hoskins's face, the horror of the truth. She cringes away from the way he's staring at her—like she's dog shit stuck to the bottom of his shoe.

"It was a long time ago," she says weakly. "When I worked for him."

"Don't worry, Paulie," Loren says. "She was boning Seever long before you came around. But I've heard that when you have sex with someone, it's like you're going to bed with everyone they've ever fucked. Isn't that gross? Imagine rolling around with Seever's naked body pressed up against you. God, that makes my stomach turn."

"Black told me to come here and help, not to listen to your shit," Hoskins says, pushing past her and Loren, heading for the back of the house. "I'll meet you inside."

There are others back there, she can hear their voices, low and hushed, because it's dark outside, it's getting late, and they're trying to be mindful of the neighbors, even in the face of a murder investigation.

"Don't worry. Paulie's a big boy," Loren says, watching Hoskins walk away. "He'll get over it."

"You're such a bastard," she says.

"And you shouldn't be here."

"Why're you dressed up like Seever?" Sammie asks. "What's going on?"

Loren looks down, as if he'd forgotten about the suit he was wearing.

"Wouldn't you like to know," he says, pulling the silver watch from its pocket and swinging it jauntily on the chain. "Maybe you *would* like a ride on the ol' baloney-pony, so I can pass the story on to Seever? Let him do some vicarious living before he meets his maker?"

"Go to hell."

"And you should go home."

"I came to talk to Hoskins. I'm not leaving until I do."

Loren looks at the house, in the direction Hoskins disappeared, considering.

"You're gonna have a long wait." Then he walks away, leaving her standing alone in the middle of the street. Farther down, a van pulls up, and a man jumps out with a big camera propped up on his shoulder, followed by a woman holding a microphone. It won't be long before the street is crawling with media, every reporter in the city will be looking for a story. It's a race against the clock now, so she scrambles, unlocks her car, and fumbles around in the dark, searching for a pen and paper. She's going to find out what's happening, even if it means standing out in the cold all night.

"Why're you doing this now?" Hoskins asks when Loren joins him in the yard behind the house. They're standing ankle-deep in snow, looking at the house, at the police swarming in and out. "You never did that shit for Seever before."

"I never had a chance last time," Loren says. "We didn't have to hunt for Seever at all, he was practically dumped into our laps. You should see how the ladies drop their panties at the sight of these suits. Especially my powder-blue one."

"Very dapper," Hoskins says dryly, but he knows Loren's not giving him the whole truth, he's holding something back. Loren doesn't do anything without a reason, and he must think Jacky Seever is connected to all this, otherwise he'd be in his own clothes, without all the shitty gel in his hair. But Loren isn't going to come out and say what's going on, Hoskins knows him better than that—no, Hoskins will have to figure it out on his own.

"Since you're here, you might as well take a look," Loren says, generously. He hooks a finger into the tiny pocket sewn onto his vest. The same way Seever used to do it. "I shouldn't send you home without at least getting a peek of what's going on. For old time's sake, you know?"

"Yeah, right," Hoskins mutters, following Loren as he steps out of the snow and onto the sidewalk. The crime scene isn't in the main house but the tiny building behind it. It's a guesthouse, a few hundred square feet built so the owner could take a tenant, make some extra income. The victim is just inside, but it doesn't feel right to call her the victim; this is Carrie Simms, this isn't like coming to a crime scene and seeing a stranger, someone you don't know, someone you'll *never* know. It's easy if you don't know the victim, if you don't recognize the freckle on the bridge of their nose or the amber color of their eyes, those little things can be easily dismissed if you haven't seen them before. A corpse you don't know is nothing. Less than nothing. It is something to study, to examine, to look over for evidence. It is stiff limbs and fingernails gone black and brittle, it is hair and blood and skin and organs, everything swept neatly into separate compartments, because it isn't a person anymore, just a body. A thing. But this is different, because he *knows* Carrie Simms, he'd recognize her voice if he heard it, he remembers how she laughed. This feels wrong somehow, seeing a girl he once knew like this, curled up on her side like a shrimp, her mouth filled with blood that's gone clotted and black. She could be sleeping, except for the awkward angles of her arms. And the blood. Oh, all the blood. It's not suicide, no, Carrie Simms didn't do this to herself. This is murder, cold-blooded and vicious.

"Looks like most of it occurred in the bedroom. How do you think she ended up in here?" Loren asks. He's standing in the doorway that leads from the kitchen and out into the yard, out on the concrete stoop, the toes of his loafers barely on the other side of the door's transition, he's pulled a pack of cigarettes out and sticks one between his lips. "Dragged?"

"You don't have some ideas of your own?" Hoskins asks, pulling a pair of gloves from his pocket and smoothing the latex over his hands, making sure to work it down into the valleys between his fingers. He hasn't been at a crime scene in a long time, but he's still got the old habits, still keeps the trunk of his car stocked with everything he needs. "I thought you were letting me look around outta the kindness of your own heart."

"Don't bust my balls, Paulie. I ain't in the mood."

"Then tell me what I want to hear."

"What's that?"

"Tell me that you need me," Hoskins says. "Tell me you need my help with this."

Loren looks at him, quickly, to see if Hoskins is joking. He's not. He wants to hear those words come out of Loren's mouth, because Loren *does* need him, Chief Black knows it, Hoskins knows it—hell, even *Loren* knows it—but it's one thing to know it, and another to say it out loud. It was true what he told Black—Loren's a good detective. Maybe the best there is. But Ralph Loren is also a wild card; he needs someone to rein him in the way a naughty boy needs a strict mother, otherwise things get fucked. Like this. Loren's dressing like Seever, picking up his behaviors, his quirks. The smoking, keeping that long cigarette pinched between his pointer and middle fingers, and the way he puckers his lips to blow the smoke out at the sky. Hoskins has seen Loren play this game of dress-up before, on a few other cases, but it was never this bad. This shit gives him the willies, to see Loren mimic Seever so effortlessly, so it doesn't look like an act at all. If Loren had a partner, someone who'd noticed this, they would've sounded an alarm, raised some questions. But Loren works alone, he does what he wants.

"You love to have me by the balls, don't you?" Loren says. He's sweating, even though it's cold outside and there's snow on the ground, there are beads of sweat standing on his forehead, on his upper lip. "You're like a fucking woman. You never quit your nagging."

There is something terribly wrong here, because the Loren Hoskins knows would never act like this. Sweating and shaking, with a constipated look on his face. Wanting help, but not able to ask for it. The old Ralph Loren would've told Hoskins to go fuck himself, he would've laughed right in Hoskins's face, flipped him the double bird. Loren's sucking on that cigarette like it's a pacifier, watching Hoskins with something like—desperation? It can't be, but there it is, no one else might see it but Hoskins does, he was partners with this man for fourteen years—not *friends* the way some partners were, they never hung out after work and had beers and watched football, but in some ways he knows even more about Loren because of that distance that always existed between them. He can see that Loren's out of control, he's in some deep shit, he's right on the edge of a bottomless hole. The kind of hole you fling yourself into, and you never, never make it back out again.

"I'll give you a pass this time," Hoskins says. "You won't get so lucky again."

Loren laughs roughly, shakes his head. Doesn't look at his old partner, who's now his partner again, but Hoskins thinks there might be some relief in that laugh, relief in the line of his shoulders. Or maybe he's imagining it. You can never be sure with Loren, the same way you could never be sure with Seever. Two men, wrapped so deep in themselves that you can never know what's true and what's not, unless you're watching closely.

And Hoskins, now that he's seen Loren like this, he's paying attention.

Loren asks everyone to clear out for a few minutes, so Hoskins can take a look around, and they're all huddled in a tight circle, out in the dry cold by one of the silent patrol units, smoking their cigarettes. There are cops and technicians and photographers. The medical examiner.

How many people does it take to solve a murder? As many as you can get. Someone had brought out a thermos of coffee, and Hoskins sees the steam wisping into evening sky before he ducks into the house, and he wishes he could be out there with them, shooting the shit, or in his basement office, nose-deep in an old file. Looking at the mess of it all, reconstructing the last few moments of Carrie Simms's life, he's reminded of how much he misses this work, and how much he hates it.

There's blood mashed into the carpet, a trail of it leading from the single bedroom before forming a small pool around Simms. Most of it had probably soaked through the carpet and into the pad beneath, and then into the concrete. It would always be there, it'd never go away. They'd have to destroy the house to get rid of it for good.

"Judging by the marks, I'd say she crawled," Hoskins says. "She was probably out of it. Trying to get away. Running on survival instinct."

"Crawled out of the bedroom and into the kitchen."

"Yep. And he was following her. Watching her struggle." Hoskins points at the bloody shoeprints. Most of the prints are in the wake of the blood trail, dried and messy. But there are two prints, off to one side and out of the way, like the guy had stepped clear of the mess, tried to get a good seat. He was a spectator. "They look about a size eleven. If you run them through the system, I'd guess they're running shoes you can get at any mall in the country."

"She lost a lot of blood."

"Yeah, she did. A lot of it before she died. I'd bet he finished her with the toaster over there. You see it? There's blood and bone fragments smeared all over it. A lot of hair. He got tired of watching her struggle, started hitting her over the head until she was dead."

"Christ on a cross."

"No shit." Hoskins doesn't chew gum. Instead, he sticks a ballpoint pen in his mouth, and gnaws on the end until it's too warped and broken to work anymore.

Hoskins stands up, his knees popping. Simms's hair is thrown over her face, and he's thankful for it. He's seen plenty of dead over the years, but there's always something awful about it, that final death grimace. Her left arm is thrown forward, her pointer finger stuck straight out, like she was trying to get them to look at something, although there's nothing there except a blank wall. Her right arm is tucked under her body, out of sight. She's wearing a white sleeveless undershirt, and one of those sweatshirts that zips up the front, but it's pulled open and hanging loosely from her thin shoulder. It's almost *flirty*. Sexual. Her bottom half is naked, except for a pair of ankle socks that had once been white but are now a rusted brown from all the blood. There are marks around her wrists, red swatches cut deep in the flesh. Rope burns, but most likely twine judging by the width of the lashes. There are bruises all up and down her limbs, cuts in her skin.

"It was twine on the other two, right?" Hoskins asks.

"Yep."

"How long's she been dead?"

"Rigor's passed, so about twenty-four. Not much more, though. We'll have a better idea when we get her on the table."

"Rape?"

"Oh, definitely."

There's a cut screen, a window that'd been jimmied open. Whoever he was, he'd crawled in and found Simms. Maybe she'd been sleeping, or in the shower, and he'd gotten in without her knowing. The last time anyone had seen Simms was four days before, when she'd gone to class at the community college. She hasn't been dead long. So she'd been alive the last three days, trapped in her own home, wishing she were dead while cars drove by on the street, while people walked their dogs, not very far from where she was. And she'd known what was coming, because she'd been through it all before, with Seever.

Christ.

Hoskins picks his way carefully around Simms, giving her a wide berth, careful not to put his foot down in any of the blood. He takes his cell phone out, snaps a few pictures. It's an old habit, he's always done it, years ago it was with the bulky old camera he carried around with him, and now with his cell, but it's the same, he does it without thinking, and Loren doesn't protest. He stands back, lets Hoskins do his thing.

Simms looks so small on the kitchen floor, so thin and fragile. He remembers the first few victims being carried out of Seever's crawl space. One of the boys had a woven bracelet around his wrist, something he'd probably braided for himself out of parachute cord, and that's what made it real for Hoskins, that's what made it worse. Because that boy had once been alive, he'd once decided that wearing a bracelet was cool, he'd played with it when he was nervous or excited, he'd spun it around his wrist until his skin was raw.

"She's had some fingers cut off," Loren says casually, pulling the pack of cigarettes from his pocket and tamping them against his palm even though he's already got one in his mouth. "Just the way Seever used to do it."

"She's not missing anything on her left," Hoskins says.

"It's her other hand. Seever got the pinkie. This guy got two more."

"I want to see it," Hoskins says, and Loren motions to the group out in the yard. Two of the technicians break off, set down their coffees, and slip on latex gloves. They ease through the kitchen, step around Hoskins, careful because it's so tight, so close. They're both young and professional, their faces blank, even as they hoist Simms up off the floor and onto the stretcher they've brought in. Good at their job. There's a loud sucking noise when they lift her, because the blood doesn't want to let her go, and Hoskins turns away, fights back his rising gorge. He's been to dozens of crime scenes, hundreds, and it doesn't much matter—that kind of shit will *always* be gross.

Hoskins grabs Simms's right hand by the wrist, gently, holds it up so everyone can see. The hand is purplish-red and swollen, filled with blood from being trapped under the body. The pinkie is gone, but that's nothing new, that's how Simms came to them. Seever had already taken that part of her. Hoskins counts the fingers once, then again, even though it's not necessary. Simms only has two fingers now, the pointer and the thumb. Her fingers make the shape of a gun, he thinks. A smoking gun.

He slowly lays her hand beside her and turns away, rubs the back of his wrist against his eye, watchful of his gloved hands, covered in the muck of death. He needs some coffee, or a nap. And he needs to call home, check on Joe, make sure the nurse is still there.

"This doesn't feel like Seever," Hoskins says, watching the techs carefully zip Simms into a black body bag.

"What makes you say that?"

"Seever kept his victims. Buried them under his house. He wanted them close, and he wanted to keep under the radar. But this." Hoskins takes a breath, slowly, but not deeply. "This guy isn't even bothering to hide the victims. He tied those last two together, he wanted them to be found at the same time."

"Okay."

"He's targeting people, specific people. This guy wants us to find these women and immediately connect it to Seever. You saw that article this morning about Brody and Abeyta? People are already making the connection to Seever."

"It's a lot of work to set up these murders so it looks like Seever's involved," Loren says. "Why would this guy go to all the trouble?"

"I don't know," Hoskins says. "I stopped trying to understand the shit people do a long time ago."

"You should see one more thing," Loren says, putting the cigarette out against the side of the house before stepping inside. "Down here."

Hoskins follows Loren, slowly picking his way out of the kitchen and down a hall—so short it could barely be called that, a few feet at most—and into the only bedroom. It's small. A futon bed pushed against the wall takes up most of the room, a cheap dresser eats up the rest. There are textbooks on the dresser, a calendar tacked up on the wall. It's probably a freebie from a bank, but the pictures are good. *Scenes of Colorado,* it says. It's open to November still, the photo of jagged red rocks jutting up out of snow-covered pines.

The blankets are wadded at the end of the bed, caught in the no-man's-land between the mattress and the frame, the bottom sheet covered in fans of dried blood.

"Up there," Loren says, and it takes him a moment to notice the words written above the flimsy metal headboard in heavy black letters. He wonders if the guy had written them up there while Simms was still alive, if she'd had to look up at those words as she'd been fighting, trying to survive. He hopes not.

It'll never be over.

"There's no way Seever's in contact with anyone on the outside. He doesn't write letters, he doesn't have access to email. No one visits him anymore except his wife, and half the time he's so drugged up he can't find his own dick. I don't see how he could have anything to do with this." Loren sighs. "But then there are the fingers. No one ever knew about those."

"Yeah, but there were plenty of guys working that crawl space. Any one of them could've let it slip, told someone. It was in the case files. There were photos taken. It could've gotten out a dozen different ways."

"What about this shit?" Loren asks, pointing at the words above the bed. "*That* never made it into any of the reports at all. That was between me and you and Seever."

"What're you saying?"

"How would this guy know to write those words up there, unless he'd heard them before?"

"If you think I'm guilty of something, say it," Hoskins says. "Don't be a pussy. Ask me."

"You never told anyone about him saying that, did you?"

"No." Hoskins answers immediately, without thinking, and realizes that's a lie a moment too late. Because he *did* tell someone—Sammie. "I never told anyone."

"I never told anyone either," Loren says.

Loren looks at him, then away. Another throwback to when they were partners. Being suspicious of each other. It's hard being chained to one person for so long, and there were times they hadn't handled it well.

"You think I killed Carrie Simms?" Hoskins asks. "Is that what you're getting at?"

"Did you?" Loren asks.

"You're really going to ask me that when you look like Seever's doppelgänger?"

"Don't act like this is new, Paulie. You know how I work."

Yeah, I do, Hoskins thinks. Seever's the best thing that ever happened to him. Seever made Loren's career, it got him a promotion, a private office, a nice raise. Seever made Loren a legend, and after it was all over, after the hunt was done, everything seemed so bland in comparison. So tame. These three dead women are perfect for Loren; he gets to go back to Seever, life is one big carousel and here they are, back where it started, like star football players reliving the playoff game.

"Bullshit," Hoskins says. "It was never like this before. And now he's in prison, so you can cut the crap."

"Okay," Loren says. "Maybe I dressed up like Seever for you."

"What?"

"You and Seever, spending all that time together in that room. Which one was it? Interview Room Two, the one all the way at the end of the hall, right? Good ol' IR2—isn't that what everyone calls it? Seever was filling your ear with all his dirty secrets, and you haven't been the same since then."

"What the fuck are you getting at?"

"I wanted to see your face when you saw me like this," Loren says. "I thought you were going to shit your pants out there. You and your girlfriend both."

Hoskins bites the inside of his cheek, hard, because he's going to start laughing if Loren doesn't stop talking. It'll be hysterical, horsey laughter, and he's not sure he'll be able to stop once it gets started. Loren and his stupid shit, his fucking crazy ideas. If you tried to make someone like Loren follow the rules and act normal, you'd end up with a bomb strapped to your car's undercarriage.

"I didn't kill anyone," he says wearily. "So you can put that stupid-ass idea right out of your head. This is a copycat killer, plain and simple."

"I know you haven't killed anyone. I had you cleared first thing, when Abeyta and Brody were pulled out of the water," Loren says. He puts his forefinger on the center of the glasses and pushes them up his nose, like Seever always did, and that one movement is so damn *true* it's nearly surreal, and Hoskins is hit by a wave of fear so hard it feels like a stomach cramp, nearly makes him double over. "But there's someone out there who admires Seever, wants to finish his work."

Loren had him *cleared*, and that pisses him off, but he doesn't argue, doesn't question why the hell Loren would suspect him first, out of anyone. Maybe he'll bring that up later, but now he's too damn tired.

"I've got to go," he says.

"You remember Alan Cole?" Loren asks.

Hoskins shakes his head.

"He used to work with Seever, supplied the uniforms for the restaurants. The two of them were real good pals, did a lot of partying together, but we were never able to pin anything on him."

"The real skinny guy, with the mustache?" Hoskins asks. "Yeah, I remember him."

"Jesus, I wish I would've ripped that pussy tickler right off his face."

"Why do you bring him up?"

"Cole was charged with sexual assault and attempted murder a year after Seever got locked up," Loren says. "He bolted, been on the run ever since. I think he's our guy. The one behind this shit."

"Any sign of him?"

"Not yet, but we'll find him. Turds like him always turn up, you just have to sniff 'em out." Loren pauses. "And I don't want you telling your girlfriend out there about this. That's the last thing I need, it getting out that we're looking for Cole, give him a chance to run."

"If you've already got a suspect, I don't know why I'm here at all," Hoskins says. "Sounds like you've got it under control."

Loren looks at him.

"The chief's orders," he says shortly. "He doesn't think it's Cole, still wants us to follow up on other suspects."

"Okay."

"I already have a task force put together," Loren says. "You can meet them all tomorrow. In the conference room on eight."

"Fine. I need some air."

It's the smell of blood that's bothering him, the smell of death and piss, but more than anything, it's the smell of Simms in the room that sends him reeling. It's not perfume—she probably hadn't been able to afford anything nice—but just deodorant, powdery and light, and laundry detergent. Basic smells, clean and fresh, and they seem so out of place here, with all the blood, and those words, those fucking words up on the wall.

Outside, there's a Korean guy standing in the driveway, leaning against the bumper of a car, getting his blood pressure taken by a paramedic. His mouth is frozen in a *wah-wah* shape, like one of those unhappy masks they use in theatre, and every time he weeps, clouds of steam come puffing out from his face, only to immediately rise and disappear. Frank Cho, who said Carrie Simms was a good tenant. That she was always thankful for the kimchi and the bean sprouts he'd bring over, that she was quiet and respectful. He'd been hoping she'd renew her lease and stay on another year.

Those words on the wall, and the missing fingers—they're small, but it's the small things that are usually the worst, the ones that cause the most damage, like tumors hidden away in the meatiest parts of the belly, patiently waiting for the right time to spew their poison and kill the host. But it's not only those things—it's Loren dressed like Seever, acting like him. This isn't how it's supposed to be. It's not fair. He needs to be able to move on with his life. But it'll never be over, like Seever had said. And, somehow, he'd been right the whole time.

Hoskins's hands are shaking, and he can't keep the image of Seever out of his head, sitting there with his wrists chained to the table legs in Interview Room Two, smiling, and probably doing the same thing with Loren, out at the prison. Talking nonstop, barely any pauses between his words, stuffing their heads full of shit. Seever had fucked Hoskins up real good, and now Loren too.

I'd choke them until they were almost dead, he'd told Hoskins. *Then I'd bring 'em back. Resuscitate them. I took a class on it one time, down at the Y. And when they'd come back they'd be so thankful, they'd cry, they'd think I was ready to let them go. They thought I was done.*

"You bastard," Hoskins mutters angrily. He's wasted so much of his life on Seever, so much of his time, and now it's like he's back again. The snow has started, falling from the gray sky, and the flakes get caught in his eyebrows and melt into little daggers of icy pain. The paramedic with Cho glances at him over his shoulder, then goes back to his patient. "You fat fucking bastard."

"You all right, Paulie?" Loren says, but Hoskins has already started walking, out down the driveway, where Carrie Simms's rice burner is parked, past the main house, because if he doesn't walk he's going to lose it, he has to walk even though it's cold and the wind is blowing and the tips of his ears are already numb. He has to get Seever out of his head, even if it's just for a few minutes, a few blocks. When he walks he can tune it out, Seever's whispers, he's been listening to them for the last seven years and he hears them still, they've never ended.

He ducks under the yellow police tape and fights his way through the crowd that's gathered at the sidewalk. There's quite a few out there now. People are drawn to crime scenes like flies to horseshit, regular people looking for excitement, and the freaks, and then there's the media, always looking for a story, with all their questions, getting into everything, like kids sticking their fingers in light sockets just to see what happens. Sammie's one of them; she might be the worst, always putting her nose where it doesn't belong, showing up at the wrong time, and he can't stop thinking about her and Seever, together, that asshole on top, between her thighs, splitting her open, grinning and grunting, deep in his throat, oh, Hoskins doesn't need to *know* what it would be like because he can imagine, and that makes it so much worse.

Hoskins has only the vaguest impressions of the crowd as he pushes through it, the hands grabbing for his sleeves, trying to force him to pause for their questions. He wishes they'd turn off the flashing lights on the patrol units, it's like they're trying to attract more people. Loren will be right behind him, he knows, on the other side of the police tape, snapping photos of the crowd to look at later, because some killers like to watch the chaos they've created, to take part in it, like a ghoul feeding off the misery of others. Hoskins is thinking about this as he sidles past a woman carrying a baby suckling on a bottle, Hoskins is looking around, his eyes sliding across the crowd, seeing but not really *seeing*, so he doesn't see the face of the man who turned away from him, quickly enough that it caught his attention. The guy has his shoulders hunched against the cold, and he's walking fast, away from the scene, and there's something strange about that, no one else is leaving, not until they get some idea of what's going on. Hoskins is still watching when the man looks back over his shoulder, a little *too* casually, and Hoskins sees that it's Ted, the guy in the next office over who's always so curious, who's so nice, who wants everyone to call him Dinky.

Ted, who has access to everything in the police database.

Ted, who'd just been talking to him about Seever.

Ted, who sees Hoskins is watching him and breaks into a run.

It's not even a contest—Ted is young but Hoskins is quick, and besides that he's angry; all he can think is that he's been working with this kid, he's been nice to him, he even bought him lunch one time, and here he is. It doesn't matter to Hoskins that this *isn't* how police work is done, you can't fly off the handle and manhandle people, Hoskins has been through this before, he should know better.

He rams into Ted, knocking him off the side of a car and onto the ground, and then he's on top of the kid, sitting on his skinny chest with his knees pinning his shoulders, he's got his hands around Ted's throat, and Ted is screaming, *trying* to scream, but Hoskins doesn't hear any of it, all he can hear is Seever—*they thought I was going to let them go, they thought I was done, they were wrong*—and then there are hands on his shoulders, pulling him away, and something slammed across the back of his skull, hard and metallic, and it makes a hollow echo in his head that he hears before he actually feels, and the pain makes him let go of Ted's throat and he stands up, takes a few stumbling steps away on the sidewalk. And then there's Loren, shouting something he can't understand, it's all gibberish, nonsense, and then Loren pushes those glasses up his face—those goddamn glasses and that hair, and Hoskins thinks that it is Seever here, and not Loren, maybe it's always been Seever—and hits Hoskins across the face with the flat of his hand, knocks him out cold.

SAMMIE

Sammie barely makes it to the bathroom in time. She shoves back the metal door of the stall, hard enough that it bounces back and hits her shoulder, nearly knocking her over. The food that dredges up from her stomach and out of her mouth is thick, ropy. Some of it looks the same as it did when she ate it—strands of lettuce, hunks of salami, thick pieces of tomato.

She flushes, washes her hands, and rinses her mouth, swishing to get all the sour taste out, even the stuff caught in the far back corners, the leftovers tucked between the fat of her cheek and her gums. She's sweating, hot beads clinging to her upper lip and scattered across her forehead, and clawing through her purse, looking for gum or a mint, because she doesn't want Hoskins to smell the vomit on her breath. If she ever gets to talk to Hoskins. There's a stick of gum at the bottom of her bag, still mostly wrapped. It'll have to do. If the bathroom were stocked with paper towels she'd press a wet one against the back of her neck to help with her nausea, but there are only the dryers that blow hot air. Global-fucking-warming, she thinks. Can't even get a paper towel anymore.

She'd still been waiting for Hoskins when he'd walked out of the house, she wasn't going to let him get away without trying one more time, and she'd seen him shove through the people, there were so damn many, but she didn't see what happened, only heard the screams and felt the push of the crowd. He attacked a young man, she heard someone say. For no reason at all. Grabbed him and threw him against a car. Tried to strangle him.

Then an ambulance had shown up and scooped Hoskins up, and she'd followed it all the way to the hospital, and she's been sitting around ever since, waiting for some word on Hoskins. She'd let the bored employee at the front desk know she was waiting for him, but the woman had seemed supremely uninterested and waved her off. So Sammie had sat in the hospital waiting room, watching *Divorce Court* quietly act out its drama on the old TV hanging in the corner and out-lining an article on the backside of a receipt she'd dug out of the trash. She doesn't have anything to write about, nothing that Corbin would actually run, except *this*, if only she can find out what happened behind that line of police tape. It has something to do with Seever, she knows it—why else would Loren be dressed up like that, why else would he bother visiting him in prison? She has to find out what it is before Chris Weber does, because he surely knows about her talk with Corbin by now, he must know he's got some competition. Corbin probably called Weber as soon as she hung up, just to rub it in his face. But Corbin's that type—he'll do anything to flay a good story out of his writers.

Of course, she thinks, it doesn't much matter if she gets anything out of Hoskins. She has the story of the year, of the decade, if only she'd write it: *I slept with a serial killer.*

If she gets that desperate, she'll do it. She'd put all her dirty laun-dry out to dry, write a big story about working in one of Seever's restaurants, of the flirting that went on, the charged comments, until there was finally a night when they ended up alone in the restaurant, and they'd had sex on the stainless-steel counter in the kitchen. She was only nineteen when it happened, and Seever was older, much older, and she'd always been attracted to that, age and power and money, and she'd let it go on for months before she was offered a job at the univer-sity library that she couldn't turn down, and she'd quit the restaurant and just like that, it was over. She didn't see Seever in person again until his trial, and she'd always sit in the back of the courtroom, where there were plenty of people separating them and he wouldn't be able to spot her.

Oh, she could write about Seever, and she'd have a captive audience; people would be eating right out of her hands. She could write about the way he'd held her naked hips, the rough feel of his hands grabbing them so he could nudge in a little deeper. Or she could write about the way he'd liked to tie her up, or when he'd asked her to fix the sleeve of his shirt around his neck and choke him while he masturbated, but she can't. She wants to write again, but her pride keeps her from going that far, because people would look at her and they'd *know*, and Dean would too, and she doesn't want to see the revulsion in his eyes. It makes her cringe, the idea that one day everyone could know these things about her, and how would she defend herself? By saying that she was so young, that she'd wanted a good time, that she hadn't known he was a killer? And all those things are true, but no one will care, because all that matters is the juicy story.

She'd been turning this over in her mind when her stomach had started churning, and she'd run for the bathroom. It's because of Seever, she thinks. The vomiting. That's all she can think, because it started after she started pursuing the Seever story, not long after she'd started sleeping with Hoskins, and it's tapered off over the years since then, mostly disappeared. But still, even now, if she thinks about Seever, if she thinks about that period of her life, her tongue gets thick and heavy, and her stomach flops helplessly. When it first started, she'd attempted to diagnose herself, got online and looked up symptoms, tried to get in her own head and make sense of the cloying taste on the back of her tongue after meals, the way her throat would clench, and the strange pleasure of emptying her belly after filling it with food. Maybe, she thought, she did it because Seever got so fat as the years passed, or because Seever had such huge appetites—for food, for murder, for life—or maybe it was stress, because it was hard to write about a man everyone hated so much, even though she hid the difficulty, made it seem easy. Or maybe it didn't have anything to do with the men in her life at all, or her job, it was just her, trying to make herself smaller somehow, to pare back everything she was, to shrink until there was nothing left of her at all.

Her cell phone rings as she's leaving the bathroom. It's Dean.

"Where are you?" he asks, concerned. This is the best part of marriage. You always have someone waiting at home for you.

This is also the worst part of marriage.

"Are you at the hospital?" he asks. "Is everything okay?"

It hadn't occurred to her, when Dean surprised her with a new phone a few months before, that it wasn't just a nice gift from her husband. It was brand-new, in a hot-pink case, fully loaded with all the bells and whistles. She hadn't found out until later that he could find out where the phone was anytime, pull up the information on a website and check her location, like she was an animal implanted with a tracking device. All the phones have it, he said, and she believed him, and if that's what he needed, that glowing blue dot on a computer screen that was her, she'd let him have it.

"I'm fine," she says. "There's nothing wrong with me. It's—Heather." There's only the slightest hesitation as she spins the lie. She's out of practice these days, but she can't tell her husband what's going on. If he finds out it's Hoskins she's waiting for, there'll be all kinds of trouble, because even though they've gone to counseling and talked it out and did everything imaginable, Dean thinks she still wants to be screwing Hoskins.

"Heather?"

"Yeah, you know. The woman I work with? The one who sells those oils? The, uh—essential oils?"

"No."

"You know, the pretty one. I've told you about her. I think she got food poisoning. Bad piece of fruit she ate during her break."

"Is she okay?"

"I'm not sure. I'm out in the waiting room. I can't leave yet, I don't know if her husband's coming to pick her up."

"What time do you think you'll be home?"

"No idea," she says. Someone steps into the waiting room, catching her eye so she looks up. It's Chris Weber, and the moment he spots her his face goes bright red. "Here she is. I've got to go, I'll try to be home soon."

"I figured Corbin was full of shit when he told me what you're up to," Weber says, walking quickly up to her, his legs stiff. He's wearing slacks and a blazer, a turtleneck. When he'd first started at the *Post*, all he'd wear were blue jeans and sweatshirts. Street gear. He's moved up in the world. A serious reporter. "What the hell are you doing here?"

"I'm waiting for a friend to be released from emergency care," she says coolly. "Why are you here?"

"I know it's Detective Hoskins back there," Weber says, stepping close. "This is my story, and I'm going to make you very sorry if you don't back the fuck off."

He's taller than her, bigger, and he's probably used to intimidating people with his size. But she spent years in the newsroom, teaching herself to talk fast and act tough, to swear like a sailor and hold her liquor. When you play with the boys, you have to behave like one, and after all those years at the *Post*, a man in a turtleneck doesn't bother her in the least.

"What're you going to do if I don't?" she says. "Break my legs? Tell my mommy?"

"What kind of game are you playing here? This is my story."

She laughs, actually laughs in his face. It feels good, not to have to be pleasant, not to be kind and helpful, like she has to be every day at work.

"Are you new here?" she asks. "It's not *your* story. It's all up for grabs, anyone can take the gold medal."

"This is my chance," Weber says. "Do you know what I had to do to get this job?"

"What?" Sammie asks. "Did you have to steal? Or cheat? Suck a dick?"

"No," Weber takes a step back, taken aback at her sudden vitriol. Surely he's heard about her, the rumors, and he knows what she's had to do, he's heard what she's capable of, but he still seems surprised. "Nothing like that."

"Or maybe *you're* the killer," she whispers to him, coming closer. She's just screwing with him now, trying to get him riled up, but an emotion still flickers across his face—shock, or guilt? It's gone before she can tell. "That'd be the perfect way to get your career going, wouldn't it? Murder a few people, make it look like Seever's work. And then you're in, right?"

"That sounds like something you'd pull, not me," Weber says. "The last year has been lonely, hasn't it? All you've got now is a pathetic retail job to hang on to."

"Oh, spare me," she says, spitting out the words. She can feel the corners of her mouth twisting down, the crease between her eyebrows deepening. She is angry, and anger is ugly. "You thought this was going to be easy, didn't you? That Corbin would hand these assignments right over, free and clear, that I'd be begging to help you? That's not how any of this works."

Hoskins steps into the waiting room. He pauses, listening to the woman at the front desk, and then he looks at Sammie. There's a bandage across the bridge of his nose, he's holding an ice pack to the back of his head.

"Now, if you'll get the fuck out of my way, I have an article to write," she says, flipping her hair over her shoulder and walking away.

"What're you doing here?" Hoskins asks. He doesn't look pleased to see her, but he's not exactly angry either, and she takes that as a good sign. He doesn't seem to notice Weber at all. "Are you still following me?"

"You look like shit."

"That's what I need right now. Someone pointing out how I look after I get my face broken into pieces."

"I heard you had it coming," she says, and he stares at her, blinks. There's dried blood crusted around the inside of his left nostril. "I understand you're beating up kids now?"

Hoskins snorts, then grabs at his head and groans.

"Jesus, it hurts."

"Let me buy you a cup of coffee," she says, putting her hand on his arm and guiding him farther down the hall, away from Weber, who looks like he's been kicked in the balls so hard they've popped up in his throat. But he'll recover quickly, and she wants to be gone by then, to have Hoskins alone. "Maybe some dinner."

"And what do you get out of it?" Hoskins asks, but she can tell by the way he's looking at her that he already knows what she wants—his words. Just like old times.

"I get the pleasure of helping a good friend."

They go to McDonald's, because that's what she wants, and she's driving, so he can't put up much of an argument. She doesn't want to go through the drive-thru and eat in the car, so they go inside and sit in one of the hard plastic booths. She orders four double cheeseburgers and a large fry. A gigantic cup that must hold a gallon of Coke. Hoskins only has coffee, and watches, bemused, as she spreads a napkin onto her lap and starts shoveling food into her mouth.

"You're going to eat all that?" he asks.

"Watch me."

So he does, sits back and looks at her. There are smears of makeup under her eyes, her lipstick is bleeding at the corners of her mouth. Sammie looks older in the cheap fluorescent lighting, drawn. Some women gain weight as they age, put on a few extra pounds around their middle, but he thinks Sammie has actually lost weight the last seven years. He can see every vein crisscrossing the tops of her hands, every tendon. They're ugly hands. Witch hands. She smells like oranges. *Men love the smell of fruit on a woman*, she used to say, but he'd always thought that she was talking about *him*, not other men. She used to spray her perfume behind her ears, on her wrists, the soft spot where her thighs came together.

Did Seever like it when she smelled like fruit?

He doesn't ask.

"So who was killed in that house?" she asks, her mouth so full of food he can barely understand the words. "Is it connected to the other two women? Brody and Abeyta? Is it a copycat killer?"

He picks up his plastic spoon, puts it down again.

"I know why you attacked that kid, but it's not him, Paulie." That's what Loren had said over the phone; he'd called when the doctor was looking him over and Hoskins had answered, even though they hadn't wanted him to. There was a sign in the room—No Cell Phones—but that's one of the perks of being a cop. You could ignore rules like that. "That kid—what's his name? Ted? I checked. He was in Miami the weekend Brody and Abeyta went missing, his mom says he's been home every night for the past week."

"Why did he run when he saw me?"

"I don't know, padnah. Could it be because you'd just ripped his ass for going through the Seever files, and he didn't want another helping? You got him pretty good, he'll be out of work for a few days. Hopefully he won't press charges."

And because the doctor was waiting, and the impatient nurse was staring, he couldn't say anything, he couldn't explain himself. "I didn't know," he said instead, that seemed to be the only thing *to* say, and that made Loren laugh.

"You haven't changed, you know?" Hoskins says now. "All you reporters—you're all the same."

"What's that supposed to mean?"

"You can't stop pumping me for information for two minutes."

"That's not true. I asked you how you've been," she says, smiling.

"Please. I know exactly what you want from me. You get your jollies off seeing your name in print," he says. "If you had to choose between living in paradise for the rest of your life or seeing your piece on the front page, I know exactly what you'd choose."

"What?" Her smile is spreading, because she knows exactly what the answer is. It's the words, the writing, it's always been that way for her, like it was for almost every other reporter he'd ever met. They were like crackheads jonesing for another hit. There were times back at Seever's house when they'd pull another victim from the crawl space and she'd known she'd have more to write, and he could see the sheer pleasure on her face. She'd take her notes and talk to the guys and snap some pictures and when the paper printed her piece she'd carry the damn thing around all day, and it wasn't only that she was *proud*, she was *high as a kite*. After every piece was published she'd want to fuck; once it was in her own kitchen while Dean was at work, on the linoleum while the dishwasher hummed beside them. She'd lain on her back and propped her heels up on the seats of the kitchen chairs so she could lift her hips into him, and she'd bitten his shoulder when she came, until he'd bled.

The back of his neck is hot.

"I'm not asking for much," she says. "Everyone's going to find out sooner or later what happened in that house. I'm asking for a head start. A name. So I have something to turn in. I need this."

"We're trying to keep people from getting scared," he says. "I don't want to read some article full of lies so you can sell a few more subscriptions. Like the garbage piece that ran this morning—I hate shit like that."

"That's not the kind of stuff I write," she says scornfully. "You should know me better than that."

"Yeah, I know you. That's the problem," Hoskins says. "We're trying to close these cases up as soon as possible. And honestly, the less the public knows about all this, the easier my job will be."

She hitches up one eyebrow.

"People should know what's going on in their city," she says. "They *deserve* to know. And if you don't tell me now, it'll get out sooner or later, it doesn't matter how much you want to keep it quiet."

He could give her what she wants—and he could ask for sex. For a blowjob. Or one of those deals he'd heard some guys at work talking about once, when a woman sucked a guy off while he took a shit. A *blumpkin*, that's what it was called. He could have anything he wanted. Those were the terms they'd had before, although he hadn't been in on the game back then—sex in exchange for information. He could insist they go back to that, he could ask her to do anything he wanted, every perverted thing that'd ever crossed his mind, he could tie her up and twist her nipples like radio dials and make her scream in pain, and she'd do it, he can tell by the look on her face. She'd agree. She wouldn't like it, but she'd do whatever until she had what she wanted, and then she'd be gone.

But in the end, he doesn't ask for sex. He doesn't ask for anything. He tells Sammie what she wants to know because she's right, it doesn't matter, it'll all be out soon enough. And because he still loves her, even though he wishes to God he didn't.

"The victim is Carrie Simms," he says, keeping his voice low, casual. There isn't anyone sitting close by, but you could never be sure who was listening.

"Carrie Simms?" Sammie frowns. "Simms? That name—oh my God. That's the girl who got away from Seever."

"Yeah."

"What happened?"

"Someone broke into her place. Tortured her, raped her. They made sure we'd connect it to Seever."

Sammie frowns, taps her fingers on the tabletop. He can see the wheels in her brain spinning frantically. Most women would be upset by this, be horrified, but Sammie has never been that way and he admires her for it. There's something cold about her, calculating, and you don't see that so often in women, at least not like it is with Sammie, who wears it all on her sleeve.

"So that's why Loren's dressed like Seever," she says.

"Yeah."

She's excited, he knows by the way she's chewing, the sparkle in her eyes. This is exactly what she wanted from him, all she's ever wanted from him. But nothing in life is free. There's gray hamburger meat stuck in her teeth, her lipstick is smeared all over the bottom half of her face from eating, so she looks a mess.

She looks almost like a clown.

"I have a question for you," he says.

"What is it?"

"Did you really have sex with Seever?"

She looks down, at the half-finished burger sitting in front of her, in the middle of the yellow wrapper with half a pickle sticking out of it, and puts her hand out, as if to pick it up and take a bite. But at the last minute she seems to think better of it, and drops her hand back on her lap.

"Yes," she says, softly.

"Did you enjoy it?" he asks, leaning toward her, until the edge of the table is pressed into his chest, cutting a line into his skin. He doesn't know why he's doing this, why he suddenly wants to hurt her, but he can't seem to stop himself. "What was it like, fucking him?"

Sammie looks away from the hamburger, turns her gaze up to him. She has beautiful eyes, she always has: wide, innocent eyes, like you'd see on a girl. She looks like she might cry, but he doubts it, because Sammie's tough, she takes shit and puts it right back out. No, she doesn't cry, but Hoskins is surprised when Sammie leans over the side of the table and makes a belching noise, it sounds like a bullfrog, and then vomits, all the dinner she'd inhaled coming right back up, all that chewed hamburger and foaming soda, spreading over the clean tile floor.

When Gloria was young, strangers would stop her mother on the street, call to her from their car windows. *I think you might be the most beautiful woman I've ever seen,* they'd say, and her mother would nod and move on, her purse looped over one arm and her lips pressed tightly together. And even if no one said anything to her mother, they'd still *look*, sometimes throwing glances from under lowered lashes, but most times it was open staring, and every so often there were whistles and catcalls, lewd suggestions. Her mother never talked about it, never repeated the things that were said to her. It was as if none of it had ever happened at all, like it didn't matter. Gloria couldn't understand it, didn't know how someone could shrug off a compliment. Maybe it was because she was so young, or because she was so ugly.

"A man said Mama was pretty today," Gloria once said. This was at the dinner table, when she was eight years old. They'd just sat down, the three of them at the table and the old dog curled up at their feet, snout on his paws, waiting for crumbs to drop.

"And what did your mother say to that?" Her father put his fork down so carefully it didn't make a sound when it touched his plate. Her mother, sitting on the other side of the table, didn't move. Didn't look up from her plate, even though they were both staring at her, waiting for her to say something.

"She didn't say nothing," Gloria said.

Her father was a tall man. Thin and wiry. When he came into a room it felt like he sucked all the air out of it, all the life. He wasn't at all handsome, with the dark hairs sprouting from his ears and the smattering of blackheads on his nose, he wasn't even handsome in the wedding photo that hung in the dining room, but anyone would look plain standing beside her mother, who was spectacularly gorgeous in her white gown, although she wasn't smiling. Gloria had always wondered how her parents had found each other, how her mother had ended up cooking in the kitchen of her husband's restaurant and cleaning the dreary little brick house on Ninth Street when she looked like a queen, but she never asked, not until years later, and her mother didn't have an answer, said she couldn't remember how it'd all happened. Her father could be mean as a snake, but he had his moments, he could be kind, and there were times she'd see her parents happy together, laughing and holding hands, kissing each other, her father bringing his wife coffee in bed and rubbing her feet, but things could turn fast, oh, her father's temper was quick, and unexpected.

" 'She didn't say *anything,*' " her mother said, correcting Gloria, her eyes not moving any higher than the mound of buttered peas on her plate. "That's how you should say it."

"That man was right, you know," her father said. He was staring at his wife, and there seemed to be heat in his gaze, hot and stifling. "Your mama's so pretty, I might have to kill her before some other man steals her away."

And then he laughed.

All her life, Gloria wondered what it would be like to be so beautiful that it made men look hungry, like starving dogs panting over a bone. But they didn't always look that way—sometimes they seemed angry when they saw her mother, as if her dark eyes and perfect face were purposely made to piss them off.

But Gloria didn't know what it was like to be beautiful, and she'd never know. She took after her father—tall and thin, plain-faced. When she was young, she'd overhear people say that she'd grow out of it, that ugly girls became lovely women, but that never happened with her; she was the same at forty as she was the day she was born. Her mother never said anything about it, but her father did.

"I always liked the smart girls better than pretty ones," he'd say, although they both knew it was a lie, because he liked nothing better than to stare at his wife; she was no dummy, but not a genius either. "You'll be a good wife someday."

Not that her mother wasn't a good wife, but she brought out something in her husband, something ugly and stupid and possessive, although no one except Gloria ever saw it. Like the time Gloria was ten, and her father was convinced that the butcher and his wife were having an affair, because she'd smiled as she'd ordered her roast for dinner, and even something as innocent as a smile was suspicious, and he'd asked her about it that night, *accused* her of being unfaithful, and then he'd pointed a gun at her face for three hours, one of the rifles he used for hunting elk in the fall. They'd been like that for a long time, her mother standing up against the kitchen counter, her father sitting at the table, the butt of the rifle nestled against the meat of his thigh, the TV droning on in the background and the beef in the oven. Her mother didn't cry out when she saw the gun, didn't seem at all surprised, and Gloria wondered if her mother had been waiting for that moment, if she'd spent her whole marriage sure her husband would kill her while dinner burned to a crisp.

"Go to your room," her mother had said, but Gloria had hid behind the couch in the living room instead, curled her knees up to her chest and listened, breathed in the dust bunnies and tried to keep from sneezing. She couldn't make out everything her father was saying, but she was sure something bad was going to happen. Gloria was a girl, but she'd grown up fast, she'd had to, most girls do, and she'd seen how her father's love for his wife bordered on obsession, that he treated her in the same way a greedy man treats his money, like he owned her, worshipped her. She needed to be captured, hidden away where no one else could see, like treasure in a vault. Or just destroyed.

Gloria fell asleep behind the couch, listening for a gunshot that never came, and woke up when her mother was carrying her into the bathroom, whispering that she needed to relieve herself before she went to bed, so there wouldn't be any accidents in the middle of the night. Her mother kept the bathroom light off, so there was only the glow coming from the hallway, yellow and comforting.

"Why did Daddy do that?" she'd asked, swaying as she sat on the cold toilet seat, only half-awake and struggling to make sense of anything. Her mother was kneeling on the cold tile, waiting for Gloria to finish so she could help with her pants and put her to bed, and she didn't look at all beautiful then, only tired and sad, and very old.

"I don't know," her mother said. "I guess it's because he loves me so much."

When you get married the diner's yours, her father had told her when she was young, and she'd go in and sit in a booth, one that was toward the back and out of the way, and a waitress would come by with a malted and fries for her, and she'd imagine how it would be to own all of it, how she'd make it better. She'd have the old tables replaced with nice new ones, and throw away the cheap plastic ferns that stood in all the corners. Put different things on the menu. Cakes, or pie. Gloria's mother could cook anything except cake. It was the altitude, she complained. Denver sat a mile high, and that was too far up for a cake to rise, and hers were always sunken, like someone had come by and thrown a rock in the middle.

But Gloria never had a boyfriend. There were no prom dates in high school, no Friday nights at the drive-in. Her mother tried to set her up with boys from the church, but those always fell through, and her father never said a word about it, but she knew he thought she was a lesbian. She knew because of the way he looked at her sometimes, and when, after high school, he pushed her into college. *You need a way to support yourself,* he'd said, but halfheartedly, not meeting her eye. *Just in case.*

It was the summer after her first year in college—she was a history major—when she came home and worked at her father's restaurant, waiting tables and smoking cigarettes out back, that she met Jacky.

"Can I bum one off you?" he said, coming up from behind and making her jump, because she wasn't supposed to be out there, her father didn't know she smoked and there'd be hell to pay if he found out. Her father didn't spend much time at the restaurant anymore—neither of her parents did, they mostly pottered around at home, busy with gardening and TV and whatever else—but she was still paranoid. "Left mine at home."

She pulled the pack from her apron pocket and passed it to him, more out of surprise than anything else. No one had spoken much to her since she'd started—she was the boss's daughter, after all, and a stranger—and she wasn't sure how to react to the friendly face.

"Thanks," he said. "Appreciate it."

"Yeah, of course."

He stood beside her, leaning back against the green Dumpster, one sneaker propped up against the metal side. He wasn't handsome, but there was something about his face that made her want to look at him more, something about the way he moved. He had a slip-slidey way about him, like a crab running on the beach, sidling along in the sand.

"I'm Jacky," he said. He didn't hold his hand out for her to shake, which she liked. Too many people had weak grips and sweaty palms, and she'd always want to wipe her hand on her skirt afterward but couldn't, because they'd think she was rude. "I wash the dishes."

"I know."

"And you're Gloria, right?" he asked, peering at her sideways with his bright eyes. "One of the waitresses?"

"Yeah."

If she were a different girl, she'd have something to say. She'd comment on his watch, or the weather, or the way it always smelled so bad out here, especially during the summer, no matter how much boiling water they poured on the concrete pad—something, dammit, anything to keep the words going. Or if she were beautiful, like her mother, she wouldn't have to say much at all. He could look at her, and that would be enough. But she could only be herself, and Gloria had heard one of the girls at school say that ugly girls had to try harder with guys, and the girl had meant it as a joke but it was true. But Gloria couldn't think of a thing to do, she wasn't beautiful and she wasn't clever, so they just stood beside each other, taking long inhales of their cigarettes and blowing clouds of smoke at the sky.

Three days later, Jacky invited her on a date.

"Why'd you ask me out?" she'd questioned. This was after the movie he'd taken her to, something about spaceships and aliens that she didn't understand. *You have to see the first two,* Jacky had said, shushing her when she asked questions. He'd bought her a popcorn and a Coke, and the butter had been greasy on her hands. She'd thought about licking her fingers, but Jacky had been watching her, so she'd used a napkin instead.

"Why wouldn't I?" he'd said. "I was surprised that a girl like you didn't already have a boyfriend."

Her cheeks were hot.

He took her out again the next weekend, to dinner at a nice restaurant, where it seemed like the entire staff stopped by the table to chat. She'd never met anyone like Jacky, who remembered everyone's name even if they'd only met once three years before, who could recall details and dates and events everyone else had forgotten. And he was always asking questions—about a person's work, their school, their family. People loved that, to talk about themselves. Later, she realized that Jacky saved information like a squirrel saves nuts for the winter—in case he needed it later.

"Did you used to work here?" she asked at dinner. This was after one of the prep cooks had left their table, wiping his hands on his apron and grinning. He'd been trading dirty jokes with Jacky for the last five minutes, while Gloria picked silently at her salad.

"No. Why do you ask?"

"They all know you."

"This is the first time I've met any of them," he said, smiling a little. "But now we're all friends."

Jacky collected friends like some people collect coins, or stamps. All the time, he was *on*, like a stage actor, and some people were repelled by that, sometimes all that energy came across as disingenuous, but most people were sucked right into his orbit. And she was too—charmed by his stories and jokes, and he always knew the right questions to ask, the way to turn a conversation around so the other person felt like the center of the world. He was made to work in sales, or politics, not washing dishes in a restaurant, but when she told him so he shrugged, and smiled.

"I've had heaps of jobs," he said. "I like to get a taste of everything."

He'd worked in lots of kitchens, he'd spent six months working as a night watchman at a retirement home, he'd even worked in a mortuary. Gross Mortuary, he told her, not a joke, but because it was the owner's last name—Gross. He'd done mostly grunt work there, but he'd sometimes helped with the departed. That's what he always called them. Not the bodies or the dead people or the stiffs. The departed. He would get them dressed in their Sunday best, put rouge on their cheeks, prop their heads on the satin pillows, and make sure their hair would lay right so the relatives settling the bill would be satisfied.

"It wasn't creepy?" she'd asked. "Working with dead people, I mean?"

They were walking through a park when she asked, holding hands, and he hadn't looked at her when she spoke, but straight ahead, squinting in the sunshine.

"No," he said. "It wasn't bad at all. It might've been the best job I ever had."

SAMMIE

This is the place Jacky Seever used to live, the spot where his house once stood. It was the house where he lived with his wife, where he had an office off the dining room where he kept his account logs for the restaurants, and a desktop computer—the same computer where police had found hours and hours of pornography, some of it tame but most of it the kind where women are tied up and tortured and end up dead, although you can't ever tell for sure, because the woman might be acting. Or not. This is where Seever ate dinner, built model cars in his free time, and murdered more than thirty people.

But it's all gone now, every brick has been torn down and trucked away, to be quietly used elsewhere or dumped and buried. It was done to keep the gawkers away, the sickos who come searching for a souvenir, some bit of Jacky Seever to take home with them. She doesn't understand how people can stand it, to have a bit of a killer on display in their homes. It's unsavory, she thinks. Distasteful. And it would drive her crazy, having that bit of Seever around all the time, making her think of him and things he'd done. She's already reminded enough of him, isn't she? Every day, all the time, she won't ever be able to forget, not until the day she dies.

What was it like, fucking him?

She still smells like vomit.

She's not sure why she came here after she dropped Hoskins back off at his car, parked under a lonely streetlamp in front of this empty lot in the middle of this quiet neighborhood, except that this is where it all started. Oh, if she was completely honest, this isn't where Seever's story really starts—its real beginning is probably somewhere else, years and years ago, deep in his childhood, although no one would ever know the truth of it except Seever. But to her, this makes sense. This feels like the beginning.

Carrie Simms. She wasn't the beginning for Seever, she was the very end, the one who finally got him put away. If she hadn't gotten away, if she'd died in that garage and been buried in that crawl space with all the others, Seever might still be free. And now she's dead. Murdered in her own home, seven years later. Loren is dressing like Seever. Hoskins is quiet, withdrawn, different from how she's ever known him. And Jacky Seever is locked safely away in prison. There's something going on, she doesn't understand what yet, it's like she's in the dark, groping around without knowing what she's looking for.

It looks strange, this empty lot in the middle of the other homes, even though the HOA is diligent about stopping the lawn from going wild, keeps the sidewalks clear of snow. Sammie wonders how long it'll take before they put a playground in. A few park benches, a big sand-box, a nice water feature. Maybe it'll happen. Maybe it won't. Maybe this place is too damn sad to be saved. She hasn't been here in a long time, not since before the house was demolished, when they were still pulling bodies out of the crawl space. She's been parked out front for almost thirty minutes, and she's seen only two people the entire time, a couple going for a late-night walk with their dog. When they see her, they stare. She waves, the start of a smile on her lips, but the woman pulls a face and yanks the dog away, the man flips her the bird. It doesn't upset her. They probably get a lot of strangers on this street, morbid fucks looking for a thrill. She doesn't take it personally, but she starts her car and leaves anyway, because the man is on his cell phone, he's looking at her and gesturing, he seems upset.

She needs to vomit again, get rid of the remnants of cheese-burger still left in her belly. But instead she goes into her little office, because the only bathroom in the house is stuck right between the two bedrooms, and Dean is probably awake, waiting for her, and he'd stand outside the bathroom, head cocked to one side, nostrils flaring, straining for the scent of guilt.

She can't do it in the kitchen, although the sink would do in a pinch, because Dean will know, somehow he'll find out no matter how many times she rinses or squirts bleach into the basin, and it'll be like be-fore, when she was doing it every day, and there'll be questions, or an argument, and she's not up for it, not tonight. So she sits in her office, swallowing the bile rising in her gullet. It's a small room, not even a room but more of a nook, only enough space for a small desk and a chair, and a single shelf overflowing with books.

The blinds in her office are still twisted open, and sitting in the dark she has a perfect view into the neighbor's kitchen window. A couple lives there, no kids. They must not have much money, because there aren't any window coverings, not even sheets tacked up as makeshift curtains. Or they don't care who's looking in. They're in the kitchen now, at the big tiled island that runs down the center of the room, and she can't tell if they're talking or only standing there, in the middle of an intimate moment they don't realize is being shared with an audience. She's seen them before, spent lots of time watching them, although they never do anything especially interesting. But they seem pleasant enough. Normal. They like to touch, to stand beside each other and hold hands, to eat dinner and pat each other companionably on the thigh. Watching them makes her feel like she did when she was a girl, playing with the dollhouse she'd gotten for Christmas, making the toys go through the mundane motions of a drama-free existence. The mother, cooking dinner and rearranging the furniture. The father, mowing the lawn and taking out the garbage. Cliché and boring, but somehow soothing.

She fires up her computer, opens up a blank document. The cursor blinks on the white page, waiting.

She types: *Jacky Seever has spent the last seven years in prison, but the city of Denver is still being haunted by his crimes. On December 1, 2015, Carrie Simms, Seever's only surviving victim, was discovered in her home, the victim of a brutal murder . . .*

It's good, she thinks. Fast. But good.

She emails it off to Corbin, then waits. Refreshes her email a few times, although it's unnecessary. Corbin never seems to sleep, and he's quick at answering emails. He hasn't changed in the last year—four minutes after she sends the email, she has a response.

This is good, the email says. *Very good. I'll pull some strings, run it in tomorrow's edition. What else you got?*

And then, the last line, which makes her heart leap up into her throat:

Welcome back.

Sammie and Dean are a couple who like to play games. Not sex games—after this many years of marriage there isn't much of that sort of fun left in them. And they don't play board games, or card games. Sometimes there are mind games, but that's to be expected, especially with them.

It's really just one game they play, and it's not even all that often anymore, not since they're getting older and tired, and the few minutes before sleep are often a blur of face washing and teeth brushing. But they used to play it all the time, late at night, after the doors had all been locked and the lights turned off and the house was dead quiet, except for the occasional murmurs from the furnace. It's always easier to play the game at night, when they are nothing more than two disembodied voices pushing through the dark. In the dark, they don't have to see each other.

This is a game of questions and answers, of endless possibilities. Sometimes they're hypothetical questions, sometimes they're not. They've played it since before they were married, teasing and laughing, poking at each other and ripping away the sheets so the cool night air would make their bodies ripple with gooseflesh. But sometimes this game turns serious, and they both get upset and angry, the bedroom seems too warm, even with the ceiling fan whirring ceaselessly above their heads.

"Are you still in love with me?" Dean asks. She'd come to bed an hour before, after getting the email from Corbin. She'd snuck into bed, thinking that Dean was asleep, but now she can hear the flicker of his eyelids in the dark, up and down, the wet kissing sound they make as they open and shut.

"What?" she asks, turning over, yanking the blanket out from where it's twisted under her arm.

"Are you still in love with me?"

"Why would you ask that?"

"Because I want to know."

"I'm married to you, aren't I?"

"What is that supposed to mean?" he asks. "Not everyone who gets married is in love."

"If I didn't love you, I'd leave. I'd go find another man to be with."

"Would you?" he asks, sounding amused. She wishes she could see his face, even for a moment. "I think you've done that already."

This is about Hoskins, she thinks. Somehow, Dean knows she was with him. She wishes she could tell him the truth, tell him everything, but he'd lose his mind, and there'd be trouble. Because she *does* love Dean, no matter what he believes. She fell in love with him because he was quiet and strong-willed and seemed to have it together—not like so many of the other men she dated back in college, when the guys were more interested in getting wasted and taking care of their cars and seeing how often they could get laid. Dean had plans, even back then—he wanted to settle down, to buy a house and have a good job, to be an adult. She wanted those things too, but it wasn't until after they married that she realized that being an adult wasn't all that much fun, that saving money meant not spending it, that making plans didn't necessarily mean they'd work out. She knows what Dean thinks: that when she's unhappy it's because of him. And it's not true, not entirely, although he won't believe her.

"Believe it or not, you're not the center of my universe," she'd said once, when he'd started complaining that she wasn't satisfied, all because she'd made the mistake of wishing out loud that they had the premium movie channels on the TV, when they couldn't afford it. He accused her of being disappointed in him, in wishing that he made more money, that he had a better job, although she thinks those are thoughts that he has about himself, ideas he's projecting onto her.

"Maybe," he'd said, "you wish you'd married someone else. Someone better."

The idea of being married to someone else has crossed her mind— who hasn't had those kinds of thoughts? But would it be better to be married to someone else, or to be alone? In the end, her answer was always no, although Dean doesn't seem to believe it, and she's tired of pleading her case to him. *I chose you,* she wants to say, but doesn't. *I could have left anytime, I could be with Hoskins, but I chose you.*

Oh, they haven't had a perfect marriage, but Dean—and Hoskins— are the only men who'd never treated her like nothing more than a piece of ass. Dean listened, and he'd encouraged, and he'd always tried so hard, and she wishes she could be honest with him, but he's so afraid. So insecure.

"I'm writing again," she says. "Corbin called, because of those women who've been killed. They think Seever might be connected."

"You're writing again." Dean shifts his feet under the covers, away from her, so they're no longer touching. "About Seever."

"Yeah."

"Do you think that's a good idea?"

"Why wouldn't it be? I've been waiting for a chance like this." But she understands what he's asking. He wants to know if she'll be seeing Hoskins, if they'll be sleeping together again. He's apprehensive, and maybe that's to be expected, after everything she's done.

"I guess."

"Have you ever hurt someone?" she asks, pushing the words out of her mouth and into the dark, because she has to say something, and that's the first thing she thinks of.

"Physically?" Dean says, surprised. "Yeah, I guess so."

"What happened?"

"In the third grade I shoved another kid into a wall, he got a bloody nose."

"Not kid stuff. Like, lately."

"Lately? No."

She stretches out, touches her toes to his, then pulls away again.

"Would you ever kill someone?"

There's a long pause, so long that she's sure he's fallen asleep again.

"Yeah," he finally says. "I would. If I had to."

"What does that mean?"

"Like, in self-defense," he says. "If someone broke in and tried to hurt us, I'm entirely within my rights to defend myself."

"How politically correct of you."

"And I'd do it for you."

"What?"

"I'd kill someone if you wanted me to," Dean says. "Sometimes I feel like that'd be the only way to get your attention. Start murdering people so you'd have a story to chase."

She doesn't say anything, but his words set off a faint alarm in her head, make her think of something else, although she can't think what. They've both said strange things under the cover of dark, admitted to things they wouldn't normally. Instead of another question, she gently pushes him over to his side, so his back is facing her, and she presses against him, their bodies perfectly aligned, and she pushes her forehead into the spot where his neck widens into his back, and they fall asleep that way, like one body under the covers instead of two.

He goes straight to his car when Sammie drops him off, sits behind the wheel and watches what's going on. The crowd has mostly dispersed, driven away by the lack of excitement, but there are still plenty of cameras, lots of media. Lots of cops going back and forth on the property, pairs of them walking down the street. They're going to be at it all night, going door-to-door through the whole neighborhood, asking every resident for their whereabouts, if they'd seen anything suspicious. There is a process to catching a killer. There are steps. They've secured the crime scene; now it's time to find a witness. That was always the part Hoskins hated the most—pounding the pavement, ringing doorbells and trying to coerce people to remember things. Most people walk through life wearing blinders; they don't see much besides what's in front of their own face, but it has to be done, because there's always a chance that someone saw a strange car parked out front, or a guy they hadn't seen around before.

And there will be more cops inside, he knows, taking photographs and dusting for prints and looking for any bit of evidence they can, because it's almost impossible for a perp to *not* leave behind DNA, unless they're incredibly careful. And this guy—he was careful, he'd kept Simms locked up with him for days and no one had suspected a thing, but maybe he hadn't been careful enough. Loren had said the last two victims—Abeyta and Brody, Hoskins had to remind himself, because it's so easy to think of them as *bodies*—had both been raped, but the medical examiner hadn't been able to pull anything off them. The guy could've used a condom, or their time in the water had washed everything clean. But this time it might be different, and he'd left something they could run through the database and hope for a match. But it might not matter if they find his DNA, because even if the guy left a fucking *bucket* of semen on the front doorstep, if they don't have him on file already, it'll be a wash. It's hit or miss, Hoskins thinks.

Sometimes worth the trouble, but not typically a lot of help in making an arrest.

A part of him wants to stay, to get back into the thick of things right away, but he's spent so much of the last few years running from Seever that he can't. Even if he tried, he doesn't think he'll be any more use tonight; it'd be best to go home, to nurse his sore head and bruised face, come back to the investigation in the morning, when he's thinking straight, when he can do the job right.

When he gets home, Joe's asleep on the couch, a melting bowl of ice cream balanced on his lap. "He's been hiding tuna cans again," the caretaker woman says before she leaves. "He's been digging in the trash and hiding them in his room. He won't even let me wash them out first."

Hoskins gets a trash bag and goes to his father's room, and the smell of fish hits him, overpowering the musky aroma of old man. The empty cans are stacked in the closet, starting in the farthest corner, where the suit his father used to wear to church hangs, wrapped in clear plastic and knotted at the bottom, to keep the ends from dragging. There are dozens of them—when did Joe have a chance to eat this much tuna? Hoskins gets on his knees, starts putting the cans in the bag, trying to be quiet about it, so by the time Joe realizes what has happened these flat tins will be far away, buried under a mound of other garbage.

"What the hell do you think you're doing?"

Joe's voice scares the hell out of him, the same way it did when he was fifteen and had brought a girl home with him, and they'd been in his bedroom, fooling around, because Joe shouldn't have been there, he usually worked late into the night, but he came home early that day, Hoskins never found out why, and he caught the two of them in the middle of their funny business. He'd stormed into the bedroom, shouting, and he'd put the girl out of the house, but gently.

"I'm throwing all this junk away."

"Get out."

"You can't live like this."

"I'm a grown man. I'll live any way I damn well please."

"These have to go, Dad."

"No."

Joe's eyes are shining, he's breathing hard. He's never been a violent man, never used his fists or was mean, is hardly ever rude or angry, but Hoskins thinks he might be ready to fight now, that there's a good chance the two of them will end up on the floor, rolling around, swearing and punching, all over a bag of cans, their insides smeared with drying tuna.

"I need those, son," Joe says, instead. There's no fight in him, none at all, and Hoskins realizes that the shine in his eyes isn't anger, it's tears, because he's ready to break down. "Please."

"Why? It's nothing but trash."

Joe sits on the foot of his bed—not *sits*, really, but more of a sink, slow-motion and graceful, and he's crying, thin old-man tears that run down his face and over his huffing lips.

"But I need them."

Seever cried when they arrested him, real tears, and Hoskins thinks it might be the only time he ever saw the man being sincerely himself, with all the bullshit wiped away. He didn't want to leave his home, didn't want to be pushed into the back of the patrol car parked in his driveway. *They're mine*, Seever had said, weeping. His forehead was mushed into the window, and he'd left behind a big smeary mark on the glass. *They're mine.*

"Why are you doing this to me?" Joe asks, covering his eyes. His hands are veined, spotted. Trembling. "Please don't do this."

Hoskins doesn't know what to say, how to make this better. He's still holding the trash bag, and when he moves for the door the cans shift, clinking against one another with hollow metallic chimes.

SLOPPY
SECONDS

HOSKINS

December 3, 2015

He tries to be quiet in the mornings so he doesn't wake up Joe, creeping around his own house like a thief. He's careful not to slam the bathroom door or to drop anything in the shower, and he usually shuffles around in socks and puts on his shoes last thing, but it doesn't matter, it's a shot in the dark, because there are times Joe is already awake, waiting at the kitchen table, his hands folded together patiently. Hoskins isn't sure what he's waiting for, and Joe doesn't seem to know either—he was never the type of man who'd wait to be served, he'd never had a woman around to make coffee or iron his clothes—no, Carol Hoskins was a real flake, she'd been seventeen when Hoskins was born and she'd only put her life on hold long enough to marry Joe and shit out a baby, and then she was gone. As far as Hoskins knows, his parents are still married, and he sometimes wonders if Joe's been waiting all this time for Carol to come back, to be ready to settle down. It doesn't look like it'll happen, though—she's had forty years to come back and she never has—and Joe has gotten used to doing everything himself, but he still waits.

Joe isn't at the table this morning, though, and that's good, because things are easier when the old man's asleep. Like the thermostat. When Joe's still asleep, that's his first stop. It's on the wall of the tiny dining room, which seems the stupidest possible spot to put a thermostat, but maybe that was the standard when the house was built. He doesn't know. He changes the temperature every morning, at least for a little bit, because Joe always looks at the thermostat, at least once a day, usually in the mornings.

Seventy-eight? Joe had shouted the first morning after he'd moved in. It was March, and even though it was spring the nights were still cold. Sometimes freezing. *You stupid, Paul? Do you know how much the gas bill is going to be?*

You're cold, Hoskins had said, but that only made his father angry, and Hoskins remembered all the times when he was a kid, when his dad would see how far into the winter season they could go before firing up the furnace, and then he'd keep the heat in the house so low they'd expel hazy clouds every time they let out a breath. And if Hoskins kept the front door open a second longer than necessary when he was going outside, or if any of the plastic sheets taped up over the windows was peeling up at the corners, Joe would spend the rest of the day in a severe state of piss-off, and nothing would make it better. *You need to be comfortable.*

I'll put on another sweater, Joe said, so Hoskins ticked the thermostat down to sixty-three, what his father considered the perfect temperature, and watched as the numbers took a dive and his father huddled deeper into his wool sweater, his lips turning a gummy purple shade. Hoskins didn't argue. It wasn't worth it, never was. Instead, he compromises, because that's what he does, he's always been that way. So he gets up early, turns down the heat so his father will think it's been there the whole time, and then once the old man's up and around, absorbed in something else, he cranks it back up again. It could backfire anytime, all his father has to do is walk over to the thermostat at any point during the day and he'll see what's going on, he'll take a look at where the dial is sitting and know, but it hasn't happened yet.

He's been meaning to buy a new coffee machine—he still has the old kind that uses the tissue-paper filters and a glass pot with the scorched bottom. One day, he figures, the damn thing'll break and he'll have to spring for a new one, one of those fancy stainless-steel jobs he's seen that takes only plastic pods, and will make just one cup at a time. He turns the dial on the thermostat, then starts the coffee. He hates doing it—pulling out the filter, rinsing out the pot, dropping in fresh grounds—he tries to remember to do it at night before they go to bed, so all he'll have to do in the morning is flip a switch, but he never manages to get to it. He's rinsing the pot—the damn thing always has grounds swishing around the bottom of it, no matter what he does—when Joe shuffles into the kitchen, rubbing his eyes. The old man's hair is wild, sticking in every direction, but he refuses to get it cut. *They buzzed it all off when I enlisted,* Joe always used to say. *I decided then I'd have long hair for the rest of my life.*

"Is Carol here?" Joe asks, scratching absently at his wrist, where the skin is raw and torn from being worked over by his nails. Colorado winters are hard and dry, and tough on the old man's skin. He's carrying the newspaper in his arm, cradling it like it's a baby wrapped in a blue plastic sleeve. "I thought I heard her."

"Dad, stop," Hoskins says, gently pulling his father's hand away, and Joe looks at him, surprised, as if he'd forgotten his son was there at all. "You're only making it worse."

"Where's Carol?"

"She's not here."

"Where is she?"

"Mom's been gone a long time."

Carol's not gone, not exactly. She's not dead, but she definitely isn't here, not anywhere near here, not if she can help it. The last he'd heard, Carol was out in Nebraska, running a pool hall with her latest boyfriend. Hoskins had last seen his mother when he was ten, and all he remembers from that visit is her long tan legs and her laugh, throaty and hoarse from cigarettes and late nights. She'd sometimes send postcards, or photos of her standing beside whatever guy she was fucking, and Hoskins had always hid those from his father, not wanting to see the hurt on his face. Once, she'd sent Hoskins a package for his birthday, but when he'd peeled the box open it was empty, and he'd never figured out if she'd done it on purpose, to hurt him for being born, or if she'd just forgotten.

"Yeah, I guess she did leave a long time ago," Joe said. He shakes the paper out of the sleeve and it falls open automatically, and there on the front page, in big black letters across the top, is a headline Hoskins never thought he'd see: SEEVER IS BACK. So much for Chief Black's wish to make an arrest before people can go nuts—if anything can push the public into a frenzy, it's something like this. He scans through the article, quickly. It's mostly about Seever, and how Carrie Simms was connected to him, and there's a name for this new murderer, because that was what reporters always did. They liked to give killers snappy nicknames, and this one might be the worst he's ever heard: "The Secondhand Killer."

"Oh, shit," Hoskins says. He'd known Sammie would write the story, that it would run, but not this fast, and not like this. This is fearmongering in the worst possible way, and she'd promised it wouldn't be like that, and he'd taken her word for it, when he should know better. The story takes up half the first page, credited to Sammie and a guy named Chris Weber, although it's only Sammie's photo that's been printed beside the byline—her old photo, the same one they always used before, the one that makes her look like Miss America. "You bitch."

"I think it's about time you stopped being so pissed off about your mom."

"No, Dad. It's not that. I don't give a shit about her."

"Yeah, you do," Joe says, sighing. There's yellow splattered down the front of his shirt—eggs from the morning before. He'll have to remind the caretaker woman to have Joe change his clothes. "We both do."

"Nope."

"Didn't you say she's running a strip club now?"

"I think it's a bar."

"Oh." Joe starts to scratch the dry spot on his wrist again, but sees Hoskins watching and folds his hands together. "I bet she doesn't wear a bra to work. That woman never did like to wear a bra."

"I don't know," Hoskins says. For a moment he thinks he might laugh, but then it passes.

"Never a bra for Carol," Joe says, sighing again. He leans back in his chair, closes his eyes. "I wish she was here. I'd like to see her."

"You still love her?"

"Nah. I want to remind her that she's old as fuck and shouldn't let her tits hang out anymore."

There's a cut under Trixie's eyebrow, shallow and raw.

"How'd you get hurt?" he asks, taking the coffee she's holding out to him. "It looks bad."

"I tripped," she says, looking away. A lie, he knows. Over the years he's come to understand that there *are* clumsy women, but not as many as anyone would have you believe. The cut on Trixie's face wasn't made by the tub or a door, or whatever other foolishness she'd try to make him believe if he pressed her. That was done with a hand, something with a ring on it, a big stone, probably, flat and dark, the kind that glitters meanly and will have blood dried into the prongs.

"Are you okay?"

"Yeah."

"Would you tell me if you weren't?"

She smiles at that, and the dimple on her chin makes an appearance. It makes him think of the girl in the closet, killed by her own mother. She'd had dimples in her school picture, the one the news had run, the same one that'd been blown up and framed for her funeral. He rubs a finger down the bridge of his nose.

"Probably not," she says, and that's also like the dead little girl, because she'd never said one word, she'd gone to her first-grade class every day and never once asked for help, never once said anything was wrong. No one suspected a thing, she was smiling until the very end and then she was dead. "I'm fine."

He pulls away from the window and parks in a spot where he can still see the shop, he can see Trixie leaning out the window and passing out the cups of coffee. He has a headache, and at first he thought it was from lack of caffeine but now he thinks it's because of *everything*. Loren and these new murders, Trixie and the cut on her face and the girl in the closet and Seever, because everything leads back to Seever, at least for him it does, and maybe it'll be that way forever.

"What the hell is this *Secondhand Killer* business?" Sammie says. She should be getting ready for work, putting on her makeup and fixing her hair, but she can't focus, because Corbin has run her article like he promised, but he's also made a few of his own additions, and added Chris Weber's name to the byline, as if they'd worked on the piece together, like they were partners. She'd called Corbin first thing, let the phone ring until he finally picked up. "I didn't put that in."

"I did," Corbin says. "Actually, it was Weber's idea."

"Weber?"

"Yeah, he's been trying to come up with a nickname for this guy. You like it?"

"No," she says, trying to keep the angry tremor out of her voice. "If I'd known you wanted a name for this killer, I would've come up with something myself."

"Listen, I wanted to run the piece this morning, and I needed something fast. Weber had already worked it up. What's the problem?"

She bites her lip. Corbin's amused, she can hear it in his voice, but she might be pushing her luck. It's the first piece she's had published in a year, maybe it's better to let it go. It's not so much about the name, although it's bad—you might as well call him the damn *Sloppy Seconds Killer*—it's because Weber came up with it.

"I was surprised," she says. "You ran my stuff—does this mean I'm back on staff?"

"You have a week to get me another piece," Corbin says. "I'd take something sooner, if you could crank it out that quick. But I'll need it soon—Weber's got a lot of stuff lined up. Enough to print daily."

"You didn't answer my question."

"I'm going to call you a freelancer for now. Prove yourself, I might bring you back on. Do this right, there's an empty office down the hall from mine—it could be yours."

"I don't give a shit about having an office."

"I'll remember you said that. Weber's been on the phone all morning, told me he'd scored an interview. Something good, I guess."

She looks at the clock, dismayed. She has forty-five minutes to get to work, and then she'll be stuck there for at least six hours. She'd call in sick and spend the day pulling together another article, but she can't afford to. They have bills to pay, they need to eat. That's the problem with chasing a dream, she thinks. Reality is always right behind you, nipping at your heels. And its teeth are sharp.

"A week?" she says. "Okay. You'll have something in a week. Less than a week."

You can make a person believe anything. She knows this is true. She's seen it herself, done it herself. She does it at work every day, makes the women who come in believe she's interested, that she's checked in while she rubs lotion on their skin, dusts their faces with powder, tells them how good they look. And these women, most of them who've never felt beautiful for a single day in their lives, they take her words, tuck them away and hang on to them, come back when they need more kindness.

Like today, for instance, when Sammie can't help watching the clock, when she's anxious to finish up and jump in her car. Every minute that passes puts Weber that much further ahead, and if there's one thing Sammie hates, it's falling behind. She's so absorbed in her impatience that she's not listening to the woman in the chair in front of her, a client who comes in every week and buys anything Sammie puts into her hands, but she isn't there for makeup, she's there because she's lonely, she wants to talk, to tell Sammie about her life, about her doctor's appointments and her son's eczema, about the way her brake pads keep squealing no matter what the mechanic does.

"You're a good person," the woman says, and this catches Sammie off guard, because she never talks about herself here, never interrupts the unending flow of words that come from some of the women.

"You don't even know me."

"I don't need to know you. I can tell."

Sammie pauses, caught in one of those moments when it seems like something is wrong, or missing, or that somehow this moment is important, and she feels like she should say something, although she doesn't have a clue what that might be. And then someone in the store laughs, high-pitched and abrupt, breaking the magic of the moment, and Sammie brushes more color onto the woman's cheeks, feeling vaguely confused, like she'd lost something, although she doesn't know what it is or even what it's called.

They let her go home early when she begs—fifteen minutes, and the manager acts as if she's been granted a huge favor—and she literally runs out the door, out the back, where the employee parking lot is. She stops when she hears someone yell her name, even though there are tiny shards of ice whipping down from the sky and the temperature is dropping like a stone in water. It's Ethan, the kid from the sandwich shop, hurrying out the door she'd come from, popping open an umbrella.

"Let me walk you to your car," he calls, and then comes running up, stopping close beside her and stooping low, so the umbrella shields her from the snow and wind, and it's suddenly dim under the cover, and they're standing very close.

"What're you doing out here?" she asks, yanking her scarf over her mouth. "It's freezing, go back inside."

"I'm waiting for Kelly. She should be off any minute," Ethan says. "But if you don't want me to walk with you, I'll stay here and wait."

"No, that's not what I meant," she says, looping her arm through his. The umbrella doesn't help with the cold, but at least she's out of the weather—instead, the ice is peppering against the nylon canopy above them, sounding like grains of sand. "I'm glad you saw me."

He smiles, and it lights up his face, but she doesn't see it—she's too busy looking down, making sure she's taking careful steps on the icy ground. If she'd seen this smile, Sammie would've pulled away, because it's the look of a kid in love, and she doesn't want to lead him on, doesn't want him to think there's a chance they'll ever be together.

But she doesn't see his face.

"I saw your article in the paper," he says, raising his voice against the wind. "It was amazing. So well written."

"Thank you."

"Can I get your autograph before you get famous?" he says, and with a flourish pulls a copy of the *Post* out, and hands her a pen. She tries to scribble her signature across the front, but the paper is already wet from the snow, ruined. "Oh, don't worry about it. I bought a few copies—I'll get you to sign some other time."

"Okay. You'll have to excuse me, I have to get going—"

"This is so exciting," Ethan says. He's smiling, *beaming* at her, and she doesn't think she's ever seen him so pleased. "I know it's your writing, but reading it makes me feel like I'm a part of the whole thing. It's stupid, I guess."

"No, it's not," she says, squeezing his arm and then quickly yanking her hand away, because Kelly is hurrying up behind them, her eyes narrowed against the wind, and she doesn't look happy to see them together. "Listen, we'll have to catch up later—"

"Yeah, sure. I've got to get going anyway."

She runs the rest of the way to her car, turns on the engine, cranks the heat as high as it'll go, and waves at Ethan as he turns to Kelly. Her lipsticked mouth is moving furiously, the words spilling out between her red-rimmed lips, and Ethan isn't even looking at her but down at the ground, his face buried deep in his coat's collar, hidden from the cold.

Carrie Simms's mother lives in the Happy Trees Mobile Home Park, which is a misnomer, because Sammie doesn't see a single tree in the whole place, and if there were, she can't imagine they'd be happy. She's seen nice trailer parks, with well-kept homes and lawns and swing sets, but this is all concrete and desperation. There's a pile of loose trash near the front gate, weighed down by snow, and a ditch of standing water that might be a pond, but probably isn't. Simms's mother—Delilah Simms—lives in Number 15, a faded pink trailer down at the end of a long street. There's an aluminum silver Christmas tree in the front window, a wreath made of plastic holly berries pinned to the door.

"Mrs. Simms?" Sammie says to the woman who answers her knock. She has dark hair, but it must be from a bottle, because her roots are gray. "My name is Samantha Peterson. I'm a reporter with the *Post*."

"Is there something he forgot to ask me?" the woman says. She doesn't look like she should live here, Sammie thinks. She's well put together, wearing a pantsuit and a simple gold chain, but she's also tired-looking, as if life's been too much for her.

"I'm sorry?"

"Mr. Weber—did he send you with some more questions?" She glances at her watch. "I don't have the time to speak right now, and I don't know what else I could possibly say. I haven't spoken with Carrie in almost four years."

"I'm sorry to bother you," Sammie says, backing down the steps. This is not how she imagined this would go, but what else could she have expected? It's standard procedure, SOP. Someone is killed, you interview the family. Get what you can out of them. Readers eat up family stories—the more emotional, the better. Of course Weber would've made this his first stop. "My mistake, we do have everything we need."

She runs lightly to her car and pulls away without buckling her seat belt, because Simms's mother is still watching her, one hand resting on the tarnished doorknob, the other arm crossed over her waist and cupping the opposite hip, as if she's in pain. Sammie drives until she can't see the pink trailer anymore and then pulls aside. Her stomach is turning, but even if she pushed open the door and leaned out there is nothing in her stomach to bring up, except the half cup of coffee she'd drunk hours before. She swallows the gathering saliva in her mouth, once and then again, and her stomach settles.

Talk to the families, that was standard. Weber would write a nice piece about the emotional impact on the family, a real sob story, even if he had to stretch the truth. He was going by the book, doing exactly the same things she'd do in his position. He was already outpacing her, and he'd keep ahead unless she started doing things differently, and she's drawing a blank now. The victim's family—done. She'd tried to get a hold of Simms's landlord, the man who'd discovered her body, but she'd had no luck on that end. She could hunt down the families of the first two victims, Abeyta and Brody, but she has a feeling that Weber already has those bases covered. She despises the guy, but he's not stupid—and that makes her hate him even more.

A dog lopes by, picking its way carefully over the snowdrifts. She unrolls her window and whistles. It is brown and skinny, too skinny. No collar, but it still pricks up its ears, looks in her direction and starts barking. It doesn't stop, even after she rolls her window back up and drives away, but chases her for a while, snapping at her bumper.

Dean is still at work when she gets home, and the house is empty, cold. She sits at the kitchen table. It's old, they'd picked the table and chairs up at a garage sale for ten dollars when they were first married, and Dean had fixed it up; he'd spent hours sanding it down and staining it, he'd called it his *labor of love*, and she'd laughed and kissed him heartily on the mouth. It'd looked new when he was done, but now it's worn and beaten; there are water rings left on the top and stains on the cushioned seats. She wonders how it got that way, how she'd never noticed it getting so run-down.

She digs her cell phone out of her purse and opens up the Internet browser, types in a few words. The icon spins for a moment, considering, and then pulls up pages and pages of information, two hundred fifty million results. It's amazing, how easy it is to find anything online now, without hardly any effort at all.

She sees what she needs, taps on it, and her phone automatically dials. She doesn't know why it had never occurred to her before, she needed Ralph Loren to remind her, but she has access Chris Weber will never have. She is approved to visit Jacky Seever.

"You've reached Sterling Correctional Facility," the automated voice says in her ear. The voice is sexless, robotic. She can't tell if it's supposed to be a man or a woman. "If you know the extension of the party you're trying to reach, please dial it at any time. Our visiting hours are Wednesdays, ten to one . . ."

"If you're tired, we can go to sleep," Gloria said. It was their wedding night, a year after their first date. It had been a long day—throwing a bouquet and dancing and cutting the cake and standing up in front of all those people, Jacky knew so many people and it seemed like he'd invited everyone he could, something her father wasn't very happy about because he was footing the bill. It was finally over, and they were technically on their honeymoon, although they weren't leaving Denver at all, just staying at the Brown Palace Hotel for a few nights, in the Roosevelt Suite, which had sounded awful fuddy-duddy to Gloria but had turned out lovely. "We don't have to do anything tonight. Unless you want to."

"What do you mean?" Jacky was watching her from the foot of the bed, his bowtie flapping loose around his neck. He'd spent the entire wedding in a state of hyperactivity, he'd danced and talked and laughed more than she'd thought anyone was capable of, but now that they were alone he was quiet, looking at her in a way she didn't quite understand. For a moment she thought it was fear, but that seemed silly, because why would he be afraid of *her*?

Oh, *she* was afraid. Yes, she was. She was twenty years old and still a virgin, had never gotten to second base, even with Jacky, who didn't seem to have all that much interest in petting. He'd kiss her when they went to the movies, but he'd pull away when things got too heavy, and he'd hold the popcorn on his lap, looking embarrassed.

She gestured, lamely, tugging at the hem of her wedding dress. She'd heard about doing *it* from girls at school, but it's not as if hearing about it was the same as the actual act.

"I don't know," Jacky said. He looked at her, then at the door, and for a minute she thought he was going to run. She'd never seen him nervous before, even when her father had promoted him from dishwasher to head cook, with more promises of management. *Owner*, her father had said. *He'll be running it all in no time.*

"Are you okay?" she asked.

"Yeah."

"Should I turn out the light?"

"I don't know. Yeah, I guess."

He came to bed once the lights were out, came to her, his skin smooth and cold under her fingers. He was trembling, and finished fast, his breath hot in the cup of skin between her neck and shoulder.

"I didn't know," he said.

"Know what?"

"Nothing. Nothing."

Jacky will only have butter in the restaurant, and at home. Real butter, not margarine or oleo, not even the good stuff no one can tell isn't butter. She tried to fool him once, to replace the stuff in their butter dish with margarine, thinking that he'd never know the difference and she could save money on groceries, but somehow he knew, he knew even though she'd thrown the evidence away. And not even in their own trash but in one of the bins outside the grocery store. She'd leaned way over the side of the can, shoved the empty box way down deep, covering it over with greasy bags of fast food and crumpled newspapers, looking over her shoulder as she did it, as if Jacky might be standing right behind her in the parking lot, watching her, knowing exactly what she was up to. She covered her tracks, did everything perfectly, but somehow Jacky still knew, and he'd thrown the nice crystal butter dish they'd gotten as a wedding gift at a wall and screamed at her for lying, for trying to trick him, and flecks of spit had gathered at the corners of his mouth.

He'd picked up all sorts of quirks like that after the wedding, mostly about things at the restaurant. Her father, who handed the keys and the deed over three months after they were married, says it's good. That it shows Jacky's a discerning man. He's got what it takes to make the restaurant run properly. And even though it hasn't been that long since he took over, Jacky's already talking about expanding, taking out a loan and opening up a second location, in a newish building where there used to be a barbershop, and a bar.

"Do you think that's a good idea?" she asks, but Jacky doesn't answer. He doesn't pay much attention to her these days, and she understands, he's busy at work, making a living to support her. He needs space, she thinks. But the only time he really seems to *see* her is when he wants *it*, fast and hard, and then he lets her keep the TV on while he takes care of his business, and she's glad for that, because she still doesn't understand the appeal of it, even though the women on her soaps love to taunt men with it, and it's all the men seem to care about.

A year passes before she catches pregnant. She's exhausted during those first few months, so she spends most of her days on the couch with the TV on, watching Erica Kane prance through life in Pine Valley, her feet propped up on a pillow and her hands roaming over her belly. It's not changed much, still flat and taut, but she can feel the tiniest push, a little extra something nestled under her belly button. She sees pregnant women every day, at the grocery store, out walking through the park, and she wants to be one of them, to have a round belly and wear those ridiculous smock tops that balloon out at the waist. And then there'll be a baby, a boy who looks like Jacky, and later they can have a girl. One of each flavor. She's already started buying clothes, tiny socks and bottles of tearless shampoo, and the checkout girl doesn't ask but she has to know, she looks at those things and then at Gloria's belly, beaming, and it's like they understand each other without saying a word.

And then, as quickly as it happened, it's over. She wakes up one morning thinking that she must've had an accident because there's a wet spot in the bed, she hasn't done that since she was very small and her father had hung all the bedding outside so the entire neighborhood could see she was a bed-wetter. But when she throws back the covers all she sees is red. It seems to her in that moment that the entire bed is filled with blood, an ocean of it; it's actually not that much but it's enough, and the baby is gone. The doctor tells her to rest, that they can try again soon, that these things happen all the time. Jacky is sympathetic at first, but he's confused by how upset she is, how sad, and says that he doesn't understand why she's acting like this, over something she never even had.

She bleeds for a week, and every time she goes to the bathroom she searches the toilet bowl before flushing, although she doesn't know what she's looking for. There's nothing but urine and clotted blood and other bits she doesn't have a name for, but she keeps looking anyway, expecting something more.

———

Marriage, she thinks, is a careful balancing act. If you put too much weight on one side, lose your focus, everything falls.

"Don't touch me," she tells Jacky. It's been nearly six months since the miscarriage, but she doesn't want to try again. She's careful—sleeps fully clothed, always goes to bed before Jacky, quickly moves out of the way when she feels him getting close.

"I need you," he says. She found a magazine under his side of the bed not long before, where it had dropped after he fell asleep. On the cover was a photo of a woman, naked and tied, a black rubber ball jammed into her mouth. The woman—and every other woman in the magazine, all tied up and being whipped or pinched or hurt in some way—looked terrified.

"I'm not feeling well right now." She didn't say anything to Jacky about the magazine—she'd been finding things like that for a while now, surprises he'd left behind. It was like finding a big green booger wiped on the bottom of a chair, she'd thought the first time. A nasty, crusty thing that had been left behind, and it was worse because it was *Jacky* doing it, it was her husband doing those disgusting things. "I need to go to sleep."

She turns over in the bed, tucking her hand under her cheek, but Jacky isn't letting her off this time. He grabs her shoulder, pins her back on the mattress. A hank of her hair gets caught in his watchband and rips right out of her scalp, making her shriek in surprise.

"What are you doing?" she says, but he's busy, working on the drawstring of his pajama bottoms with one hand and holding her down with the other. "Let me go."

She pushes at him, tries to fight him off, but Jacky's stronger than she is, and his arms are longer. When she manages to sink her nails into the meat of his cheek he slaps her, hard, and she puts her hands over her face and cries, sucking in air so hard she can hear it wheezing through the cracks in her fingers.

"Let me see your face," Jacky says, grabbing at her wrists and trying to pull her hands away, his hips not slowing down, and she realizes that this is turning him on, that she's like one of those girls in the magazine, she's scared and crying and trying to get away, and Jacky doesn't just like it, he loves it. She doesn't let him pull her hands away, even when he pinches her, taking flesh in between his fingers and squeezing until the skin squirts out of his grip and she screams, but she doesn't lower her hands. "I want to see your face."

Jacky doesn't wake her up when he leaves for work the next morning, so it's almost noon before she gets up, smeary-eyed and groggy. She slept like the dead, but she's still exhausted. She pads into the kitchen, turns on the coffee machine, and watches it slowly drip into the pot, not noticing that her robe is untied and open, and that she's naked beneath, or that she's swiveling her hips back and forth, tufts of her pubic hair skimming the lip of the counter. And she certainly doesn't notice the dried blood on her thighs.

She thinks her husband might've raped her. Or not. Can that even happen? She's not sure.

She slops the coffee over the mug's rim when she pours, burning the back of her hand. She could leave Jacky. Ask for a divorce. Those things happen. She doesn't know any women who've actually left their husbands, but she's seen it on TV, knows it's possible. All day she thinks about this, about leaving, and she gets a suitcase out of the hallway closet and puts a few things in—just some panties and blouses, a few pairs of slacks. If she packed all her clothes, she thinks, that means she'd made up her mind, that she was ready to go.

But she's still not sure.

Later that night, when she's sitting across from Jacky at the dinner table, watching him shovel food in his mouth, she decides she has to say something. That's what women are supposed to do, aren't they? Speak their minds? Get their feelings out in the open? She thinks she might've read that tidbit of wisdom in a magazine somewhere—probably in the waiting room at the dentist's office. Clear the air, it said. Work things out. Or be a modern woman, and leave. She didn't need a man who'd treat her badly, the magazine had said.

"About last night—" she starts, but Jacky won't let her finish, because he suddenly has an awful lot to say, even though he hasn't said a word since sitting down.

"I don't know what I was thinking," he says quickly, standing up and coming around the table to her. She flinches away when he tries to hold her, and she sees the pain in his eyes. "I didn't mean to hurt you. We haven't been together for so long, and I've been wanting you so badly."

I guess he does it because he loves me so much, her mother had said.

"I'll move into the guest room until I find somewhere else to live," he says. "I won't touch you again."

"I don't want you to do that," Gloria says. This is not going the way she thought it would, not at all. It's one thing if she plans on divorcing him, but it's something completely different if he's trying to leave her. How could he do this? He's in the wrong, after all. Isn't he? *Isn't he?*

"I don't think you're attracted to me anymore," Jacky says. He looks ready to cry. "If there's something wrong with me, if you don't want to be with me, I understand. There're a lot of men out there—"

"I never said anything like that."

"But you didn't enjoy it last night."

"I never said that." She can't believe the words coming out of her mouth. The lies. But is she lying, telling him that she enjoyed his crushing weight on her body, the sandpaper-pain as he forced his way between her legs? She doesn't know. It's like she can't remember anything anymore, and the only thing she feels is an overpowering need to hold on. She had all sorts of intentions, but they've jumped ship. "When did I say that?"

"I guess you didn't," Jacky says slowly. "But you've been so cold to me lately, I thought—"

"How about you don't assume anything about me," she snaps, scooping more green beans out of the bowl and thumping them down on his plate. "I've got my own mind, and if I don't like something I'll let you know."

"All right, then," he says. "You'll let me know."

"I'll let you know," she says firmly, and then says it again. She remembers the half-packed suitcase upstairs, excuses herself from the table, and goes up. She doesn't bother taking out the clothes but sticks the suitcase back in the closet, quietly, so Jacky won't know what she's doing, so he'll never know.

The next day Jacky brings her flowers, and he keeps doing it, a new bouquet every few days. He buys whatever's in season—daisies in the spring, mums in the fall. Carnations all year long. Tall, fresh flowers, their heavy heads drooping over the sides of a glass vase, their delicate stems barely able to hold them upright.

"I don't need a new vase every time," she says. "If you bring the flowers wrapped in paper, they'll be fine."

But he doesn't listen, and keeps coming home with more glass vases, and she feels bad tossing them out with the trash, so she instead stacks them in one corner of the garage, in a careful pile. They get dusty there. Dirty. She doesn't touch it, this precarious mountain of glass that grows bigger every week, but sometimes she goes out into the garage to look at it, the bottoms of her bare feet cold and dirty on the concrete, her arms crossed over her breasts. After the first few times, she noticed that spiders would climb inside the glass, not knowing that they'd never be able to get out again, that they'd end up dead at the bottoms, their legs crinkled up close to their bodies, the whole rest of the world right there, close enough to see, but still not close enough.

THE

HUNT

HOSKINS

December 7, 2015

It's quiet in the basement without Ted in the office next door, and it seems darker than usual. Probably a psychological thing. When he gets in there's a manila folder on his chair; inside there's a few handwritten pages of notes, done in Loren's fancy Palmer script on unlined computer paper, and a yellow sticky note on top. *Take a look?* it says. *This is the best the numbnuts on the task force could come up with. I'm out today, headed down to Pueblo. We got a call that Cole might be down there, hiding out.*

Hoskins shuffles through the pages, runs his fingers down the cover memo, and laughs. Numbnuts, Loren was right about that. If the task force can't come up with a better list of suspects than this, the whole damn city is in trouble.

The suspect is a man, the papers say. *No shit.* Age eighteen to fifty-five, which seems like a pretty big gap to Hoskins. Caucasian. A man with deep-seated sexual perversions and an inferiority complex, which Hoskins guesses covers most of the men living in Denver. After this is a list of suspects, men to check out. It's a short list. Every investigation has to start somewhere, it's not just something that *happens*; a case is built, brick on top of brick, until another door opens up and a new possibility is revealed. But these names—they're a joke.

The first is Tom Bird, a local businessman in the running for the upcoming election for mayor. He's been spending a lot of time shaking hands and kissing babies, and he's done quite a bit of grandstanding about the crime rate in Denver, promising it'll dip lower when he's elected. Hoskins takes a pencil, draws right through this name. If Bird had gone to the trouble of murdering three women to draw attention to his platform, he should be running for the fucking president, not mayor.

Next is Pastor Jack Pelton, who'd spent the last twenty years playing big-time to the Bible thumpers in town, until he was caught in an undercover sex sting involving underage girls not long before. His church had given him the boot, but Pastor Jack was on the rise again, because everyone likes a repenting sinner. Church attendance always went up when people were scared, and could Pastor Jack be trying to throw a scare into Denver just to get more asses in the pews? Hoskins drew a line through this name too. There were easier ways to fill the collection plate.

Person of Interest Number Three: Frank Costello, Esq. Jacky Seever's lawyer, who'd represented his client in court and collected his fee, but his business had gone down over the years. He'd had a good hike after Seever's trial, and maybe that's what he was looking for again—getting Seever's name back out there would be advertising gold. But Costello is about seventy years old, and he'd broken his hip twice. Hoskins didn't think the guy would be able to take down a toddler, much less a full-grown woman. Another strike.

Next is Dan Corbin, the editor in chief over at the *Post*. Circulation at the paper is down, hell, everyone knows that, the *Rocky Mountain News* had disappeared a few years ago and the *Post* looked like it was headed in the same direction. A huge story involving Jacky Seever, three dead women, with Sammie Peterson, former star reporter on the case—it was a wet dream come true for Corbin. But Hoskins has met Corbin—he's a loser, the kind of guy who'd be too afraid to go skydiving so he'll watch videos online about it instead. He was safe. A guy who'd deny that he ever jerked off and then go home and do it into a sock in the back of his closet. The kind of guy who'd spent his whole life hiding behind words.

Another line, right through Corbin's name.

He knows what Loren and his team are thinking—that the Secondhand Killer is doing this for some kind of gain. Financial, maybe. Or notoriety. Seever's name held a lot of weight in Denver, any mention of him makes people sit up and take notice. But Hoskins had been inside Simms's house, he'd seen her body. He'd seen the marks left on her, those bloody shoe prints on the carpet. And the words. Simms makes him think of the time he'd gone out to a place in Texas, a couple hundred acres where corpses were left out to the forces of nature, so doctors and detectives and anyone who had a good enough reason could go to see how a human body decomposes. They called it the *body farm*, which had struck Hoskins as a helluva awful name when he went out to visit. It sounded more like a strip club, and he doesn't remember much from his time there, except for the dead woman laid out in a field of wildflowers, the hem of her dress fluttering in the breeze, the empty holes where her eyes had once sat pointed toward the sky. A cage had been put up around her, made out of chicken wire. To keep the animals out, someone had said. So she wouldn't get dragged off.

"Every one of these bodies has something to tell you," the guy in charge had said during the tour. "You just have to figure out how to listen."

Hoskins has six photos of Carrie Simms saved on his cell phone, mostly extreme close-ups. Looking at them makes his head pound, and he thinks it might be time for a break, time to go outside and walk a few laps around the parking lot. There's one picture of the gashes around her wrists, left by the twine that'd held her, another of the backside of her skull, caved in like a hollow gourd. One of her right hand, the last three fingers missing. The others are the same, except the final one; he must've taken it by accident when he was moving, because it's blurry, like a painting done with watercolors and then smeared when still wet. It's Simms's face in the photo, and it's blurred enough that she still looks alive, she almost seems to be laughing, or maybe she's screaming.

What he thinks Simms is trying to tell him, what Loren and the task force are overlooking: The Secondhand Killer *might've* started out killing for some kind of gain, whether it's financial or personal, but it doesn't seem that way anymore. There's only one thing he seems to be looking for now—pleasure. No one tortures a person for days unless they're getting their rocks off, and there was a sort of frenzied glee in Simms's murder. Hoskins closes his eyes, thinks of the toaster sitting on its side, dented and covered with hair and bone, blood. Whoever Secondhand is, he's had a taste of pleasure, and now he knows he likes it. He raped those three women, tortured and murdered them, he was cruel about it, he made it last.

And he's going to do it again.

There's one more name on the list, ridiculous, but somehow not.

Jacky Seever.

"You know what I like about you, Paulie?" Seever said once. This was near the end of their time together, before the trial started and after Hoskins had gotten everything he could out of Seever, although it sometimes felt the opposite, as if Seever was the one wringing him like an old dish towel. "You understand. Not like Loren. You understand me."

"I think you're mixed up. I'm not here to understand you. I'm here because I have to be. This is my job."

"I don't know," Seever said, smiling. "I think there's a part of you that enjoys being in here with me."

"I wouldn't say that."

"You ever jerk off to the stuff I tell you, Paulie?"

"What?"

"I see how you look when I talk," Seever said. "I get the feeling you wouldn't mind trying some of it yourself."

"I'm not like you. I'd never do the things you've done."

"Oh, I wouldn't be so sure. You've got potential, I can see it."

It's important to establish a victim's timeline, the days and hours and even minutes leading up to their death. This can be problematic, because you can't *always* know what someone is doing. You can't always know who they talked to, or what they were thinking, even technology these days can't catalog every second of every minute of every hour of a person's day, although Hoskins is sure Apple is working on that.

Like some of these cold cases he has on his desk. Murders that happened ten or twenty, thirty years before. It's not as if he can pick up the phone and ask people where they were on a particular date decades before, or what they were doing. Time passes, people forget. Evidence is destroyed. And then, years later, those files end up on Hoskins's desk.

"We don't have shit," Loren says. They're in a conference room at the station, Loren on one side and Hoskins on the other, going over the list of suspects, working through everything point by point.

He hadn't found Cole in Pueblo, Loren said. No sign of him. Hoskins doesn't like to look right at him, because Loren's still dressed up like Seever, pressed and proper in his suit, a tiny flower tucked into the lapel, but what can he do about it? Nothing, because even if he says something to Chief Black, even if he moseys on down to Human Resources and files a complaint, they'll shake their heads, laugh at him. Because he'd be complaining about Loren's suit, the glasses he's wearing, and the slick part in his hair, and those things don't mean anything to anyone but him, because Hoskins sees Seever in everything Loren's doing, in the clothes he wears, the way he smokes, the way he sucks his saliva through his teeth. Those are Seever-isms, they don't belong to Loren, but they don't alarm anyone except him. "Five days since we found Simms, and still nobody knows anything, nobody sees anything. I hate when this happens. We end up waiting for another victim to turn up."

It's not that they're *waiting*, really. They're putting together a timeline on Carrie Simms, but she's the worst kind of person you'd ever have to track. She didn't have a credit card so they could see her purchases, no cell phone that would've marked her locations. The last time anyone had seen Simms alive was school. Biology class. Most of the students didn't know her name, only recognized her if they were shown a picture. Simms was quiet, didn't have friends. Hadn't had contact with any of her family in years, and none of them were surprised to find out she was dead, even her mother.

"If it makes you feel any better, I don't think it'll be a long wait."

"Jesus, Paulie. Don't let anyone hear you say shit like that."

"You know how it goes. This guy's rolling into third gear. He's getting into his groove."

"Why do you think he's doing it, Paulie?" Loren says. "For attention?"

"I don't know."

"I'm starting to wonder if we're ever gonna find this guy," Loren says. "He's probably yukking it up right now, thinking we're too stupid to catch him."

"We'll get him."

"Yeah. Listen, we've got the team from the field coming in to debrief in five. You sitting in?"

"Yeah. Of course."

"I hope this guy knows how much time we're spending on his ass. Make him feel good about himself, stroke his ego."

"Yeah, right," Hoskins says, rubbing a finger over the bone in his eyebrow, where it's still sore from Loren hitting him. "Gimme a minute. I'll meet you down there."

Loren shoots him a look before he leaves, but Hoskins doesn't notice. He's too busy considering; he has the maddening sense that there's something here he should be thinking of, like a word on the end of his tongue that he can't manage to dredge out. Something that Loren said reminded him of something else, the ego thing, and it seems important, but then it's gone, as suddenly as it was there, before he could pull it out of the shadows and make sense of it.

"Every decision I've ever made has been the wrong one," she said once. This was to Dean, after she'd lost her job at the *Post*, when she was still upset and vulnerable, not considering the words coming out of her mouth before it was too late. "My whole life, I've never done anything right."

"You'll find another job."

"Why don't you make more money?" she'd asked, although she already knew the answer. Dean was a good guy, but he wasn't good enough. He was smart, but not smart enough. In the grand scheme of things Dean was just another guy, forgettable, low on the totem pole at a marketing firm that was low on an even bigger totem pole, and he'd always be that way. He didn't know how to move up in the world, and he didn't have much interest in it. He was happy where he was, answering phones and building spreadsheets and whatever else he did—his title was Marketing Sales Coordinator, no one even knew what that meant, it was a mystery—he could never understand why she was always pushing for more, for herself, for him. "Every man I know makes enough money to support his family. Except you."

"Is that what you want?" He looked sick. It was wrong, she knew it was, she was hitting below the belt, making him feel like less of a man because of his salary; her mother had always warned her not to do that, not to belittle her husband, but it felt good. She couldn't keep the words from spilling out of her mouth. "You don't want to work? You want to stay here, be a housewife?"

But she didn't want to be a housewife, she'd never wanted that, she liked to work, didn't mind it. And it wasn't about the money but the *idea* of it, although she didn't know how to explain herself in a way that made sense. She wanted Dean to gather her up in his arms, to tell her everything was okay, that she'd been good at her job, that she wasn't a failure—but instead, Dean seemed as scared as she was.

"What I want is a man who can take care of me."

It takes her two and a half hours to get to Sterling Correctional Facility, the prison where Jacky Seever will live for the next fourteen months, until he's put in an armored transport and taken south to the prison in Cañon City, where he'll be strapped to a bed in the middle of a room full of witnesses and injected with poison, and everyone will wait until he falls asleep and his heart rumbles to a stop. Sterling is east of Denver, a downward slope away from the mountains and onto the plains, where the land becomes nothing but scraggy bushes and yellow dirt, houses that hunker close to the ground and hold on with all their might. It's colder out here, where the wind blows without breaking, although there's less snow on the ground than in the city, only a dusting that blows across the interstate, whipping around in tiny ice tornadoes before disappearing. This place makes her eyeballs ache. It's all that sky, she thinks, unending gray stretching from one side of the world to the other, with nothing to break up the monotony. She feels like she's suffocating under all that sky, like a fishbowl has been turned over and plunked right on top of her head.

She's been to a prison before, when she was fourteen. It was part of the "scared-straight" program her high school had, although there weren't enough delinquent kids to take, so everyone went. Not one kid had tried to get out of it, because any excuse to cut class was a good one, even if it was to visit a prison, so everyone was separated, boys on one bus and girls on another, and they went their own ways. Sammie doesn't remember much from the field trip, only that one of the girls started weeping when she was patted down, big gulping cries that echoed off the concrete walls. And she doesn't remember much about the prisoners who spoke to them, except that they were pleasant and vaguely boring, not all that different from her own mother, and none of them had done anything all that exciting to end up behind bars, except one, who was small-boned and pretty, who didn't seem all that much older than they were.

"I killed my husband," the woman told them. She wasn't nervous standing in front of the group of teens, but matter-of-fact. "I thought it was an accident, but they said it wasn't."

They, Sammie quickly figured out, was everyone else, everyone who wasn't living inside the woman's head.

"I did it with a knife," the woman said, after someone asked how it'd happened. "He was asleep."

Then they were taken to the prison's cafeteria for lunch, where they were served macaroni and cheese, a green salad, and cartons of chocolate milk like they had at school.

"It's not usually this good," the husband-killer said. "They made a special lunch, just because you guys are here. Like we're having a fucking party or something."

The prison is not what she expects. She's read about it, looked up photos of it online, but she isn't prepared for how big it is, how empty it seems. That's an illusion, she knows, because the place is full up with prisoners, too many of them, but they're not out in the fenced yard, not in this snow and cold.

There are parking spots for visitors, and she pulls into one but keeps the engine running. Checks her hair. She'd had trouble choosing lipstick—the color a woman wears on her lips is important, like she tells customers at work. It can make your teeth white, your smile glow. Lipstick can change everything. She'd spent a long time picking through her bathroom drawer, looking at all the tubes, each color with its own name printed on the bottom. Lust. Sin. Defiance. Gorgeous. Perverted. They're all sexual, tawdry. DTF. Down to fuck. There's nothing called Intelligent or Brainiac. No Failure or Idiocy. Disgusting. Nothing like that. After a while, she slid the drawer shut, didn't put on lipstick at all. But she wore good shoes—black flats with silver studding around the edges. Classic, expensive. They look nice, but they pinch around her toes. She has her leather purse, she's wearing a brand-new blouse. It's stupid, she thinks, to get all done-up to visit a man in prison, but she didn't think blue jeans would do it. Seever had always noticed when women dressed nicely, and complimented them, and she wants this to go well.

Sammie gets out of her car, pushes the button to lock the door, and starts toward the prison. There's a woman coming her way across the parking lot, walking fast, her head down to keep out of the wind. Another visitor, all done for the day. There's something familiar about the woman, and it isn't until they're a few feet away that she realizes who it is—Gloria. Seever's wife.

Gloria looks much like she always did, is even dressed the same. Sammie had seen her a few times when she worked at the restaurant, when she'd come in with Seever, on his arm, and she'd sit in a corner booth and pick through a salad, or tear apart a hamburger, only eating the meat and skipping the bun, and always with her mouth pinched as tight as a drawstring purse, disapproving. Sammie didn't officially meet Gloria until after Seever's arrest, when she was scrambling, when every reporter on the planet was desperate for an interview, and Gloria had agreed to sit down and speak with her. It hadn't gone well, and it'd only lasted a few minutes, but surely, Sammie thinks, Gloria won't recognize her. It's been so long.

But Gloria does. She's walking across the lot, hurriedly, and she seems upset. Or she's chilled from the wind—there are two spots of color high in her cheeks, her lips are pressed thin—but when she sees Sammie she stops short, takes in a sharp breath. She looks like a woman preparing for a fight.

"Mrs. Seever," Sammie says, coming forward, her hand already stretched out. She could turn and run back to her car, part of her wants to do exactly that, but she's found it's sometimes better to react against her instinct. It throws people off. "How good to see you again. I'm not sure if you remember me, Samantha Peterson. I'd love to speak with you, if you have a moment."

Gloria doesn't blink an eye.

"He told me you were coming," she says, her teeth set as she speaks, clamped together so only her lips move. Her voice is different, Sammie realizes. Gloria's the kind of woman who usually speaks in a soft voice, a feminine tone. High-pitched and girly, almost a whisper. But now she sounds harsh and gritty, and Sammie realizes it's because she's about to burst into angry tears. "Said he's anxious to see you after so long. Could barely sit still from the excitement."

Sammie is struck dumb. Gloria Seever is jealous. Every word she says, every movement she makes is oozing with it. Jealousy is always a terrible thing, but this seems so much worse, this ugliness over a man who'll be put to death soon enough.

"I'm here for an interview," she says. "To talk."

"Can you imagine, after everything I've done for him," Gloria shrieks into the wind, and Sammie flinches back from the sound of it. "He's looking forward to a visit from *you*."

And then, just like that, it's over. Gloria totters away across the blacktop on her sensible heels and climbs into her Buick. Her car squeals when she backs it out, when she turns onto the street. She needs brake pads, a whole new car. Sammie can't seem to get her legs to move for a moment after Gloria is gone, but is frozen in place, her purse smacking against her thigh and her heart pounding against the inside of her chest.

"I'll need to hang on to your purse, sweetheart," the guard at the front says, smiling shyly at her. "Standard procedure, you understand."

"No worries," she says, handing over her bag and lifting up her arms, so he can wave a metal detector up and down her body, searching for whatever it is people might try to sneak into a prison. She scratches the loose bun on the top of her head while her arms are up, and the guard catches the movement.

"Can you let your hair down, please?" he asks, eyeballing her head carefully, as if she might be hiding a shank in the coils of hair.

"Sure," she says, but less enthusiastically than before. She'd wanted to keep her hair up, so she'd look severe, older, not with it all tumbled around her shoulders. She pulls the pins out and the guard sticks his gloved hands right into her hair, digging around and massaging her scalp, running his fingers along the backs of her ears, pulling the ends. He sniffs, he might be smelling her hair, although she's probably being paranoid.

"You look familiar," the guard says, staring. "Have we met before?"

"I write for the Denver *Post*," she says, a little self-conscious, but still pleased he knows her. "You've probably seen my photo printed there."

"Yeah," he says, not sounding convinced. "Except I don't read the paper."

"Is it usually like this?" she asks the guard when he brings her into a room split in two by a glass partition. There's a small desk on each side, and a plastic chair. An old rotary phone mounted on the wall, just the receiver. She thought Seever would be right in front of her, so she could smell his breath, see the network of wrinkles under his eyes, but he'll only be a voice in her ear, a man on the opposite side of the smeary screen. "With visitors, I mean?"

"No, not usually," the guard says, his hands on his hips. "Most prisoners get to see their guests in the common room."

"But not Seever." Not a question, not exactly.

"Nope, not him. He's had some—problems in the past."

"What happened?"

The guard gives her a pitying look. *I'll spare you the details,* that look says. *It's not a story fit for young ladies.*

"Seever's old and fat, but he's quick. Slippery. He ain't allowed to see anyone anymore, not unless they're on the opposite side of some bulletproof." The guard smiles, shows off a mouthful of dentures that look more like alligator teeth. "Because he's still dangerous."

Seever is so different that it's almost like meeting a stranger. She remembers one time, when they were alone in the restaurant and she stripped down to a rubber apron and yellow gloves that ran up to her elbows, and slowly washed the dishes in the big basin sink, and when Seever came around the corner and saw her there, suds dripping down her bare breasts, he made a choking noise, and his face had turned very red. This fat old man sitting across from her, his wrists chained together and then looped around the legs of the desk, he can't possibly be Jacky Seever, who wouldn't let her take that apron off when he fucked her, so it made a watery squeaking noise as they moved against each other.

He knocks on the glass with his fist, points at the phone. She picks it up, presses it against her ear. It's slick in her hands, smells like rubbing alcohol.

"Sammie," he says. She closes her eyes, thinks of his voice traveling into the mouthpiece, down into the wires and cords and then spilling directly into her ear. She almost puts the phone down and walks out, but then she thinks of Weber, of his smug face and his interview with Simms's mother, and how she has nothing to write, nothing at all, not without this. "It's me, Sammie. Jacky."

She never called him Jacky. Oh, plenty of other people called him that, he insisted on it, he liked to be on a first-name basis with everyone, but she'd always called him Seever.

"Oh," she says, opening her eyes. "Hey."

She can hear him breathing through the phone, see the rise and fall of his chest, but the two things seem somehow disconnected, separate. Like a video recording when the audio is off, just a bit, not enough to matter but still annoying.

"It's good to see you," Seever says. "God, you look exactly the same as you did fifteen years ago."

"You don't," she says, and Seever laughs. Not the big belly laugh he used to have, but a soft, wet chuckle.

"Yeah, that's what I've been told." His tongue pokes out, bright-pink, sweeps over his bottom lip. "Why'd you come all the way out here, Sammie? You've been an approved visitor for a long time, you never showed up before."

Have someone else go out, she'd told Corbin years before, because she was getting everything she needed from Hoskins, he told her everything Seever said in the interview rooms, and Corbin had tried to send another reporter, but Seever had refused to talk to anyone except her. But she wouldn't go, the thought of seeing him made her physically ill, she didn't think she'd be able to stomach it. It would've been an exclusive; Seever had never talked with anyone else from the media, and maybe that's why Sammie had ended up on the chopping block, because she'd refused to play along. But she was here now, wasn't she? They'd finally gotten her in, Corbin would get the story he'd wanted so long ago.

"Have you heard about the murders in Denver?" she asks, picking up her pencil and tapping it against the desk. A few sheets of paper and a pencil was all the guard would let her bring in. She hates writing in pencil.

"The Secondhand Killer, isn't that what you called him in that article?" Seever asks. "Because he's picking at my leftovers, I guess?"

"I didn't come up with it."

"Good. It's a terrible name."

"I know."

"I don't know who he is, if that's what you're here to ask," Seever says. "Detective Loren comes to visit me once in a while. He had some crazy ideas, thought I might've had a partner, or mentored someone, and now they're starting up where I left off."

"Did you?"

"Did I what?" Seever's smiling, he knows what she wants but he's going to force her to spell it out for him.

"Have a partner? When you—when you murdered all those people—were you working with anyone?"

"No." He shrugs, and her gut thinks he's telling the truth. She might be wrong, she's been wrong before, but maybe she's not. She decides to let the question be.

"Are you in touch with anyone?"

"Like who?" he asks, amused. "My wife is the only one who visits me anymore, and she wants to tell me about the soap operas she's watching, and how much it costs to fill up her gas tank."

"Maybe you're telling your wife things, and she passes them on to the Secondhand Killer."

An emotion flickers across Seever's face, but is just as quickly gone. His face falls back into slack lines.

"Leave Gloria out of this."

"You don't write letters? Send emails?"

"Nope. Nothing like that. You can confirm all that with the prison officials."

Seever isn't going to tell her anything she doesn't already know about the Secondhand Killer, and she had a feeling it would be this way but she came anyway, because there's always a chance. She looks down at her paper, taps the pointed lead end against it so there are tiny dots all over the top, small smudges. She's not normally this way in an interview, so quiet and hesitant, but this is different because this is Seever, and she knows him.

"I figured you'd have more questions for me," Seever says, smiling. He looks like a kindly old man, white hair and glasses, but there's a monster hiding behind that smile, and she hadn't wanted to come see him for that reason; it gives her a sort of creeping horror to know what this man has done, what he's capable of, and she'd never known, the whole time she'd been sleeping with him she'd never had a clue. "I thought you were the reporter-extraordinaire. I expected more. I hope when your boyfriend Hoskins comes out to talk to me, he'll actually make it worth my time."

He's taunting her, throwing out a line and waiting for her to take the bait. That's how Hoskins always put it to her, that talking to Seever was like playing Russian roulette—you could never be sure when that bullet would come, when a truth would show its face among all the lies. Seever could twist your words, leave you so confused and out of sorts that you'd forget what you were talking about; he'd plant ideas so deep in your brain that you'd never know they were there until they'd start hatching and rooting around, like maggots. But she's ready for this, she's got questions, she wrote a list, and she's prepared for his head games. That's the most important thing.

"Oh, I have plenty of questions," she says, and Seever's eyes widen when she turns over her sheet of paper, when he sees everything she has written down. "Are you ready?"

"Shoot."

The first question isn't on her list, it's not something that'll ever be published in the *Post*, but it's a question she's had since she'd found out what Seever had done.

"Why'd you let me live?"

"Did you get everything you needed out of him?" the guard asks.

"I think I did." She rifles through her purse, makes sure everything's there. "Seever—he doesn't get any visitors?"

"His wife. And you." The guard holds up his fingers, counts off the names. "Sometimes that cop stops by. Loren."

"No phone calls? He doesn't write letters? Or get packages?"

"Nope. I mean, his wife brings him things."

"Like what?"

"Food, sometimes, when the warden allows it. Cookies, those kinds of things. And art supplies. But that all gets inspected, so we know there's nothing bad coming in."

"Art supplies?" She'd forgotten about Seever's art. It'd been big news when he first started, it was like having a monkey at a typewriter, pounding out a novel, and at first his paintings had sold for lots of money, but it wasn't long before the newness of it had worn away. She hadn't realized he was still doing it. "What does he paint?"

"He used to paint all kinds of nasty things. Dead people and blood and—and well, *you know*," the guard says, and she catches his hesitation, he doesn't want to say anything *too* nasty in front of her. "But that only lasted till the docs amped up his happy-pills."

"Now what does he paint?"

"Nothing all that interesting anymore."

"What happens to all his work?"

"His wife takes most of it with her. I heard she sold some for cash, but I think she hangs on to most of it."

"None of it's here, to see?"

"Nah. If his wife don't take them, we chuck them into the incinerator. I wouldn't want to take home anything that man made. It'd give me the creeps."

"Okay. Thanks."

She'd come with a long list of questions, everything she'd wanted to ask but hadn't when he was first arrested, about the victims and his desires and his upcoming execution, and Seever had been surprisingly cooperative. But he'd never answered her first question. The most important question, in her opinion. He'd stared at her, his eyes glassy, with tears, or maybe it was a trick of the smeary glass partition. He'd opened his mouth and then quickly shut it again; she'd been able to hear the harsh snap of his teeth as they came together, even through the phone. They'd sat in silence until she knew that he wouldn't answer, that he'd never answer, and she asked another question, moved the conversation along to something else, and she thought it might be because he didn't know *why* he'd let her live, he didn't have an answer, even in his own head.

It was when she was coming toward the end of her questions when she knew Seever was getting tired and impatient, she could see it in his eyes, and she'd known that was coming because that's how interviews went—you could only pump someone for information so long before they were through, but she had to do this in one shot, because she never wants to come back to this prison, never wants to have to see Seever again.

Did you ever—

If I could get you in here would you suck me off? Seever interrupted, leaning forward until his nose was nearly pressed against the glass. His eyes were bulging and wide and he was breathing quickly, and she thought that she was seeing the monster now, desperate and hungry; this was the man who'd raped and tortured for so long, who looked like a normal man but was rotten and putrid inside. *When you climb on top of Hoskins and push his dick up inside you, do you pretend he's me?*

She didn't respond to this, only set the phone carefully back down in the receiver and gathered her things. She didn't look up when Seever started rapping his knuckles on the glass, or even when his muffled shouts came to her ears. She'd been expecting something like this to happen. The interview was over.

She's going to write one hell of a piece with this, Weber will never be able to come close.

FULL

CIRCLE

December 8, 2015

He's downstairs, back in his basement office. Mostly because there's no office for him upstairs, and also because all those people bother him now, the hustle and bustle of the detectives running in and out, the pings of emails coming and the steady whir of the printer. He used to thrive on the chaos up there; he couldn't think straight unless there was loud music while he worked, but things have changed, and now he prefers the cool silence of this windowless room. He should be upstairs to help with the Secondhand Killer case, but being up there all day is pointless, because he gets all the reports in emails, in group texts on his phone. Besides, Chief Black didn't tell him to run the case, just to make sure everything was going well, and it is. Except for Loren dressing up like Seever, which doesn't bother anyone but Hoskins. Loren's always been a little off-kilter, he's done a lot of crazy things, and this is another example of it.

Despite Loren's hijinks, the investigation is moving in exactly the way it's supposed to—methodically, with each step on the list being checked off as it's done. There is a team canvassing Simms's neighborhood, another tracking down anyone who knew her. And a third team, calling and visiting anyone who'd once been connected to Seever, anyone who'd spent time in his company, because any of them could be a suspect, but any of them could be in danger too. This is how most murder cases are cracked, with questions and answers, with phone calls and knocks on doors, but Hoskins has to wonder if that'll be enough this time. Sometimes you can follow all the rules, you can make sure every *i* is dotted, every *t* crossed, but there's still a chance it won't be solved. Hell, he only has to look around his office to know that, see all the murder cases that've gone cold, victims buried without justice, killers still on the loose. They're running with the assumption that the Secondhand Killer knew Seever before he was arrested, that he'd known about the fingers, because it's all they have now, they're grasping at straws. Grasping at fingers, although Hoskins doesn't think any of the detectives will find that so funny.

He sits behind his desk, flips on the table lamp that he brought from home, because the overhead lights aren't enough down here, not if you need to actually work. The batteries in the wall clock must've died the night before, the hands are frozen at twelve and one. He fires up his computer and opens a file folder. Shuts it. He hasn't been able to stop thinking about what Loren had said the day before: *I hope this guy knows how much time we're spending on his ass. Make him feel good, stroke his ego.*

Hoskins turns away from the computer and picks through the pile of folders on his desk, shuffles through some pages. He ends up looking at one of the oldest cold cases they have on file in Denver—1952, a young woman left a cocktail party to run an errand and disappeared. She was found dead a month later, nearly thirty miles away. There are notes scrawled in the margins, left by other investigators over the years, some of them faded away to almost nothing. Hoskins runs his finger down them, tracing his nail along the words. There's one that catches his eye, about halfway down on the right, written in blue ink. *Based on this, I don't think it's his first rodeo.* There's an arrow beside this, pointing at a typed sentence from the medical examiner, stating the body had been carefully washed before being dumped, probably in water mixed with bleach. And that note was right on; it probably hadn't been that killer's first rodeo, he'd known what to do to keep from getting caught, nearly sixty years had gone by since then and the cops had never arrested anyone in connection to the murder. He was either dead by now or a very old man, and he'd stayed free because he'd known what to do, he'd probably honed his technique over several murders. His first kill had probably been sloppy, but he'd learned from it. Seever had done the same thing. His earliest victim had suffered a head wound, but she hadn't died from it—the examiner thought she might've been buried before she was actually dead; she'd been smothered in the avalanche of crawl-space dirt shoveled over the top of her because Seever was still inexperienced, he'd probably been scared and nervous, but he'd learned, oh yes he had, and quickly, the same way a dog will learn not to piddle on the floor when you smacked him on the nose with a rolled-up newspaper.

And that was the thing, wasn't it? This Secondhand Killer—and it seems like that's what he's going to be called, whether any of them like it or not—was careful, he was thorough. He hadn't let anyone see him, and he hadn't left much, or anything, behind, although the tests are still being run on the samples they'd taken from Simms. He was good, very good; some people might say he was lucky, but over the years Hoskins had come to understand that a person makes their own luck, especially if that person is a killer.

He turns to the first page of the file, looks at the photo of the woman who'd disappeared in 1952. She had dark hair and big eyes. A lush mouth filled in with lipstick, probably red, although he couldn't tell in the black-and-white photo. Whoever killed her had been experienced. He'd done it before. And maybe, he thinks, it's the same with the Secondhand Killer. Maybe he'd killed, and then he'd switched gears and decided to go after people connected to Seever, he'd even started doing it the way Seever did it. Why?

Because he wants his ego stroked.

Lots of killers crave attention, for people to sit up and notice them. They do it for the blood, they do it for the sex, but it's also driven by the ego. It sounds like some crazy Freud shit, but it's true. There was the Zodiac Killer out in California, BTK in Kansas, both had sent letters to the police, they'd taunted and teased, because they wanted the attention, like a kid screaming for candy. And Secondhand was sending them messages too, because he'd chosen to mimic Seever, but he wasn't hiding the victims like Seever did—no, he was leaving everything out for anyone to see, because he wanted them to notice. He didn't want to be caught, oh no, he wanted to stay free and keep doing what he was doing, but he wanted everyone to be talking about him, he probably went to bed at night smiling because he was so damn satisfied.

Hoskins taps on his keyboard, wakes his sleeping computer back up. He'll comb the database of unsolved murder cases involving a female victim that happened in the last five years, possibly even less. The last two years. There wouldn't be too many—Denver is still a safe place to live, not safe enough to keep your doors unlocked at night, let's not get crazy, but safe enough. He waits, hoping the computer will get its ass going, but it just sits there with a half-loaded page, not doing anything, even when Hoskins tries to reboot it.

"I need a few things, it won't be long," Ted says, and Hoskins looks up in time to see the kid walking past his office door, his cell phone stuck against the side of his head. He hadn't expected to see Ted anytime soon, he'd figured the kid would still be at home, but this is good, he wants to apologize, to clear the air, and besides, he needs his help. "Give me two minutes."

"Hey, I didn't expect to see you here," Hoskins says, standing in the office door. Ted freezes, then slowly looks over his shoulder. If a person could look like a scared rabbit caught in a snare, that person would be Ted. "I'm glad I caught you."

"I thought you were working upstairs," Ted says, turning full around. There's a clean white bandage crossed over an eyebrow, and a ring of purple bruises around his neck. The whites of his eyes are red from burst blood vessels. Hoskins winces, touches his own face. His upper lip is swollen, his nose sore, and there's a lump on the back of his head, but Ted looks worse, and it's bad because he was the one to do this.

"No, I'm still working from down here."

"Oh, okay." Ted pulls a ring of keys from his pocket and unlocks his office. "See you around."

"Hey, wait."

Ted pauses, looks at him warily.

"I'm sorry about what I did," Hoskins says. He doesn't have any problem with apologizing, never has—even when he doesn't mean it. But this time he does mean it. "I saw you at the crime scene, and I lost it. It's not an excuse, but I've always had a hard time dealing with things connected to Seev—to that particular case I worked before. Not an excuse, but that's what it is."

Ted's lips move but no sound comes out. He looks at the clock on the wall, then at Hoskins.

"My mom thinks I should quit," he finally says. "After what you did to me."

"Don't do that, man," Hoskins says, taking a step closer. He stops, holds up his hands when Ted shies away. "You're good at this job. You work hard, and everybody appreciates you. Don't let my stupid shit get in your way. I promise nothing like that will ever happen again."

Ted sighs. "I like it here."

"Then don't quit. I can call upstairs if you want, see if they'll move me to the other side of the basement. Or maybe you could go upstairs, get a nice office with a window. But don't quit because of what I did."

"What you did to me, was it like before?" Ted says. "When you got kicked out of Homicide?"

Hoskins pauses, lowers his hands to his sides and folds them up into fists. Of course Ted would know about that, everyone does. Not like it's a big secret.

"Yeah, I guess it was like that time."

Ted looks down at the toes of his sneakers. Sighs again. There are some people who will hold a grudge their whole lives, coddle it, never spit it out, as if they're holding a piece of steak in their mouth until the meat has gone gray and unrecognizable, a tasteless lump, but Ted isn't one of those people. Hoskins can tell by the slope of his shoulders, by the crease between his eyebrows, that he wants to let things go back to the way they were before.

"Okay," he says. "Apology accepted. Honestly, I've been beat up worse by my brothers."

"Great." Hoskins claps his hands together, and he's glad to see that Ted doesn't flinch away from the sound. "I'm glad you're back, because I need your help with my damn computer."

Slowly, a smile spreads across Ted's face.

"It'll take me some time," Ted says when he hears what Hoskins is looking for. "You can't pull those up yourself?"

"With the clearance I have now I can only look at cases that've been officially marked cold, or have been put under my authorization," Hoskins says. "Some of the murder cases in the last five years, they're still active. I just want to take a look."

"I could get in trouble for this, you know."

Hoskins raises his eyebrows.

"And you could still get in trouble for snooping through Seever's case files."

"Oops, guess that's true," Ted says. "Okay, what should I be looking for again?"

"Unsolved homicides involving female victims within the state of Colorado. And send a request out to police departments in nearby states, see if we can have temporary access to their systems. Secondhand might've done some traveling, even lived somewhere else."

"That's it?"

"Isn't that enough?"

"You don't want to be more specific? That might give us a lot of results. I can narrow down the search parameters if you have more."

Hoskins thinks of the missing fingers, the words on the wall. Those were things specific to Seever, but what if Secondhand had done it before, and they'd missed it, it'd been overlooked? What if Secondhand had been killing the same way for a long time, but he was tired of being ignored, so he'd only recently started going after victims associated with Seever, thinking they'd sit up and take notice? And they sure did, sat up like good dogs begging for a treat.

"Wait. Female homicide victims who were found missing fingers," Hoskins says. Seever had liked to do it, and so does Secondhand—and cutting off fingers wasn't something that a killer would do randomly. No, it was a trophy for him, Secondhand probably would've done it each and every time, or not at all. "Start with that, but we might need to do another search if it doesn't pull up anything."

"Missing fingers?" Ted grimaces, his hands hovering above the keyboard.

"Yeah. Missing fingers. Seever did it to every one of his victims, and now Secondhand is too. I thought you read Seever's case file."

"I didn't get through the whole thing, a few pages in—it's a big file. I didn't have a clue about the fingers."

"We never released that detail to the public," Hoskins says, grabbing a pencil and spinning it on the desktop, until it settles to a stop, the sharp lead tip pointing right at him, dead at his heart.

"Why not?"

"Because it's gross. And sometimes it's best to keep information back, in case you need to use it later." Hoskins scoops up the pencil, drops it back into the cup, tip down. "Like now. Secondhand knows that Seever took their fingers, so he's doing it. So he must've known Seever before, worked with him."

Ted rolls his eyes, crosses his arms over his chest.

"What if Secondhand found out about these fingers some other way?" Ted asks.

"How would he do that? We kept pretty closemouthed about it," Hoskins says. "Made sure only a select few knew. And all those people still work for the department."

"Okay," Ted says, rocking back in the chair. He's got his thinking cap on, his tongue is sticking out one corner of his mouth, and it makes Hoskins want to laugh, but he doesn't. Sometimes a good idea can come from the strangest place, even from a kid with tight-ass pants who wants to be called Dinky. "So let's say everyone kept their mouth shut.

It could've gotten out a different way. Someone might've hacked into our database. It's happened before."

"When?"

"A year and a half ago," Ted says. "We were never able to figure out exactly what information was stolen. Seever's file might've been something that was copied. It might be published on the Internet somewhere, for anyone to see."

"That happens?"

"Oh, yeah," Ted says, sitting up straight. "Man, you can find everything online. Crime-scene photos, autopsy reports. Everything. If you think something's secret, you should search for it online. You'd be surprised."

"Have you searched for stuff on Seever?" Hoskins asks. God, he feels so old talking to Ted, not understanding half of what's going on. It doesn't seem like all that long ago that no one had a computer or a cell phone, and if you wanted information you went to the library, took a long stroll through the card catalog or the microfiche.

"Yeah, but I didn't find much. I can peek around some more if you'd like, see if I can find anything about this finger thing."

"That would be great," Hoskins says, standing up and clapping a hand on Ted's shoulder. It's nice to have the kid back in the basement. "Good man. I'll run out for lunch while you do this. Chinese all right?"

Ted's still working at Hoskins's desk when he gets back, and he groans and gratefully holds out his hands for the takeout box of lo mein.

"You ever consider there might be something wrong with you?" Ted asks, waving at all the pictures on the wall, the case files Hoskins has torn apart and pinned up. "I don't know how you can stand to work like this, with all these dead people watching you."

"That's why I'm a detective, and you're in IT," Hoskins says. "You get anything back yet?"

"Our system needs updating," Ted says, sighing and ruffling his hair. "It takes so damn long to pull up anything, especially if it's a wide search like this one."

"Oh, take your time," Hoskins says, sitting down and ripping open a pack of chopsticks. "It's not an emergency, there's just a serial killer on the loose and we don't know when someone else will turn up dead. No big deal."

"Sarcasm hurts, you know?" Ted says, turning to glare at him. "I *get* it. I'm working as fast as I can."

"Okay."

"Oh, you had a visitor while you were gone."

"Who?"

"Your old partner. Loren?"

"He should've called me."

"I told him that," Ted says, jamming noodles into his mouth and slurping them down, making them vanish like hair down a shower drain. "He said he did."

Hoskins pulls his cell phone out of his pocket. Three missed calls, all of them from Loren. He hadn't even heard it ring, and he had it cranked all the way up.

"Did he say what he wanted?"

"Nope. But he left that for you." Ted points with his chopsticks at a package leaning against the wall beside the door.

"What is it?"

"He didn't volunteer that information," Ted says, carefully dabbing the corners of his mouth with a napkin. "This might be a surprise to you, but Ralph Loren isn't exactly the friendliest guy around."

Hoskins snorts, drops into a chair, and grabs the package, holds it across his thighs. It's flat and rectangular, taller than it is wide, and wrapped in brown paper. He jams his finger under the flap and rips it open, and then he must make some kind of alarming noise, although afterward he can't remember doing it, because Ted jumps up, his face twisted with concern.

"What's wrong?" Ted says, but Hoskins can't answer—he feels like a fist has been jammed down his throat, choking him. "What is it?"

Hoskins hands him the package, he doesn't want to hold it another second more than he possibly has to.

"What the fuck is this?" Ted cries, revolted, but Hoskins can't dredge up the words. His chest is tight, he feels like he might be having a heart attack, but he's pretty sure it's the horror of seeing this, of having cradled it in his lap. Loren has brought him a Seever painting, a Seever original. Hoskins hasn't seen one since the Christmas after Seever was arrested, when a painting was delivered to the station, addressed to both Hoskins and Loren, and they'd set it up in the conference room, where it had sat for a week before it finally disappeared, because no one wanted to touch it. It was a clown, and he was pinned to a crucifix, tears running down his white painted cheeks as snow fell from the canvas sky. The clown had Seever's face, and that wasn't at all a surprise, because nearly every painting that came out of the prison those first few years had Seever's face, as if he were trying to get free by sending his likeness out into the world.

"It's pretty good," Chief Black had said. "I'm surprised he's that talented."

"Yeah, maybe if I pull down my pants and bend over, you can poke a brush up my asshole and I'll paint your portrait," Loren said. He was glowering at the painting, and if he'd put his fist through the clown's face, Hoskins wouldn't have been surprised. Or upset.

"You always gonna be a foulmouthed bastard?" Black asked.

"Looks that way, don't it?"

"Hitler was a pretty good artist too," Hoskins said, and Black made a noise in his throat and went back into his office, slammed the door.

"Fuck a duck, kid," Loren said, but he was grinning. "You sure know what to say to kill the mood."

Seever had taken up art not long after his arrest; he used watercolors and charcoals and paints, whatever he could get his hands on. Most of the work he put out was pleasant, nothing you'd expect to see from a killer—Sleeping Beauty in her bed, her hands folded sedately across her chest; a mountain stream; Seever himself, looking into a mirror and smiling. But Hoskins had heard that Seever created dark stuff too. Dead people and zombies and clowns, always there were the clowns, and this painting has a Seever-clown too, eyes smiling from those white greasepaint diamonds. And it wouldn't be so bad if it weren't for the bunch of balloons the clown is clutching, but two of those balloons pulling on their strings and bobbing on the breeze aren't balloons at all, they're heads, decapitated heads, blood dripping from their raggedly cut necks. Those two heads, their eyes are white and blank and dead but they are smiling anyway, having a damn good time being pulled along on their strings—*Look, Ma, no hands!*—and any fool can see that one of those heads is Ralph Loren; Seever got every single detail right, from the mole on his forehead to the scar on his upper lip. Seever is good, he's not fucking Michelangelo, but he's good, and he's good enough that Hoskins knows that the other balloon-head, the one that seems to be laughing, is his own.

"Loren's got a shitty sense of humor," Ted says, holding the painting up so he can see it better, look at every detail. "This explains why he was all dressed up."

"In one of those fancy suits?" Hoskins asks, thinking of Loren playing dress-up, in his three-piece and glasses, but Ted shakes his head, confused.

"No, he was in a clown costume," Ted says, still looking at the painting so he doesn't see the jolt Hoskins gives, how gray his face becomes. "Like the ones Seever used to wear, like the clown in this painting. He was laughing, said something about clowns getting away with anything. What's that supposed to mean?"

Hoskins tries to stand up but his knees buckle and he drops back in the chair, dizzy, his head swimming like he's been spun around a hundred times, a *thousand,* he's come full circle and he's back right where he started, where it all began.

"Where the hell is he?" Hoskins shouts. "Where did he go?"

"I didn't even know he'd left," Jenna says, jumping to her feet and coming around her desk. She's the girl who works the Homicide desk, answering phones and filing and making sure everything runs smoothly, she's been around since before Hoskins was tossed downstairs, and she's a vast improvement over the girl they had before, who was like one of those spiders curled up under a rock, waiting for some unsuspecting victim to wander by. That girl had accused the entire department of sexual harassment, said that she couldn't perform her job, she needed a big cash settlement to feel better. It was a hell of a mess to clean up, but now they have Jenna, and she's a good girl. "That's nothing new, he's always been that way."

"He didn't say where he was going?" Hoskins asks.

"No."

He pushes past Jenna and goes down the hall, rattles the knob on Loren's office door. It's locked, of course—Loren doesn't like anyone in his personal space, he doesn't want anyone going through his things. But the doors are a joke—flimsy and thin, and all Hoskins has to do is kick against the knob and it snaps back, the cheap plywood splintering. There's a shriek from behind him—Jenna, with her hands clasped at the base of her throat—and a group of detectives gathered together, watching. None of them try to hold him back, or even talk him down from his rage; they watch, bright-eyed with interest. No one seems all that surprised at his anger—it's almost as if they've been waiting for this to happen, they've been wondering when the shit was going to hit the fan. Most of them were around when Loren and Hoskins were partners, they've seen the arguments and the brawls, but even the new guys would've heard the stories.

Why are you so upset? Ted had asked after Hoskins had opened the painting. *I don't understand.*

And Hoskins doesn't understand why he's so mad either, only that everything about this is wrong. This isn't supposed to be about Seever, this is about a new killer, but somehow Seever's back anyway, leering at him out of the painting, his name printed in the newspaper, everyone talking about him again. Hoskins thought he was done with Seever for good, but there was Loren, all dressed up in those three-piece suits, his hair slicked back with so much gel you could see the white of his scalp peering through, and Sammie, digging for more information and writing that damn article, getting people all worked up, even after he asked her not to. Loren and Sammie both thought Secondhand was connected to Seever, that he was finishing Seever's work, but Hoskins thinks Ted might be right: Secondhand knows about the fingers, but it's not through Seever directly. Secondhand isn't connected to Seever, he'd seen an opportunity and jumped on it. He doesn't think it's Alan Cole behind the murders; Cole had put on his boogie shoes and split, he was already on the run, had been for years. Hoskins can't imagine he'd be back in Denver, begging for the spotlight. No, whoever the Secondhand Killer is, he is doing it for the attention, he is doing it because he wants people to look.

He is doing it to have his ego stroked.

"Holy shit," Hoskins says. He freezes after one step into Loren's office. He feels like he's been told there might be land mines under his feet, ready to blow him straight to hell. "What the fuck is all this?"

It isn't the view Hoskins notices first, the same good one he used to have from his office. No, what he first sees are the corkboards on the walls, barely visible because of all the papers tacked to them, the photographs. There are photos of Seever's crawl space, of the victims being carried out, of Seever's house. Some of them are newspaper clippings, but most are photos Loren must've taken himself and then printed. Hoskins takes another step into the room. There are autopsy photos and reports tacked up, he's seen them all, he was there when it was all happening, those are burned into memory, but they're still a shock to see. An unpleasant shock.

And then there's the painting, the original clown, nailed up over Loren's desk, in a place no one could possibly miss it. Hoskins had always figured someone had thrown the damn thing away, but here it is, watching him. Smiling.

"Fuck me," Hoskins croaks, backing slowly out. Distantly, he realizes that his own office looks almost exactly like this, only his walls are made up of many different cases, but it doesn't matter, it's all shit in the end. Loren might be crazy, he thinks. But then so am I.

He turns, feels the pinprick eyes of all the victims posted up on the wall following him. This office is giving him the creeps, and he wants to go outside, stand with his feet in the snow. He grabs for the knob, then sees what's hanging on the back of the door and recoils. It's a costume, satin fabric, half blue and half red, with a big ruffled collar and fuzzy yellow pom-poms sewn down the front instead of buttons. A clown suit. Always with the fucking clowns.

Hoskins touches the costume, rubs the silky fabric between his thumb and first two fingers. There's dried blood on the sleeve, ground into the lace cuff.

This room, full of Seever's victims, Loren dressing like Seever, acting like him, it isn't good. He's worked with Loren for a long time, he's seen the guy do some strange stuff, but not like this. This is obsession, plain and simple. Bad things are born out of obsession.

"I know where he is," Jenna says, sticking her head in the door. She has her cell phone in one hand, and her other keeps tucking her hair behind her ear, nervously.

"Where?"

"He's over at St. Luke's, on Nineteenth," she says, and he's already past her before she can finish, his car keys jingling in his hand. "Visiting with patients."

"You ever been in love, Paulie?" Seever had asked him once. They'd been together every day for two weeks straight, Seever filling Hoskins's ear with names and details and stories, half-truths and nightmares, about the victims and the murders and his childhood, more than Hoskins had ever wanted to know about Jacky Seever, more than he could stomach.

"Yeah," Hoskins said, leaning back in his chair, one foot balanced on the opposite knee. "Couple times."

"You want to tell me about them?" Seever asked, and winked. "Give me a few nasty details, something to keep me warm at night?"

Seever held up his hands and shook them, made the handcuffs jangle on his wrists. He was handcuffed, and then chained to the table when he was in IR2, Hoskins made sure of it. The other detectives thought it was overkill, that Seever was nothing but an old man who'd passed his prime, but Hoskins had seen what he was capable of, and he didn't trust him. Seever had recounted his childhood for Hoskins, he'd told him about the father he'd never had, the boys in high school who'd laughed and thrown rocks, he'd rambled on endlessly about his restaurants and his marriage, he'd made himself sound like a nice guy, a normal guy, but Hoskins still didn't trust him. Because Hoskins knew that you could know things about someone without really *knowing* them, and that's how Seever had operated his whole life. He'd put on his expensive suits, he'd worn his clown costumes, and people had never bothered to see past that.

Seever was the wolf posing as Grandma.

"I don't think I'll be sharing anything," Hoskins said. "This is supposed to be about you, Seever. Not me."

"Oh, right." Seever grinned. "Sometimes that slips my mind."

"Have *you* ever been in love?" Hoskins asked, curious. He expected that Seever would say he'd been in love a dozen times, a hundred, that he'd loved every person he'd murdered. That he was in love with his wife, that he was in love with Carrie Simms, and Beth Howard, and all of them, but Seever shrugged instead, as if puzzled by the question he'd asked himself.

"I don't know," he said. He looked down at his wrists, gave them another shake. "I'd meet someone, work with them, and I wouldn't be able to stop thinking about them. It'd drive me crazy, I'd become obsessed. Is that what love is? I don't know. Maybe it is. I don't know."

Hoskins is almost sure it's 2008 again, those days when they'd watch Seever clamber out his front door in a clown costume, and they'd follow him to the hospital and watch him entertain the kids, blowing up balloon animals and singing songs, and it almost seemed like he might be innocent, that a man who'd volunteer to help sick children couldn't be capable of anything bad. But there was something *off* about Seever, something that didn't quite *jibe*, even when his painted face was smiling and he was squeezing his nose and telling jokes, but Hoskins couldn't put his finger on it, not at first.

The realization came while he and Loren watched Seever prance around the children's unit, giving horsey rides. It was his face that was all wrong, the makeup he'd smeared all over himself to create a mask. The paint around his mouth was too red, like blood, and the corners of his smile weren't rounded, but had points as sharp as daggers. He looked like a clown who'd stick a knife in your throat and defile your corpse. Oh, people smiled when they saw Seever coming down the halls at the hospital, but Hoskins started noticing the way they turned their faces in distaste when he came close, like he was a bad smell, like deep down, subconsciously, they knew what he really was.

Hoskins shakes his head, trying to clear it, because he's *not* crazy, he's not—it's 2015, and he's coming up behind Ralph Loren, who's swaggering through the hospital in a clown costume, and Loren's done his makeup the way Seever used to, with all the sharp angles and all that red paint, too much red. Loren's laughing, that stupid-ass donkey laugh of Seever's, and Hoskins would like to pull his gun from the holster and shoot the clown right in the back of the head, his hand actually twitches toward his belt, but he grabs Loren by the shoulder instead, spins him around.

"What the hell kind of game are you playing?" Hoskins shouts, and Loren looks surprised, and then guilty, although that's gone so quickly it might've never been there at all. "Why are you doing this?"

"Haven't you figured it out by now?" Loren asks, brushing his white-gloved hands along his ruffled collar, making the lace stick straight out from around his neck. "I'm becoming Jacky Seever."

"Seever's in prison," Hoskins says through gritted teeth. "You're wasting your time."

Loren's mouth drops open in feigned shock.

"How *dare* you," he says, putting his hand on his chest in a *lil ol' me* gesture. "I'm *helping* people here. And if it just so happens that I'm investigating a case at the same time, even better."

"You're not looking for Jacky Seever," Hoskins says, grabbing Loren's arm, and two nurses who'd been walking toward them turn and walk the other direction so abruptly it would be funny if Hoskins were in a laughing mood. "You should be looking for Secondhand. He's out there while you're fucking around with this shit."

"You remember what I used to tell you?" Loren says, pulling his arm out of Hoskins's grip. "I'm hunting, Paulie. *Be vewy, vewy quiet.* I think we're close, *vewy* close. Did you know Alan Cole volunteered with Seever a few times? Dressed up like a clown too. Danced the motherfucking jig for the kids."

"You found him?"

"Not yet," Loren says, and he chuckles. He's lost it, Hoskins thinks. This case finally sent him over the edge. "But we'll have him locked up before the weekend. Scout's honor."

Loren pops three of his fingers up in a salute and waggles his eyebrows, up and down, then grabs the red bulb on the end of his nose and honks it twice, sketches a bow, and skips away, his long clown shoes slapping against the tile floor.

"Where have you been?" the caretaker woman asks. He's late, much later than he'd thought he'd be, because of the shit with Loren. "This will put me into overtime for the week."

"I'll pay it," he says. "How was he today?"

"He urinated in the kitchen sink," she says. "He said it was too far to walk to the bathroom. And he laughed about it."

"I'm sorry."

"He did it all over the dishes I'd just *cleaned.*"

"I'm sorry. I'm not sure what else I can say."

But she must not think Hoskins is sorry enough, because she leaves in a huff, without saying goodbye. All over some hot water, he thinks. Sooner or later she won't come back and he'll have to call the service again, ask them to send out someone else.

"Is she finally gone?" Joe asks. He's sitting on his bed like a kid, knees drawn up, the newspaper propped up on his thighs. "All day, all she does is nag. It's like being married."

"It's cold in here, Dad. You should be wearing socks."

"I'm fine."

"Yeah, I know you are."

Hoskins gets a pair of clean socks from the dresser and starts to roll them over Joe's feet, but the old man's toenails are long, and yellowed, so he stops and gets a pair of clippers from the bathroom. He could ask the woman to do it in the morning, but the last time he did that she'd ignored his request, so he won't bother. He doesn't want to get into it with her, it's not worth his time.

"Hold still, I don't want to cut you," Hoskins says. He sits at the end of the bed, takes Joe's feet onto his lap. The old man's heels feel weird in his hands—like sandpaper, rough and ridged, but somehow still soft.

"All right, all right. You don't have to pinch so hard."

"I'm not pinching."

"It tickles. Don't touch there! Goddammit."

"Sit still. Quit acting like a baby."

"I'm not a baby."

"You sure as hell act like one. Don't move."

Joe sits for a moment,

"I've got money, you know. Savings."

Hoskins straightens up, looks at his father.

"Yeah, I know," he says. "So?"

"We could take that money, get me a spot at one of those retirement places," Joe says. "There're some nice ones in town."

"We're not doing that," Hoskins says. "I've seen some of the shit that goes on in those places. You can't trust anyone. It's better for you to stay here."

"There'd be people taking care of me."

"I take care of you."

"I know."

"You used to say how you'd rather die before moving into an old folks' home," Hoskins says. "What made you change your tune?"

"You've got a lot going on. You've gotta work, get a woman. I have a feeling I'm the worst cockblock there is."

Hoskins smiles a little at that.

"It's not like you've had too many chances to put your blocking skills to the test."

"True." Joe pauses. "That woman tell you I pissed in the sink?"

"Yeah."

"I did."

"Why'd you do it?"

"I wanted to make her mad. It was quiet today. We needed some excitement."

"Got it."

"This going crazy business isn't all bad, you know," Joe says. He's looking at the newspaper again, running the tip of his pencil along the crossword clues. "It's really not that bad at all."

SAMMIE

Corbin said she had a week to write another article, and it's done, but she hasn't emailed it over yet. Instead, she's tinkering with it, moving around words, deleting, and then adding back in again, second-guessing herself, worrying that it might not be good enough, that it needs another tweak. She's never felt this way, but she's also never had to compete with anyone before, she's only ever had to worry about keeping her own head above water. She's on her lunch break, sitting in the food court with her laptop open, trying to ignore the crowds swarming all around her and pecking at the keyboard and wishing something bad would happen to Chris Weber. Not that she *really* wishes for anything to happen to him, it's more like when she's driving and gets cut off, and hopes that the other driver will get pulled over and have to pay a big ticket while she lays on the horn and waves her middle finger around—that's what she wishes for Chris Weber. That he'd suddenly take ill—nothing fatal, of course—or decide to give up writing altogether, and then her life would suddenly be easy, and Corbin would have to accept her work, no questions asked, and she could stop worrying.

"You don't look very happy," Ethan says, pulling back the chair across from her and sitting down. He's carrying a tray with his own lunch, it looks like he means to stick around, so she shuts her laptop and pushes it to one side. "How's the writing going?"

She crinkles up her nose.

"It's okay."

"What's your next article going to be about?"

She sighs, traces a finger on her laptop's apple icon.

"I visited Seever in prison," she says.

"You visited Seever?" Ethan says, impressed. "Like, sat down and actually *talked* to him?"

"Yeah."

"Wow. What did you talk about?" Ethan's leaning so far over his food that his collar is nearly dipping into his bowl of clam chowder, his face is rapt, she's definitely got his attention. It's silly but it makes her feel good, because when was the last time she had anyone interested in what she had to say, so fascinated that it's like they're wearing blinders, like the rest of the world no longer exists? The last time anyone had listened to her the way Ethan is now was when she'd read her work out loud at the Tattered Cover, when the room had been so quiet except for the sound of her own voice and she could almost *feel* the audience straining to hear her words, to catch every inflection, every breath she took. No one is all that interested in hearing her talk about her work these days, even Dean is uninterested, he's a little *hostile* about it, because he's been through this before, he ended that period of his life with the knowledge that his wife had been unfaithful, so that's to be expected. "Has he heard about the Secondhand Killer? What does he think?"

"If I told you I'd have to kill you," she says, teasing, and Ethan doesn't like this, not at all, but she hardly notices because she's looking over his shoulder, searching; it feels like someone is staring at her, hard, and her eyes skip right over him before snapping back, because Jacky Seever blends right in, he always has, that's how he got away with killing for so long.

But it's *not* Seever, it's Loren, in a nice suit with his hair all slicked back, he's already played this trick before, she should know better, but it's not something a person can get used to, having him all dressed up like a man she'd once known, a man who she'd once held in her body, a man who'd killed so many. It would be an unpleasant shock if she'd caught only a glimpse of Loren dressed like this, making his way through the swelling crowd, shopping or eating, but this is worse because he's staring right at her, he's watching her, waiting for her to notice him. Loren winks when their eyes meet, slow and flirty, the way Seever always did it, and her arm jerks in surprise and knocks into Ethan's tray of food, upends his bowl of soup, and there's a moment of chaos while they clean, Ethan inhaling irritably as he mops up the mess, and when Sammie looks up again, searching, Loren is gone.

GLORIA

They're married for a few years when Jacky gives her a credit card, a rectangle of plastic to use instead of cash out of the bank account. She can use the checkbook too, if she needs it, but he prefers her to use credit, because it makes things easier.

For accounting reasons, he tells her. *You don't have to write anything down. I'll look it over when the statement comes.*

How much can I spend? she asks.

Jacky shrugs.

Just don't go crazy, he says. *You should be fine.*

At first, it's scary to shop, to go up to the register and wait for the employee to ring everything through and then give her credit card a swipe, and then there's a long moment of waiting while the computer hums and thinks and the cashier stares at the screen and Gloria thinks that this is it, this time the cashier will take out of a pair of scissors and cut up the card and tell her to get lost, that she doesn't have enough money to pay for any of it, that she never will. It's her worst nightmare, that second before the computer spits out the receipt for her to sign, when it seems like the whole world is made of glass. But the card never comes back declined, it always goes through and the cashier smiles and hands her a pen to sign and Gloria smiles back, more than relieved that everything is still okay.

There are always people at the house, sometimes professionals from one of the different clubs Jacky belongs to, other business owners looking to network, or sometimes kids from one of the restaurants, teenagers who come over for dinner and stay late, watching TV and drinking beer with Jacky, talking and smoking and laughing about sports and movies and everything, because Jacky can make conversation about anything, that's always been one of his gifts.

Ever since he took over the restaurant, Jacky likes the house full of people, the floors groaning under the weight of shuffling feet and thick with the smell of perfume and cigarettes, he was never like that before, he always liked their privacy, he liked to come home from work and eat dinner and relax, read the paper and watch the news. It's called networking, he says, it's for the business. But she thinks this change might be because they've never caught pregnant again, even though they've been trying for ten years, even though the doctor says there's nothing wrong with either of them, and their plans for a family are quietly shelved, then disappear altogether. The house is too big, too empty without the happy sounds kids would make, and he wants it to fill it up, kill the silence.

So he puts out an invitation to everyone, and at first not many show up, but Jacky keeps pushing, keeps cajoling, and more and more come, until every night is a party at the Seever house, plenty of food and beer, Jacky sitting at the head of the dining-room table like a king, his face red and jolly, and it all seems so ridiculous and sad, and there's something desperate about it too. She doesn't like Jacky very much when there are other people around—she actually doesn't like him at all, with his deep, gusty laugh and moronic jokes, and she feels embarrassed for her husband, because he's busy making a fool of himself, although no one else seems to mind. They all think he's one helluva good guy, a real gas, like her father used to say. They laugh and slap him on the fat of the arm and sit around her nice cherrywood dining-room table and eat and leave behind wet rings with their glasses because they won't use the coasters she puts out *every damn night.*

You should join us, Jacky tells her, but she won't. She cooks the food, puts it out on the table before they all sit down, and then cleans up, after everyone has moved to another room, so they don't watch her picking up their messes and wiping up their spills, like a maid in her own house. She loads the dishwasher, wipes down the tables and counters once, and then again, and heads upstairs, puts her hair up in rollers and applies her cold cream. She doesn't like the noise, their talk about people and places she doesn't know, will never know. She'd rather be in her own bed, tucked down under the comforter with the ceiling fan whirring companionably overhead.

It's easy to spend money, easier than she ever knew. Her father is a man who uses cash to pay for everything, who has a big steel safe in his bedroom full of greenbacks. He doesn't trust banks, but that's not a surprise, because he doesn't trust anyone. He jeers when Gloria shows him her credit card, his face mean as he mashes his cigarette into a saucer.

"You're coming up in the world, are you?" he says. "Managed to trick a bank into lending you money you don't need?"

"It's not like that—"

But her father shouldn't be one to judge, not when he never let her mother treat herself to a new dress, never let her tithe extra to the church. Her father always called himself frugal, but she sees now that he's stingy, that he wouldn't let a dime squeak out of his wallet to make anyone happy, even his own wife. At least Jacky isn't like that. He likes to give people things, wants to help them—she can't count the number of times high school kids have stopped by the house for career advice or guidance, or because Jacky promised them a few bucks to mow the lawn or rake the leaves, even if it'd been done only a few days before. She's heard people say that you sometimes have to sacrifice to get ahead (she's not sure where she first heard that saying, and even though she thinks it's about chess, it still applies to her husband), and that's what Jacky is doing. Sacrificing. Spending a few bucks to make other people's lives better.

She still wants a baby, more than anything, but they can't, so why not get a job? Or go back to school, become a teacher. Bring home her own paycheck, contribute to what they have going on, have something going on that could fill her days. But Jacky tells her no, gently, in a soft voice, reminding her that he provides everything she will ever need. Everything she could ever want. And that's true, but sometimes Gloria thinks there should be more than this, than grocery shopping and planning meals and watching television and ironing, that she wants more than this, that she never thought this was how her life would turn out, even though women friends are always saying how lucky she is, what a good man Jacky is. And he is. She feels guilty when she thinks otherwise, because he pays attention to her, and takes her out for nice meals and opens doors and pulls out her chair, and he's always careful about putting the toilet seat back down when he's finished. And there's the things he doesn't do, let's not forget, heavens no, because the things a man doesn't do are just as important as the things he does—he doesn't complain when she comes home from JCPenney and Montgomery Ward with armfuls of bags and he doesn't care when she burns the casserole and he doesn't mutter when she wears a flannel nightgown, the one that covers from her chin to the tops of her toes, and tells him that her head hurts, that she wants to go to bed, that she's not in the mood. There's never been a repeat of that episode so long ago, no more sex that might be rape but probably isn't, and he doesn't say that she's so beautiful that she deserves to die, and he doesn't hold a gun up to her head and promise that after he shoots her he'll shoot himself too and the police will never find them, two bodies lying side-by-side on the cold linoleum, their bodies so close it'll be impossible to tell one person from the other.

She wakes up one night, suddenly, not sure why. Her heart is caught high up in her throat, and she's scared, *terrified*, and she's not sure why, and that's the worst of it, to not have a reason for the fear. Jacky's side of the bed is empty, and the house is quiet, so he might've fallen asleep downstairs on the couch after everyone went home, it wouldn't be the first time. She considers getting up, putting on her robe, creeping downstairs, waking her husband, and bringing him back with her, but she doesn't want to leave the safety of the bed, as if the blankets might offer some protection against whatever monster is out there.

Someone screamed, she thinks, but the thought is barely there before she's asleep again, already gone, and she won't remember any of it in the morning.

The doorbell rings one afternoon, and there's a young man standing on the front steps, a handsome one with light hair and good skin. Not zitty and pockmarked like some of the other boys she's seen, who're constantly scratching and picking at their faces. At least it's not a girl—there was a time when Jacky would have sent home any number of young women, girls he'd met while he was out doing whatever it is he does during the day, sent her to Gloria to do things around the house for cash. Beautiful young girls with lean thighs and bright smiles, who'd come over in short skirts and thin T-shirts, not clothes to work in but to be seen in. Once, she caught Jacky staring out a window at a group of girls working in the garden, and it's not that she minded so much—all men looked at young women, hell, cars passing by on the street slowed to watch the girls at their raking—but did he have to do it right in front of her? But she didn't say anything, didn't tell him that it hurt her feelings, that it made her feel insecure. She was forty-five, and she felt every minute of it, every year. In the creaking of her knees, in the bags under her eyes. And those young girls, they made her feel terrible, but what could she say without looking like a complete fool?

"Mr. Seever isn't home from work yet," she tells the boy. She's flustered, even though she's dressed and has her makeup on—young men always make her feel awkward, especially the good-looking ones. She knows it shouldn't matter what a boy half her age thinks, but somehow it still does. "You can wait for him here, if you'd like."

The boy follows her in, sits at the kitchen table, and enthusiastically drinks the Coke she pours over crushed ice. She's irritated at Jacky, because she was in the middle of reading a novel, one from the library that seemed like a stinker but she checked it out anyway; it was like a puppy with big, drooping eyes at the pet store that she had to take home. And now, after starting to read with the lowest of expectations, the book is turning out to be something great, but she can't leave the boy alone in her kitchen so she can get back to reading—instead, she has to sit there and make small talk and be friendly and keep from glancing at her wristwatch, desperately listening for the sound of Jacky's car pulling into the driveway.

But the boy seems to sense how uncomfortable she is, and makes it easy.

"I'm here to do some chores for your husband, ma'am," he says. "If it's all right, I'll get started and let you get back to whatever you were doing."

"That would be nice," she says, relieved.

There's a pause, and Gloria twists the tissue in her hand. It's moments like this, she thinks, in which important things happen. Choices are made. She could take a step forward, throw her arms around the boy's neck and slip him the tongue. Drag him up to her bedroom and undress for him, slowly, and move her mouth over all that tight, young flesh. It would serve Jacky right, to have his wife sleep with the boy he sent home to work, because he's been cheating since the beginning, she knows it and ignores it, and she usually tries to put it out of her head, because it's just sex, and every man has to have fun, but then there are days when Jacky will take her to the restaurant and she'll see him looking at one of the waitresses, and the girl will stare right back at him with her dark eyes, and Gloria can practically feel the heat in those looks, and she'll see how she's being neatly pushed to one side. Jacky thinks she's a stupid, unsuspecting housewife, but she knows everything. She's half-tempted to do something crazy to get back at Jacky, but doesn't when she realizes it's probably her library book influencing her even though it's on the other side of the house. It's the kind of book where anything is possible, where animals talk and houses fly; the kind of book where a woman can get any man she wants, even if her own father called her ugly and fat, even if that man is a boy wearing a faded T-shirt and a pair of bright-white sneakers. She wants to do something, but instead she doesn't do anything at all. That's her deal, like they used to say.

"So what does my husband have you doing today?" she asks, delicately clearing her throat.

"I'm digging."

"Digging?" For the first time, she realizes he has a shovel propped up against his chair, the worn metal edge balanced on her kitchen floor. It's smallish—she can't remember what it's called, a shovel like that. Not a trowel—a spade, like in a deck of cards.

"Yeah," the boy says, wrinkling his nose in amusement, like he's giving her the punch line of a joke he doesn't quite understand. "Mr. Seever wants some holes dug in the crawl space."

That boy who digs the crawl space, he comes to the house a few times, and he's always friendly, always smiling. And then he's gone. When Gloria asks about him, Jacky is vague and distracted.

"Oh, he won't be back around," Jacky says. "He found something else that suits him better."

Every marriage has rules, not ones that are written down or set in stone, but they're there just the same, creating invisible fences that only two people can see. And if her own marriage only had one rule, Gloria thinks, it is this:

Gloria knows nothing.

So Jacky does what he wants, he always does, he always will, and she knows nothing. It's easier that way, to let things ride, and Gloria realizes that this same rule may've been part of her parents' marriage, that she not only inherited her mother's long fingers and blue eyes but also her ability to keep her mouth shut too. To not ask questions.

It's not that she doesn't love Jacky—because she does. It's a faded love now, gone soft and worn from going through the wash so many times, but it's there. And what does it matter if that love isn't what she imagined when she was a girl? The love they have is the familiar sound of Jacky clipping his fingernails over the toilet, the rumbling of his snores when he's especially tired. The smell of the lotion he always works into his knuckles, especially during the winter. It's the way he leaves his boxer shorts crumpled outside the shower, even though it irritates her, even though she's asked him a *million* times to take the three extra steps and throw them in the hamper, because it means she has a husband, she has a man taking care of her. And besides that one time, Jacky's never been cruel to her, he's been nothing but loving, and she's sure he depends on her, he loves her back. He *needs* her. He wouldn't know what to do without her, that he never wants to be apart. And she feels the same.

But.

There is sometimes blood on his boxer shorts. Not a lot, but enough to notice when she's throwing the clothes in the wash and checking for stains. It's not around the rear end—if it were, she'd insist that Jacky go see a doctor, he could have something terribly wrong if he were bleeding from back there—but around the front, the part where the fabric splits for that ridiculous hole that always makes her laugh, because she can't imagine a man trying to poke out through *that* to go to the bathroom when they could just pull down. She asked him about it once, but Jacky shrugged, he said it must be dye from the fabric, running. *Cheap shit*, he'd said. *Buy American next time. Then we won't have that problem.*

And then, the month before, she was sitting by the open window in their bedroom, reading, and the night wind was tugging at the curtains, and the hem of her skirt was slipping against the back of her calf like watered silk. She heard Jacky coming up the stairs, his feet heavy, but she only looked up from the words when he was standing in front of her, his hands reaching out for her like a child. There was blood grimed into his knuckles, dried blood, but some of it was fresh, and she shrieked, concerned that he'd hurt himself, but when she took him into their bathroom and made him sit on the closed toilet lid and wiped him down with a damp washcloth she saw that he wasn't hurt, not at all, that the blood couldn't be his. *Almost got away*, Jacky whispered, nearly hysterical, and there was something in his eyes that frightened her, that made her want to take her car keys and drive as far as she could, away from this man. But instead she washed him, carefully, then made him lie down in their bed. And even though he said he wasn't at all tired he immediately fell asleep, and she took his bloody clothes—and the washcloth, don't forget that!—down to the laundry room and ran them through a cold cycle, dumping in an overflowing capful of bleach during the rinse. She didn't sleep with Jacky that night but went to the guest room, slept on top of the blankets fully dressed, facing the door, her hands tucked carefully under her cheek. She thought that when Jacky woke up she'd ask him about the blood and what he'd said and all the traveling he did, even though he didn't need to, and she'd make him be honest, finally get the truth out of him. But when she woke up Jacky was in the shower, singing jubilantly, and before he left for work he put his hand on the back of her neck and kissed her, the way he used to, and she saw that the blood had come right out of the clothes, like it had never been there, no problemo, so what was the point in bringing it up at all?

But there is also the garage, the one he's converted to his party room. The boom-boom room. He's said he doesn't want anyone in there when he's not home, that it's his space, his *privacy*, that she should respect it. *I don't go rifling through your drawers,* he says, and this makes sense, although she doesn't have a padlock on her dresser like he has on the door going from the house into the garage. There's only one key to that lock, and she doesn't know where he keeps it. There are times during the day, when she's vacuuming or dusting or doing nothing at all, and she'll go to that door, lift the heavy lock, hold it in her hands, and test the cold weight of it against her palm. She tugs on it to see if it'll pop open, but it never does. Why would it? Jacky is always careful, he always locks it up tight, never leaves the house or goes to bed without checking it.

But even the most thorough person can have a slip-up.

It's a Tuesday when he forgets, he's in a hurry, he overslept and doesn't even have time to grab a coffee before he's out the door, and she hears his car tearing down the driveway. And somehow the padlock hasn't been pushed shut; he's forgotten to do it, it's dangling there, holding the door shut but no longer keeping her out.

She doesn't go in, not right away. She drinks a cup of coffee, watches the morning news. She scrubs the bottom of the tub, even though it's not that dirty, and then showers herself, carefully rubs her lilac-scented lotion over every part of her body. She does her hair, applies mascara.

Then she goes downstairs, back to the door. Part of her expects it to be locked, that Jacky might've come home during the day, he sometimes does. Maybe she wants it to be locked, so she doesn't have to see what's behind there, but it's still open, and it takes her a moment to pull it free of the metal loop it's hanging through, because her hands are shaking so damn bad. She is Bluebeard's wife, who was told to not open a certain door but couldn't resist the temptation, and found out the terrible secret her husband was hiding.

She takes only a single step into the garage, and stays in the room for less than a minute. Then she leaves, locks the door firmly behind her, and goes to the kitchen. Washes her hands and starts peeling potatoes. She is making a roast for dinner, with red potatoes and French bread. It's Jacky's favorite.

She comes home from the prison, upset and tired, not sure what to think of that reporter woman visiting Jacky, but what can she do about it? Nothing, that's what she can do. Absolutely nothing. He's a grown man, he can see whomever he wants, do what he wants.

He always has.

She climbs out of her car, her keys in her hand, thinking that she'll go inside and brew a cup of tea and watch some TV. Not the news, it's all about these murders, the Secondhand Killer, that's what they're calling him, and she knows they're trying to connect it to Jacky, although she's not sure how. The police have even come by with questions, and left disappointed. By the sad looks on their faces, they were hoping she was behind it all, or that she knew where Alan Cole was, who'd apparently been one of Jacky's old friends although the name isn't at all familiar to her. Oh, she sent them packing, because how is an old woman like her going to be any help to them?

She's already got the key slid into the lock before she notices the words spray-painted in red across her door. YOU KNEW, BITCH, it says in straggling letters. It's already dried, so it's been there most of the day already, for anyone with eyeballs in their head to see.

The world finally found me, she thinks, but she knows that's not *completely* true, it's not as if she were lost at the bottom of the ocean, or hiding under an assumed name. Anyone who bothered to look could've found her, anytime, and they have before, like whoever broke in and stole all her things. A search on the computer, even a quick flip through a phone book, and she could've been found. But these new murders are upsetting people, and everyone needs to be angry at someone, and she might just be the right person.

She could get a bucketful of soapy water and a rag, get to work on scrubbing the words away. Three words, it wouldn't take too long. An hour, maybe less. But does it really matter?

Instead, she goes inside, locks the door behind her. Puts a kettle of tea on the stove and turns on an old black-and-white movie, rests her feet up on the coffee table. And she pretends those words aren't on the door at all. The easiest lies are the ones you tell yourself, after all, and Gloria's gotten very good at that over the years.

WE

DON'T

MAKE

MISTAKES

Six hundred thousand people living in Denver. Maybe it's too damn many. Lots of people from California migrating in, that's what residents say. All those West Coast people with their bad driving habits and their liberal ideas, taking over. That's why this city is going to hell, the natives say. That's why housing prices are going up, why people keep getting killed. Look at what happens out in Los Angeles, they say. All that violence. And now it's happening here.

But really, it can happen anywhere.

For example: a quiet street in a suburb of Denver. The houses are small and older, mostly made of brick, and the lawns are big. There's an elementary school a block away, and kids play outside without being watched too closely by adults. There are no children out today, because most of them are in school, and the others are inside, probably in front of the TV, because it's too cold to be out. Many of the houses have Christmas decorations, lights and wreaths mostly, and one house has a plastic nativity scene in the front yard. It's not life-size, but it's pretty close, and the baby Jesus has been stolen and replaced with an empty milk carton wrapped in a blanket, although no one has noticed it yet. It's a nice place to live, not too far from the glitter of the big city but far enough. A good neighborhood to raise a family.

There is a man walking down the street—he *is* a man, legally, twenty on his last birthday, although he has the acne-ridden face and scrawny arms of a boy. He is pale and small and his hair needs to be washed. He'll beef up in the next few years, he'll hit the gym and start lifting weights and eating plenty of protein, and he'll wash his car with no shirt on so everyone can admire all his hard work.

That is, it's what he'd do if he lives that long.

This boy is Jimmy Galen; he doesn't have a car and has to walk everywhere, point his feet in a direction and go. He doesn't like to walk on any of the main streets, tries to stick to the side roads and shortcuts, through neighborhoods and parks, over fences and along sewage drains. He doesn't like anyone to see he doesn't have a car, doesn't like to think of the pitying looks he gets as people drive by, seeing his shoulders hunched up against the wind, his eyes squinted against the sun. So he takes the back routes, in the hopes he'll never see anyone he knows.

"Why does it matter what anyone thinks?" his mother asks when he complains about his lack of wheels. "So what if you have to walk?"

"You don't understand," he says. "You don't have to walk anywhere."

And she doesn't, because she already has a car. He loves his mother, doesn't want to fight with her, but how's he supposed to get anywhere without a car in this city—how's he supposed to get a girlfriend?

"You're still young," his mother says. "Walking will do you good."

"You have a car."

"I have to get to work."

"So do I," he says. "You could buy me a car, you know."

She snorts and waves her hand, goes back to watching the local news. That's all she's been watching the last few days, ever since that Simms girl turned up dead. It wasn't all that long ago that she wouldn't even talk about Seever, wouldn't let anyone mention his name, because it could've been Jimmy buried in his crawl space, he could've been one of those poor kids on that long list of names.

I only met him once, he'd say when she'd start in about those dead kids, usually after some wine, but she didn't want to hear it. *We lived down the street from him for six months before we moved. I mowed his lawn twice.*

My Jimmy's a lucky boy, his mother had told the nice lady reporter from the newspaper all those years before, when Seever's trial was on-going and everyone was talking about him, and his mother had been so pleased when her name had actually been printed, she'd clipped out the article and saved it. *Seever didn't take a shine to him. He let my boy live.*

"You know we can't afford another car," his mother says now. "If your father was alive—well, that doesn't matter. We don't have the money."

Jimmy shrugs into a coat, not wanting to see his mother have an-other breakdown about his father, who fell asleep behind the wheel on the interstate and never even saw that tree coming. It's been three years since then, and she still brings up her dead husband every time Jimmy asks for money, as if they'd be straight-up millionaires if her husband were still alive. He figures he'll save up for a car, although it'll be years before he has enough for something good. *Tough titty, said the kitty,* as his dad used to say.

"I'm outta here," he says, but his mother isn't listening, she's so caught up in the news about that girl. He thinks about ripping the plug out of the wall, reminding his mother that *he* might be next, that whoever went after Simms might need another victim, that's what the cops had said when they'd called that morning, that Jimmy and his mother should be careful, that they were contacting anyone who'd ever been connected to Seever, just in case. He thinks about telling his mom that she'd better drive him to work so he'd stay safe. But if he said that her imagination would start running wild, and then she'd be all over him, she'd want to take him to work every day, and then pick him up, and she'd sneak into his bedroom at night to check on him to make sure he was okay. So he doesn't say anything, just shrugs into his coat and zips it up as far as it'll go before heading outside, out into the cold. It's the middle of the day, and the Second-Story Killer, or whatever they're calling him, seems to be after only women, so he's safe.

Outside, it's freezing. It often gets cold here, but this—this is something else. It hasn't been cold enough for the schools to close yet, but they'll probably be shut down tomorrow; they don't want kids getting frostbite while waiting for the bus or walking to class. But at least they're all inside now, not out here with him, trudging through the piles of snow his dickhead neighbors never bother to shovel off their sidewalks, and by the time he gets to work his feet'll be soaked through and he won't be able to feel them until they start to thaw and hurt like hell.

It's mostly the thought of his feet that makes him decide to take the bus, although he hates everything about public transportation. He hates the extra-long buses the city has, like two worms connected in the center by an accordion, and he hates the fact that even though most of them are brand-new, they still smell like piss. He doesn't know why that is. The plastic seats are shiny and free of gum and the floors are mostly spotless, but they still smell. Like some guy stood in the middle of the bus, right in the springy thing that keeps the whole thing connected, and unzipped, spraying urine everywhere.

But what does Jimmy Galen hate most about the bus? That anyone can see him riding it. *Anyone.* And riding a bus is even worse than walking, especially if your friends see you doing it, and they blast by while you're waiting inside the clear plastic walls of the bus stop and shoot you the finger, screaming and laughing, because their parents bought them a car to drive, and you're the fucking loser waiting to take a bus to your job at the mall, where you sell shitty sports memorabilia to lame kids or single old guys with nothing better to spend their money on.

"If you signed up at the community college I might let you take my car to class," his mother said that fall, after everyone went back to school and the streets seemed empty.

"I just graduated."

"Two years ago," his mother said, snorting. "If you want to get a good job, you have to go to college these days."

"You never did."

"Things were different back then," she said. "Times have changed."

"I'll think about it."

But he didn't think about it, because he had no interest in college. College was for smart kids, kids with brains, and Jimmy isn't all that bright. At least that's what his dad had always told him, and that's what the teachers in high school had said too. Actually, the teachers had usually said something about him not living up to his full potential, which in real-speak meant he was a fucking numbnuts, which was how his dad always put it. And even though his mom told him not to believe it, told him that no one understood him, he thought all those people were probably right. He'd spent an entire year in middle school wondering if he was retarded, like full-on short-bus retarded, but then realized he was stupid. Not stupid enough to actually benefit from the lack of brain cells, but pretty stupid. So why waste the money on college? He figured he'd stay at the store, work his way up. It wasn't a bad gig, and he liked most of the other employees. They were nice to him, didn't make him feel like an asshole. He doesn't need those dipshits he went to school with, who just want a punching bag. He'll make new friends, work his way up into management. Get an apartment, a girlfriend.

He's thinking about these things while he waits at the bus stop, huddled in a corner, the sleeves of his coat coiled over his hands and his face nuzzled into the collar, his breath leaving a damp patch on the fabric. He's alone in the plastic booth, because everyone else is either too smart to be out on a day like this or has a car. He's so occupied with this, so furious that his mother will spend hundreds of dollars on boxed wine every month and not even consider cosigning a car loan for him, that he barely notices the person come into the booth and sit right beside him, even though there're three other metal benches, all of them empty. He doesn't notice anything until there's a sharp point digging into his side, poking all the way through his coat and T-shirt and into his skin.

"What the fuck's your problem, man?" he says, trying to jump up, but the guy has one hand on the back of his neck and the other pushing the knife deeper into his side. The year before, one of Jimmy's friends had been accidentally stabbed in the thigh at a house party, and he'd told everyone that it'd taken a while to feel the pain, that he hadn't felt anything until he looked down and saw the steak knife sticking out of his leg. But now Jimmy knows that's bullshit, because the pain is immediate, even though the knife can't be very far in, an inch, maybe not even that.

"There's no problem," the guy hisses. "No problem at all."

"I don't have any money, man," Jimmy says. He's sweating, big beads of it running down his back and into the crack of his ass. "I'll give you my wallet, but there's nothing in it."

"I don't want your money." The hand tightened when Jimmy tried to turn his head, so he was left staring out at the falling snow. The guy's breath smelled like cigarettes, and he was wearing a cologne that smelled familiar, or an aftershave. Jimmy didn't know.

"Then what do you want?"

"Oh, you'll see."

He's going to piss in his pants. He's never been so scared, and his bladder is about to let loose and soak his pants, run down his leg and into his shoes. Maybe, Jimmy thinks, he'll laugh later, because he thought his socks would be wet from the snow, he couldn't even imagine how bad things could get. Now, having a little bit of snow in his shoes sounds like a luxury.

"This is what I get for taking the fucking bus," Jimmy says.

"Shut up." The guy forces him to stand, makes him walk out of the shelter and back into the cold. There's no one around, no one on the street so he can scream for help, there's not even any cars driving past. It's like everyone is dead and they're the only two left alive on the whole planet, trudging across the frozen ground under a slate sky. It makes him think of that TV show his mom likes so much, where most everyone is dead and there're groaning zombies lurching down the streets. That show makes the idea of everyone being dead seem almost nice, like it could be a great time, but this is different, this is wrong and he doesn't like it at all.

"Where are we going?" Jimmy asks, but it's too late, the guy is shoving him hard, and kicking him in the back of the knee, so Jimmy crumples forward, slumping into the open trunk of a car idling at the curb, a neat and easy trick, like the guy had planned the whole thing, practiced the move until he got it perfect. He tries to sit up, to get up and run, but he can't because he's lying on some slippery fabric, and when he gets a handful of it he sees it's silk, bright colors with fuzzy pompoms sewn up the front, like something a clown would wear. He doesn't think about this long, because he's gotta get out of this car, he's heard that you should never let some psycho take you to another location, somewhere secluded where they can have their way with you, and although the advice is usually given to girls, he thinks it probably holds for him too.

"Hey man," Jimmy starts to say, and—

Jimmy wishes he were dead, and he thinks that'll come, sooner or later. He doesn't know where he is, or how much time has passed. He is tired and he is hungry and he is in pain. And he is cold. He doesn't know when he was undressed, but everything is gone, even his socks, and he must be in a basement or somewhere underground, because the floor is plain cement and he can hear the guy climbing stairs in the next room every time he leaves or comes in, his feet slapping against the bare wood steps.

"I'm not gay, I want you to know that," the guy says, crouching beside him, his hands dangling between his thighs like they were having a *normal* conversation, and Jimmy nods, because he doesn't *care*, he doesn't give two shits whether the guy is gay or not, he wants to go home. He wants to sleep in his own bed and eat his mother's meat loaf and lumpy mashed potatoes, and he'll never ask for a car again, not ever, if he could go home to her. "This isn't about you."

"I don't know," Jimmy croaks. He's thirsty, and his throat is nearly swollen shut from all the screaming. He knows he's not making sense, but it doesn't matter, because the guy nods, thoughtfully, like Jimmy told him exactly what he wanted to hear. This guy likes to talk, and he's told Jimmy all about his life, his job, but mostly about a woman.

"I'm doing this for *her*," he says. He has some tool in his hand,

Jimmy doesn't know what they're called but they look sharp and they look mean and they look pinchy. He squeezes his eyes shut, trying not to see, but the guy slaps him lightly on the face until he looks again, because if there's one thing this guy hates, it's to be ignored. "She *needs* this, and I'd do anything for her."

"Please, no more," Jimmy says, but this guy, whoever he is, isn't the type to respond to begging, or even to reason, and there's more, of course there is, it feels like hours but it might only be minutes, because pain warps time, it draws it out like a taffy bender at the county fair, stretches and then bends it so there's no beginning, and there's no end.

Just before Jimmy loses consciousness for the last time he sees the easel in the corner, and the stack of canvases on the floor beside it. It reminds him of his father, who used to lie on the couch in front of the TV and pop a DVD in of that painting guy—he'd been dead a long time but his dad had liked him so much he'd ordered the full set of videos—the guy with the afro and the soft voice, and his father almost always fell asleep to that show, because he said it was soothing, the soft noise of the brush against the canvas. What did that afro-guy always say? Jimmy tries to remember, he doesn't have the strength to open his eyes but he *needs* to know, he can remember his father's socked feet propped up on the arm of the couch and the way his mother would try to be quiet as she moved around so her husband could nap, and Jimmy would sometimes sit on the floor and eat through a sleeve of crackers and watch the guy paint and scrape out the shapes of trees and shadows, and those were good times for him, maybe the best times.

We don't make mistakes. Jimmy remembers, this is what the guy always said, and it makes him smile. His mouth is full of blood, but he still smiles, to think that he could remember, even though the words seem to come to him from a howling distance. *Just happy little accidents.*

December 10, 2015

Hoskins is in the dark of his own bathroom, fumbling for the light switch. He doesn't find it right away, and for a moment he's gone back in time, to when he was a kid and there wasn't anything worse than the dark, and he was always sure that something was going to reach out and grab him from the shadows. But now he's a grown man, a cop, for Christ's sake, and the last thing he should be afraid of is the dark, but he still feels a touch of panic as he runs his fingers along the wall. He's never felt this way, this touch of fear at the base of his spine, but now he's sure someone's in the bathroom with him, because cops are always being targeted; they found a cop murdered in his own garage last week, shot in the back of the head and—

His fingers find the switch.

He looks to make sure there's no one with him, then into the mirror, and runs his fingers along his chin, over the puffed skin beneath his eyes. There's the old familiar tingle inside his mouth, where the fat of his cheek rubs against his teeth. He gets canker sores when he's under stress, not one but many, oozing wounds that line the inside of his mouth and make it nearly impossible for him to speak without pain. He'd gone to the doctor for it, years before, not able to pry his lips apart without a yelp of pain, hoping for some help.

"I'm not a magician," the doctor said. "You'll have to wait it out. Gargle saltwater."

"But—"

"I don't have some magic pill I can slip you."

"I don't need magic. I need help."

He's awake because he was dreaming about Carrie Simms, and the two other girls, their faces bloated and black, and they'd been chasing him, although he didn't know why. And then he'd tripped, he'd fallen but it was in slow motion and he couldn't move, it was like being frozen in time, and then he was awake, the blanket stuffed into his mouth to keep from screaming. He twists the sink's faucet, then waits for the water to get hot, his fingers gripping the sides of the basin so tightly they're white and bloodless. He stands there a long time, not moving, watching the reflection of the room behind him, as if there might be something waiting back there, ready to jump out of the shadows and come for him. It's only when the water starts steaming that he snaps out of it, sticks his hands under the tap and then yanks them away when it burns.

"Why'd you kill all those people?" Hoskins had asked Seever, more times than he could remember, it was the question they kept circling back to. Seever had a different answer every time; he would lie and scream and sometimes he'd not answer at all, but even in silence there's some truth.

"I don't know," Seever had said, and it was the best answer he ever had for the question. "I started, and then I couldn't stop."

Hoskins could understand. That's life, being addicted to something, even to *someone*, and not being able to stop, not ever, even when you want to.

When the water has cooled down enough, he splashes some on his cheeks, rubs the tender spots under his eyes, then presses his face into the hand towel hanging from the rod, breathes in the smell of mildew. He's been too busy with work the last few days for anything else, and the house is going to hell. He needs to do laundry, load the dishwasher. He pays the woman who comes to keep an eye on Joe enough, you'd think she might lift a finger to help out, but of course she doesn't. But it's not part of her job description, people don't like doing more than the least of what's expected, he gets it. Doesn't mean he likes it.

He heads back into the bedroom and picks his cell phone up off the nightstand. It's flashing silently, letting him know that at some point while he was asleep he got new messages. Two texts. The first is from Ted. It's short, to the point, about the cases he was searching through. NO VICS MISSING FGRS IN LAST 5 YRS, it says. SRY. ☹

"Shit," Hoskins says, deleting the message. He'd hoped he was on to something, that there'd be some missing link between old cases and this new one, but it was nothing but another dead end.

The second text is more interesting. It's from Sammie; it could mean anything, or nothing at all. She's called him a few times over the last few days, left messages, and he's deleted them all. He isn't going to help her with another story like he did the last time.

I NEED TO TALK TO YOU. IT'S IMPORTANT.

He sits on the edge of the bed, his phone in one hand, still running the towel over his face and breathing in that musky smell that's both bitter and homey, considering Sammie's text, and then he hears the scream; at first it sounds like a woman but then he realizes that it's his father, something is wrong with Joe.

He grabs his gun from its spot in his nightstand and runs down the hall, a big man in pajama bottoms and a plain white undershirt, sprinting toward the sound of his father's screams. *I need to start exercising more,* he thinks in the moment before he bursts into his father's bedroom, *or I'm going to have a heart attack.*

Hoskins is sure that Joe is being hurt, that someone broke in, wanting to steal a TV or money and instead found the old man sleeping in his bed. He's so convinced of this that it takes him a moment to understand Joe is alone in the room, he's curled up in a corner and he's terrified, he's pointing at nothing, shrieking like an old woman.

"He's here," Joe was screaming, those were the only words Hoskins could make out through all the gibberish, and even when he took Joe by the shoulders and gave him a good hard shake it didn't seem to matter, the old man kept on screaming, the whites of his eyes showing all the way around and the spittle gathering in the corners of his mouth in white chunks.

Hoskins doesn't know what to do, the doctor had mentioned something about hallucinations but he hadn't said anything about *this,* the screaming that won't stop and the old man doesn't seem to recognize him, only keeps his hands hooked into claws and won't stop shrieking, pointing at things no one else can see, so he hits his father. Hard, across the face, thinking that it might snap him out of it, and there's a satisfying crack when his fist connects, and then the screaming stops, as suddenly as if it'd been severed with a knife.

"That shut you up, didn't it?" he mutters, and he immediately thinks that those words aren't his, they're Seever's, and Joe is slumped back on his pillows, there's blood coming from his mouth, some from his ear, and Hoskins realizes he did the wrong thing, he made the wrong choice but it's too damn late now. He's had moments like this before, those times he'd rewind his life ten seconds if he could, he'd make it right, he'd do something different.

His father is slumped back on the pillows, maybe he's dead, but then the old man opens his eyes, suddenly, as if nothing had happened at all, and looks right at Hoskins.

"Who are you?" Joe says, and then starts screaming again, but this time Hoskins doesn't hit him, he backs out of the room and stands outside the door and tries to slow the frightened thump of his heart in his chest.

Later, at the hospital, the doctor will tell him that this is common in people with his father's diagnosis, that it may only get worse.

"Dementia is very serious," the doctor said. "He could hurt himself the next time he has an episode. Or someone else."

"I see."

"Mr. Hoskins, I don't think you can continue caring for your father on your own. An assisted-living facility would be best for him. I have some information you should take home and look over. I can answer any questions you might have."

The doctor shoved a few brochures into his hand, shiny booklets with happy, smiling white-haired folks on their pages. *You can't take care of one old man*, is what Hoskins hears. *You've royally fucked it up this time.*

"Thank you."

"He'll need to stay the rest of tonight, and possibly tomorrow night for observation. Do you happen to know how he hurt his head?"

Hoskins pauses. Slips his hand into his coat pocket so the doctor can't see the bruises on his knuckles.

"I don't."

"Okay," the doctor gives him a half-smile, and shrugs. He knows, Hoskins thinks. He knows exactly what happened. "It's not a big deal, just thought I'd ask."

"Okay."

Idaho Springs is northwest of Denver, the first town on the map as the city disappears and the mountains crowd in. There's not much to it—a handful of gas stations, a single supermarket, a few clustered neighborhoods of older homes. It's a nice little town, but it's the kind people pass straight through to get to the ski resorts, a town where no one really lives. Hoskins veers off I-70 once Denver's nothing but a gritty haze on the skyline behind him, ending up on a two-lane road that snakes south, into an area where the homes and businesses peter out and the wildlife squeezes back in. He drives slowly, worried that another car might speed around the next blind curve, but there's no one on the road, either in front or behind. It's strange out here, Hoskins thinks. He doesn't like it so much. He's more comfortable with concrete and asphalt, buildings made of steel and brick. Not this. All these trees, crowded in so close there's a solid wall of bark and leaves on either side, so thick you can barely see anything in the distance.

He eases slowly around a switchback in the road, pulls off on the packed dirt beside the blacktop, where two police patrols are parked, low and sleek, mean metal grilles attached to the fronts. Local cops, and the units look brand-new, but that isn't much of a surprise. On the east side of Denver you had kids in rags, starving to death, but out here there was money. A hundred and fifty years before there'd been the gold rush, and then silver, and now there was skiing, tourism. Different delivery methods, but the same results.

He parks farther down, past the units, out of the way, and turns off the car. It's colder out here than in the city, but there's less snow on the ground, under the cover of all the pines and evergreens. A gray moth lands on the windshield, spidery legs ticking along as it walks. Hoskins smacks the flat of his hand against the glass, but it doesn't move. Doesn't even flutter its wings. He leans closer, trying to get a good look at its underbelly, and there is a metallic tap on his window, just beside his head, and he jumps, startled. The moth flies away.

"Roll it down," the officer shouts, one of the locals, and Hoskins is bemused to see him make the cranking motion with his hand, because when was the last time he'd seen a car with one of *those*?

He opens the door instead, stands up. He'd gotten the phone call when he was leaving the hospital, he'd planned on going home and back to bed, but here he is, because another victim has been found, and it looks like another one belonging to Secondhand.

"Detective Hoskins?"

"Yeah."

"Loren's already here. He wanted me to wait for you, walk you out to the site."

"Has he been here long?" Hoskins asks.

"About ten minutes."

"Okay."

"We got an ID on the victim," the cop says. "James Galen. Jimmy, that's what people called him. He was going to work, his mom said. Never made it there."

"Did the kid know Seever?"

The cop shrugs.

"All right." Hoskins sighs, zips his coat as high as it'll go. "Let's go take a look, see what we've got."

The kid out in Idaho Springs had been found by a couple taking a walk, although from the looks of them, Hoskins thinks it was probably more likely that they'd parked and went looking for a quiet place off the beaten path to get high, maybe squeeze a little sexy time in. There isn't much snow out that way, especially under the cover of all those trees, but the ground is damp and soft and spongy, and that's where the couple had found Jimmy Galen, thrown onto a bed of wet pine needles, his arms and legs thrown out wide so he looks like a starfish.

And then there is Loren, dressed in a Seever-suit, a pair of glasses pushed high up on his nose, standing over the body, his hands perched on his hips. It is a Seever-pose, and Hoskins wonders how much Loren had practiced to get it down, if he stands in front of his bathroom mirror and works it.

"Left the clown suit at home this time?" Hoskins asks, and Loren laughs, a fat chuckle, then yanks up on the thighs of his slacks and kneels over the dead boy.

"His mom said he's been gone a few days, but she said he'd done it before. Up and disappeared. That's why she didn't report it sooner. Said they'd been fighting about a car, and she figured he was mad," Loren says. "He's been gone for a few days, but dead less than twenty-four hours."

"Any word on locating Cole?" Hoskins asks, curious. And hopeful that they'll make an arrest soon, although he still doesn't believe Alan Cole is their guy.

"I've got a team on it," Loren says. "They'll have him in custody real soon."

"I guess we'll just watch the victims pile up until then?"

Loren flips him the bird.

Hoskins's phone vibrates in his pocket, against his chest. He pulls it out, glances at it while Loren's still talking, telling him about the victim, Jimmy Galen, who'd mowed Seever's lawn a few times. Galen's mother had been in the paper, answering some questions about Seever years before, Loren said. Sammie's the one who'd interviewed her.

"What's that?" Hoskins asks slowly, looking up from his phone. He'd heard Loren say Sammie's name, and that was funny, because the text he'd gotten was from her; he'd read it three times already, trying to make sense of it.

"I said, your girlfriend's the one who interviewed this kid's mother for the paper."

"I got a text from Sammie," Hoskins says, frowning.

"Speak of the devil and she *shall* appear," Loren says. "If you wanna be some help around here, why don't you put your goddamn phone away?"

CALL ME, Sammie's text said. I NEED TO TALK TO YOU ABOUT LOREN.

He sees Loren's lips moving, but he can't seem to hear what he's saying. Instead, Hoskins's ears are filled with a high-pitched whooshing sound, like the wind tearing through a tunnel, and later he realizes the noise is his blood rushing, faster and faster, pumping through his head and back to his heart at dizzying speed.

HE'S STILL DRESSING LIKE SEEVER, Sammie had typed. Two minutes ago, maybe less, depending on how long it took for the words to be beamed up to a satellite in space and then reflected down to his phone. I SAW HIM LAST NIGHT. HE WAS FOLLOWING ME.

"You with me, Paulie?" Loren says, coming over, until he's close enough for Hoskins to see the twisted hairs of his eyebrows and smell the bacon on his breath. If there's one thing Loren hates, it's to be ignored, and he's pissed now. "You gone deaf, Paulie? I said, put your fucking phone away."

SHOULD I BE WORRIED? Sammie had texted, and that was it. Hoskins wondered how long she'd debated sending this last sentence, because Sammie wasn't that type. She'd once told Hoskins that she was the middle child, born between two other girls, and she'd been the tomboy, the one who never cried, the only one not afraid of the dark. But now Loren was following her, all dressed up like Seever, and there were people turning up dead, people who'd once been connected to Seever, and who was more connected than Sammie? She'd waited tables at Seever's restaurant back in college, she'd written all those articles about him for the paper, enough to fill a book. And she'd once been his lover. The task force on this case had been busy, trying to reach every person Seever had known before the Secondhand Killer did, and not once had anyone considered that Sammie should be warned, that she might be the next one in danger.

Loren was following Sammie.

Loren, who'd put in a good word and saved Hoskins's job when he was ready to get the boot. Loren, who called women bitches but still held doors open for them, who'd made more arrests than any other cop in the department. Loren, who'd been dressing like Jacky Seever, who'd been putting on a clown costume and makeup and heading to the local hospital to prance around, who hunted suspects by *becoming* them, and Hoskins had always wondered what would happen if the play-act went too far, it was a thin line between crazy and not, and Loren was constantly teetering between the two. Loren, who was the only one besides Seever who ever called him Paulie.

"You left me that painting," Hoskins says slowly. "You left that painting Seever made."

"Yeah?" Loren says, confused. "Seever sent that thing to me years ago, I figured it'd make you laugh. He's painted a lot of . . ."

Loren trails off, looks away, as if he's lost his train of thought, and Hoskins grabs his shoulder and pinches down, hard.

"You've been following Sammie," Hoskins says, but Loren isn't listening, it's his turn to be staring off into the distance, lost in his own head, until Hoskins gives him a hard shake. "Why have you been following her? What are you up to?"

"He paints," Loren says, softly. "Seever paints, all the time."

"What? Yeah, we already know that, Captain Obvious."

Loren's phone rings, and he pulls it out of his pocket, glances at the screen, frowning.

"I need to go," Loren says, trying to push him away, but Hoskins isn't letting go. "There's something I need to check."

"What are you up to?" Hoskins says, pinching down as hard as he can, but Loren hardly seems to notice.

"Get off me," Loren says, shaking off his hand and shoving him away. "You wanted back into Homicide, here you go."

"Where are you going?" Hoskins shouts, everyone nearby is watching, standing with their heads turned and their eyes bright, so they look like curious animals peeping out of their underground burrows, checking out the commotion. "Where the hell are you going?"

But Loren doesn't answer, he's already halfway across the clearing, his arms swinging by his sides, and it's his own walk, at least, not some more Seever mimicry. Loren's distracted enough to forget to keep up his charade, something about painting, and Sammie—

"Should we go after him?" another detective asks, sidling up beside Hoskins. The guy looks ready for a fight, anxious to knock Loren on his ass, but that won't help anything. No, Hoskins wants to know what Loren's up to, and it won't do a damn thing to drag Loren back now. Hoskins glances back at Jimmy Galen's body, his glassy, horrified eyes rolled up to the clouded sky, and sighs.

"Just follow him," Hoskins says. "I want to know where he's going. What he's doing."

Desperation is not a pretty thing. It's the burlap sack of emotions—no one looks good wearing it. Sammie can't think of one time in her life when she's felt as desperate as she does now, and maybe that's a good thing, to have lived most of her life free from it.

"I don't know," Corbin is saying. She puts the phone on speaker and places it on the table in front of her. She can't stand one more second of Corbin speaking right into her ear, especially when he sounds like he's gearing up to reject the article she'd emailed over. "I mean, it's a solid interview. But there's nothing about the Secondhand Killer in it."

"Seever claims he doesn't know who Secondhand is."

"Yeah, I get it. And Seever's big news, but he's only back in the paper because of Secondhand. Whatever you're writing—it's gotta have both of them in it to work. It needs to be current."

"But if there was a book about Seever—"

"Yeah, I know this would be perfect for a book about him. But what I need now is a piece about the Secondhand Killer. *And* Seever. Look, if you would've gone and talked to Seever seven years ago, yeah, *that* I could've run. Front page, above the fold. But this—I mean, there's nothing in this interview we don't already know. It's interesting stuff. But nothing new."

She stands up, slams her fist into the front of a kitchen cabinet. It drives her fucking *crazy*, to be back in this place, fighting for a story and the chance to make her career again. Maybe it'll always be like this—the constant paddle upstream, the struggle to stay afloat. She's not sure if she likes the idea.

"Sammie? Are you there?" Corbin asks, alarmed. "What was that?"

"Nothing," Sammie says, sitting down again, cradling her sore fist between her breasts. "If this isn't working, what should I write about?"

"I don't know. You're the writer, not me. But I can't run this. Not when Weber's got some really great stuff in the works . . ."

"What's he got that's so great?" Sammie asks. Weber has had a new piece in the paper every day, about Secondhand, about Seever. It's good, well written, although she hates to admit it. "Has he figured out who Secondhand is now?"

"No, but if you figure it out, I'll never publish anything else Weber writes," Corbin says, laughing. "I'm not going to tell you what he's working on."

"Oh, c'mon. What do you think I'm going to do? Sweep in and steal his story?"

"That wouldn't surprise me in the least."

"Fine," she says. A little hurt. "Don't tell me."

"Okay," he says, more smug than she would like. "I won't."

She hangs up the phone and puts her head down on top of her folded arms, but her eyes are still open, staring at the table's rough wood grain. She has to be at work in a few hours, she's trying to use her free time for writing, but it's not happening. The more you want something the harder it gets, and she wants to write a good story for the paper so badly it almost hurts.

"You're perfectly safe," Hoskins had said when he'd called her back, right before she'd gotten on the phone with Corbin. "I have some officers keeping an eye on Loren, and I'll know if he gets anywhere near you."

"Are you with him?"

"No," Hoskins said, drawing the word out.

"Do you think he's the Secondhand Killer?" Sammie asked, and he was silent for so long that she thought he might've hung up, except the phone was still picking up the background noise. The sound of the wind, and of people working, speaking in hushed, serious voices, the crunch of tires over gravel and slamming car doors. They were sounds she recognized.

"He's not," Hoskins finally said. "Loren's insane, but he's not a killer."

"And you know that for sure?"

"He's not Secondhand, Sammie. I had someone clear him after I got your text, made sure he had alibis for the times the other victims went missing. And he does." Hoskins sounded strangely satisfied. "Like I said, Loren's crazy. But he hasn't killed anyone."

"Are you at a crime scene?" she asked, and Hoskins paused, thrown off by the sudden change in questions.

"Yeah, it looks like another Secondhand victim."

"Why didn't you call me?" she'd asked. "I'm trying to write these pieces for the paper, I would've come out—"

"That guy you're working with just got here," Hoskins said, and she wearily closed her eyes. "You know, the one you wrote that last article with?"

"I'm not working with him," she said. "I have to go."

She'd cradled her head in her hands, felt the tears coming on. Chris Weber, who'd gotten his name attached to her byline, was already at the crime scene; he'd managed to snake his way into the place before she'd heard a single word about it. Maybe it's a sign that she's not cut out for this work anymore, she doesn't have the time to call the police department every few hours, hoping for news. It was different when the paper was her full-time job, when she had all day to chase leads and track down sources, but she doesn't have that luxury now. But that's an excuse—a lousy one, because if she wanted a story more than Weber she'd find a way to make it work, and it wouldn't matter if she had a job or not.

Or maybe she has to get creative. She did it before, and it got her into Seever's house, she'd landed the story of the decade. That's all she needs now. She had to chase it differently from how most people would've, but in the end she got what she wanted. Maybe she's going at it wrong, though. Maybe she needs to stop *reporting*, and start investigating. Corbin said he'd never publish Weber again if she found out Secondhand's identity, and she knows he was joking—but what if she did find out?

She rubs her fingernails on the top of the table, making an irritating rasping sound, but she's so deep in thought she doesn't hear it. She can't keep up with Weber, so it's best to let him go running around the crime scenes, trying to squeeze whatever information he can out of the cops. Let him wear himself out, skipping around in endless circles. She'll chase this story down, reach between its legs and squeeze till it screams, until it tells her who the Secondhand Killer is.

ALBERT Q. THOMAS, the sign above the art gallery's door says. She'd looked it up at home, flipped through the website, scanning the list of artists who've had their work featured there.

Halfway down the list is Jacky Seever.

"Can I help you?" the man behind the counter asks when she steps inside. He's tall and serious-looking, with a thick beard, the kind that makes it hard to tell how old he is but also makes most men look like crazed lumberjacks. This man is no exception. "I'm about to close up shop for the night."

"Oh, I'll be quick," she says, smiling so big her cheeks ache. "I saw online that you sell Jacky Seever's work."

There's a pause, a long one, and she thinks she might've said the wrong thing but she can't be too sure, this man has a poker face, more like a *dead* face, and she can't figure out what he's thinking.

"You a cop?"

"What? No. Why do you ask?"

The man narrows his eyes at her.

"I had this cop stop by earlier asking the same thing," he says. "He had all kinds of questions about Seever."

Loren, she thinks. Hoskins has been busy at the crime scene.

"So, you do sell Seever's stuff?"

"I used to," he says slowly. He grabs the flap of his ear and rubs it. "I haven't lately, though. There used to be a lot of interest in his work, those things were flying outta here like hotcakes, but that petered out after a while. I've had a few calls in the last few weeks asking if I have any of his work—Seever's wife brought in a few pieces last week and they sold for quite a bit, but the good stuff would go for a lot more. And I could sure as hell use the cash."

" 'Good stuff'?" Sammie asks, genuinely puzzled. "What's that?"

"Oh, when Seever first started it was all blood and gore. Sexual. Portraits of his victims. Morbid stuff, but it sold fast, and for a lot. But then it was all landscapes and bowls of fruit, and people stopped buying."

"No interest in fruit?" she asks wryly.

"Oh, people would buy a square of toilet paper if they think Seever wiped it on his ass. Especially with these new murders going on."

"Yeah?"

"Oh, yeah," he says blandly, staring out at the nearly empty parking lot. "That's all it takes. A few dead women and people are constantly calling for Seever's stuff. I should've started killing a long time ago."

She blinks, tilts her head to one side as she looks at him.

"Not that I've ever killed anyone," he says when he notices her watching. His neck had gone blotchy red. "That would be crazy."

She drums her fingers on the counter and looks around, tries to think while she keeps an eye on the guy behind the counter. His words might not mean anything, he might've just been thinking out loud, but you could never be too safe. Cold, hard cash was as good a reason as any to kill, and she'd have to mention this guy to Hoskins, make sure the cops were keeping an eye on him. The gallery is small, dingy, the art on display covered in dust. It's a business in desperate need of a few good sales.

"You sure you're not a cop?" the man says, yanking on his beard. He seems nervous.

She tilts her head, considering.

"I'm not with the police, I'm with the paper," she says, "I'm writing a piece on Jacky Seever, and the new Secondhand Killer. And if you can help in any way—well, I'd appreciate it."

He looks down at her hand like she's a strange bug he'd never encountered before, and she wonders if she's going about this all wrong.

"How could I help you?"

"What's your name?" she asks.

"Simon."

"You're not Albert?"

"That was my dad."

"Okay, Simon. You mentioned you get calls about Seever's work?"

"Yeah. Quite a few lately, since these new murders started up." He taps his knuckles on the counter. "For a long time it's just been one guy. Same dude, every week. He calls and asks if I have anything new from Seever. Every week, never fails. Anytime there's a piece available he buys it over the phone, has me ship it to him."

"One guy?"

"Yep. Same one, all the time. He must have a real hard-on for Seever."

"How long's he been calling?"

"Oh, for a while now. The last few months, I guess."

"Do you have his shipping address on file?"

"Nope. It's never the same one, so I don't bother taking it down."

"You know his name?"

"I don't remember, and I'm not even going to wager a guess. If my computer was up and running I'd tell you, but it crashed a few days ago and I haven't had the cash to get it fixed."

"Did you tell the cop all this?" she asks. "About this guy who calls?"

"No," Simon says, pursing his lips. "He never asked about that, and I didn't think it was important. Besides, I didn't like him very much. He was *rude*, right from the moment he walked in, demanding information. I didn't get into this business to be a slave to the police. Have some manners, or it's *good day to you*, sir."

She laughs at that, and Simon's eyes light up.

"You've got a great laugh," he says.

"Thank you," she says, reaching over and touching the top of Simon's hand. She feels so stupid, trying to flirt with this guy, but she'll do whatever it takes. "You're sure you don't know how to reach the guy who always calls about Seever?"

Simon sighs. "No, but I'm sure I'll get a call from him any day now, and if you want I'll take down his number and make sure it gets into your hands."

"You'd do that?" she says.

"Oh, yeah," Simon says. He smiles sweetly. "For a fair exchange."

Here it comes, Sammie thinks. She'd been waiting for this.

"What do you want from me?" she asks. "Dinner, or something?"

He snorts, laughs so hard his beard trembles.

"I'm not so sure my boyfriend would like that idea," he says. "How about you write something about me for the paper?"

"Like, an advertisement?" she asks.

"No. More like an article about a struggling local business. I need to get some customers through these doors." He gives another laugh. "And this article, I want it on the front page."

"I don't decide those kinds of things," Sammie says, tapping her knuckles impatiently on the counter. "I can't promise anything like that."

"You seem like a persuasive woman. I mean, it seems like you *could be*, if you want me to put you in touch with this guy."

Sammie chews on the inside of her cheek. If she gets a good story out of this, she might be able to swing it. Besides, there's always the chance that Simon won't hear from the guy again, and this trip will be a complete loss. Better to blow on the dice and give them a roll.

"I can try."

"Good enough for me," he says, and pulls a business card out of his pocket. "Here. Write down your info. I'll text you as soon as I hear from him."

"You're the cherry Lifesaver," she says, scribbling down her number. That nervous pit that's been eating at the inside of her stomach for the last few days is gone, and she's starting to think that everything might be okay. If this guy actually gets a call and remembers to text her the info, she'll have a story and her ass will be saved. Better late than never.

"What does that mean?"

"It means you're the best," she says, and winks. "And I always save the best for last."

The idiots he had following Loren have already lost track of him. He's not sure how it happened—maybe it's because Loren's squirrelly and Denver's a big city with plenty of places to hide, or because they're not putting all that much effort into it, because Hoskins isn't anyone important these days; he's been down in the basement long enough that the other detectives don't want to follow his command anymore, he can see it on their faces, tell by how they react to his orders. He's a joke these days, and not even a funny one.

"He drives fast," one of the detectives tells Hoskins in a slow, drawling voice. An *I-don't-give-a-shit-about-this* voice. "It looked like he was heading toward the station, but he's not there now."

"Check his house," Hoskins says. "There's a bar down on Wynkoop where he likes to go. Why do I have to tell you how to do your fucking job?"

He hangs up without waiting for a response, because if he has to spend one more minute listening to the useless prattling of these morons he's going to lose his shit. It's all running away from him, being lost in chaos, and he didn't want to work this case to begin with, he was *ordered* to do it. He's called Ted, had the kid confirm Loren's whereabouts when each of the victims went missing, and Loren's clear. He's not the Secondhand Killer but he's definitely not right in the head. He's called Chief Black, told him his concerns about Loren, how he's dressing up like Seever and following Sammie and now vanishing, but the boss man isn't concerned, says that's how Loren is, it's to be expected, that the Secondhand Killer is still out there, so shouldn't Hoskins be focusing on *that* instead of babysitting his partner? And that shit makes Hoskins so mad he's ready to tell Black to go fuck himself, to turn over his badge and his gun and call it done, he hasn't been this mad in a long time. This was never supposed to be his problem, yet here he is, Loren's gone and there's a dead kid being zipped up in a bag and Sammie is upset because there's another reporter here and

Hoskins wants to go home, to catch up on the sleep he missed when he took Joe to the hospital. It's been a long day, long enough that when he thinks back to that morning, to Joe screaming, terrified and sobbing, it feels like it happened weeks ago, not in the last twelve hours.

He makes sure Jimmy Galen is all loaded up before he gets in his car and drives, heading back to the station but instead ending up at the coffee shop, and he doesn't go through but parks and watches. Trixie's working the window, wearing a yellow polka-dot bikini, like the one from the song, and her skin is perfectly tan and smooth, even though it's the dead of winter. He'd gone through the drive-thru the day before, on his way into work, and he saw the new bruise on Trixie's shoulder right under the strap of her bikini, where it looked like someone had poked her, hard. Too hard.

"Do you have a boyfriend?" he'd asked her then, and her face had closed up, right away, snapped shut, and he'd seen that look before from other women, women who were afraid of the men in their lives, always scared they were walking into a trap.

"Yes," she said immediately, and Hoskins knew that if he pushed her she'd say her boyfriend was *protective*, but he knows that code, you aren't a cop without seeing that shit all the time, men who think that women belong to them, like the way you can own a house, or a banana. He sits in the car and his eyes start to drift shut, he's tired and he imagines Trixie going home to this guy, but in his head *he's* the boyfriend, and he pokes her, smacks her in the face and chokes her, sticks her fingers in his mouth and bites down until those delicate bones start to break.

Where the fuck are these thoughts coming from?

He gets out of his car, paces back and forth across the parking lot a few times, and circles the Walmart, his head ducked against the wind. The walking's not working the way it usually does; he's still on edge, he feels like he's chewing on glass, so he finally climbs back into his car and watches Trixie pass out coffee and make change and swipe credit cards, and he nods off, his head dropping down to his chest, and that's not much of a surprise, because he's exhausted, he was at the hospital all night with his father and spent the morning with Loren, he's running on nothing but adrenaline and caffeine, and those are both in short supply.

But his dreams—God, his dreams. He's being jacked off in this one, and while this isn't unusual—most of his dreams are about sex, have been since he was thirteen—there's something about this that isn't quite right. And when he looks down, he sees what the problem is right away—it's Seever's fist pumping up and down on his dick, and he's got a cigarette clenched in his mouth, in the odd way Seever always smoked, biting down so hard Hoskins can see the indentations left on the filter.

"What the fuck are you doing?" Hoskins asks, but he doesn't push Seever away. It feels too damn good for him to want it to stop, no matter who's doing the deed.

"What's it look like I'm doing, dumbass?" Seever growls, grinning around the cigarette. He pushes his glasses up his nose. "Sometimes I wonder if you're slow."

"God," Hoskins says, and he's close, he's so damn close, Seever has got both hands in on the action, he's really working it now, and then suddenly he lets go, and Hoskins's dick is standing straight up, hard as a rock, and it's funny, the way it waves in the air, indignant.

"You're like me," Seever says, slapping away Hoskins's hands when he tries to grab himself to finish the job. "Once you start, it's so hard to stop."

"What do you want?" Hoskins says, nearly screaming. One touch, that's all he needs, and he'll come, he'll squirt like a fucking geyser. "I'm not anything like you."

And then he wakes up.

The first thing he sees is Trixie walking by, out of the coffee shop and toward an old car parked off to one side. She doesn't see him, and he's thankful for that, because if she'd come over to the window and taken a good look at him, hollow-eyed and sick-looking, a raging boner ready to split his pants, she would've run away screaming. But she doesn't see him, and she slips behind the wheel of the old car and revs the engine. It doesn't sound like much, he bets it never gets warm enough inside and will probably give up and die at some point in the near future, but what else could she possibly afford on her salary? He wishes he could help her.

Help her? Seever's voice speaks up, from somewhere deep in his brain. *Yeah, I bet you'd like to help her. Help her bend over and stick her ass up in the air.*

"Shut up, shut up!" Hoskins shouts, slamming the flat of his hand against the steering wheel, not noticing the frightened looks he gets from people walking by. "Leave me the fuck alone."

He should go home, or back to the station, but he can't stop thinking of Seever shoving him away, but it *wasn't* Seever, he tells himself, it was Loren. Wasn't it? It all seems so twisted up in his head now, and even his memory seems off. It was Loren dressed as Seever, and he'd been following Sammie, but that didn't seem right because it was Seever who used to fuck Sammie, it was Seever's voice he couldn't get out of his brain, it was always Seever, that bastard had been riding on his back like a monkey for the last seven years, whispering dirty secrets even when Hoskins couldn't hear him.

"I'm not a bad guy," Hoskins says, not even aware he's saying the words, or who he might be talking to. He's thinking about the woman who'd killed her daughter, and how good it'd felt to hear her scream, and Joe, too, how he'd fallen silent as soon as Hoskins had hit him. It's wrong to want to hurt people, he's known that since preschool, but everything feels different now. Mushed around the edges. "I'll show you. I'm not a bad guy."

He flips on his blinker, turns out onto the street. He's gripping the wheel, his nails are cutting into the leather. Trixie's car is just ahead.

Trixie lives in the kind of apartment building that would be called a tenement in a big city, but here, in the middle of Denver, USA, with a view of the mountains and a shitty park nearby, it's called an urban up-and-comer, like people expect it to suddenly get better any day now. It rises six stories up, and the only way into the apartments is through the long hallways that snake through the building, hallways that always smell like feet and urine and curry. He watches as Trixie gets out of her car and goes inside, and he's right behind her, close but not too close, because if he loses sight of her in this endless maze of doors, he'll never find her. But it's easy, she's on the first floor, he sees her open a door—15A—and slip in, and she doesn't lock it, there's no telling snick of a deadbolt being pulled. Something tells him to wait, not to burst right in, so he walks farther down the hall, his hands in his pockets, strolling, like he belongs there. He sees a few people, but no one gives him a funny look, or asks any questions—that's one of the good things about a place like this, maybe the only good thing.

After fifteen minutes he goes back to Trixie's door, twists the knob in his hand. It opens easily, and he goes inside. He is only in the apartment for a few minutes, and there's mostly silence, except one scream, a woman's scream, and then Hoskins leaves, closes the door gently behind him. There is blood on his hands—not a lot, but enough—and the blood isn't his.

Two hours into her shift at work and if somebody handed her a knife she'd probably stab someone. Or herself. She can remember a time when she thought shopping the weeks before Christmas was fun, as if being sardined into a mall and hunting for elusive gifts was a game, but now she's on the other side of it. The seedy, ugly underbelly of the retail world. She'd write about that if people were interested, but all anyone wants is blood and gore and death. Jacky Seever, and the Secondhand Killer. And she's stuck. She'd spent an hour with Seever, asking him every question she could think of, but it's not what Corbin wants. And Weber's out there now, sniffing around at crime scenes and putting together something good, and she's stuck here, waiting for a call from the guy at the gallery that she'll probably never get, and she can't think of what else she could possibly do, who she should speak to.

"There's a guy here to see you," one of the girls says, and she weaves through the crowds of shoppers, trying not to make eye contact so she won't get stopped with a question. She gets to the front of the store and looks around, thinking that it'll be Loren waiting for her, Loren-as-Seever, and she looks right past Hoskins at first, it's like he isn't even there, staring a hole through her, and then her gaze snaps back, she really sees him.

"What're you doing here?" she asks. "What happened to your face?"

There's a bruise rising on his cheek, his eyelids look swollen and red, as if he's been crying, although she can't imagine that. He reaches for her, slowly, like he's moving through water, and she grabs his arm. The sleeve of his coat is cold, covered in half-melted snowflakes.

"Is he here?" Hoskins asks, and she has to duck close to hear the words. He's looking around, his eyes darting from one corner to another, searching.

"Who?" she asks, worried, because Hoskins looks like he's hiding, like someone's following him and he's on the run, scared.

"Seever," Hoskins whispers. "You said he's been following you. Is he here?"

"Have you been drinking? You should eat something. I think we've got cookies in the back—" She tries to turn around, but Hoskins grabs her elbow hard enough that she gasps in surprise.

"I'm sorry I didn't call you about the new victim," he says, his voice shaking. "I should've called you. I love you, I should've called."

"It's fine," she says, trying to back up, but there are so many people around that there's nowhere to go, not unless she turns tail and runs.

"All I ever wanted to do was help," he says. He grabs her by the shoulders, his fingers digging into her flesh, needy, trying to pull her closer, it reminds her of the way he used to touch her when they were in bed together, and she feels the palms of her hands go hot and damp. "That's all I ever try to do."

He's not drunk. He's exhausted, reeling on his feet.

"Help with what?" she says, trying to untangle herself from his arms. "You're not making any sense."

"Yeah," he says. He's still reaching for her, trying to touch her face, but she shies away. His knuckles are shredded, bleeding.

"Oh my God. What the hell did you do to yourself?"

"Come here." Hoskins spreads his arms, and without thinking she steps into them, is enfolded in the familiar smell of him. She's short enough that she can press her forehead into his breastbone, feel the rumble of his heart. "Let me hold you."

"Hoskins?" a man says, and she turns. It's a uniformed cop, his hat still on his head, and another one a few steps behind. They're both young, hardly old enough to shave, Sammie thinks, but everyone looks young to her these days. They're both embarrassed. "Detective Hoskins?"

"Yeah?" Hoskins says. He runs his hand down over his face. "Hey, Craig. Mark."

"Listen, I hate doing this," the cop says.

"Yeah. Yeah, I know." Hoskins looks sheepish.

"What's going on?" Sammie asks.

"We have a warrant for your arrest," the cop says to Hoskins. He's looking down at the blood on Hoskins's hands. Sadly, it seems. "I don't like to do this to one of our own, but we don't got no choice in it."

"What did you do?" Sammie asks, stepping back, out of the circle of his arms.

Hoskins ignores her and sticks out his wrists.

"We don't need cuffs," the cop says, wincing. "I don't think you're a flight risk."

"Do it," Hoskins says. He nods at the crowd that's gathered around them, the people holding up their cell phones and recording the exchange. "Give these people a little excitement."

"What did you do?" Sammie asks again, grabbing at Hoskins's arm as she watches the cuffs circle his wrists. Then, a terrible idea settles into her brain. "You're not the Secondhand Killer, are you?"

Hoskins laughs.

"Wouldn't that be an amazing story? I can see the headline now—detective picking up where Jacky Seever left off. You'd better get on writing that."

There is a moment after the police have gone and the crowd has started to disperse that she wonders why Hoskins came to her, she has her arms folded across her stomach as if she's cold, or in pain, and then she sees Dean, standing off to one side, watching her. Watching her as she was watching Hoskins be led away, and in the few steps it takes for her to reach her husband she wonders how long he's been there and what he's seen, what Dean saw on her face, and for some reason she feels guilty, although she's not sure why, because she was standing in Hoskins's arms, and although it wasn't the embrace of two lovers, it might've looked that way. It *probably* looked that way.

"What are you doing here?" she asks. "You never visit me at work."

He holds out a bouquet of flowers. Red roses. Love triumphant, she thinks. But the way he's looking at her, it doesn't look like love. He looks wearily disgusted, like he's smelling something bad.

"I wanted to surprise you," he says dully. "I got a promotion. And a raise."

"You never mentioned it before."

"I wanted to surprise you," he says again.

"I didn't know."

"You don't know a lot," he says bitterly. "You don't know half the things I've done to try to make you happy."

He pushes the flowers into her hands.

"I'll see you at home," Dean says.

He doesn't kiss her goodbye.

She's afraid to go home. Not afraid of Dean, because she doesn't think he'd ever hurt her, but afraid of what he'll say. She's spent the last seven years swearing to her husband that she's not been in touch with Hoskins, and for most of that time it's been true. But this makes her look like a liar, and she could tell Dean the truth, the whole truth and nothing but the truth, but she'd still look a liar, because she's kept it from him. She never told him about following Hoskins to Simms's house, or going to dinner with him, and if he hadn't been watching she never would've told him about Hoskins coming to her work. And withholding information isn't lying, or maybe it is, and she's just trying to pull a fast one.

So she doesn't go home. After work she finds a table in the food court and nurses a cup of lukewarm coffee. There are still plenty of customers, the smell of French fries and hot pizza is thick in the air. A person might think it's impossible to be lonely while in the center of such a crowd, but that's wrong. You can be lonely anywhere.

"What's wrong?" Ethan says, pulling out the chair beside her, not lifting so the legs scrape across the floor, making a horrible sound that makes her teeth come together in a snap, and she realizes that she feels the same way she does when she's sick, or when she hasn't had enough sleep. Like the world is made from exquisitely blown glass, and she wants to put her fist through every last piece of it.

Stay the fuck away from me, she almost says, viciously. *Go back to making sandwiches and cleaning tables, and leave me the fuck alone.*

But instead her mouth drops open and she finds herself telling Ethan everything. She has to talk, to get it all off her chest, she doesn't have anyone else to speak to, and one person is as good as the next, as long as they'll sit and listen, nod their head at the appropriate places and look sympathetic. Ethan's so young and he can't possibly understand, but she tells him anyway, about Corbin not wanting her latest article, about Weber being a better reporter than she is, about visiting Seever and seeing Gloria, about Dean, about her job. She keeps her voice low, and speaks quickly, barely pausing for breath between one word and the next, because if she does she's going to cry, she'll break down in the middle of all these people and that's the last thing she wants. To have people looking at her, wondering at her tears, nudging one another and whispering. *Look at her,* they'd say. *Can't hold it together.*

"Detective Hoskins, the cop I told you about, he was arrested earlier, right in front of me," she says, shaking her head slowly. "I'm sure he's not the Secondhand Killer, but maybe I ignored all the signs. I guess he could be—"

"Tell me about the guy working for the paper," Ethan says. "Weber, is that his name?"

"Yeah. Chris Weber. God, I hate him. If he wasn't around things would be going a lot smoother."

"I'm sorry you're having a tough time," he says, and clasps his hand on top of hers. He's trying to be nice, thoughtful, but his hand is moist and warm, and she wishes he wasn't touching her, so she pretends that her nose itches and pulls away, then drops both her hands into her lap.

"Thank you for listening," she finally says. It's late, and the tables around them are mostly clear. A young woman in uniform is pushing chairs out of the way so she can sweep, and a few of the restaurants have their lights off and the metal grates pulled down. "I needed that. To get everything off my chest. I owe you one."

"I know exactly how you can repay me," Ethan says. She draws back, cringing, expecting him to suggest something that she won't want to do, dinner and sex, or just sex. "It's nothing weird, I promise. I've been doing some writing, and I was hoping you'd read some of it, give me your feedback."

"Of course," she says weakly. She's relieved, but she also feels guilty, because what kind of life has she lived, to immediately assume a man is going to ask her to spread her legs to pay back a favor? Maybe, she thinks, that's the reality every woman faces, or it's her. Oh, who is she kidding? It's *definitely* her. "Here, give me your phone, I'll program my number, and I'll take yours. We could meet sometime, have ourselves a writing workshop for two."

"I'd like that," Ethan says, smiling so sweetly that she can imagine what he looked like as a little boy. "And then I'll owe you one, I guess."

TWO
BIRDS,
ONE
STONE

If this were a movie, you'd know some bad shit was about to go down, because the music has gone low and haunting, and your heart starts beating at that same rhythm, even while your hand is digging into your greasy popcorn and you're smelling the god-awful perfume of the woman sitting two rows down. You know it's going to be bad, because the camera sweeps down through the morning sky, and it's actually blue today, a nice break in the winter habit, down to a car parked at a pump outside of a gas station, a nice SUV that burns through gasoline faster than it said it would on the dealership sticker, and it's Chris Weber squeezing the handle and dumping E85 into his tank, pissed that it's $3.49 a damn gallon and hoping that it'll get better before it gets worse, although things never seem to work that way. If gas prices keep heading up, he'll either have to sell his car and buy a bike—not a motorcycle, but a bike with pedals—or find another job. He wants to write, loves to do it, but it doesn't pay shit, and his father keeps telling him to get his real-estate license, that's where the real money is. His dad's even offered to pay for the courses, but Weber still keeps pushing back, because he doesn't want to sell houses, he wants to sell stories, and he thinks this Secondhand Killer story might lead him to something big, there's a possible book deal dangling out there, there's a lot of money. Once he writes that book his father'll have to drop the real-estate lecture, he'll have to back off. He'll see that writing for the paper isn't some phony dream. Even now people recognize him, like the guy who'd pulled up to the pump beside him, who'd peered at him for a long moment before speaking up.

"Don't you write for the paper?" the guy had asked. "Weber, right?"

"Yeah," he'd said, surprised and trying to hide it, because no one had recognized him before. "Yeah, that's me."

"Cool," the guy said, and then he'd slammed his car door and headed for the convenience store, whistling as he bopped across the parking lot, swinging his keys on his finger, round and round in a motion that made him think of a watchman swinging a nightstick. Weber had watched him, bemused. So that's what it's like to have people recognize you, he thought. He couldn't decide if he liked it or not.

He finished filling up his car—$75.84!—and pulled back onto the road. He has an interview this morning, with Gloria Seever, and he'd worked hard to get it, he'd had to talk fast to get her not to slam her door in his face.

"Gloria Seever?" Corbin had said when Weber told him. He hadn't been able to tell if Corbin was impressed or confused, not at first. "Like I told you, these pieces aren't exclusively about Seever."

"I know," Weber said quickly. "But I'm pretty sure she knows something about the Secondhand Killer, I think I could get it out of her."

That wasn't entirely true, but Weber thought a little white lie couldn't hurt anyone. With the way Secondhand was operating, he figured the guy must be communicating with Seever somehow—but everyone else thought the same damn thing. The cops were being closemouthed about it, not that they were ever helpful, and he knew Sammie had gone to visit Seever at Sterling; Corbin had called him the day before, specifically to tell him, because a sit-down with Seever might turn into something big. That's the kind of reporter Sammie is— flay the meat from the bones, go right for the jugular. Hell, that's the kind of reporter *he* wants to be, although he knows better than to compete blindly with Sammie, who is still good, even after nearly a year out of the game. Sammie knew cops, she had pull, she was able to get in to interview Seever, no fuss, no muss. He'd showed up in Idaho Springs when he'd heard about Jimmy Galen, but the cops had turned him right around, shooed him back onto the interstate and into town. But, he thought, if he were Sammie Peterson, he would've gotten a front-row invitation to the crime scene.

God, he hated her. Everything about her. Before she had the idea to pit herself against him, he'd shown up at her work, thinking that she'd help if he took her out for lunch, kissed her ass some. But she hadn't been there at all, and then Corbin called her and things went right to hell. But that was this business—if you didn't keep one step ahead, you might as well throw in the towel.

He hated Gloria Seever too, but he also felt sorry for her, because when he went to her house, hoping to speak to her, there were three words spray-painted across her front door—YOU KNEW, BITCH—and he thought it must be hard to live that way, with everyone thinking you were guilty and despising your very existence. But that didn't mean she had to slam her door right in his face when he'd knocked and said he was with the *Post*, so then he'd been forced to stand out on her front step and press his nose into the spot where the door met the frame and yell, more out of frustration than anything else.

"Please!" he'd shouted. "I need this!"

And then the door had pulled open again, maybe it was the desperation in his voice that brought Gloria back, he'd dated women like that, who operated solely on sympathy, who'd do anything if they felt sorry for you.

"Come back this evening," she'd said. Her mouth was pinched so tight that a sunburst of lines radiated out from the center, pointing out in all directions, and he realized that she was in her robe and slippers, curlers in her hair. "Around seven. I'll talk to you then."

So here he is, his tank filled and his hands freshly washed to cut the smell of gasoline, sitting on one end of Gloria Seever's sofa in her pristine living room. She's very prim, this woman, with her ankles demurely crossed and the heavy strand of pearls around her neck. There's a silver framed mirror on the wall behind her, hanging above a side table, and he can see a spot on the back of her head where the hair has parted and her scalp shines whitely through, and his own face. He looks wan, frightened, crouched on the flowered cushions. He has the strange urge to grab one of the pillows from beside him and hold it to his stomach, the way he did when he was younger and he'd constantly be sporting wood, although he doesn't have an erection now, and being in this house makes him feel like he might never have one again.

"Thirsty?" she asks, and he doesn't have a chance to answer before she starts gathering refreshments anyway, bringing them in from the kitchen. Weber can remember hearing that she'd attended every day of Seever's long trial, that she'd never cried, never showed any emotion. She was cold. Jacky Seever was a scary bastard, but Weber had to wonder what kind of woman it took to be married to him.

"I don't know anything about these new murders," she says before he has a chance to ask his first question. She was bent over the coffee table, pouring tea into fine china cups and taking cookies from a tin and arranging them on a plate. "If that's what you're here to ask me about."

"I didn't—"

"And I don't know anything about the things my husband did."

"You don't?"

"No," she says. Puts her cup down, right in the center of the saucer, so there's not the slightest sound. Gloria Seever is a careful woman.

"Then why did you agree to talk to me?"

"You said you need this. And I need this too." She takes a cookie off the plate—vanilla with pink sugar frosting—and presses her lips to it. Not a bite, but a kiss. "I want you to write about me, that I'm innocent. That I never knew about any of the things my husband did."

Weber pinches the web of flesh between his thumb and pointer finger, the same way his mother always did. She said it was a pressure point that would relieve a headache, but he never did buy it. Still, he keeps doing it.

"All right," he says finally, sighing, and flips open his notepad. This is completely pointless, no one is going to believe that Gloria Seever was in the dark about anything, and he doubts that anyone even cares at this point, but he'll go through the motions anyway, because sometimes a story sprouts out of nothing. "Let's see, where should we start? You go visit your husband at the prison, don't you?"

"Yes," she says, smoothing her skirt down over her knees.

"And how do those go?"

"We talk, catch up."

"About what?"

Gloria's thin shoulders rise up and down in a fluttery, nervous motion.

"Nothing much. I tell him if anything's happened to me. Jacky tells me about the other inmates, and the guards. What he's reading. What he's painting."

"I didn't realize your husband still painted."

"Oh, yes," Gloria says, jumping to her feet. "He's *prolific*. Someone broke in a few months ago and stole most of the work I'd brought home, but let me show you what I have left."

"Oh, that's not necessary—" he starts, but she's already gone, in another part of the house, in one of the bedrooms, he can hear her rustling around, sifting through boxes and papers. Weber leans over to grab a cookie, and the toe of his shoe hits something. At first he thinks it's the coffee table, but it's instead a wood frame with a canvas stretched over it, a *painting*, shoved under the table. He slides it out and holds it up.

"Oh my God," Weber says. He was expecting a landscape, or a few dancing clowns, not this. The subject of this painting is a nude woman, lying on her side with her arms curled up beside her head, her hair spilling over the floor—*mermaid hair*, he thinks—and the woman might be sleeping, or she might be dead, because there's blood, there are two fingers missing on her left hand and they're spouting smears of red paint. Finally, he looks at the woman's face—she's beautiful, even with her eyes closed, and she looks familiar, like someone he knows—

"It's Samantha Peterson," Gloria says. She's standing, other canvases under her arm, watching him, for God knows how long. "She and my husband were involved, once. Jacky might've been in love with her."

Weber looks at her, shocked, then again at the painting. It *is* Sammie, he sees it now.

"You know, he's never once painted me," Gloria says, sitting down. She's sad, and jealous, he can't blame her. This woman has stood behind her husband for so long, through everything, and he's obsessed with another. "He likes to paint her. He made that one a long time ago, and I've hung on to it. All this time, I've kept it with me."

"I'm sorry," Weber says, it's a stupid thing to say, but nothing else comes to mind.

Gloria makes a choking sound, low in her throat, and he half rises from the sofa, concerned; she looks like she's having a great shock, a stroke or a heart attack, an aneurysm, although he wouldn't know the difference. Her mouth is slack and her eyes open so wide he can see the red pools surrounding the whites, and he then he catches a flicker of movement in the mirror and glances up, and at first none of it seems to make sense, because there's a man standing behind him, it's the man from the gas station, the one who'd recognized him, and he's holding a golf club with both hands, raised over his head like an ax, and that seems so ridiculous that Weber smiles, he feels his cheeks creaking up as if they were made of stiff leather and sees his reflection do the same, and then he hears the man say something—or maybe it's his imagination, some nonsense about birds—and then the man brings the club down, with enough effort that the tendons in his neck are standing out like ropes, and the metal head of the club comes down with a scream and buries itself into Weber's skull with a crunch.

If this were a movie, the screen would now be fading to black.

ALRIGHT,

ALRIGHT,

ALRIGHT

"Time to wake up."

Gloria moans, tries to pull back from the hand stroking her face, but she's pinned, and when her eyes flutter open it's Jacky, a few inches away from her face. She tries to scream, but a hand clamps down over her mouth, and another pinches her nose shut, cutting off her air flow, and she struggles, tries to break free, but she can't. He's too strong. He always was. "Wake up, sweetie-pie."

She nods frantically, because she needs a breath, the darkness is already creeping in around the edges of her vision. And he's as good as his word. Once she stops struggling he lets her go, and she takes a long gasp of cool air. She can also smell Jacky—the manly, excited sweat of him, but that doesn't matter so much. The only thing that matters is that she can breathe.

"Good girl," Jacky says, rubbing his fingers through her hair. She's laid out on the couch, her head up on one arm and her feet propped on the other, and it occurs to her that the last person to sit here was Chris Weber, that nice young man from the paper, but what had happened? And then she remembers—the golf club whistling through the air and the crunch of bone. Gloria had screamed, she'd screamed until it felt as though her chest were ready to burst, and then there'd been the merciful darkness. She pinches her eyes shut, trying to get the image of Weber's last moments out of her head, but Jacky slaps her, lightly, on one cheek and then the other. "Oh, no you don't. I want you to look at me."

She opens her eyes again, but this can't be Jacky, it's dim in the room, the blinds are drawn and it must be a trick of the light, a trick of her mind. She looks at Jacky, but it isn't him, not really. Jacky is fat and old now, he's far past his prime. And Jacky is in prison, don't forget that. He's hours away from here, sitting alone in a cell, behind a locked door and four walls of concrete. This isn't Jacky but somehow it is. This man is Jacky when he was young, Jacky when they were first married, in those first few years when everything seemed so uncertain and exciting. It is Jacky, but then she blinks and it's not, it's only a boy wearing torn jeans and a sweatshirt with his hair parted sharply to the right, like Jacky always did.

"What did you do?" she whispers, and the boy smiles, there's something in his eyes that is missing, something that is dead, and she never saw Jacky like this. But then she thinks of what she found in the garage. That girl, blindfolded, and she'd known Gloria was there, she'd asked for help, and Gloria had turned and left, she'd gone back into the house and locked the door and kept her mouth shut. Gloria had never seen Jacky look like this, but that girl surely had—and what about the rest?

"This is our little secret," the Jacky-boy says, and he slips a hand up her skirt, and she slaps him, claws at his face, but he means serious business, and he is strong, and in some ways it is like the other time Jacky hurt her, but in other ways it is worse, because she thought she was safe, she thought it would never happen again, but now she knows better.

It'll never be over.

SAMMIE

Dean wasn't there when she got home, the house was empty and cold, and it had that smell a place gets when no one has been there all day. Like dust, she thinks. The flat mineral smell of water standing in toilet bowls. The furnace whooshed to life when she opened the front door, and she screamed in surprise, then laughed at herself, a little too loudly. It was unnerving, to hear all the sounds of life around her, even when she was still. The humming of the fridge, the slow drag of the wind against the siding. And a clicking sound, it reminded her of Dean clipping his toenails, and she spent an hour wandering through the house, trying to catch up with that sound before it finally disappeared.

She tried to call Dean's cell phone, but he never answered. She didn't know who else to call, or what to do. If your husband goes missing, what do you do? Search for him? She almost did that, walked out to her car with her key in her hand, and then turned around and went back inside. Denver was a big city, and he could be anywhere. She had no idea where to begin. There were hundreds of places to hide in the city, thousands, and it would've been a waste of time. Dean was angry, he was hurt, and maybe it was best to let him be that way, to wait until he came home. He knew how to find her.

So she went to bed. The sheets were ice-cold and she couldn't seem to warm up until she lay on her stomach and crossed her hands under her belly, with her face toward the big numbers on the digital clock. She fell asleep that way, and when she woke up she was sure it was morning, but only ten minutes had passed. She tried to call Dean again, but it had stopped ringing altogether, and went straight to voicemail.

"Goddammit," she said after the beep. "I know you're angry, but don't do this. Come home so we can talk about it."

Twenty minutes later:

"I've seen Hoskins a few times, but it was only because of this stuff I'm doing for the paper. But nothing's happened, Dean. I swear. Nothing happened."

And then, later:

"Go fuck yourself."

She doesn't get out of bed until the watery gray sunlight is peeking through her blinds, even though she's been awake for hours. There's no sound of a car in the driveway, or a key in the door. She pads to the bathroom and sits down on the cold toilet. Lowers her head down to her knees. Almost. She's not as flexible as she used to be.

She starts the coffeepot, sits on the sofa. The Christmas tree is still in the box, pushed halfway under the coffee table, winding pieces of packing tape holding it all together. She nudges it farther under the table with her toe. They usually put up the tree on Thanksgiving, opening up the boxes of ornaments they've collected over the years and snapping the plastic branches together, but somehow they'd forgotten it this year. They'd eaten their turkey and stuffing, and the can of cranberry sauce with the ridges still cut into the jellied sides, the same as they always did, but instead of putting up the tree they'd gone to bed, and a few days had passed before Sammie remembered what they'd forgotten. It's hard to start a tradition, to create a thing you come back to every year, but it's so easy to let it go. To give up and let it disappear, like it'd never existed at all.

She picks up the phone, calls Dean. No answer. Calls the art gallery, following up on her lead. It goes straight to voicemail. Calls the county jail and police department and Hoskins's cell, wanting an update, but there's either no answer or no one will cooperate. There's nothing more frustrating than sitting in your own home, punching numbers on the phone and expecting results and getting stonewalled. She doesn't have anything else to do but sit and *wait*; she can't leave because Dean might come back, but she should go, she still needs a piece to turn in to Corbin and there's no story here in the four walls of her own home.

All of it pisses her off, Dean and Corbin and Weber and Hoskins and the whole situation, and the tree's still in its box, just to top it all off. If Dean were here they could put it up right now, but he's not, because he's angry at her for something she didn't even do.

A text comes in, makes her phone beep and she lunges for it, snatches it up. It's from Dean.

I'm married to a whore, it says, and that's all, because Dean knows it would hurt her, that single word, he'd called her that once before, during their weekly session of couples therapy, and she hadn't cried but she'd been upset, and now it makes her furious, because she didn't do anything and she can't even explain herself; she knows that if she tries to call or text him she'll be ignored.

The coffee machine beeps to let her know it's done, but she ignores it and goes back to the bedroom, yanks on a pair of jeans and boots, a sweater. She's not thinking of the Secondhand Killer or Hoskins or Corbin or how she needs to head to work soon—she's so angry that everything else has been booted from her head, she can't focus on anything else except that one word, *whore*, that's what her husband thinks she is, and maybe she'll have to prove him right, so he can see that she doesn't care what he thinks, she'll *show him*.

He'd spent the night in a cell at the jail, lying on a thin cot that's hanging from a freezing concrete wall, and dreamt of Sammie. This isn't unusual, because he dreams about her a lot, but it's never like *this*—usually Sammie is laughing or fighting with him, or holding his dick, sliding it slowly into her mouth—but this time Sammie is *dead*, she's on the floor and her skull is smashed in on one side, so her head has the misshapen look of a deflated basketball, and it's not just blood oozing out of her head but yellow stuff too, and when he sees that several of her fingers have been cut away Hoskins opens his mouth to scream, but then there's a hand on his shoulder, shaking him awake, and it's the same cop who apologized for arresting him, Craig, and his eyebrows are drawn together over his hawk nose, worried.

"Wake up," he says, shaking harder. "You're having a bad dream. Wake up."

Hoskins sits up, his head swimming.

"What's going on?"

"It's time for you to go," Craig says. "Your bail's been posted. Here, I brought you some water. You look sick as a dog."

"Where have you been?" Ted is in his face the moment the elevator opens onto the basement. "I must've called you twenty times."

"Thirty-one, actually," Hoskins says, going straight into his office and tossing his paper sack of belongings onto the desk. Ted is right behind him. "I spent the night in jail."

"You were arrested?"

"I didn't stay for the five-star accommodations."

"Why were you there?"

"It's not important. What's been going on here?"

Ted eyes him with what seems to be pity. Looks at his wrinkled slacks and the blood still smeared into his knuckles, and it looks like he has more questions, but instead he presses his lips together in a disapproving line.

"I searched online for mentions of Seever, about him cutting off his victim's fingers."

"What'd you find?"

"Nothing," Ted says. "I must've looked through thousands of links and images about Seever, and none of them mention fingers."

"Dammit," Hoskins says, sitting at his desk, heavily. He got sleep, but it wasn't great, and he can feel his bones creaking in protest as he moves. "I was sure you'd find something."

"Well, there is this one website I've heard about—lots of crime-scene photos, torture porn. People sell the real nasty stuff to that site for big bucks. But I wasn't able to check it out."

"Why not?"

"You have to pay to be a member. And I don't have my own credit card—my mom gets all the statements. And if she knew I was looking at that kind of stuff, she'd kill me."

Hoskins blinks. Waits for Ted to say he's joking, but the kid's dead serious. In his twenties, afraid his mom will catch him doing something naughty.

"Just curious—do you go to any porn sites?"

"Only the free ones," Ted says warily. "Do you want this website or not?"

"Yeah, what is it?"

"It's called alltheprettyflowers.com. Spelled like it sounds."

Hoskins raises an eyebrow.

"And this is a website where we're going to find something that might lead us to Secondhand?"

"Yeah," Ted says. "Lots of websites give themselves an innocent name. So if someone's going through their browsing history, it doesn't stick out."

"But it shows up as a porn site on your credit card statement?"

"Yeah." Ted grins sheepishly. "I found that one out the hard way. I won't even tell you how pissed my mom was."

"All right, what was the site again?"

Hoskins's phone rings, and he holds up a single finger—wait one second.

"Hello?" he says, frowning. "Hello? Is someone there?"

There's a long moment of silence, and then Loren is there, sounding irritated.

"That was fucking weird. The damn thing didn't even ring."

"Loren?"

"Yeah. So you're out, I guess? Back at work?"

"Yeah." Hoskins closes his eyes, presses down on his eyelids until there are flashes of purple. "Where the hell have you been?"

"Well, I spent this morning getting together the cash to bail you out," Loren says, sounding amused. "Nice one, by the way. I always like to see a douchebag get his ass kicked for beating on a woman. How's the girl doing?"

Hoskins sighs, rubs his knuckles on the underside of his chin. He'd certainly given Trixie's boyfriend a few broken bones and some bruises to teach him a lesson, but Trixie hadn't seemed all that appreciative about it. She'd demanded that Hoskins leave, she'd been crying, the tears and snot mixing on her face.

"She's fine," Hoskins says. "But I get the feeling she didn't want my help."

"That's a woman for you—blowing cold one second, hot the next. Or even worse—not blowing at all." It's a joke, a bad one, but Loren doesn't laugh. Neither does Hoskins.

"Why'd you disappear yesterday?" Hoskins asks. "You walked off that scene, and no one knew where you'd gone."

"Yeah, I like it like that," Loren says. "Don't send guys out to follow me again, Paulie. It won't ever end the way you hope."

"Enough of this shit!" Hoskins shouts, suddenly furious. He sees Ted flinch back. "You've been acting crazy, Loren. You need to tell me what's going on. Right now."

"Alan Cole is dead. He died last year, I just got confirmation. Heart failure."

"What?"

"It's not Cole, Paulie. It's Sammie."

"Leave her out of this."

"Can't. Ever since she showed up at Simms's, I haven't been able to stop thinking about her."

"Stop it."

"When I visit Seever, he talks about Sammie all the time. Not his wife, not any other woman. Just Sammie. And did you know Seever paints her? I flashed around Sammie's picture at the prison, a few of the guards recognized her from the paintings he does. They said she's usually naked in the pictures. Sometimes she's dead."

"Where are you going with this, Loren?"

"I guess Seever's wife got her hands on one once, and just about shit her pants. Now, after he paints Sammie, they throw them in the garbage. Destroy them."

"I had no idea," Hoskins says, fishing out his wallet and handing it to Ted, who's pushed him gently to one side so he could get on the computer. Alltheprettyflowers.com. The page that pops up is simple—a cartoon gravestone, *RIP*, with a single white daisy sprouting from the patch of grass in front of it. It makes him think of Seever in a clown costume, a daisy pushed into his lapel.

"Seever's obsessed with Sammie, and it got me thinking, because Secondhand's obsessed with Seever. At least, that's what it looks like."

"And now you're obsessed with her?" Hoskins is watching as Ted types in his credit card information—two hundred dollars a month, it says, plus a termination fee when he cancels—scrolls through the terms of use, inputs a username and is finally in. The site is simple, nothing special, there aren't even ads running up and down the sidebars, until Ted clicks on the search tool in the top right corner and types in two words: Jacky Seever.

"I'm saying, Sammie's the common denominator in all this," Loren says, and Hoskins hears both this and the whir of his computer as it loads thousands of images onto the page, pumping everything the site associates with Seever onto his screen. Some of the pictures don't have anything to do with Seever at all, but most do. "She wrote about every one of the victims for the *Post* before, and now all of them are dead. She was fucking Seever. Her career took off because of what he did."

"Sammie didn't kill anyone," Hoskins says numbly, his eyes darting over the computer screen, horrified, taking it all in. There are crime-scene photos from Seever's crawl space, he recognizes most of them—hell, he'd *taken* some of them, those photos had all been stored in the PD's files, they were supposed to be secure. And there they are, the answer to what they'd been wondering—there are photos of victims' hands, zoomed in and cropped, the stumps made front and center.

"I didn't say she did," Loren says. "But I think Secondhand might've started all this because of her. Maybe because he caught on to Seever's obsession with her, decided to keep it going. She's back at the paper, isn't she?"

"Look at this," Ted whispers, scrolling down. The page goes on and on, into infinity, it seems, the most recent additions at the bottom. According to the time stamps, a dozen new photos have been added in the last twelve hours, all by the same user, all uploaded at the same time. SecondHand is the username, of course it is, of course he'd want to show off his work, because he wants his ego stroked, maybe he thought he wasn't getting enough attention and the sick fucks on here would give it to him, would give him a goddamn standing ovation.

The first photo added by SecondHand is of Carrie Simms, her face covered in blood, lying on her kitchen floor. Hoskins took a picture very much like it with his own phone. Hoskins scrolls quickly through the rest—Abeyta and Brody, and the boy they'd found. Jimmy Galen. There are two photos of the boy, but he's not out in the woods like they found him, he's tied up on a concrete floor, his mouth is a big circle, he's screaming, alive. Hoskins grimaces and clicks to the last photo uploaded.

"If he was doing it for Sammie at first, he's not anymore," Hoskins says. There's pressure building up behind his eyes, and he hopes he can get a few minutes alone with the Secondhand Killer, it doesn't matter that his hands are swollen and painful, he'll teach the little prick a lesson he won't forget. "We have to find her. She's in danger."

The last upload, it's Sammie, but it's *not* her. It's a painting of Sammie, propped up against a wall, Seever's signature in the bottom corner. She's naked in it, her eyes closed, and bleeding from where two of her fingers have been cut away. But it's not the painting that bothers Hoskins so much, but the caption beneath it.

She's next? SecondHand had typed. And then, added after the words, somehow making it all even worse: ☺

Sammie's gone. Hoskins met a unit at her house first thing, battered down the door when no one answered and searched the place, but no one's home. He's called her cell, called her work, called the security out at the mall, and no one's seen Sammie. He has the team at the station working on getting a hold of Dean, of her parents. Anyone who might know where she is.

He's coming out of Sammie's house when his phone rings.

"We found another victim," Loren says. "About thirty minutes ago."

"Is it Sammie?" Hoskins asks dully.

"Christ, no. Guy named Chris Weber. And you'll never believe this shit—it was Gloria Seever who called it in. He was over at her house last night, she says he was there to interview her for the paper, a piece about Seever and the Secondhand Killer. She says he left after the interview, she didn't notice he was still parked out there until this morning. He's crammed on the backseat of his own car with half his face bashed in, and all the fingers on his right hand are missing."

"You believe her story?"

"I don't know what to believe, Paulie. I went by, but I didn't talk to her—figured if she caught sight of me she'd clam right up. There're detectives with her now, trying to get to the truth of it, but you know what a closemouthed bitch she is. But we shouldn't consider her a suspect. I don't think she's strong enough to turn this guy's face into raw hamburger. That's what it looks like, *padnah*. This whole thing's gonna make me swear off red meat."

"I thought Sammie was writing about Secondhand for the *Post*."

"She was. And so was this guy. They were competing against each other for the same job, I guess. That's the story Dan Corbin fed me, anyway."

Hoskins takes a pen and a scrap of paper out of his pocket, writes *Chris Weber* down on the paper. Circles it. Draws a line, then writes Sammie's name. Ted's back at the station, trying to get a hold of the people running alltheprettyflowers.com, see if they can find out exactly who is registered as SecondHand, but it doesn't look promising. People who run websites like that prefer to remain anonymous, and they extend that courtesy to their clients. Hoskins figures it for pointless, but they have to try.

"Any word on Sammie yet?" Loren asks.

"Not a thing," Hoskins says. Something pulls against his ankles, makes him jump. It's a stray cat, mewling to be picked up, and he kicks at it, furious. "She's gone, her husband's nowhere to be found. It's not looking good."

"I didn't think you'd be okay coming over here," Ethan says, standing back so she can come inside. "I could've met you somewhere, you know."

"This is a nice neighborhood," she says, unwinding her scarf from around her neck and dropping it on a side table, beside a framed photo of an older couple, posed in a studio in their Sunday finest. The man is in a nice suit and has the sharp look of an educated gentleman, and the woman looks kind. Her white hair is styled in soft curls that seem to melt away from her face. "Who's this?"

"Who?"

"This." She points at the picture. "Your grandparents?"

"Yeah, that's them. This is their house."

"Where are they now?"

"On vacation in Florida. I'm housesitting."

"Oh." She peeks into the living room. It's a nice house, small. Lots of knickknacks and doilies, wallpaper with cabbage roses. "It smells weird in here."

Ethan rubs his hand on the back of his neck. "I need to take out the garbage."

She walks farther into the house and he's right behind her, like a puppy dog. He's nervous, she can practically feel it coming off him in waves. She'd tried to call Hoskins again, before she'd even pulled out of her driveway, wanting to see where he was; if he'd been released from jail she would've gone to him, probably fucked him, that's what Dean thinks she's been doing, so why not? But there was still no answer, and she'd been considering what to do, whether or not to go back inside and wait or head down to the police station when her phone rang in her hand, it was Ethan, calling just when she needed it most, and he invited her over to talk and now here she is, walking through his grandparents' house.

They sit, side by side on the couch. There are clear plastic covers on the arms, to keep them from too much wear, and Sammie smooths down the one on her side. Ethan is sitting so straight he could have a pole up the back of his shirt, and sequins of sweat are clinging to his forehead. When was the last time a man was so nervous around her? High school, probably, but she can't remember. It's nice, to have that kind of effect on a man. She'd forgotten how it was, that prickle of anticipation that comes before sex with someone new.

"Are you all right?" she asks, and when she touches his knee he jumps like he's been spattered with hot grease. "Do you want me to leave?"

"No. I've—I've never had anyone *want* to come here."

"What about Kelly?"

He blinks, looks away. "We broke up," he says. She waits, thinking he might say more, but he doesn't.

"I'm sorry."

"It's okay. It's for the best. We're not interested in the same stuff." He clears his throat. "I should go get my notebook, let you read what I've written so far."

"Wait."

She's never been good at starting these things. It's always the man who starts it, who touches her, kisses her. But Ethan is so young and so nervous, and he's terrified, she can see it in his eyes, and he's never going to touch her, and if she doesn't do something soon she'll end up going home. Already she can feel her resolve dissolving, this petty revenge was a stupid idea, but then she thinks of Dean, and how he's punishing her for something she didn't even do, and she wants to get back at him, even if Dean never knows she's here, even if he never finds out what she's done, *she'll* know, and that'll be enough. She slides her hand from his knee up his thigh, until she's cupping Ethan through his pants, and that's easy because he's already hard.

"Sammie," he says weakly, and she puts her hand loosely over his mouth and holds it there. There's a cut over one of his eyebrows, shallow and mean-looking.

"Shut up," she says, and he groans when she undoes his pants and he springs free, his eyes roll back in his head and he's already trembling, lifting his hips into her hand so she'll take more. "Sit still, don't move. Let me do it."

But it's already over, before she can do anything else, it's gone before it's even there, deflated to nothing in her hand, and he's crying, Ethan is actually weeping from embarrassment, and he grabs her hand, wipes it clean on his shirt, leaves a gleaming smear across the fabric.

"I'm sorry," he says. "I've never been with anyone like that."

She's not sure if he means he's never gotten a handjob, or if he's never had sex.

"It's fine," she says, pulling away. "It happens all the time. Really, it's fine."

She pats his back awkwardly, wanting to be kind, but she's already wondering how soon she can leave, what excuse she could give to get out the door. And then her phone rings, *perfect*, she pulls it out of her purse and glances at the screen. It's the Denver PD calling, maybe she'll finally know what happened to Hoskins, where he is.

"Excuse me," she says. "I have to take this."

She gets up and steps outside the room, tugging on the bottom of her shirt as she puts the phone up to her ear. It's funny, how quickly things can go wrong, although she's never had it go bad quite that fast.

"Hello?" she says, but there's no answer, only a low-pitched hum. "Is anyone there?"

"You'll have to go outside if you want to hear them," Ethan says from the living room. "Phone service is hit or miss in this house."

"Oh. Okay. I'm gonna go wash my hands, and then I'll step out and call them back."

There's a powder room off the front hall, and there's a dish of soaps shaped like seashells beside the sink basin, the towels on the rack are looped off at the middle with thick lengths of raffia ribbon that've been tied into bows. It reminds her of Seever's house, because Gloria had decorated like this—carefully, thoughtfully. She washes her hands, turning one of the soap-shells in her palms to get a lather going, and dries her hands on the thighs of her jeans.

She comes out of the powder room and pauses to look at the photos nailed up on the wall before going outside. There are a lot of them—pictures of the grandfather in a business suit, the grandmother rowing a boat on a lake. It looks like Ethan's grandparents are travelers, but there are no children in the photos. Lots of friends, it looks like, lots of good times. Sammie peers at a few of the photos, looking for Ethan's face among the old ones, but she doesn't spot him. But Ethan's shy—maybe he doesn't like his picture taken.

The wall of photos, it makes her think of Seever's house. Again. She hasn't thought of the time she'd spent in that house for a long while, but now it's come up twice in the last few minutes. Why? This little house is nothing like Seever's McMansion.

Her phone buzzes in her hand as she's looking over the photos, but it's a text this time, from a number she doesn't recognize. I'D FORGOTTEN I HAD THE GUY WHO CALLS ABOUT SEEVER'S STUFF STILL SAVED IN MY CALLER ID. HERE'S HIS NUMBER.

The art dealer, she realizes. Simon. She'd thought he might not get back to her at all, that she'd have to search out a new angle, but it looks like things are about to turn around. Fuck you, Weber, she thinks, tapping on the number Simon had sent over and starting a text.

HI, she types. I WAS TOLD YOU'RE LOOKING TO BUY SOME OF SEEVER'S ARTWORK. PLS CALL OR TXT ME BACK. THX.

She finishes, hits Send. Then, she hears a muffled, canned voice, coming from somewhere nearby.

Alright, alright, alright. She recognizes the sound—it's a cell-phone alert, the kind you download and use instead of the standard ring or beep. She's heard all kinds of them, usually while at work—alarms set to sound like Christmas music or belches or even the revving engine of a racecar—and she's even heard this particular one before, used by a woman who blushed bright-red when the man's voice bellowed out of her purse. *It's from* Dazed and Confused, the woman had said. *I love that actor, but I can never remember his name.*

"Was that your phone?" Sammie asks.

"I must've gotten a text," Ethan says.

She can hear Ethan moving around, shifting pillows and books, hunting for his phone.

"Oh. Okay."

I'D REALLY LIKE TO MEET WITH YOU, she types. Hits Send.

Alright, alright, alright.

"I didn't realize you had that ringtone," she says slowly. It can't be a coincidence, that she sends a text and Ethan's phone immediately goes off. Can it? Oh, stranger things have happened, she's crazy for even thinking it, but she still takes a shuffling step toward the front door.

"I actually have two phones. I pay for one, my mom pays for the other."

"I've never heard of someone having two phones," she says.

Or maybe she was crazy for not thinking it sooner.

"It helps me keep things separate," he says. "Otherwise it gets confusing."

I HAVE A QUESTION.

Send.

Alright, alright, alright.

Ethan. She never found out his last name, doesn't know anything about him except that he made sandwiches for a living. But he'd known all about her, right from the very beginning, because he'd read all her articles in the *Post*, he'd especially enjoyed the ones about Jacky Seever. And she'd liked the attention, she'd told him things about the case, more than she should've, Ethan was good at listening, he was kind, and he'd been interested in her writing, and he had a crush on her, it felt good to have a man look at her like that, even if he was just a kid, he was harmless.

Wasn't he?

"Maybe I should go over your writing some other time," she says, still typing into her phone. She can't stop, not now. She has to know.

ARE YOU THE SECONDHAND KILLER?

Send.

Alright, alright, alright.

She should run, but she can't seem to move. If this were a movie, she thought, I'd be screaming at the dumb bitch not to stand there like an idiot but get moving. The killer's in the next room, you've got to go. Good advice, but sometimes life is more like a movie than most people realize, and she's frozen to the spot, watching her phone and waiting.

Her phone vibrates in her hand and the screen lights up. She has her answer.

YES. Then, a beat, and another message: I DID IT FOR YOU.

Sammie barely has time to read the text before Ethan comes loping around the corner, and she finally tries to run for the front door but it's too little too late, he's fast and the hall is short and then he's on her, dragging her deeper into the house, and she's screaming, fighting, and it's only then that she realizes why she's been thinking of Seever. It's the smell. This place smells like Seever's did when they were digging up the crawl space.

Piece together the victim's timeline. That's what Hoskins keeps telling himself as the minute hand on his watch ticks forward. Find out where Chris Weber had been in the hours before his death. The minutes. He repeats this to himself, mutters it under his breath until people are looking at him like he's crazy.

Sammie is still nowhere to be found.

"Don't think about her right now," Loren says. "She's probably out shopping. At the spa. Turned her phone off. You need to focus. Weber's been dead less than twelve hours. He's our best chance of finding the Secondhand Killer. Maybe someone saw them together before Weber was killed."

But Loren knew as well as he did—Sammie wasn't at a spa, and she wasn't shopping. Sammie was probably dead, her fingers cut off and her head smashed in. Seever might've loved Sammie, cared for her, he'd painted her picture and kept her name on his visitor's list, and the Secondhand Killer had picked up on that, maybe he loved Sammie now too. Hate is a dangerous thing, Hoskins knew, but love can be even worse.

Chris Weber lived on his credit cards, used them for everything. Rent, food, his online shopping addiction. He was close to maxed out on several of them, barely keeping from drowning in debt. Not that Hoskins is judging—he's toting around plenty of financial garbage himself, even ten years after his divorce.

But one good thing about all that debt: it makes it easy to track Weber once the banks start cooperating and sending statements. According to his boss, Weber had spent most of the day before at the *Post*'s office downtown, then left late in the afternoon, without telling anyone where he was going. But they could see what he'd done by where he'd spent money—thirty-two on an early dinner at a Mexican restaurant, then seventy-five on gas.

"These are the last places he went before he stopped at Gloria's place," Loren says. "Let's meet at the gas station, we'll work backwards from there."

It's a kid named Davey working the front counter, who'd been the only employee around when Weber had come through. He's pulling hot dogs off the rollers when Hoskins and Loren come in, dumping them right in the trash and putting new ones on.

"Does anybody ever eat those things?" Hoskins asks, grimacing.

"Oh, yeah. There's this whole subset of people supporting the popularity of gas-station food. It's an underground movement." Davey eyes him, taking in his slacks and pressed white shirt, the gun holstered at his belt, then at Loren, who still hasn't given up Seever's suits. "I'm sure you guys aren't familiar with it."

Hoskins grins. He likes smart-ass kids.

"You remember seeing this guy yesterday?" Loren asks, holding out his phone. It's a photo of Weber, snatched right off the *Post*'s website.

"Most people pay at the pump, I never see them," Davey says. "And I don't remember that dude coming in."

"You got cameras?"

"Oh, yeah." Now Davey is excited, walking fast through the store toward the back room, his orange smock flapping out behind him. "State-of-the-art shit, man. The owner put it all in a few months ago. The best there is."

"I need to see footage of the pumps. See if this guy talked to anyone, if he was acting strangely."

"He dead?"

"Why would you think that?" Hoskins asks.

"Because the only time I ever see cops come around is if someone's dead or getting high," Davey says. He takes the bulky headphones from around his neck where they'd been hanging like a noose and spins them on his forearm. "This something to do with that Secondhand Killer?"

"We can't tell you that."

"Okay, okay. But I want you to know I have an alibi for the last twenty-four hours."

"I'm not accusing you of anything."

"No, sir. You're not."

"You afraid of us, kid?" Loren asks.

"Nah," Davey says. "But my momma told me that if a cop ever comes around asking questions, I should keep my mouth shut and smile real pretty."

She turns on the shower, waiting for the hot water to make it through the pipes, and looks at her naked body in the mirror. She'll turn fifty-six next year—not bad, a goodish age. Not old enough to be out of her mind, but still old enough. Her breasts were the first to go—they went from high and firm to loose bags of flesh hanging from her chest, and she could've had plastic surgery, had them fixed for all eternity; they'd had plenty of money for that, but she didn't. She didn't like the idea of going under the knife, so instead she bought bras and creams and cure-alls, although nothing worked the way it was supposed to. And her stomach was always so flat, nearly concave, but is now a pooch that rounds out uncomfortably even though she's never given birth to any babies, never been overweight. But that's getting old, she thinks. Her eyes are bad, her lips lined. She's spent thousands of dollars to make herself look better, but for what? None of that matters. She looks in the mirror and sees only herself.

Today's reflection is different from usual, though. The sensitive spot of flesh below her nose is swollen from where the Jacky-boy had clamped his hand over her mouth, and there's a bruise rising on her left cheekbone, but it's not much, nothing that couldn't be covered with makeup. All it took was a dab of concealer and she was good; the detectives who'd had so many questions about Chris Weber for so long had never even mentioned it. But that was men for you—they only saw what they wanted to see, they overlooked the little things. Like the bruises on her face, and the way she'd moved, slowly and carefully, favoring her right hip, because she was sore and tired—some of it was from what the boy had done to her, but most of it was because of the cleaning she'd done after he'd left. Oh, it would've been easy enough to leave Chris Weber on the floor where he'd fallen; she could've called the police and told them exactly what happened, they would've had to believe her, all they'd have to do is examine her and they'd know she was telling the truth. But she hates the police, hates the way they treat her when they realize who she is, so before she put much thought into it she was taking care of the problem herself, the way she always has. She dug Weber's keys from his pocket and pulled his car into the garage, careful that the door had shut all the way before rolling him onto an old comforter and tugging it through the house. It took her three hours to move him thirty feet, she almost quit a dozen times, but the thought of having a corpse in the house with her was so revolting that she couldn't bring herself to stop. Besides, it was too late to call the police—they'd want to know what she was doing with the body, why she was moving it. So she dragged him out, wadding the blanket up in her hands and pulling, wincing when the back of his skull cracked against the steps leading down into the garage, but she finally managed to bundle him into the backseat, and even though her back was twinging painfully and she'd never been more exhausted in her life, she cleaned up. Threw the comforter into the washing machine and got out her cleaning supplies and wiped up the blood—there wasn't all that much of it, except in the spot where Weber had fallen to the ground, and she was still able to get most of it up off the hardwood, except the faintest maroon shadow, and that could've been mistaken for a red wine stain, but she still scooted the rug over it. Of course, if the police decided to run their tests on her floors they'd know the truth in a second—she was a good housekeeper, but not *that* good. Then she pulled Weber's car out of the garage, planning to drive it across town and abandon it in some parking lot, or on an old dirt road, but instead left it out front, in the same place Weber had parked. She didn't consider herself a lazy woman, just tired, and she didn't think her brain was capable of carrying out any sort of plan, not in such an exhausted state. The last thought she had before collapsing onto her bed and falling to sleep was about Jacky, and wondering how he'd kept it up for so long.

She'd called the police when she woke up, and covered the bloodstains left on the sofa with a big velvet throw. The two cops had sat on that couch, right on top of the evidence they needed, one of them even complimented how soft the blanket was and she'd had to bite her tongue to keep from laughing. What a joke it was—not necessarily a good one, but still. It might've been easier to skip calling the police, but the thought of someone discovering Chris Weber out there—a *child*, heaven forbid—forced her to pick up the phone and dial. And the police came, they poked around and seemed satisfied with her reasoning that she'd always been targeted because of Jacky—*look at what some-one spray-painted on my front door, officers*—that maybe this Second-hand Killer was trying to send a message, she knew they'd be back sooner or later, but they would stay away for a while, because she's not a suspect, not an old lady like her.

She looks in the mirror, runs her fingers over her cheeks and pulls her skin taut. She's aged, of course, but that doesn't make the reflec-tion any different from the day before, or the day before that. No, the real changes aren't so obvious. It's in the tightly drawn skin around her eyes, the valleys that're suddenly bracketing her mouth. For the first time she looks old. She never looked like this before, even when Jacky was first arrested, those terrible months when he was on trial and she wasn't sure what was going to happen to her.

The bathroom is filled with steam now, billowing out over the top of the shower curtain, and she swipes her palm against the mirror, leaving behind a clear fan shape. The Jacky-boy had kissed her when it was over, gently, on her eyebrow, and absently patted the side of her face. *I'll be back soon,* he'd said, and then he'd left. She stayed there on the couch for a while, holding her torn skirt against her chest and feel-ing the rush of warm air from the vents against her bare legs. It oc-curred to her then, looking at the popcorn-textured ceiling, that Jacky would always be a part of her life, in one way or another, and that's how it would be, until the end of time.

This is our little secret, the boy had said, and she'd always been good at keeping secrets, she'd kept all of Jacky's for so long, she'd kept him safe, it might've been the only thing she was ever good at. She'd kept his secrets their entire marriage, until she saw the girl out in the garage, tied and blindfolded, and even then she'd been prepared to stay silent, to stand behind her husband *till death do us part,* until she dreamt that night of going into the garage again, of going to the girl and yanking off her blindfold, but then she saw it wasn't a girl at all, she was staring into her own eyes.

There are pills in the medicine cabinet, some of them were prescrip-tions filled in Jacky's name that she'd never bothered to throw out, she'd toted them all over, one home to another. Pills are funny in that way, you save them, *hoard* them, even when you no longer remember what they're for, even when the expiration date has gone by, *just in case.* And she needs them now, takes all the orange prescription bottles out, lines them up on the top of the toilet. She fills the cup she uses to rinse after brushing her teeth and starts, shaking a few pills from one bottle into her palm and then swallowing, drinking the water so fast a spike of pain settles into the center of her forehead, until her belly feels bloated and full, swishing with liquid. She thinks of the garage as she swallows the bitterness down, the boom-boom room, and of the girl with the ropes around her wrists and ankles, the blindfold over her eyes. She'd known Gloria was there, and she'd asked for help, and Gloria had left, she'd made dinner and then went to bed and the next morning she'd gone straight to the public library and asked to use the phone, because she couldn't think of anywhere else to go—she hadn't seen a pay phone in years, didn't have a clue where to find one, and she didn't want to do it from home, not for this. The woman behind the counter was more than happy to let her make a call, because the Seevers made generous donations, and Gloria smiled and waited for the librarian to wander away before she dialed.

"I have information on a case you're investigating," she'd said quietly. Pleasantly, so no one would think anything was wrong and come over to eavesdrop. A little boy ran by and smiled at her and she returned it, twiddled her fingers, like everything was normal, just another day, but she'd never felt quite so cold inside, so empty. "Those missing people, the ones the police are looking for? I've seen them, going into a house, and they never come out again. Yes, I know the address. And also, I'd like to remain anonymous."

Gloria opens another bottle, shakes out more pills. More and more, until the cup of her palm can't hold any more.

"You love him, don't you?" the boy had asked, as he'd been buttoning his pants. He'd shaken his head—in awe, or admiration. "Everything you did for him. You're the perfect wife."

That girl in the garage—she'd been cold. There were goose bumps on her bare skin. She'd been wearing nothing but panties and a T-shirt, and her lips were purple.

Gloria presses her face into the towel hanging from the rod. It's one of the rough ones, and the fibers scratch at her face—she usually saves those for mopping up spills and isn't sure how it ended up here, but it doesn't matter this time. She goes over to the shower and turns on the faucet.

The girl, she'd begged for help. And Gloria had gone back inside the house, snapped the padlock back in place. And then she'd made dinner. And now that girl is dead. Finally dead. Gloria saw it on the news, not too long before.

She pulls back the shower curtain, carefully steps into the tub. The water is turned up as hot as she can stand, and she lets it run over her shoulders, burning down her body.

She's kneeling beside a steaming pile of her own vomit.

"What the hell am I supposed to do now?" Ethan demands, pacing in front of her, three steps to the left, and then back again. They're in the living room, where just a while ago they'd been ready to do the dirty, but now it couldn't have gone further in the opposite direction. The coffee table is pushed out of the way, and Sammie is kneeling where it had stood, one of her knees sunk into the divot left in the rug. Her thighs are spread painfully wide, and her wrists are tied behind her back and to her ankles with a length of twine that Ethan had pulled from his pocket. He was prepared. "Why'd you have to be poking around in things that aren't your business?"

"I was chasing a story," she says simply. She's not crying, her eyes are hot and dry in their sockets, more like loose marbles than what she uses to see. "Besides, the police will catch up with you sooner or later."

"The police?" Ethan laughs wildly. "Those idiots can't find their own assholes. I'm not worried about them."

She's never seen this side of Ethan. With her, he's always been kind and sweet, soft-spoken. Not like this. But maybe he's right. Hoskins and Loren might never catch him. He might go on operating for a long time, the way Seever did.

"Why're you doing this?" she asks. "You're a good guy."

He stops his frantic pacing and stares at her like she's an idiot. Like the answer should be obvious.

"I started all this for you."

"What?"

Ethan drops down to his knees on the rug so they are face-to-face, only inches from each other. From this close she can see the black-heads scattered across his nose, the one hair in his eyebrow that's so much longer than the others. It's funny, she hadn't noticed any of that before, when she was ready to sleep with him, but now she's repulsed.

She tries to shift back, to put some space between them, but he has her locked down tight.

"All you'd ever talk about was working for the *Post*," he says slowly. His eyes are glowing with a fevered light, and when she tries to look away he pinches her cheeks and forces her to look at him. "About your work on Seever. I knew that if people thought Seever was back, the paper would let you write again. And they did, didn't they? That's exactly what happened."

"You didn't have to. No one asked you to do any of this."

"No, no one did," he says, grinning, his eyes rolling. "But I did anyway. And you got to write again, didn't you? I've never seen you so happy. And I was the one who made you that happy. *I* was."

Ethan's hair is stiff with gel and hair spray, his scalp is shining whitely beneath. It's the same way Seever always wore his hair. When did he start doing it like that, and why didn't she notice?

She tilts her head back as far as it will go, until the tendons in her neck scream in protest. Maybe, she thinks, Seever was meant to kill her. She'd asked why he'd let her live, and he didn't have an answer, there wasn't an answer; he didn't *let* her live, it was just delayed a little. She'd managed to put it off for a few years, but it's all already been written, and a person can hide from fate for a while but can never be free of it altogether.

Maybe, she thinks, she always belonged to Seever, and she always will.

"I love you," Ethan says, running his thumb down her exposed throat. It makes her shudder, in revulsion, and in fear, but with something else too. Anticipation? "I love you so much, so I gave you a story to write. I got rid of that Chris Weber. You hate him, you told me that. I did it for you. All of it."

He tilts his chin up at a childish angle, daring her to argue with him. She doesn't.

"This isn't your grandparents' house, is it?" she asks. Tries not to think about Weber, or Carrie Simms, or anyone else. She's not going to ask, she's not giving him the satisfaction.

He blinks, twice in a row, hard. "How'd you know?"

"You're not in any of the pictures."

That makes him smile. "You caught me," he says. "I'm staying here for a while."

"Where are the people who live here?"

"Oh, they're around," Ethan says absently, and she has to bite her lip, hard, to keep from moaning. That's what the smell is, she should have known.

"If you love me, let me go," she says instead. "Untie me and let me go."

"I do love you," he says. "Seever loves you too. I saw one of his paintings yesterday, of you. Have you seen it?"

"No."

"He made you beautiful." Ethan ducks his head and smiles, a coy smile that makes her shudder, and then it disappears, and everything is dark. "And he made you dead."

"Please, let me go. I want to go home."

"No." Ethan gives her a sly look. "If I let you go, you'd go to the police. You'd tell them everything."

He leans closer. He smells of sweat and piss, of food gone bad. It's the smell of insanity, she thinks, as if his pores have opened up and bloomed with crazy.

"You would tell on me, wouldn't you?" he asks. "You'd turn me in?"

He's waiting for her answer; her life depends on it. She could lie and tell him no, that she'd never turn him in, thank him for everything he's done. She's been telling lies her whole life, she's been weaving her stories at the loom and pulling the threads tight, she's good at it, she could make Ethan believe, and he might let her go, but he might not. He has an eager look in his eyes; he's waiting for her to say something, to tell him she loves him, to plead for her life, because he *loves* her, that's what he says. It's a boyish look, the desperate look of a man terrified of rejection, but there's something else there too, buried deep under that charm but still peeking through, just around the edges but it's enough for her to see.

It's nothing. Nothing at all. A screaming void that swallows up everything it can. He's used her as an excuse, said that he killed all those people for her, that she'd wanted him to, and maybe he believes it, but it was really for himself; he'd probably been fantasizing about killing for a long time and needed an excuse to soothe what scraps of conscience he might've had, and he'd latched on to her. And even if she lies to him, it'll be the same. He doesn't love her. He'd been the one to call her, he knew she was coming over, he'd already had the twine in his pocket. He was prepared. It's all the same to him. He wants her to beg and cry, but it'll be the same in the end. *Do you like it fast or slow?*

Seever had asked her once, and she'd found it funny then, but now it's horrible, it has a completely different meaning.

So she doesn't bother lying. Not because she's a hero, not because she wants to die, but because she's so damn tired of it all. And she's angry that she'd fallen right into this, that she hadn't had a clue, and now here she is, and she wants to hurt him.

"I would go straight to the police, I'd tell them everything," she says. "I'd tell them that you killed all those people. That you're a sick fuck." She blinks, slowly. "I'd tell everyone that you couldn't get it up, even when I was jiggling your dick in my hand."

He flushes, ugly red from his scalp all the way down his neck, and he leans over, pulls open the side-table drawer, and grabs a pair of wire cutters with bright-yellow handles. They could be brand-new, except for the dark spots on the blades. It could be rust, she thinks. Could be. But who does she think she's kidding? They look sharp, and she knows they'll have no trouble cutting through her flesh and bone.

"Pause it, right there," Hoskins says, leaning over Loren to get closer to the TV screen. They've been sitting in the front of the bank of video equipment for the last two hours, moving backward and forward through the recordings of the day before, in the ten-minute window when Weber was there. It should've been simple enough, but the owner had installed a lot of cameras, and there were a lot of pumps to watch— twelve of them total—and although the credit card statement told them *when* Weber was there, it didn't tell them *where* he'd been. There was a lot of footage to zip through. But finally, Davey had found something. "That's him. That's our guy."

It's Weber all right, alive and well, his head a few hours from being beaten in. He sticks the pump into his tank and starts it up, then looks up at the sky, shades his eyes with the flat of his hand. He looks disgusted, as if he's completely disappointed with the winter weather, then turns and climbs back into his car.

"He didn't talk to anyone," Loren says. "He filled up his tank and drove off."

"Rewind it a bit," Hoskins tells Davey, who twists a knob and pushes some buttons. "Look. Right there. He stops for a second. See how his head moved? Like he's listening. Someone at the next pump said something, and he nodded. He might've said something, but we can't see his face from this angle."

"Can we look at this from a different camera?" Loren asks.

"I can do a lot better than that." Davey pounds on the keyboard, his fingers moving faster than Hoskins can see, and then there's suddenly a new image frozen on the screen. It's a still of a young man, dark-haired and dark-eyed, his face a ghostly smear on the recording. "This is the guy Weber would've been talking to. And there's his license plate."

"I've seen him before," Loren says, getting so close his nose is nearly touching the screen, the image is all pixelated at that distance, worthless, but Loren doesn't back up. "He was with Sammie. At the mall. They were at dinner. He's just a kid."

Davey passes a slip of paper to Hoskins with the license plate number.

"Good work," Hoskins says, patting the boy on the shoulder. "You should come work for the PD one day."

Davey shrugs, smiles. It's a smile Hoskins knows exactly how to read: *Thanks, but no thanks.*

He'd turned his phone off the night before, so he wouldn't be tempted to answer when she called, and checked in at a motel. It was one of those extended-stay places, where there's a whole living room setup, and a small kitchen table. A coffee maker with the smallest pot he's ever seen and those tiny bottles of shampoo and conditioner that're never quite enough. Life in miniature. There's something desperately sad about a place like this, because a hotel isn't supposed to be a home, or even a shadow of a home, but he'd gone there anyway, checked in then went to the bar next door and picked up a box of buffalo wings and brought it back to his room, flipped through the TV and couldn't find anything because the channels were all out of order and not what he's used to, and ended up going to bed. But he didn't sleep, not much, because Sammie's not there beside him. They've had their problems, but they've always slept in the same bed every night from the beginning, and he's used to the weight of her next to him, the smell of the perfume she uses.

All of this, Sammie's unhappiness, her infidelity, it's because they didn't have a wedding, he thinks. It's not all of the reason she's unhappy, but it's part of it. They'd dated for eight months when he proposed, and she'd been so excited, so ready to look for a dress and a cake and then he'd had to tell her that they couldn't afford it, it was silly to spend the money on a single day, just a few *hours*, really, and she'd agreed, and he'd thought that was the end of it. They signed the papers and ate a nice dinner and both of them went right back to work the next day, and he'd thought it was fine, being married was hardly different from dating, and he liked it that way. No bump in the road. But then, after they'd been married for two years, Sammie started bringing home magazines full of wedding gowns and floral arrangements, she said they could have a ceremony and renew their vows, but he'd still thought it was a waste of money, and she dropped it. Sammie didn't nag; when she was angry she didn't talk at all, she wanted to be alone, and he sometimes couldn't tell when something was wrong until it was too late, and she'd scream until her face had gone an alarming shade of red and he thought she'd pass out from the effort.

She was unhappy because they didn't have a wedding, but it was more than that. It was because he was a disappointment. Like his job. He'd worked at the same marketing firm for the last ten years, he'd never been offered a promotion or even had interest in one, because he was good at his job, he was happy, he didn't think life was all about work, but he knew Sammie saw it as a flaw. She had girlfriends whose husbands made a lot of money, guys who were lawyers or doctors or executives, and those women went on nice vacations and had nice cars, and Sammie didn't complain, no, that wasn't her, but he could see it in her eyes. The disappointment.

She'd brought it up only once, when they were side-by-side in bed. The lights were all out and they weren't touching, the blankets were tamped down between them, keeping them apart.

"I thought you were a different man when I married you," she'd said. "I didn't expect things to be like this."

She wasn't cruel about it, only matter-of-fact, and then she rolled over on her side, away from him, and went to sleep. He'd wanted to grab her shoulder, to see the startled look in her eyes when she woke up, and demand to know what she meant, that she explain how he was so different, tell him what she wanted.

But he'd let her alone.

And then she'd started sleeping with that cop, and later she'd told him that it wasn't because of him, it wasn't because he made her unhappy but because of work, that the pressure to get the story drove her to it, and he'd forgiven her, but forgetting is a completely different thing, and he sometimes still asks her about Hoskins when they're having sex, asks what it was like to fuck Hoskins, if he went fast and liked to prop her legs up on his shoulders, if she let him push it into her asshole, and she never answers, just turns her face away, and sometimes he thinks she might be crying but if he runs his hand on her cheeks it always comes away dry. That's why he finally asked for that promotion—because his wife is so disappointed in him that it doesn't even make her cry anymore.

He gets up after a night of broken sleep, and showers, brushes his teeth. The water coming from the tap tastes strange and there are tiny ants circling the drain.

Maybe all this is my fault, Dean thinks. He's always bringing up Hoskins, making Sammie think of him. He turns on his cell phone. Lots of missed calls, and a few voicemails.

Nothing's happened. I swear.

And, Go fuck yourself.

He decides to go home. They'll fight, he thinks, and then they'll make up. Things can go back to the way they've always been, because maybe she's telling the truth. She's been writing for the *Post* again, covering the Secondhand case, and maybe that's the reason Hoskins had gone to see her at work. Even if it's not, they can work things out, they always do. They've been married too damn long to just throw everything away.

But Sammie's not home. And she's not at work. Not answering her phone.

So Dean does what he does, he signs onto the computer and tracks her phone. It's amazing, the things technology can do these days, and it pulls her up immediately—well, not *her*, but a blue dot that's supposed to be her. It's not that he doesn't trust his wife, but it's addictive, and he likes to sign in at random times and check in, see how accurate it is. Pretty damn spot-on, he knows that, even if she's walking around at work with her phone in her pocket he can sit in front of the computer and watch the blue dot move.

His phone rings as the screen finishes loading. She's in a house, not too far away, and it feels like the blood is all rushing to his forehead, thundering through the veins there. She's with Hoskins, he knows it, when he didn't come home she ran right out so she could jump into bed with him—

His phone rings in his hand.

"Goddammit, Sammie—"

"Mr. Peterson? This is Jenna at the Denver Police Department." The woman is talking fast, so he can barely understand what she's saying. "I've been trying to reach your wife—"

"She's with that goddamn detective," Dean cries. "That's where she is. Detective-fucking-Hoskins."

There's a pause, a long one, and then the woman speaks again, sounding strange.

"Actually, it's Detective Hoskins who asked me to call you."

"She's not with him?" There's a heavy feeling settling on his chest, like he's being slowly suffocated. Something is very wrong, because the police wouldn't be calling otherwise, it's bad when the police call a person; he knows that from Sammie. *If I've been murdered, they'll call you right away,* Sammie had told him once. She'd been joking, and he'd told her to shut up, that he didn't want to talk about those things happening, it was like a wish, in reverse. If you talked about it, it *would* come true. *They'll probably ask if you know where I am, because the spouse is always the main suspect, at least at first.*

"No, sir. It's very important that we locate her. Do you happen to know where she is?"

That blinking blue dot.

"Sir?" the woman says. "If you know where she is, please tell me."

If I've been murdered. Sammie would laugh about things like that, make it into a joke, even after he asked her to stop. He doesn't think those kinds of things are funny. *They'll call you right away.*

Dean hangs up. The blue dot isn't moving, but it's still blinking. He's going to find his wife.

The blue dot has led him to a house that is small and brick, set far back from the street, and there's Sammie's car parked out front, the black car with the crack running through the left side of the windshield, he'd wanted to get it fixed but Sammie had said no, that it didn't interfere with her line of sight, that she didn't want to have to pay the deductible. He's scared, his stomach is roiling in his gut but he still pulls right into the driveway and climbs out without bothering to turn off the car. The front door is unlocked and he pushes it open, expecting someone to greet him with a gun; he'll be shot because he's trespassing—*This is private property, son, get out*—and he wonders why the hell he'd rushed out of the house without bringing a weapon. Not that he owns a gun, but it would've been easy enough to bring a knife, or one of the golf clubs from the set Sammie had bought him a few years ago. He wishes he had something in his hands, anything, the weight would be comforting to hold, but the only thing he has with him is his wallet, and how could it possibly help, to clutch a square of leather in front of himself like a nervous woman holding a purse? In the end, Dean goes in with nothing but himself, and his fear.

But no one meets him at the door, except for the smell, it's bad enough that he has to press the back of his hand over his nose to keep from being sick. He's trying to keep his gag reflex under control so he doesn't hear it at first, he doesn't hear *her*, it's Sammie. She's crying, and she's very close, just in the next room, and he runs down the hall and is so surprised by what's going on in the living room that he's frozen for a moment, there's a man kneeling over Sammie, busy and not paying attention, and Dean's not sure what to do, there's so much blood and he's not a violent man, he's not prone to action, he's a cubicle jockey who sits at a desk and types ninety words a minute. Not a man who knows how to deal with this.

But it turns out he doesn't have to know how to deal with a situation like this, because instinct takes over and he grabs the floor lamp sitting by the door—it's the kind of lamp old women seem to prefer, tarnished gold with a thick glass bubble halfway up, twinkling crystal droplets hanging from the shade—and he hefts it up like a baseball bat, the heavy bottom propped up on his shoulder. Dean went to college on a baseball scholarship, they called him Big D back then, and he swings the lamp easily enough, it's much lighter than the old maple bats he used to practice with, practically flies through the air of its own accord. His muscles remember the familiar movement and slide easily against one another, even though it's been years since he hit a ball. He swings that metal lamp hard enough that he feels something tear painfully inside his shoulder, and there's a moment Dean will always remember, when time seems to slow down, to nearly stop, when the crystals that've come loose from the lampshade are turning end-over-end through the air, sparkling as they catch the light, and the base hits the man in the temple, right in the sweet spot. And then everything speeds up again, like a rubber band snapping into place, and the man is facedown on the floor, not moving.

The medical examiner's verdict: Ethan Hobbs was dead before he hit the ground.

Dean's old baseball coach would've been proud of that swing, he would've shouted and hollered if he saw it, he would've ripped his hat off his head and thrown it up in the air in celebration. *Swing, batter-batter, swing,* Dean thinks vaguely as he crumples to the ground, not far from his wife—it's not only the pain that's bringing him down but also the realization of what he's done. Dean has kept his word to Sammie, that he would kill for her, if he had to.

The car is registered to Glen and Ruby Wachowski. The vehicle hasn't been reported stolen, but they're an older couple, retired, no immediate family—exactly the type of people a criminal would target. Hoskins thinks of the pale, blurry face talking to Weber across the pumps at the gas station. That face could belong to the Secondhand Killer.

Hoskins and Loren ride together to the Wachowski place, in Loren's car, just like old times. There are a few close calls, when Hoskins grabs the door handle and curses because Loren drives like a bat out of hell, he's going to kill them both, but Loren throws back his head and laughs, calls him an old lady.

"Reminds you you're alive, doesn't it?" he says gleefully.

There's a car in the driveway—Sammie's, the one Hoskins always called the Mitsubi-*shit*, and they don't bother knocking, Hoskins kicks in the door and they rush in, guns drawn and ready to pump someone full of lead, but they're too late, the exciting part is already over. There's no chance for them to play hero. There's a man on the floor, dead; Sammie, her eyes dull and her lips pale, is clutching her hand to her chest and Hoskins thinks she must be going into shock but there's an ambulance behind them and the paramedics sweep in and take her away, and her husband too, who is weeping softly and has to be led from the house like a child.

The dead man is on his belly—ignored by the paramedics since there's nothing they can do for him, their business is with the living—so Hoskins and Loren flip him over—it's harder than it looks even though the guy isn't that big—and they take a good look at his face. It's surreal for Hoskins, to see Seever standing above this kid, looking down at the guy who tried to pick up where he left off.

"You piece of shit," Seever says, and Hoskins's eyes clear, and he sees it's not Seever at all, but Loren, and the guy on the floor is the Secondhand Killer, and he's finally dead.

It's over.

WHAT

YOU

DON'T

KNOW

If this were a movie, the end credits would be rolling and the lights in the theater would be coming up and you'd be trying to decide whether you should wait until the massive herd of people creeping down the stairs is gone or if you should fight your way through, because the line for the bathroom is going to be *long* and the drive home is bumpy and you had a big Coke during the movie—not even the large but the *extra*-large, the size that makes other countries laugh and point and make fat-American jokes. But you wait, despite your throbbing bladder, because sometimes there's something cool on after the credits—like the time all those superheroes were sitting around eating lunch after they'd saved the entire planet, no one saw *that* coming, did they? And honestly, you want to know what happened to these people after everything was said and done, you want to know it all, so you stay, you almost piss your pants but you stay, and you are not disappointed.

His full name was Ethan Rhodes Hobbs, and that's what would've been printed on his gravestone—if he'd been buried. Instead, he was cremated, and his mother came all the way out from Minnesota to bring the ashes home. Ethan's mother—one Patty Hobbs, née Haven—had always thought her son would end up in a bad way, but not like this. Ethan had been in and out of trouble all through school; he'd always been violent and sullen, and there'd been that incident with the girl, and that other time with that neighborhood dog—but she'd always blamed it on his friends, said Ethan was easily influenced, that he was a normal boy trying to find his way in life. But once she was told everything he'd done after moving to Denver, Patty was forced to revise her opinion.

So Ethan's ashes were given to his mother, and that night she'd slept in the hotel with the plain ceramic urn on the nightstand beside the bed. She thought it'd be nice to have one last night with her son, to say her final goodbye before she took him home and scattered his remains on the wind, and no one knows for sure what happened over that night, but when Patty Hobbs checked out of the hotel the next morning she stopped at the first fast-food restaurant she saw and tipped the entire contents of that urn into the trash bin sitting outside the drive-thru. She left Denver that same day, drove straight through to Minnesota with the empty urn on the seat beside her, but when she got home it was full again, maybe it was sand, maybe it was cigarette ashes, maybe it doesn't matter.

And Ethan? Most of his ashes ended up twenty miles outside of Denver, in the Tower Landfill out in Commerce City, mixed in with the shitty diapers and empty milk cartons and mildewed newspapers and buried under layers of soil and sand and rock. But before the garbage men came, some of Ethan's ashes were picked up by the winter wind and were sent whirling through the city, and those bits of Ethan Hobbs are there still, they'll be dancing in the streets of Denver forever, because you can burn evil, you can cut it and crush it and think it's gone, but you'll never be rid of it completely, not really.

What Dean never tells anyone, partly out of shame and partly because he's not sure how to put it into words: He'd almost let Ethan Hobbs kill his wife. He'd considered this when he saw Sammie on the floor and Ethan kneeling over her, cutting away her fingers—oh, he wouldn't have left her entirely, he would've gone out to his car and called the police and waited, but she would've been dead by the time they arrived, there's no doubt in his mind. It was only a single stray moment, lasted no longer than a heartbeat, but he'd still thought it, and afterward, when Ethan's dead and Sammie's recovering in the hospital and people are calling him a hero, saying he'd saved his wife, he feels like a coward, he feels guilty, and that'll stay with him for the rest of his life. He'll never tell Sammie, though, because he loves her, and this one time he's not a disappointment.

Three days after Ethan's death, the police break down Gloria's front door. They'd come to follow up, to tell her that Chris Weber's killer had been found, but she never came to the door, and wouldn't pick up her telephone. It smells like something's gone bad in there, the cops tell one another. She might've fallen. Broken a hip and couldn't get up, doesn't have anyone checking on her. Those sorts of things happen all the time. So they kick in the door.

But they weren't expecting the carpet to be soaked through, and there is something floating on the surface of all that standing water, like the scum of grease on a pond. Later, the medical examiner will tell them that it was skin they'd seen, thin layers of epidermis that had been flayed away from the flesh by the pounding jets of water from the showerhead. The shower's still running, they can hear it quite clearly, and when they push open the bathroom door one of the officers stumbles away, gagging wetly on his own breakfast. It's not only the smell, although it's worse in the bathroom, stronger, but it's more the sight of Gloria Seever, who has swollen up like a balloon, her skin gray and pulled taut, splitting in certain areas where the maggots are already roiling and feeding. The shower curtain is ripped down—she fell, the examiner later guesses, when all those pills took hold she lost her balance—and she's half out of the tub, stiff and swollen as a waterlogged piece of wood, but the worst part, the absolute worst is her mouth, wide and gaping and cracked, partly open, so it no longer looks like a mouth at all but a bottomless maw, hungry and demanding and angry.

Later on, they'll have to identify her by her teeth, since the rest of her is so bloated and warped that she's not recognizably Gloria Seever. She no longer even looks human—she's more like a monster. And maybe—probably—she would've taken some comfort in that.

Ethan Hobbs had thirty-one of Seever's paintings in his possession, he'd turned the Wachowskis' dining room into his own personal art gallery. He was the one who'd broken into Gloria Seever's home and stolen them, and if the police had taken her burglary report seriously, if they would've launched a full investigation, they might've arrested Ethan Hobbs before he was able to kill anyone, but that's life—there are the paths you take, and the paths you ignore, and that's that.

The paintings were of the clowns Seever liked so much, frolicking and grinning and blowing up balloon animals, and landscapes, one of the night sky. Harmless, and worthless. The violent paintings had all sold at the gallery or were taken by police, and Gloria had kept the one of Sammie hidden, and maybe that was best, because if Ethan had seen it to begin with, if he'd realized what Seever had intended for Sammie, she might've been his first victim, not his last.

At least, that's the theory Loren and Hoskins come up with.

The pinkie and ring finger on her left hand are gone. Most times it doesn't bother her at all, until she catches someone staring at her mutilated hand, wondering what the story is behind it, and she'll tuck it behind her back, out of sight. The fingers sometimes ache, even though they're gone. *Phantom pain*, the doctors call it, and she's tired of being haunted by things that aren't really there.

She should write the book, Corbin says. And the articles. Everything, as soon as she's able. There's no more competition, because Weber is dead, and besides, she has *the* story of the year. She was Seever's lover, she reported his arrest, she was the one who got away. The girl who lived.

But the words seem to have dried up.

Dean goes back to work and she stays home, watches a lot of TV, takes a lot of naps. Dean has taken the kitchen table out to the garage and is sanding it down when he has free time. He's going to refinish it, put new fabric over the seats. He's going to make it beautiful again, but it will take time. All good things take time, he says, watching her. For the first time, her husband has gray in his hair, at the temples.

Six months after Ethan's death, she sits down at her computer. Slowly types in a word, pecking at the keyboard with her pointer finger. *Seever*. All of this is about him, it started with him and ended with him, and she thinks it might be time to suck the poison from the wound and get rid of him, once and for all. Write about Seever and Ethan until they're both worked out of her system. It'll be slow work, but that's life, isn't it? You get dressed one pant leg at a time, you live one breath at a time.

And Sammie, she'll heal one word at a time.

And what about those fingers, you might be asking? Between Seever and Ethan and all the death they left in their wake, that's a helluva lot of missing digits. What happened to them all? That, unfortunately, will remain a mystery for all time, because it doesn't look like either of the two men who know the actual truth are talking.

Glen and Ruby Wachowski are found in their basement, near the furnace. The police found evidence that Ethan had held the others—

Abeyta and Brody, and Jimmy Galen—down in the basement as well; he'd turned the place into his own personal torture chamber, where he could do whatever he wanted without interruption.

And Ethan had also started doing art in the basement. He'd set up an easel, bought watercolors. There are dozens of paintings, but they're nothing like Seever's. They are crude, sloppy. Mostly they are houses, brown boxes with curlicues of smoke rising from the chimneys, big loopy clouds in the sky and a smiling yellow sun in the corner.

Those paintings, they are the work of a child.

Frank Cho, the man who owned the guesthouse where Carrie Simms was murdered, had it torn down not long after her death. It was bad luck, he thought, to leave such a building standing, and he was probably right. Thirty minutes before the cottage was torn down, Cho walked through it one last time, stepping carefully over the bloodstains left on the floors, and stopped to read the words still scribbled on the bedroom wall.

It'll never be over.

Those words didn't mean anything to Cho, although the police had fussed over them enough, he'd heard them arguing over how they'd ended up there, until finally they'd let the matter drop. None of them ever guessed that it was Carrie Simms who'd written the words above her bed, balancing on her mattress not long after she first rented the place. Seever had first said the words to her in the garage, although she didn't remember it, but some part of her *must have*, because they echoed through her dreams, they drove her crazy until she got them out of her head and onto the wall, but every time she looked on the phrase she felt an unsettling anticipation, as if she were waiting for something, although she didn't know what.

Ethan first read the words after he'd knocked Carrie Simms unconscious, when he was sitting on her chest and listening to her rattling breath drawing in and out and waiting for her to wake up again. He puzzled over them, then forgot them entirely. He was busy with other matters, you see.

So the little house was torn down and the debris was carted away and Frank Cho sold the entire property for much less than it was worth, but he felt a pressing need to get away, and he wanted to move closer to his family. Particularly his granddaughter, a pretty nine-year-old who called him Pop-Pop, and when she disappears a year from now, vanishes into thin air on her walk home from school, Frank will listen to his daughter's haunted cries and look at his trembling hands and remember those words on the wall, and he'll think that it's true, it'll never be over, that there's never an end to suffering.

But perhaps it's best to save that story for another day.

Detective Ralph Loren finally stops dressing like Seever. He puts away the three-piece suits and the tinted glasses, throws away the hair gel. Loren goes back to normal for him, which isn't very normal at all, and for the first time, Hoskins is thankful for it.

One spring afternoon Hoskins drives out to Sterling Correctional Facility. Seever is in the hospital wing, confined to his bed—he had a heart attack not long after getting the news about Gloria, and about Secondhand, crimes that had nothing to do with Seever but had *everything* to do with him, and he's been bedridden ever since. It's still about a year until his execution, if it doesn't get caught up in legalities and pushed back, but Hoskins has a feeling Seever won't be making it to his own execution. Seever's a man on his way out, his heart getting one beat closer to finally bailing. In his hospital bed Seever looks more like one of the victims they'd pulled from his crawl space than his old self.

"Hey, you fat fuck," Hoskins says, and Seever's head turns on the pillow to look at him, but there's no flare of recognition, no answering gleam. This man in the bed isn't Seever—this is a pale specter, a man who's been giving bits of himself away—to Hoskins and Loren, to Sammie, and Ethan, little slivers that stuck with them like rusty needles, jammed in their hearts and wouldn't let go—and there's not enough left here to make a whole man. Not anymore. "This is it. I came to say goodbye. I'm never gonna waste my time thinking about you again."

Seever's lips are moving, he's trying to say something or maybe he's delirious, but Hoskins doesn't stop to listen, because he doesn't care. He's wasted too much of the past few years dealing with the damage Seever has done to his life.

He leaves the prison, points his car back toward Denver. He needs to check on his father, but Joe's adjusting well to the old folks' home, he's better than he's been in a long time, he's happy. Hoskins'll stop in and see him, then he'll go home, put his feet up, and watch some TV. Take a nap and meet Ted for drinks, do some work. He wishes he could forget Seever, forget how Sammie looked on the floor of that house, her eyes distant and shiny as Dean screamed, and Ethan Hobbs, on his side, a single runner of blood leaking from his nose. Hoskins wants to forget it all, but he'll be happy enough if it would blur and fade, like a photograph left out in the sun. That would be enough.

FADE

TO

BLACK

Summer 2007

He throws one big party during the summer, holds it in his backyard, a place he's made perfect for people to gather. When they first moved in, the backyard was nothing but rocks and sand, and it took years and a goodish amount of money to level things out and put down sod and plant trees and have the pond dug, but anything that looks effortless is always expensive. But even with the perfect backyard, it takes time to get set up for the annual summer barbecue. Tables have to be set up on the lawn, fairy lights strung through the branches of the shrubs, tiki lanterns plunged into the ground, floating candles set loose on the pond. And the food—there's always more than enough, because if there's one thing Jacky doesn't like, it's the thought of people not having enough to eat, of having anyone walk away from his house and not be bursting at the seams.

The barbecue invitations go out three weeks before, and this year it's a luau theme, and Gloria is wearing a grass skirt and passing out those flowered necklaces at the door. And there's a pig, an actual pig with a metal pole jammed right down its mouth and poking out its ass, and it seems to be grinning, pleased as punch to be included in the ceremonies. But there's a grill too, for anyone who doesn't care for pork, where Jacky stands and flips hamburgers and hot dogs, chicken legs soaked in BBQ sauce. Everyone stops by to speak to him, at least once, because Jacky's the master of ceremonies at these things, he's the man of the hour, the Grand Poobah. They tell him how much they appreciate the party, how much everyone looks forward to it all year long. They hug Jacky, clap him on the shoulder, slap him on the fat of the arm. And Jacky glows from the pleasure of it, of all these people having a good time because of him, what he's done, and he stands at the grill with a spatula in one hand and a cold beer in the other, looking out over the crowd, watching the pretty girls spin to the music and the men put their heads close together and laugh, and he's not thinking how low he'll be tomorrow, how he'll shut himself in the guest bedroom and lie in the dark for two days straight, how he's already hidden three bags of potato chips and boxes of malted balls under the bed because that's all he'll want, he's been through this before, he knows what to expect. He's not thinking of that now, because right now the sun is out and the breeze is cool, and nothing smells bad, no one's going to complain today, the only thing anyone can smell is the roasting meat, and Gloria is waving at him, smiling, her wedding ring catching the light. And soon it's late in the afternoon, the sun is low and the wind has picked up but people still keep showing up, parking three blocks over, sometimes more, but Jacky doesn't mind, he waves everyone in, saying that everyone's welcome, there's always room for one more.

Acknowledgments

My deepest thanks to Stephanie Cabot, Amy Einhorn, Christine Kopprasch, Ellen Goodson, Rachelle Mandik, Jamison Stoltz, Mark Haskell Smith, Tod Goldberg, the friends I made at UCRPDMFA, and the girls at store #133. And most of all, thank you to Cade, Jacob, Lauren, Gunner, and Beau, who know exactly when to create a distraction; and my husband, who doesn't read but always listens. To anyone I have forgotten to mention: I apologize, and please accept my most sincere thanks.

Recommend *What You Don't Know* for your next book club!

Reading Group Guide available at

www.readinggroupgold.com